THE KING'S BLADE
QUEENMAKERS SAGA X

BY
BERNADETTE ROWLEY

THE KING'S BLADE
Bernadette Rowley
Copyright © 2022 Bernadette Rowley
All rights reserved.

First published 2022 by Bernadette Rowley

ISBN: 978-0-6450742-2-2

Printing/manufacturing information for this book may be found on the last page

First Printing 2022 by Bernadette Rowley
Cover Design by Dar Albert wickedsmartdesigns.com
Interior Design by
Business Communications Management bcm-online.com.au

VC:TKB-2022-06-20

ACKNOWLEDGEMENTS

Deep thanks must go to my beta readers and biggest fans,
Nic Page and Rachel Cass.
Their generosity in being my first readers for The King's Blade and
their enthusiasm for my words are inspirational. Thanks also to these
ladies for their critical feedback during cover creation.

To Duncan Carling-Rodgers for his assistance during the edits of
The King's Blade and for the formatting.

To Dar Albert for her stunning cover.

To my husband, Michael, my sons, and their ladies for their
unending love and support and for sharing in the disappointments
and triumphs of a writing life.

TITLES BY
BERNADETTE ROWLEY

(in suggested reading order)

TABLE OF CONTENTS

CHAPTER ONE

ALECIA woke in Vard's arms, her body chilled by the night air. They lay on his cloak in the clearing, their bodies entwined and the scent of sex upon them. She played with the fine hairs on his forearms, recalling the glorious moments when she had surrendered to him.

A sudden feeling of uneasiness wound its way up from her stomach. If another child resulted from their lovemaking, it would be a big complication to her plans.

She sat up, Vard's arms falling from her body, and felt around for her clothes. He stirred and ran his hand down her back, making her shiver.

"Let me fetch your clothes, my love. We should return to the camp."

In seconds, he retrieved her garments and helped her dress. His hands were gentle, reverent, as if the act of dressing her was a kind of worship. Once she was clothed, Vard pulled on his breeches, shirt, and tunic, then donned his boots.

"You're quiet, my love," he observed.

She felt his eyes upon her, though it was too dark for her to see his expression. The sliver of moon had long set.

She sighed. "I'm just trying to understand how making love just now changes things between us. Apart from the obvious, if I should conceive. That must be faced if it should occur."

He was silent for long moments. "You talk as if we've just conducted a business transaction, Alecia." There was a cold, hard edge to his voice.

"I didn't mean to sound that way, but I can't help wanting to know what's next—and worrying how this will change things. Or *if* it will change things."

"Do you want it to?"

"Honestly? Part of me wants it with all my heart." She took a step toward him. "But another part, the part that you hurt when you deserted us, is terrified of being broken again."

He gripped her upper arms. "Each day has been torture since I left you on the farm. You must believe I thought about you and Iona each day; hated myself for leaving you. I knew you'd think I had abandoned you again."

"You *had* abandoned us." She shrugged and pulled away, hoping some distance would help her think.

"But for your own good. The bear wouldn't leave me, and I couldn't risk going feral again, as I did with the wolf. I couldn't endanger you and our daughter, so I acted to guarantee your safety from the threat I posed."

"I know you love us."

His shoulders slumped. "I hear a 'but' coming." He drew the cloak from the ground and placed it around her shoulders.

She shivered. "I can't see a path for us at this moment. You're working for the king, and I have my own dreams. Perhaps when I'm queen, you can be my prince consort. You can have whatever position you wish, and we'll have more children."

He shook his head. "Come to Wildecoast with me, Alecia. I'm sure the king will give us larger quarters. He'd be delighted if you'd join your life with mine. It's time we made that commitment official. I can train Iona, or at least be there to watch her grow. Father can join us, and Iona will have a grandfather."

"It sounds marvelous, Vard. Perhaps one day we *can* be a family, but for now I know my path lies separate from yours. I need to be free to choose my next steps."

He lay his palms along her jaw, his fingers lacing through her hair. "And *I* need you with me. Together, we can be stronger than we are apart. And I must see my daughter."

"You're welcome to see Iona whenever you wish. I'd never deny you access to her."

"What about access to her mother?" The intensity of his words trapped her. How was she saying "no" to this man she loved? Her resolve wavered as she imagined a simple life with him and Iona. And then she took hold of her humble fancies. Her life could never be uncomplicated. But this man assaulted her defenses and broke them down so easily. She must stay apart from him as much as possible if she was to complete her goal.

She took a step backward. "Please don't ask that of me. I find you hard to say 'no' to. You're everything... almost everything... I want in this world. But now is my time. I feel it in every particle of my being. This was what I was born for—to be queen. If you can't support me in that goal, then I must deny you for now."

Alecia made herself hold his troubled gaze, knowing he would clearly see her resolve. She might stray from her path from time to time but would always return to it.

He breathed out, hands on hips. "I fear for you, my love. You need help, and it's help I can't give, not while I work for the king."

She stood before him, shoulders back. "I must do this on my own. I don't want your help. It's best if we keep our distance from each other, except in our roles as Iona's parents."

"If that's what you wish, I'll try to respect your request. But it won't be easy standing by while you place yourself at risk." He bent and kissed her cheek. "We should seek our rest."

Alecia nodded, and they walked back to the camp, close but not touching. She relived the moments in the clearing as she walked, wondering if Vard did too. Her resolve wavered as she recalled the heady moments when she was with him, the heights they climbed together, and the delicious ecstasy of being one. Could she deny him, deny the love they shared? It was clear their hearts still beat as one.

He was her soulmate, perhaps the only one she'd ever know. Was there still a place for their love in this world if she pursued her dreams?

Troubled thoughts kept her company on the last leg of their walk back, so it wasn't surprising that Lin greeted her with a frown.

"What's wrong?" she asked.

"Nothing, Lin." Alecia crossed to her saddle, removed the bed roll, and prepared her pallet. All she wished was to close her eyes and let sleep take her.

Arelle finished threading the last branch in their makeshift shelter before joining them.

"You seem worried," Arelle said. "Did Lord Anton have bad news for you?"

Lin snorted. "Bad news indeed. You're such a child, Arelle. Can't you see they've been intimate?"

Alecia spun to face her friend. "That's enough! It's really none of your business. I'd appreciate it if you'd hold your tongue and allow me some peace."

Lin's eyes widened, and Arelle snapped her mouth shut.

"That's where you're wrong," Lin said. "As your advisor, I must know all there is to know. How can I do my job if you keep secrets—even of the most intimate moments?"

Alecia drew a long breath, then let it out to bring her anger under control. Lin may not be completely correct in what she said, but she did have more rights than the others. And her relationship with Vard could threaten her path to the throne.

She turned to Lin. "We talked of many things."

Lin didn't have to know the most intimate moments. Perhaps Alecia would feel more able to share what had happened with Vard later. First, she must process it in her head and heart. "He wants me back, wants a life with the two of us. I said no." She drew a ragged breath. "I can't conduct a relationship with Vard while he works for King Beniel. At least I don't see how I can. I need distance from him and from the king to build my support base. So, for now, I've said our relationship must be for the sake of Iona and nothing more."

Lin's eyes held unshed tears. "That must have been difficult. I don't imagine he was happy to hear it."

"He wasn't, but I believe Vard will respect my wishes. Now all I must do is stay strong."

Arelle hugged her. "We'll help. When you waver, all you need do is lean on us."

A tear slipped from Alecia's eye at the generosity of her friend. Lin hugged her from the other side.

"What she said," Lin whispered, sniffing. "You'll be a magnificent queen."

* * *

The days slipped by as they approached the tree city of Selinore. Vard fell into the rhythm of the trail, rising before dawn to explore the paths ahead, usually as the hawk. It was the most effective form to scout in, but his most vulnerable. He couldn't quite shake the nagging feeling he was being watched, but saw nothing. Perhaps it was merely the worry he held for Alecia's safety—but he didn't think so.

Soon after dawn, he would return to human form and report to the scouts. Breakfast was a brief affair, and they took to the road, the ladies in the center of the group. Sometimes Linnet scouted the trail with Vard's Rangers. She was competent and improving, according to his men. With Alecia, he only exchanged brief pleasantries. She watched him—he felt her eyes on him throughout the day. But he'd play by her rules unless she changed them.

Nearing luncheon on the fourth day, Ruven Magbalar approached. He was another who watched Vard, as if he was some mysterious new beast. If only he knew the truth. Vard pretended to be oblivious. Perhaps the elf would let something slip to explain his interest.

"Morning, Magbalar," Vard said and was pleased to see the elf's small jump. "How fare you on the trip? You must've been busy these last three days."

Ruven cleared his throat and brought his horse alongside Vard's. "I've been thinking about your request—regarding secret magics held by Faenwelar. I told you I wasn't the one to ask, but I have remembered something from childhood."

Vard turned to him. "Oh? Something that might explain the events which puzzle me?"

"Possibly, although you may well laugh at my suggestion. Many would."

They rode along in silence, Vard probing the elf for his emotions. He was uncertain, his scent spikey. He didn't want to tell Vard what he had recalled. Finally, Ruven cleared his throat again.

"There is a rare elven line called dragon lords. To my knowledge, I've never met one."

Vard's ears pricked at the title. It felt familiar, but he couldn't remember where he'd heard it. Perhaps in childhood? His mentor, the elf Melandrach, would know. "Why are they so called?" he asked.

"I'm unsure. Perhaps they commanded dragons in the days when the beasts existed. None have been heard of since men took over the kingdom. But with Faenwelar challenging humans for control, it made me wonder if the dragons and their masters were indeed extinct."

Vard tested the idea as he rode along. Dragons—or even one dragon—would explain much. But he'd be laughed at if he were to suggest it. A dragon could have pulled out the bars of Gorin's prison and flown away with him, leaving no trace. And a dragon could have flown in elven soldiers to ambush the king. It was outlandish—but possible.

He shook his head. "I'm sorry, Magbalar, I'd be a laughingstock if I suggested a dragon was responsible for either of those puzzles. Keep this to yourself. If I need anything else, I'll come to you."

Ruven bowed and rode away, leaving Vard no closer to solving the mystery. Perhaps he'd find the answers in Selinore.

* * *

Alecia ground her teeth, wondering if she should've returned to Brightcastle. She worried about being away from Iona. Also, if she had returned to her daughter, the tryst with Vard wouldn't have happened. As it was, she couldn't pull her thoughts from the love she and Vard had made on their first night together.

She longed for a repeat performance with him, but he'd been completely aloof since that night. It was what she had asked of him, but she couldn't escape thoughts of his hands on her, and his body over hers, sending her to paradise.

That experience was unlike any other she had enjoyed with Vard. True, much of their moments together were during times of danger, where they hadn't had the luxury of enjoying being one. Most recently, she'd been recovering from Iona's birth, and her mind was on other matters, her body healing after the trauma of childbirth. She had almost died, would have except for Vard's magic.

Dammit! She owed him so much. He had been there for her, always known what was best, and constantly tried to protect her from his animal forms. In the past, she was naïve, believing their love would see them through, and not willing to admit the truth.

She'd placed herself in a precarious position when she depended on Vard, and he'd known that instinctively. But now her body was safe from the bear, and, ironically, it was he who saw a path ahead for them, and she who denied it. She had grown into a woman who wouldn't depend on a man.

But she wanted him; oh how she *burned* for him. Her eyes followed him of their own accord. Her ladies noticed, and they tried to distract her lest she embarrass herself. But they need have no fear of that. Vard never looked in her direction, never met her eye unless he needed to speak to her. He had fully embraced her wishes. *Damn him!*

Oh, she was an idiot! She damned the man because he agreed to her demands! He was being a complete gentleman— and she couldn't stand it!

That evening, the fourth on the trail, Vard got up after dinner and didn't return. Alecia worried about him. Certainly, he could handle himself better than anyone else she knew; even so, he could be vulnerable. She sat beside Lin and Arelle and chewed her lip.

"What's the matter, Alecia?" Lin asked.

"Vard hasn't returned. I'm worried."

"You just wish for an excuse to be alone with him again," Lin whispered. "I understand, but you must leave the man be. He has agreed to your wishes, which, I might add, are perfectly appropriate."

"I can't turn off my feelings for him just like that," she said, snapping her fingers. "Don't you think someone should go and find him?"

"Alecia," Arelle said. "I'm sure he has a ranger looking out for him, or someone else. There are men on patrol around the perimeter. You need not worry."

Alecia stood. "I can't sit still any longer. I'm going to have a snoop around camp; see if I can find out where he went." She started to walk away, then turned back to them. "Arelle, you can come with me, but stay five paces behind so as not to arouse suspicion."

Inwardly, Alecia rolled her eyes at herself. She was such a ninny. The five paces thing made no sense, but that was the beauty of being a royal—she didn't have to make sense.

She stopped before a young ranger on sentry duty. The man snapped to attention. "Ranger, do you know where Lord Anton went? I need to speak with him."

"He is patrolling, Princess."

"Should he not be back by now?"

"Our leader comes and goes as he pleases; we wouldn't think of questioning him."

"Then which way did he go?" Alecia asked, folding her arms.

"He went north, Princess, but he could be anywhere now. He should return shortly. Don't fear, the King's Blade can handle himself."

The ranger tried to hide his hero worship of Vard, but failed miserably.

"I'm going to take a stroll through the woods where he left, Ranger. Could you fetch someone to accompany me? I realize you can't accompany me as that would be deserting your post."

The young man's face wore a look of horror. "That wouldn't be wise, Princess. I advise you to stay in camp. Lord Anton was most clear. You are to be always under our protection."

Alecia huffed. "That's why I asked for an escort."

"But Princess, it will take time to organize that. Please, just return to your ladies, and I'll send Lord Anton to you when he returns."

Alecia fixed him with a look that usually got what she wanted, and the man wilted under her gaze. A throat cleared beside her.

"What is the problem?" Ruven Magbalar asked.

The ranger snapped to attention again. "Nothing, Sir. The princess was just enquiring as to the whereabouts of Lord Anton."

Alecia turned to Ruven. "Good evening, Commander. I'd like to take a stroll through the woods to the north. Would you care to join me?"

She snapped her lips shut, wondering where those words came from. She had no desire to be alone with this elf!

Ruven hesitated. "What is the purpose of this stroll?"

"The princess is concerned for Lord Anton," the ranger said.

Ruven smiled, his exotic elven eyes measuring and finding her wanting… as usual. "Really, Princess. Vard Anton can fend for himself. Would it not be more prudent to await his return? He won't thank you for going after him."

Feelings warred inside Alecia. All she wanted was to find Vard, make sure he was well, and spend some time in his company. She could've just walked into the forest once given a direction, but didn't want to cause a fuss. And she was trying to behave in a way befitting a queen instead of her usual impulsive actions.

"Oh, bother! Don't worry yourselves." She turned to make her way back, but Ruven caught her elbow.

"I'll escort you, Princess." He addressed the ranger. "We won't go far beyond the trees. and the princess will be quite safe in my company."

The ranger saluted, and Alecia had no option but to accompany Ruven. They stepped beyond the first line of trees to the north of the encampment.

"Why are you doing this, Ruven?" she asked.

"I thought it a good opportunity to apologize for being rude to you when we first met. It was thoughtless of me. And so, I ask for forgiveness, Princess Alecia."

"Ah… I forgive you." Alecia paused in a pocket of light from the moon, hoping to see his expression. No such luck! Was he genuine? She couldn't shake the anger of their last encounter. "Your impertinent question regarding the degree of my political influence was one I'm sure others will ask. But I have more power than you may think."

"How so?"

She drew her shoulders back and continued her walk.

"I'm of the royal line, and there have been ruling queens in the past. I believe it's only a matter of time before the king's lack of male heirs forces him to consider me. And, in the meantime, I will form alliances."

"As with my leader, Princess Gwaethe."

She nodded. "Indeed. While other kingdom leaders scorn the elves and are barely polite to the *Lenweri, I* believe you're the key to a prosperous future."

"And your Lord Anton?"

Alecia hissed. "I'd appreciate it if you didn't call Vard '*my* Lord Anton.'"

He inclined his head. "It seems you and I are destined for a rocky future, Princess."

"It doesn't have to be, Commander. I admire your story of struggle and swearing to Gwaethe's cause." Personally, Alecia wondered if Magbalar had another agenda. Was he loyal? She would have to ask Vard; his Defender senses should be able to detect any artifice from the elf.

Ruven's lips twitched in a smile. "And yet I sense you still wonder if I am truly loyal. Well, let me assure you, Gwaethe Arenil has all my heart and commitment. I will see Faenwelar and his ilk dead or banished."

"But not brought into the *Lenweri* fold?" Alecia asked.

He shrugged. "Better to kill them all than have traitors in our midst."

She frowned. "But don't you see? If Gwaethe felt like that, she would've left you to rot in that prison."

"No, she would not. She thought we were *Lenweri*, not *Sis Lenweri.*"

"Even more reason to be forgiving to other *Sis Lenweri*, I would've thought."

Ruven laughed. "Princess, you have much to learn about elves. We are a hard people, not given to trusting easily. But when we give our heart to a cause, it is difficult to shift. Those elves who fight for Faenwelar are loyal to his cause. There may be some artisans, civilians, and females who will join Gwaethe, but they will be few."

Alecia shook her head. "And yet, here you are. Perhaps there will be more *Sis Lenweri* who return to the fold than you anticipate."

Ruven shrugged his shoulders.

"What are you doing out here, Princess?" Vard's deep voice interrupted their discussion. "Magbalar, is all well?"

Ruven bowed. "All is well, King's Blade. The princess and I were having a private discussion which is now concluded. I bid you good night."

Ruven turned and melted into the trees. Alecia shivered. She wanted to understand the elven people, but feared she never would. She turned to Vard.

"Were you looking for me, Alecia?" His voice rumbled through her, stirring thoughts of their last encounter in the forest.

She stepped closer. "I was worried when you didn't return. It's silly, I know, but…"

He frowned. "This is what you wanted—for me to keep my distance. And I have followed your wishes."

Alecia placed her hand over his heart and closed her eyes, feeling a slight skip in the beat. It was only fleeting. Perhaps she'd imagined it. She drew strength from the steady thump of his heart and opened her eyes.

"You're right. I haven't changed my mind." She drew a deep breath, trying to push aside all thoughts of his arms around her. "What took you so long?"

He paused, as if debating what he should tell her. "Walk with me."

She went without hesitation, wondering if he truly wanted to talk, or if he had other activities on his mind. She couldn't help her traitorous heart from hoping for the latter. Her hand in his felt right, and, every so often, he squeezed it. She sighed. Life with Vard could be wondrous if only she allowed him to order it as he saw fit. But she could not.

He halted beside an immense fir tree and turned to face her. "I scouted as the wolf tonight. In that form, I can access the thoughts of the local wolves. I often do this as it enables me to reach further, see more. Something unnerved them. A massive darkness overtook them and struck terror into the packs. Some mentioned a streak of fire, trees ablaze."

"I thought I smelled smoke earlier," Alecia said.

His hand gripped her shoulder. "Do you still have true dreams?"

"Not lately. I don't know why. I used to see you in them, but not since you gained control of your gift." She missed the intimacy of seeing Vard when he wasn't with her. "I'll tell you if anything should change."

"This darkness the wolves speak of, and the fire... I wonder if it could spell a dragon?"

Alecia gasped. "All the dragons died out centuries ago, surely?"

"Ruven told me there was a line of ancient elven nobility called dragon lords. He was unsure why they were so called, but it's possible they commanded dragons."

"Vard, is it possible these lords might in fact be dragon shifters?"

He shook his head. "I would've heard of it."

"What if they aren't Defenders? What if their purpose wasn't to help the innocent, but to advance their own cause?"

"It's a long shot at best. I'll be laughed at if I suggest dragons to the king, let alone dragon shifters. We need proof."

"Can you speak to the wolves? Ask them of the darkness they fear, perhaps project a picture of a dragon into their minds?"

"I've developed a connection with several of them. They shy away from me, but I'm hoping to do as you say in the coming days. I just hope we're wrong, because if there *is* a dragon, even *one*, that bodes ill for our cause."

CHAPTER TWO

SELINORE, the elven capital, was near. Vard had connected with several wolves in different packs, and one thing was sure—a dark menace spooked them, something they hadn't seen before, but they recalled in their ancestor memory. Vard had tried projecting an image of a dragon as he had seen in fairy tales as a child, but with little success.

All they could tell him was of darkness and fear. It was a massive thing, but it could so easily be a dark cloud of magic rather than a dragon. And the clouds of a storm could rain down lightning and set the forest afire. But the wolves knew storms, and they said this wasn't one.

Whatever it was only came out at night, so his hawk form was of little use. No matter how high he hovered on the warm updraughts during the day, he spied not a leaf out of place. It was maddening.

The itchy feeling that Faenwelar was planning something big and mustering his troops for a final push wouldn't leave him. He must speak to the *Lenweri* high prince, Kain Arenil, then hightail it back to Brightcastle and Wildecoast. The kingdom was almost out of time.

Alecia was another matter. She hovered near him all day, likely hoping to catch a moment to speak. But he must keep her at arm's length. She would demand an audience with him should she have anything important to share about the coming threat. Ha! Listen to yourself! *Demand an audience!* As if he were a king! Vard shook his head and tried to focus on the trees he rode through.

It was too quiet—as if the animals and birds prepared for trouble. Throughout the entire trip to Selinore, he'd had a spikey sensation in the back of his skull, a sixth sense of impending doom.

Perhaps Kain Arenil could help shed some light on his elven cousins and their plans. He also looked forward to seeing his father and Melandrach.

At lunchtime, Alecia approached.

He rose and bowed. "Princess, how are you?"

Her lips twisted in a grimace. "I'm fine, *Lord Anton.*" She lowered her voice. "The dreams are back." She thrust a piece of parchment into his hand. "I hope this helps."

She turned and stalked away. Vard opened the letter to find two paragraphs in Alecia's neat hand and a picture. A gaping mouth, rows of sharpened teeth, and a monstrous flame seemed to leap off the page. Above were two malevolent eyes, the pupils compressed ovoids. She had drawn an arrow pointing to the irises and the words "gold and crimson".

Last night I dreamed of the creature I've drawn. It was a true dream, and it was coming for me, but I don't think I was the only target. All I saw was that face, so I don't know what the beast is. It could be a dragon, or perhaps it's another enemy. I'm not sure, but I think I died in my dream. That hasn't happened before.

We must return to Brightcastle as soon as we can. I fear for Iona and my people. We must prepare. Already I fear it's too late.

Her words were close to the very ones he'd thought that morning. The itchy feeling that doom was upon them. And now Alecia had again dreamed of disaster. His heart ached at the fear she must have experienced during and after that dream. He should go to her and find out for himself that she was well. But then he recalled her words before handing him the note. She had said she was fine.

The best thing to do was to get back on the road to Selinore. Perhaps someone there would have the answers they needed.

* * *

Alecia drew her horse to a halt at the sight of the massive trees of Selinore, the elven capital. She'd heard of the great sentinels, but never imagined they could be this enormous. Some of them housed the noble elven families. Here they would find Kain Arenil and Vard's father. Excitement rattled her insides at the thought of so much strangeness in one place.

Vard had sent a scouting party ahead to warn of their approach, and, as usual, he had explored the path himself. Nothing would catch them unawares. This was a critical meeting for her in her goal of being queen. Gwaethe supported her, and now she might sway Kain to the cause of a queen on the throne of Thorius, although elves weren't known for having queens as far as she could tell. She remembered Gwaethe complaining about it during their visit. Still, anything could change.

Kain, Gwaethe's half-brother, was said to be a prickly man, but one who would see reason. As an elven leader, though half-human, he wouldn't be averse to magic as many other leaders were. He could be the voice of reason.

Lin appeared beside her. "You'll be left behind, Princess," she said. "If you wish to be seen as a leader, ride in beside the King's Blade."

Alecia huffed and kicked Silver into a trot. Daydreaming wouldn't get her to the throne of Thorius. Even though Lin's words shamed her, she knew they were true and not meant to cause her grief. She thanked the Goddess for her friend's wisdom.

Arriving at Vard's side, she pulled Silver into a sedate walk.

"I wondered when I'd have the pleasure of your company," Vard said quietly.

She smiled. "I was merely taking in the grandeur of my first sighting of Selinore. The trees are magnificent."

"Indeed, they are. Wait until you're invited inside one of them. You won't believe how interwoven the branches are, and how the elves can move from tree to tree without descending the trunk."

"I wouldn't want my neighbor being able to walk into my house at any old time," she said. "That must be horrible."

"I assume there are rules about such things; boundaries so to speak."

"Living in a tree sounds romantic, but what about fire?" Alecia asked. "It has to be a risk, surely?"

"We can ask that question and many others at the feast tonight. You're in for a treat."

He sounded excited to spend time with the elves. It was a side of Vard she'd not experienced. So often when together, they'd been fighting for their lives, on the run, or living in fear of his bear form. Her heart ached at the thought of the life she might enjoy with him now. Was she right to keep pushing him away?

"I'm excited to experience Selinore in all its glory. Is Lady Alique in residence? I heard she was setting up a hospital here. I must convey Ramón's regards to his sister."

"I believe she'll be hostess of the feast tonight along with Gwaethe's mother."

They arrived at the entrance to the tree city and dismounted. Alecia hoped she had dressed well enough not to give offence. Not expecting to attend a royal event, she had traveled light when leaving Brightcastle. She settled her red and white Zialni cloak over her shoulders and pulled its collar up. If only she had her tiara, it would have made a better impression.

"Don't fuss," Lin whispered from behind. "You look grand enough."

Alecia frowned at her comment, but nodded. When would she ever come into her own? She should know all this after years of living in her father's court. But dealing with foreign leaders hadn't been common, and she'd never had to conduct herself as an alternate ruler.

"Fake it until you make it!" Lin whispered.

Vard chuckled beside her, and Alecia rolled her eyes. "That will be enough merriment at my expense, Vard."

Her comment made him laugh harder, and she fell into annoyed silence.

A handsome man with an olive complexion strode toward them, accompanied by a beautiful blonde woman dressed in a sky blue and silver gown. She must be Alique. Alecia hadn't seen her for years since her last visit to the Wildecoast court. Alique had been a young teenager then, prone to giggling and teasing Ramón, who'd been a squire in Wildecoast. How things had changed!

"Lord Anton," Kain Arenil said, holding out his hand to Vard. "It's good to see you again. You look well."

"And you, High Prince."

Vard turned to Alecia. "Please let me present Her Highness Princess Alecia of Brightcastle."

Alecia curtsied, and Kain bowed.

"You are most welcome to Selinore, Your Highness." He turned to Alique and drew her forward. "This is my wife, Lady Alique Jazara."

It surprised Alecia that Alique was introduced with that surname. There was no time to ponder as the lady bowed low to her.

"May I also extend my welcome to Selinore, Princess," Alique said. "I hope you enjoy your stay, and that you will take a tour of my hospital while here."

"It would be my pleasure, Lady Alique." Alecia admired the firm set of Alique's shoulders and the tilt of her chin. "Your brother, Ramón, sends his regards and his hope that he may see you again soon."

Alique inclined her head, and Alecia saw a flash of pain cloud her startling blue eyes. What was that about? She hoped she might get to know this lady whilst in Selinore.

"You must be weary after your journey," Kain Arenil said. "I've prepared rooms in our home for you, Princess, and for your ladies, as well as for Lord Anton. There's a house for the officers to share, and we have quartered your rangers and warriors with my elven soldiers."

Ruven joined them. "Lord Anton, allow me to see to the men while you get settled in." Vard nodded, and they parted ways. Elven attendants led their horses away, promising to deliver their belongings to the rooms.

Alecia walked beside Alique, while Vard and Kain walked ahead toward the largest tree Alecia had ever seen.

"It must be strange living in Selinore, Lady Alique," she said. "How have you settled in?"

The woman lifted her chin higher. "I'm coping as well as can be expected. We've been welcomed with open arms which is gratifying, and my hospital keeps me busy."

"But you would rather dwell with your own people?"

Alique paused, her steps slowing. "I will be wherever my husband is, Princess. He's all I need to be happy."

Alecia decided to drop the topic. Alique appeared unhappy in Selinore, and Alecia marveled at the sacrifice she had made for her husband. Did Ramón know of his sister's discontent? Likely not.

They entered the trunk of the tree, and immediately Alecia experienced an uplifting of her spirit. A calm she rarely felt suffused her.

"Oh," she breathed, laying her palm on the nearby wall. It was faintly warm. She entered further into the large room, walking around the walls where alcoves had been cut to house treasures. The entire space was lit by curious spheres which hung from the ceiling. Most of the objects on display were pottery and statues with themes of woodland creatures and elven men and women. The exhibits entranced her. They were simple, but also beautiful and dignified.

"These are stunning."

Kain joined her. "Many were here when we moved in, but we've received some as gifts since. They represent our talented craftsmen and women. I thought it would be a good idea to store them here, so our visitors could enjoy them. It's a kind of museum and display room in one. If there's a piece you'd like to learn more about, I could introduce you to the artisan."

"I love miniatures of forest creatures, especially birds," she said, pointing to a gathering of three birds carved from wood—a robin, woodpecker and hawk. There was a wolf in the next alcove, much larger than the birds, and so lifelike. It reminded her of Vard.

He stood behind her, and when she met his gaze, his eyes glowed. "Perhaps I'll meet this artist."

"I'll have it arranged," Kain said.

"Prince Arenil," Vard said, "how do you light this space? I'm sure it would intrigue the princess to hear of the globes."

"Our lighting magicians maintain the spheres," Kain said. "They're infused by a spell that draws in light energy, augments it, and then releases it into the space around them. We can't risk candles and oil within the large trees. In other elven residences made of stone, the traditional ways of lighting persist."

"Magical lighting," Vard murmured. "I wonder what other marvels you hold in Selinore, Prince Arenil?"

Kain frowned. "It sounds like a leading question, Lord Anton. Is there something specific you wish to discuss?"

"Please, call me Vard. And yes, I'm hoping to uncover something to solve a mystery. I'll explain after we've settled in."

Much to Alecia's disappointment, they left the lower chamber and climbed the winding staircase to the third floor. Several small chambers opened off from a landing.

Alecia had a room of her own, while Lin and Arelle shared. Vard was also given a room on their floor. Alecia's meagre travel gear was already present.

Once alone, she stripped off her outer clothes and washed her face and arms, perfuming the water with one of Hetty's potions.

She brushed her hair until it shone, delighting in the mirror with carved stags and antlers around the frame. Next, she donned soft cream breeches and a matching shirt and gray tunic. She twisted her hair into a chignon and placed a comb with pearls to hold it in place. The result pleased her.

A touch of blush and kohl completed her look, and she felt ready to continue her adventure. She strode to a small table over which was suspended one of the magical globes. A rich red wine, along with fruit, cheese, and bread, lay on a tray.

After days on the trail, it was a delight to sip fine wine and partake of cheese and fresh bread. There were even nuts and berries, gathered from the surrounding forest. Alecia felt invigorated as she partook of her feast.

There was a knock at the door. When she opened it, Vard stood without, also looking refreshed. The tightness around his eyes had relaxed, and the smile on his lips was mirrored in his eyes.

"You look wonderful, Alecia."

Vard's voice never failed to send a tremor through her. She swallowed hard and cleared her throat. Time to stop acting like a teenage girl with her first infatuation.

"Thank you," she said, smiling. "This place agrees with me. I don't understand why Alique doesn't like it."

"Oh? She doesn't?"

"That's the impression I got from our brief talk," Alecia said.

He frowned. "Don't go digging around in her private life. We have enough trouble on our hands and mysteries to solve."

Alecia lifted her chin. "Of course, I won't. What are your plans?"

"You and I have a meeting with Prince Arenil, while Lin and Arelle will be shown around Selinore by one of the royals."

Alecia couldn't hide her surprise. "Really? I'm glad my ladies are to be shown such respect."

He held out his arm, and Alecia stepped into the narrow hall. It necessitated walking close to Vard, which both thrilled and frustrated her. They climbed the staircase to the next level, where a female elf in forest garb ushered them into a spacious audience chamber.

Kain was present, talking in low tones to an older elven woman in flowing robes of green and autumn gold, a crown of forest flowers on her brow. He turned to them as they entered.

"Princess, Lord Anton—please meet Queen Elora Arenil, wife of the late Orionkael Arenil and mother to Princess Gwaethe Arenil. Elora, may I present to you Princess Alecia Zialni of Brightcastle, niece of King Beniel, and the King's Blade, Lord Vard Anton."

Elora stepped forward, her bearing regal and her dark face smooth despite her age. She shook hands with Alecia, then Vard.

"I am glad to welcome you to Selinore, Princess, My Lord. We have so few kingdom visitors it is always such an exciting time when they grace us with their presence."

Alecia smiled at the queen. "It's our loss, Your Majesty. Your home is beautiful, and I thank you for your warm welcome."

Elora shook her head. "There is no need to honor me with that title, Princess. I am no longer queen since the king died. My address has reverted to My Lady, but Elora is what others call me. It is Kain's way of showing respect." She sent a fond look Kain's way.

Kain smirked. "I was raised to respect my elders and those wiser than I, Elora."

She inclined her head. "I think I would like your mother and father, then."

Alecia watched the interaction with interest. As wife of the elven king Orionkael, who had lain with a human woman and sired Kain, she had reason to resent the king's half-blood son. It seemed she had made peace with him instead.

Vard cleared his throat. "I too thank you for your welcome, Elora. I look forward to hearing some of your wisdom."

Elora inclined her head, studying Vard. Alecia noticed her gaze rested on his eyes the longest.

"I see you have other talents apart from being the King's Blade, Lord Anton. Is it you who visited with Melandrach, Orionkael's brother, recently?"

"I did. He has helped me immensely."

Elora smiled. "I'm glad. Melandrach's skill runs deep. We are fortunate to count him amongst us." She paused, her eyes tightening. "I also hear the night hounds are about."

Kain interrupted. "Let us be seated, and we can begin once the others arrive."

* * *

Vard seated Alecia and took a chair for himself opposite Kain Arenil. It wasn't long before Ruven rejoined them, as representative of Amitania. Two more female elves entered with him, one who appeared to be Elora's age wearing soldiers' garb and with a streak of white hair amongst her short black curls. The other was a stunning younger elf in a blue robe whose dark gaze held animosity. Vard stood to welcome them.

Kain rose. "Welcome Ruven, please take a seat." He turned to the older elven woman. "Rasalar, our guests are Princess Alecia of Brightcastle, niece of King Beniel Zialni, and the King's Blade, Lord Vard Anton. This is Lady Rasalar, sister to Orionkael and Melandrach, and trainer of our soldiers." Vard shook her hand. "And this is Alia Kelsis, the leader of the *Sis Lenweri* females in Selinore." He nodded his head to her and waited for the women to be seated before resuming his chair.

It was an interesting group. Vard wondered if Alia Kelsis could be trusted. From what he'd heard, the *Sis Lenweri* females captured after the battle of Amitania hadn't gone willingly to Selinore. Most were pregnant. Some of the kingdom soldiers had attacked them after one of their men was killed by the women.

It had been a mess of epic proportions, tensions running high between the *Sis Lenweri* and the humans upon reaching Brightcastle. With some of the elven females miscarrying, it had been left to Alique to treat the women.

Kain and Gwaethe Arenil had managed to extricate the *Sis Lenweri* females to Selinore, under the cover of darkness, and then smooth over relations with King Beniel.

Kain looked around the group and began speaking. "We meet in grave circumstances. I remind you that nothing we discuss can leave this room. We don't want any word getting back to the *Sis Lenweri*." He looked at Alia. "Alia Kelsis, I included you as you may have valuable intelligence to impart. You have pledged your loyalty to our cause; that of peace."

Alia's eyes flared bright, but she nodded.

"Now," Kain said, "we will discuss the night hounds. Do you have something to report on the beasts, Vard?"

Vard stood. "I have. After more than fifty years, they have returned to Thorius. I've seen them, and they're as ferocious as legends tell. As recently as last month, they've been active in Thorius. If not for the hounds, a recent attack by the *Sis Lenweri* would've succeeded in killing our king."

Alia's fists bunched in her robe. "I would know more of this attack."

Vard fixed his gaze on her. "*Sis Lenweri* ambushed the king's convoy late one night. They attacked with no warning despite the best efforts of my rangers and trackers to safeguard the campsite. *I* patrolled within the hour before the attack."

Alia glared back. "Perhaps you are not as gifted at protecting your king as you think," she said.

Elora hissed. "Alia, you will remain quiet unless asked a question."

The elven woman's lips snapped shut, and she lowered her eyes to her lap.

Vard went on. "If not for the night hounds' aid, I believe King Beniel would've perished, and likely Princess Benae of Brightcastle as well. There's no telling how many might have died. Once the attackers were dispatched, I followed the retreating hounds and found them in the company of a young woman I've met before."

Alecia turned to him, lilac gaze narrowed. "Who is it?"

He shook his head. "I can't betray her confidence. She's a witch, but the secrecy of her identity is important. She has agreed that, for now, the hounds may serve our cause."

"*For now?*" Kain asked, his tone tense but measured. "Meaning we can't rely on them."

Vard nodded. "It's a possibility. Witches can be fickle creatures."

"You sound as though you speak from experience, Vard," Kain said.

He nodded. "I've known several in my time. They're difficult to pin down. By nature, they're secretive, mysterious. But I think this sorceress has many reasons to defend the kingdom. I don't believe we need to be concerned during our war with Faenwelar."

Kain frowned. "How can we contact her?"

"She has said she will come when our need is great. She relies on dreams and her connection with the hounds to know when she must act."

Rasalar stood, her hands in fists at her sides. "We *Lenweri* have our own magic practitioners. We don't need to rely on this human witch with her hell hounds. How can we know if she can be counted upon?"

"Rasalar," Elora said, her voice low, "be at ease. The sorceress has already proven her worth by saving the king and many others. Let us not borrow trouble."

Rasalar frowned, but sat down.

Elora turned to Vard. "The hounds are known to the *Lenweri*. In the history of our people, they have been friends, but also foes. And now we know why. It must depend on who governs them."

Vard nodded. "Indeed. But I must follow up on something Rasalar said. Your magic practitioners—besides lighting, what magic can they wield?"

"Why do you ask, Lord Anton?" Elora asked, her face serene.

"I have two puzzles to solve, and magic would explain much." He told the group about the mystery of Gorin's escape from a tower in Wildecoast Keep, and of the sudden advent of the *Sis Lenweri* on the king's trip to Brightcastle. "I fear Faenwelar has employed magical arts to achieve both. However, I don't know how."

They all looked at Alia who stiffened at the attention. Her lips thinned, and her eyes hardened to flint.

"Alia," Kain said, "are you able to answer the question of what magic the *Sis Lenweri* hold?"

She snorted. "As if the elven sorcerers and lords share their secrets with such as me, a female. That knowledge is only for the high born among us. Elven children are tested at five years of age. They are taken away for this testing, so no parents ever see what it involves. Some of them do not return. We think it is magical ability that is being assessed, but no one will tell us. My sister lost a child last year. For all we know, he might be dead."

Alecia gasped. "That's horrible. Are the children ever seen again?"

Alia closed her eyes, and a tear slipped out. She seemed to gather her composure before going on. "It is difficult to know. Children change much, and they are so young when taken that they don't remember who they are. Many of us believe they are brainwashed, given another name, and are lost to their families forever."

A hush fell over the group as they digested what Alia said.

Vard turned to Ruven. "Is this your experience as well?"

Ruven frowned. "My family is heavily committed to the profession of soldiers. Even so, our children are also taken at around five. We are told they are being checked for good health. None have been kept, as with Alia's nephew." His eyes found hers, and there was sorrow in them.

"We can't assume this process is undertaken in the search for magic," Kain said. "There may indeed be a medical reason. Perhaps some children are diseased and don't return because they are…"

"Put to death?" Alecia asked, her voice higher than usual.

Kain met her gaze. "You don't know the *Sis Lenweri* as I do, Princess. They are capable of much."

"Even Faenwelar would not kill his own people, Prince Arenil," Alia snapped. "Especially not children. They are too precious."

Vard stood. "We're not getting anywhere here, so let's change focus. I want to know about the dragon lords."

Every elven face went blank at his words, even Ruven's.

"There are no dragon lords," Elora snapped. "They roamed this place centuries ago, but their beasts died of old age, or were killed in battle, and the lords met the same fate."

A curious look passed between Rasalar and Elora. Something was happening here that he didn't understand.

"Rasalar?" Vard asked. "Do you have anything to add?"

Her jaw tightened, and Elora carefully looked away.

What was going on?

Vard continued. "Because—you may laugh—but I believe a dragon could've been used to rescue Gorin. It would explain everything that puzzles us. I also think the same beast dropped the *Sis Lenweri* attackers near our campsite." He looked at Elora, Rasalar, Ruven, and Alia. "Tell me I'm wrong."

Silence greeted his words. Kain cleared his throat and stood.

"I am your lord, and you must tell me the truth," he told the four. "I see no one laughing at Lord Anton's explanation. *Is* this possible? Are there still dragons and dragon lords in this land?"

Rasalar drew in a deep breath and stood to face her leader.

"I believe Faenwelar is a dragon lord. My brothers, Orionkael and Magbalar, have shared stories with me—family stories handed down from ancient times. It is said that our father, too, had the ability, and that one of us might inherit the power to command the beasts. That is why Faenwelar could not allow Orionkael to rule any longer. He was too much of a threat, even though my brother was a peaceful leader, not interested in discovering if he contained this magical power."

Kain's face turned stony. "Why am I only hearing of this now? Did none of you think this possibility worth mentioning? This puts the battle with the *Sis Lenweri* in a whole new light!"

Vard studied the elven leader. Perhaps this news meant that Kain himself had inherited even more potent magical talents. But now wasn't the time to mention *that* possibility.

"What do we do?" Vard asked. "We must know what we're dealing with, otherwise Faenwelar may pose more of a risk than we can deal with. If there are dragons, we must plan to neutralize them."

Alecia stood. "Very few humans will believe in dragons without seeing them. Indeed, I'm struggling to believe we're discussing this. How do we confirm their presence?"

"The princess is right," Vard said. "We need proof for many reasons. It's time to focus on the hunt for evidence of dragons."

"Agreed," Kain said, turning to Elora. "Elora, please go now and consult the ancient texts for anything which might help—descriptions, locations, behavior, and who the dragon lords were. Consult the other elders in this too."

Elora bowed and left.

"Alia and Ruven," Kain said, "speak to your *Sis Lenweri* contacts here and see if you can glean any more information on the dragons and their lords."

They, too, bowed and departed.

"Rasalar, I want you to organize an expedition to Melandrach's forest home, so we may question him. See that we are well-guarded on the trip."

Rasalar dipped her head and left. Only Kain, Vard and Alecia remained.

Vard blew out a long breath. "Dragons! Who would have thought?"

"They may yet not exist," Alecia said. "It *is* far-fetched."

"The old legends are coming to life," Kain said. "I'm the last man to believe in fairy stories, but when you mention the night hounds… You've seen them in the flesh. Are they as gruesome as the stories say?"

"Worse," Vard said. "They can be killed, but if they take you by surprise, you'll be disemboweled before you can shout."

"So, we journey to Melandrach? Your uncle?" Alecia asked.

"I'm not sure you should go with us, Princess," Kain said. "There will be dangers, perhaps more than we anticipate."

"I've just tramped through the forest from Brightcastle to Amitania and then on to Selinore. I'm coming."

"I'm sure Alique would be glad of your help in the hospital," Kain said. "It's rare she gets company, and Selinore wears on her."

Alecia's eyes softened. "I'd like to spend time with her, but I also want to meet Melandrach. He sounds fascinating, and Vard…"

Vard shook his head, and she fell silent. Vard had told her Kain didn't know he was a Defender. Indeed, Vard wasn't sure if the mysterious elven Defender Melandrach had revealed his true gifts to anyone except other Defenders.

"Am I missing something?" Kain asked, brows drawn down.

"Just something that should remain in the family, Prince Arenil," Alecia said. Vard smiled at her quick thinking. His heritage, and that of Iona's, was something that shouldn't be revealed lightly.

Alecia turned to Vard. "I'm sorry, Vard."

It seemed they'd aroused Kain's interest. His eyes gleamed, perhaps at the thought of more secrets being revealed.

"Are you sure what you were about to say isn't relevant to our war effort?" Kain brought his intimidating scowl to bear, first on Alecia, then on him.

Vard's hackles rose, and a growl mounted low in his throat. He reminded himself this man was not their enemy. He was proud to see Alecia wasn't intimidated.

"Quite sure, Prince Arenil," she said. "I suggest you concern yourself with dragons and leave my family business to me. I'll be sure and tell you if I discover anything important."

Alecia's words only made the elven leader frown harder. Privately, Vard rejoiced. If Alecia sought to be queen, she'd need every bit of the spine she'd shown Kain this day. But, then again, the odds of her succeeding in her quest were slim.

Kain huffed out a breath. "Very well. Have you decided if you'll accompany us to visit Melandrach?"

Alecia adopted a lofty air. "Not yet. I'll consult with Vard and my ladies, and speak with your good wife before I decide."

At that moment, Lady Alique appeared at the chamber door. Kain went to greet her and guided her to them. She curtsied to Alecia, and Vard kissed her hand.

"Princess," Alique said, "I wondered if you'd like a tour of my hospital. We have patients who'd like to meet you. I think it would do them good to spend time with you."

Kain nodded. "Please go with my wife, Princess. We'll meet in an hour for a late luncheon."

Alecia nodded and left with Lady Alique, while Vard faced Kain.

"Well, Prince Arenil," he said, "what are the chances you have inherited the powers of the mythical dragon lords?"

CHAPTER THREE

ALECIA reveled in the peace of the giant trees as she walked with Alique to the hospital. "Selinore is quite beautiful, Alique," she said. "There's a rare tranquility here."

Alique looked up into the branches. "I suppose you're right. I need to stop and notice it more."

Alecia's ladies approached in the company of a short elven woman with close-cropped white hair. Except for the pointed ears and chocolate-colored skin, she could have passed for human. Though there were races of humans in remote kingdoms with very dark skin. The three were laughing over something Arelle said.

"Isiloe," Alique said. "I want you to meet Princess Alecia."

The diminutive elven woman's pale blue gaze, rare amongst the elves, collided with hers. "I am pleased to make your acquaintance, Princess." She was polite, but there was no other deference shown.

"Likewise, Isiloe. I must thank you for keeping my ladies company while we were discussing the dreary matters of war." She examined Isiloe's green and brown breeches and tunic. "Are you one of the famous elven warriors we've heard so much about?"

"You mean famous *female* elven warriors, Princess?" Isiloe asked, her tone cool.

Alecia refused to be cowed by the snippy tone. "Yes, if you like."

Isiloe nodded. "I am an elven warrior. We do not distinguish between male and female as you in the kingdom do. Indeed, you appear to be dressed in men's clothing. That must make you famous as well?"

"So far, Isiloe," Alecia said, "I think I may be more notorious than famous."

"Isiloe," Alique said, her tone soft, but firm, "is Julli in the hospital?"

"Yes, she has a great sense of duty, that one." Isiloe went to walk past, but Alique laid her hand on the elven woman's arm.

"Kain is organizing a trip to visit Melandrach. Can you help with that? I know you'll want to see your uncle."

"Is Kain going?" Isiloe asked.

"Yes, I believe so," Alique said.

"I will think on it." Isiloe turned to Arelle and Lin. "Come with me." She strode away without another word.

Lin and Arelle raised their brows and looked at Alecia and Alique.

"With your permission, Princess, Lady, we will accompany Lady Isiloe." Lin said

Alique laughed. "Don't let her hear you call her 'lady'!"

"Go with my blessings," Alecia said.

Her ladies hurried off.

"I'm sorry for Isiloe's abruptness, Princess. It's merely her way. She'll bow to no one, especially one not elven."

"Oh," Alecia said. "How does that affect her dealings with Kain?"

Alique shook her head. "It's rocky and has been from the start. For some reason, she has attached herself to me, especially since Gwaethe left for Amitania. Isiloe and Gwaethe are very close. I think that's the source of conflict. Isiloe's offended that Kain has taken Gwaethe's position."

Alecia frowned. "How does Gwaethe feel about Kain being leader?"

"She's overjoyed, mostly. I'm sure she'd like to lead the *Lenweri* herself, but since her marriage to Jacques Vorasava, she's content to work with him to create a place in Amitania where our two races can live as one."

"It's certainly a remarkable city now. Much different to when I was there before. What Gwaethe and Jacques have formed from the rubble is a tribute to them."

"You have traveled far lately, Princess."

"Please, call me Alecia, and I shall call you Alique."

The gorgeous blonde inclined her head. "Allow me to show you through my hospital."

They continued another hundred paces until they arrived at a low set building made of granite with a slate roof. A verandah ran along the front with many doors leading off it. Alique paused to allow her guest to take it in.

"It's amazing. You've built so much in a short time. How many patients can you hold?"

Alique led the way up the central steps. "Comfortably fifty, but, if pushed, we could care for three times that number. We'll extend in time, or perhaps build another hospital, especially for the elderly or pregnant."

"Or both?"

"Indeed." Alique led Alecia through the front doors, past a desk where a young woman sat, writing on parchment.

"Julli, I want you to meet someone," she said.

Julli stood and walked around her desk to stand before Alecia.

"Princess Alecia Zialni of Brightcastle, this is my assistant in this venture, Julli Dovara."

Julli curtseyed, and Alecia grasped her hand. "I'm so pleased to meet you, Julli. You must show me your hospital."

Julli's eyes went wide. "Oh, Princess! I couldn't presume to show you around. This is Lady Alique's work, not mine."

"Nonsense, Julli," Alique said. "I could never have done this without you. We'll show the princess together."

She held out her hand, and Julli linked her arm through hers. Together, they walked down to the first door on the left of the central hallway.

"This leads to the wards," Julli said, her voice low and calm. "They occupy this side of the building. The surgery, preparation, and consulting areas are on the right. We also house the maternity wing on that side."

Alecia spent an enjoyable hour touring the hospital and speaking to the patients. A fireplace warmed each ward and workroom, and a laundry and kitchen lay at the back of the building. It seemed Alique and her team had thought of everything. The stone had been brought from a nearby quarry, and more continued to be brought in preparation for future building needs.

After the tour, Julli went back to her patients while Alecia and Alique took tea in the office. Their talk turned to life in Selinore.

"Some of the younger elves desire their buildings to be of stone," Alique said. "It's the human influence. It also makes sense that people living in a forest are wary of fire. Kain has directed that firebreaks be made through the surrounding trees. You should have seen the fight he had over that!"

"I can imagine," Alecia said. "It makes sense, though. And I assume the wood from the felled trees didn't go to waste?"

"It didn't," Alique said. "We'll use it to make more furniture for the hospital when it's dry enough. As part of Kain's contract with the forest, we must plant a tree for each one we remove."

"What do you mean by contract?" Alecia asked.

"It's complicated to explain, and even I don't really understand. Kain can talk to the trees." She shivered, but then stiffened her shoulders and met Alecia's gaze. "They allow this sacrifice because he's special to them. Sometimes it's hard to reconcile the man I knew as army general with the man who commands the *Lenweri* today."

Alique's somber words struck Alecia. She didn't know what to say. Vard had changed in the time they were apart, but perhaps not to the degree that Kain had. Should she even comment?

"I think I've shocked you with my words, Alecia."

She met the direct gaze of the healer. "I don't know you well, Alique. It would be easy for me to say the wrong thing. Lately I've been trying to watch my words."

Alique laughed. "I'm more difficult to offend than you think. When you've been to the edge of life and back, it changes you."

"But not so much that you want to live in the forest?"

Alique looked down at her teacup. "Not as much as that. I'm making the most of my life here. I must learn to bend, so I don't snap. Kain has been wonderful. It's a difficult transition for him, too."

Alecia sighed. "It seems we're all in a period of great change. Let's hope it's for the good. If it helps, I admire what you've achieved here."

Alique smiled, but her eyes remained sad. "It helps a little. It would help even more to visit my parents, but it seems too difficult to achieve now. And they won't visit me. Father is terrified that if he leaves the estate, something dreadful will happen. You know the *Sis Lenweri* took my family. We only got them back because Kain and I agreed to be hostages. Then Father was taken again when *he* tried to help *us*. He hasn't recovered from that trauma. It has left him a changed man. His eyes…" She shivered.

Alecia reached out and took her hand. "I'm sure you'll see your father and mother soon. Instead, perhaps you could travel with us back to Brightcastle when we return. I know Ramón would love to see you."

She brightened at the thought. "Perhaps. I'll think on it."

* * *

Vard returned from his bird form to human in time to watch his father morph from the wolf. As soon as the change was complete, he stepped closer and hugged his parent.

He had waited long for this. The emotion that coursed through him took him by surprise. He still had trouble believing his father was alive, let alone a fully-fledged Defender.

He stepped back and examined the older man. "You've changed, Father. I like how the mantle of Defender sits upon your shoulders."

Lyam Anton smiled, his gaze no longer haunted as it had been. "Melandrach was everything you said. He has helped me despite how difficult it has been at times. I'm strong, but still getting used to it all. He also helped me to forgive myself for the atrocities I've committed." At those words some of the grief returned. "I can't live in the past and must keep moving forward."

Vard nodded. "It's how we all must live. I need you with me. Are you prepared to return to Wildecoast to organize the defense of the kingdom?"

Lyam squared his shoulders, and a fierce light entered his gaze. "I am, though perhaps I need more arms training. I've been sparring with Vortek Cruzen, the other Defender you sent to Melandrach, but I'm not content with my skills."

"You may have your choice of where you live. Either Brightcastle or Wildecoast will provide opportunities for learning weapons. But I'd like you with me."

Lyam nodded. "We've been too long apart." He paused. "Princess Alecia and my granddaughter are in Brightcastle, are they not?"

Vard nodded. "It's why I suggested you may like to stay in that city. As much as I long to keep you close, I'd feel better having you near Alecia and Iona."

"From what I hear, Alecia needs no protection."

Vard frowned. "She's courageous and impulsive, two traits that are dangerous when combined. But you're correct, she's fierce enough for three women."

"We should return to Melandrach and the others before we're missed," Lyam said.

"Yes, Father. One more thing. I don't want Kain knowing you're my father just yet. Can you keep this secret from him for a little longer? I'll just say you're a ranger come into my service."

Lyam nodded. "You don't trust the half-blood elven prince?"

"I don't know him, and he knows nothing of Defenders. Even though he has recently confronted elven magic, I don't know if he could handle the reality of shapeshifters. If he knew we were related, it might raise awkward questions. Being associated with me may even put you in danger, now that I'm the King's Blade."

Lyam grasped Vard on the shoulder, joy shining in his eyes. "I'm so proud of you, son. To think that my child has risen to such heights… and you've accomplished it all on your own, with no political help."

Vard cocked an eyebrow. "Actually, I don't think it has hurt being associated with Alecia. At the very least, it brought me to the king's— and the queen's—notice."

"Do I hear a story in that?"

"You know most of it. However, the king relies heavily on his wife's advice, and Queen Adriana is… fond of me." He felt heat in his cheeks. "I'm not sure if you've noticed, but women are drawn to Defenders. The more powerful we are, the more draw we have. And then there is compulsion."

Lyam gasped. "You haven't used *that* on the monarchs?"

"Only a little to escape Adriana's clutches one night."

His father's eyes widened. "Even though you belong to her niece?"

"In Adriana's opinion, all's fair in love and war."

Lyam shook his head. "I agree, we will tell no one of our relationship. Perhaps it's best I stay in Brightcastle rather than with you? Who knows of your Defender powers?"

"Alecia, of course, two witches—but I also know their secret so they will keep mine… and the admiral of the King's Navy."

Lyam's mouth dropped open. "Is that wise?"

Vard shook his head. "Definitely not. It was an accident." He told Lyam how it happened. "Another reason to stay well away from Wildecoast."

"Let us return, Vard. I'll go first and meet the visitors, and then you can follow."

Vard folded his arms and watched his father morph into the pale gray wolf. He howled and bounded off through the trees. Vard smiled to himself and formed the image of the hawk in his mind...

When Vard arrived back in camp, everyone was settled around the fire, sitting on logs. Most were eating the evening meal. A ring of elven and ranger guards stood at the edge of the clearing, far enough away that they wouldn't hear the discussion. Melandrach approached and surreptitiously removed a feather from Vard's shoulder, then introduced him to Lyam and Vortek along with two humans and three elves who were currently living with him.

Vard shook his father's and Vortek's hands as if they were meeting for the first time. No one would've known any differently. However, when he seated himself on a log beside Kain, he found Isiloe's eyes upon him. She, of all of them, might have an inkling that Vard held secrets. He had met her briefly when trying to save Jacques Vorasava's life. To say she had regarded him with suspicion was understating it.

Vard glanced across at his father, and his heart lurched. The amulet! He had given it to Lyam before he began his training, and now it lay exposed at his father's throat. Perhaps that was why Isiloe studied him. Had she seen the amber talisman? Did it matter if she knew they were linked? He could tell her it was only a stone *like* his, if she asked. But what if she didn't ask and just assumed there was a connection? He wanted to protect his father, and secrecy was a powerful way to do that.

He tried to catch Lyam's eye, but it wasn't easy when they had agreed to pretend to be strangers. Lyam was deliberately avoiding him. *Damn!*

Kain chose that moment to rise and address those gathered. "Melandrach, uncle and elder of the *Lenweri*, brother to Orionkael and to Rasalar, I bid you greetings. Thank you for the welcome you have extended to us."

Melandrach rose. He was a tall, thin elf of indeterminate age. If his gray hair was any indication, he must have been past one hundred years old. Elves lived long lives and could be effective warriors well into their seventies. The elven Defender wore long robes in a swirling green and silver pattern that would be difficult to see in the forest. He raised hands with exceptionally long fingers, and his dark eyes swept the group.

"It is with joy that I welcome the son of Orionkael, my brother. On each occasion we have met, I have found Kain Arenil to be a wise and honorable man." A buzz went around those seated, all perhaps wondering why Melandrach chose this time to praise the half-blood elven prince. "I want you all to know that every person at this fire tonight will have a role to play in the days ahead. Indeed, I foresaw this meeting in a dream, many months ago." His eyes rested on each individual for several seconds as the silence lengthened.

Vard examined the others and found varying expressions on their faces. Kain frowned as he so often did. Isiloe's eyes were wide, as she likely imagined what her role might be. None of them had expected to be told they were a part of a prophecy this night, least of all Vard. But, of course, he expected to be an integral part of the battle for control of Thorius, being the King's Blade. It was just the prophecy that was a surprise. He hadn't realized Melandrach had a talent for seeing the future.

Melandrach continued. "I see no *Sis Lenweri* here, and this saddens me. They can provide valuable information on their people, even though you fear their loyalty isn't true."

Isiloe stormed to her feet. "How can you welcome them when they killed your brother? We cannot trust any of them."

Kain spoke up. "This is why we didn't bring our *Sis Lenweri* friends tonight, Melandrach. Our people are divided as to whether we can trust those who have pledged to our cause. We must be cautious."

Melandrach nodded, but sadness cloaked his gaze. "This is true, but we must rise above suspicion if we are to reunite our people."

Vard grew impatient. They had information to uncover. He cleared his throat and stood.

"Melandrach Arenil, can I speak openly before your followers?"

The old elf nodded.

"Then we have a question for you. Are there dragons still living on this land?"

There was a collective gasp from those who were not at the meeting earlier that day. Every eye latched onto Vard, and some lips held smirks, especially Isiloe's. She remained quiet, however, likely thinking he'd dig himself deeper into the mire.

Melandrach's gaze found Rasalar's, and she nodded.

Vard sat as Melandrach stood. "Once the dragons, lesser and greater, inhabited all the world, including Thorius. They had a love of mountains and forests; they lived in vast caves within mountain ranges. Indeed, I believe the Usetar mountain range was home to several of the lesser dragons at one time."

"What was the difference between lesser and greater, Uncle?" Kain asked.

"It was as it sounds, My Prince. The greater were colossal beasts who could carry several men on their backs. They could also speak directly into the minds of their riders. Their colors were every shade of the rainbow, so beautiful that to look upon them would make you weep with wonder. They were highly intelligent and ate anything large enough to give them sustenance, but there was a covenant between the beasts and elves that no dragon would kill the *Lenweri*."

"The lesser dragons lacked the gift of mind speech and were around a quarter the size of their huge cousins. What they lacked in size, they made up for in ferocity, hunting in packs and stripping villages of residents."

"Why have we never heard of these dragons, except in fairy tales?" Isiloe asked.

"Hundreds of years have passed, niece, since the lesser dragons wandered the world. They couldn't be allowed to kill humans and elves. It was 'kill or be killed' from the perspective of elves and man." Melandrach rubbed a hand across his face and closed his eyes as if to draw strength. "Alone, the elves were doomed to obliteration, so they made an agreement with the humans to work together and cull the lesser dragons. Unfortunately, the beasts were wiped out, as far as I know."

"And what of the greater dragons?" Vard asked, riveted by Melandrach's story.

"The greater dragons lived on. They even helped kill particularly aggressive lesser dragons. Through this process, tighter bonds were made with the elves, and some even became dragon lords. These elves were given the right to ride the greater dragons."

"Then some could still exist today?" Vard asked.

Melandrach paused, frowning. "It is possible, though I believe the last died several decades ago. Our people have lost contact with those you call the dragon lords. As a result, we have no current knowledge of the greater dragons." Melandrach fixed Vard with his piercing gaze. "Why do you ask this question? Do you have reason to suspect dragons are active?"

"Prince Gorin of the *Sis Lenweri* escaped Wildecoast Keep in strange circumstances. If a dragon pulled out the bars of his prison and flew away with him, it would explain much. Also, the attack on King Beniel likewise could be explained with the help of a dragon. The beast could have dropped attackers near to us without being observed. The only other way this could've occurred is with the use of magic or tunnels."

"King's Blade," Melandrach said, "do you not think there could be logical explanations for these events beyond dragons?"

"There might be, but, so far, we've come up with nothing. Also, Princess Alecia of Brightcastle has had a dream featuring a beast that is likely a dragon. She has true dream visions, though they're sporadic."

"Your evidence is flimsy, Vard Anton." Melandrach sat and folded his arms across his chest.

Vard looked at Kain for help.

Kain stood. "Then you think it unlikely dragons patrol the skies and fight for our enemies, Uncle?"

Melandrach drew a deep breath, and met the eyes of his leader. "It is unlikely."

"But worth keeping in mind as we approach our war with the *Sis Lenweri*?" Kain asked. "Or is this a crazy idea which we must cast aside?"

Vard stiffened. Over his dead body would he lay aside this theory. Alecia's vision had sealed the evidence for him, but he could understand why others would fight the very thought of the beasts existing.

Melandrach frowned, his bushy brows obscuring his eyes. "Stay vigilant and look for evidence of the greater dragons and their lords, by all means. It is said that Faenwelar may have inherited the power to speak to dragons, to rule them. It is also said that my brother, King Orionkael Arenil, had the same power, latent though it must have been. Which means you may also have that ability within you, nephew. Faenwelar cannot allow you to rule the elves. He will bring everything he has to eradicate you. Especially if dragons still exist."

"If they exist," Kain said, "then we must gain control of them or eradicate them. How can we do that?"

"Dragons were canny creatures with an intelligence equal to ours. There was evil at their core, so it is not surprising that Faenwelar would be drawn to them; that he would try to discover and control them. If this is so, it will be difficult in the extreme for you to command them. You are not evil, Kain Arenil. The hold you would have over a dragon would be tenuous, and your elven blood too dilute to command such a beast. Perhaps you could secure the loyalty of one of the dragon lords, if, in fact, *they* still exist. As you can see, you will have a hard time convincing anyone that the *Lenweri* should follow this path."

Vard's heart fell.

Melandrach spoke again. "Do not allow this dragon quest to skew your perspective. It is highly unlikely any still survive. You are doomed to fail if you persist in looking for something which is not there."

CHAPTER FOUR

THEY gathered once again in the meeting chamber in Selinore, but without Ruven Magbalar and Alia Kelsis. Lyam and Vortek, along with one of the elven Defenders, had accompanied them back to the forest city. As well as Vard, Alecia, and Kain, Elora, Rasalar, Isiloe, and Alique were also in attendance.

The mood was somber. They sat in a circle of chairs, each waiting for another to break the tense silence. Vard's gut churned at the thought he might have drawn them all together to discuss a fantasy.

There might well be other explanations for Gorin's escape and the failure of his rangers to detect the *Sis Lenweri* before the attack on the king's convoy.

Alecia had experienced no more true dreams, or none that she remembered. Her gift of prophecy was uncertain at best and had never been developed. He must keep his mind open to other possibilities than the dragon theory.

But each time he tried to dismiss the possibility that mythical beasts were helping the *Sis Lenweri* cause, he thought of the night hounds and their presence after five decades of absence. *They* were no myth, and their appearance in the kingdom at this time must tell them something. He'd find Lady Star and see what else she knew.

Vard stood, and all eyes fell on him. "Prince Arenil, how do you suggest we proceed?"

Kain raked his fingers through his close-cropped dark hair. "Honestly, what Melandrach said has me wanting to dismiss the idea of dragons. Don't we have enough concrete enemies without looking for mythical ones?"

"So, you believe they're all extinct?" Vard asked. "Isn't it worth continuing to look for evidence? What if we engage with the *Sis Lenweri*, and a dragon threatens us? How will we combat that?"

Isiloe jumped to her feet with a hiss. "You heard my uncle! That possibility is unlikely. Melandrach is wise." Her eyes fell to the stone he now wore at his throat, having retrieved it from Lyam. "You would be brave to ignore his advice… some would say foolhardy."

Elora stood, and Isiloe quickly sat, her eyes downcast. Rasalar also glared at her daughter.

"Because you have a different view, Isiloe," Elora said, "that is no reason for rudeness and threats."

Vard cleared his throat. "I'm not offended by Ramar Isiloe's comments, Elora. She only says what many will think when they hear my theory. Despite that, I can't shake the feeling that this needs to be pursued. We must discover if dragons still exist." He turned to Kain. "Prince Arenil, with your cooperation, I wish to form a dragon task force. It will be a joint elven and human initiative. Its purpose will be to locate the beasts and their masters—if they exist—and to plan for defense against the creatures."

Kain stared at him, long enough for Vard to wonder if his plans would gain approval.

In the end, he nodded. "I'll help with that, Lord Anton. Submit your request for elven members of your task force, and I'll help in whatever way I can. I suggest you meet with Rasalar before you leave and discuss the best way to prepare our soldiers for battle against greater dragons. That way, she can adjust the training of *her* soldiers."

Alecia stood. "Prince Arenil," she said, "do you have dreamers amongst the elves here?"

Kain frowned. "I'm not sure how this is relevant."

Alecia lifted her chin. "Although my gift is undeveloped, I have experienced dreams that appear to show the future, and, other times, I know when something will happen. I'd love to spend time with your dreamers, if there are any. Also, I think we should question them about any dragon dreams."

"Ah," Kain said, "I see. There was mention of a dream you had that might have shown a dragon. Was this recent?"

She nodded. "On the trip here. I'm sure that's what my dream showed. It was a very distinctive creature, and there was fire coming from its mouth."

Elora stood. "I will take you to see our dreamers, Princess. You may spend time with them before you depart. Perhaps one of them would travel with you."

Alecia's eyes widened. "That would be wonderful, Lady Elora."

Elora nodded and sat, her hands folded in her lap. Alecia resumed her seat beside Vard, and he felt the fine tremors of excitement in her body. This gift of hers could be useful if developed.

Vard continued. "I'll spend another day in Selinore and then must leave for Brightcastle." He met Kain Arenil's dark gaze. "Might I have a private word with you, Prince Arenil?"

The others, including Alecia, rose and left, talking amongst themselves as they went. When they were alone, Vard turned to Kain.

"I don't wish to offend you, Kain, but I wanted to speak to you about the coming conflict with the *Sis Lenweri*. Can King Beniel be certain of your support when the time comes?"

Kain's eyes hardened. "I could ask *you* the same thing. I believe Faenwelar will come against the *Lenweri* in Selinore first, then attempt to take the kingdom. Can we count on *your* help in preventing his victory over *us*?"

"It would be unwise of King Beniel to deny you soldiers. I'll counsel him to come to your aid."

"And he would listen?"

"I think so. Humans and elves have worked together to defeat the *Sis Lenweri* before. We can do so again. If I have your word that you'll come to our aid, then I'll do my best to see that we do the same for you. Princess Gwaethe has provided elven warriors who will stay in Brightcastle. Perhaps you can send some who can go with me to Wildecoast?"

Kain frowned and paced back and forth across the room, rubbing his chin. He stopped and faced Vard. "That's a good idea. The more we understand each other, the more trust there will be. I'll choose both scholars and warriors to go with you."

"And I'll leave six ravens trained to return to Wildecoast Keep. You may use them for communication. Do you have any way you can get word to Amitania?"

Kain nodded. "I do."

That was all he said, but a strange look crossed his face. Vard left it at that.

"I'll take my leave now and prepare for departure tomorrow. If you can gather the elves who will travel to Wildecoast, I'll send you a list of those who might help with the dragon task force. Perhaps many can perform both tasks? "

Kain nodded. "A good idea. If they aren't ready to leave with you, they will leave within days."

Vard nodded and bowed, then left the audience chamber.

Alique waited for him outside. "I wish to travel back with you to Brightcastle."

"Does your husband know?" Vard asked.

She shook her head. "I'm about to inform him. He won't like it, but I'll take Isiloe with me. That should settle any qualms he has."

Vard frowned. "I don't want to come between you and your husband, though another healer would be welcome. And Isiloe is a fearsome warrior, I've heard. I might train her for the dragon force."

"Then you'll go ahead with this dragon task force?"

He nodded. "I must, even though many will laugh."

"Including Isiloe. I don't think she's the right one to invite."

"That remains to be seen. Who will run your hospital here?"

"Julli is very capable, and she'll be aided by an elven healer named Tuthariel. I'm confident all will be well. And I won't be gone forever."

"The situation could change rapidly, Lady Alique. You may be stranded in Brightcastle, and travel is treacherous at the best of times, let alone now."

She raised her chin and fixed him with her arresting blue gaze. "I've been to the door of death, walked through, and returned, Lord Anton. I won't shrink from this." She stared at him unflinchingly. "And now, if you'll excuse me, I must speak with my husband."

Vard bowed and descended to the base of the tree where he found Rasalar waiting. Together, they formulated defense plans for their dragon squad. Rasalar agreed to begin training and to only advise the leaders of the purpose of their drills, not the squad members.

Elves who had mastered the long bow and could shoot 250 yards would make up the force. It was decided that shooting the eye of an attacking dragon was the swiftest way to disable it.

Rasalar suggested a dozen warriors who could accompany them to Brightcastle and on to Wildecoast. She consulted with Elora who offered another six elders as diplomats and advisors.

As the sun disappeared behind the treetops, Alecia found Vard. She had donned an emerald green robe covered with swirling patterns of silver thread. He paused a moment to admire her beauty. The attire suited her, even though he would never have imagined it.

She smiled as she approached. "You've been busy all day. I have it on good authority you haven't eaten, so I'm here to invite you to a feast."

He raised his brows, taking in the failing light. "Indeed, I lost track of time. Might I say you look fetching in that robe."

She laughed, and he loved the carefree sound, even though he imagined she was far from free of worry. For one thing, she must miss Iona terribly.

"You never used to be such a flatterer, Vard. Living at court has changed you. Perhaps my aunt has had a hand in that." She frowned and studied him.

"Now, Alecia, there's no need to worry that Adriana will steal my heart. It's already given."

His words only made her frown deepen. "Then she has tried! I *knew* I couldn't trust her. How many times has she tried to seduce you?"

"I refuse to answer that question. You have nothing to fear. Besides, haven't you declined my offer of marriage?"

He immediately regretted his words. Pain smashed across her face, and her eyes dropped to the leaf litter. He raised her face with a gentle pressure to her chin.

"Beloved, I'll always be yours. I'll wait for you until the end of days. I only hope you spurn all those who will seek your attention and affection. I'm a jealous man."

"Can we spend time together tonight, Vard? I need you."

Vard's instinct was to refuse her, but the yearning in her lilac gaze found an answering need within him. Even if they couldn't lie together, they could enjoy each other's company.

"After the feast, we'll find a quiet corner where we can talk, I promise."

* * *

The elven feast, hosted by Prince Arenil, was held in the city's central square, which was an extensive park surrounded by the great trees. Alecia was glad that all who lived in Selinore had been invited. Even Melandrach came to celebrate. He couldn't be a total recluse after all.

Her eyes followed Vard wherever he went, and he was almost always in the company of females. Alia Kelsis seemed to find him fascinating, and Alique appeared completely at ease in his presence. Even Isiloe had warmed to the King's Blade. Perhaps she wasn't immune to his Defender attraction. The older female elves deferred to him as though he were the font of all wisdom, even Rasalar and Elora.

Alecia fetched a drink and returned to sit with Lin and Arelle, who had both imbibed too much wine. They were giggling over something silly that Arelle said.

"Could you conduct yourselves with a little more decorum, ladies?" Alecia asked, seating herself on a log beside them.

That sent them both into hysterics. Eventually, they sobered enough to speak.

"I'm sorry, Princess," Lin said. "It's been a long couple of weeks. We're just letting our hair down tonight."

Arelle joined her. "It's been a long month! This is just what I needed. Before tonight, I was getting so tense and moody, even jumpy."

Alecia frowned. "That's all very well, but what will people say?"

"What will the elves say, you mean?" Lin said. "All the humans here are as tipsy as we are... well, most of them."

"Lady Alique is abstaining," Alecia said. "And Vard never drinks much."

She frowned as a bewitching elven female leant closer to Vard, her eyes upon his mouth. She gasped, and her ladies followed her gaze.

"Ooh! Isiloe's sister is making a play for the King's Blade. I wonder what Rasalar will say of that?" Arelle said, hand on her heart.

"Hush, Arelle," Lin scolded. "Someone will hear you." Her eyes darted to Alecia. "You know Vard would never betray you. Don't you?"

Alecia's fists gripped her gown. "He needs to keep his distance from her. He has always been too damned attractive for his own good. Even the queen has her eye on him."

"Alecia! Surely you jest?" Lin said.

"I do not. He has assured me he's immune to her, but she's as good as his employer. I hate to think what pressure she might bring to bear on him."

"I can't see anything you can do about that except trust him. Besides, do you expect him to place his life on hold until you see fit to include him in yours?"

Alecia gasped. "How dare you!"

"Well," Lin said, "isn't that what you're doing? Vard would have you tomorrow. He'd move you and Iona into the palace at Wildecoast. You told me he offered to do just that."

Finding Lin's observation painful, Alecia changed the subject. "You said that was Isiloe's sister? I never knew she had one." The elven female looked nothing like Isiloe, but she could see the resemblance to Gwaethe—tall, lithe, dark curly hair, and stunning.

"Yes, that's Chandrelle," Arelle said, "and we've spent quite a deal of time with her today. She can shoot a longbow almost as far as the males. Vard and she fought each other with the sword. You should see how quickly she learns. She's a born warrior."

"Please don't tell me she's coming with us?" Alecia asked.

"We're not privy to that information," Lin said.

Alecia fell into a glum silence as she watched Chandrelle run her finger down Vard's bicep. "Why doesn't he step away? I've a good mind to go over, and … and…"

Lin's brows shot skyward. "And what would you do? Cause an incident that would upset elven and human relations? She's just flirting. It will lead nowhere."

Alecia lapsed into silence, contemplating how to deal with what she was witnessing. Her ladies were correct in everything they said. Vard was loyal to her; he had rebuffed the queen's advances. And this night, he couldn't afford to upset the elves by overreacting to Chandrelle's interest.

And neither could she.

As much as she wished to stalk over and scratch the elven beauty's eyes out, she must be calm. Drawing a deep breath, she held it a moment, then let it leave her body.

"That's better, Princess," Lin said. "You must be the essence of serenity tonight."

Arelle snorted, and suddenly they were all laughing, even Alecia. It was good to truly relax after the months of pressure and responsibility. She longed for more of this joy in her life and less of the constant worry. But that life was still far off.

Lin sobered first. "You know I'm right. Vard would marry you tonight and you could enjoy a life much less fraught than this one."

Alecia met her friend's serious gaze. "Perhaps. Perhaps not. The future is by no means certain. Vard is the King's Blade now, but what if Uncle Beniel dies? I guarantee he won't have a role in the new administration. Ramón would never allow it. And then there's Piotr. If he makes a play for the throne, none of us can predict what will occur. Allowing Vard to care for me doesn't ensure my future or that of my daughter."

She regretted bringing their happy moment to an end. "But you're right. We need this night to celebrate and give thanks for our life and health. With friends like you, I know I'm well supported."

For some reason, that made her tipsy ladies laugh again. Soon they were all giggling fit to burst.

* * *

Vard heard laughter and glanced toward the sound. It surprised him to see Alecia and her ladies giggling uncontrollably. His love wasn't given to public displays of hilarity, although her ladies, not being high born, couldn't be expected to have the same standards.

He studied them for a time. It seemed his hope that the female attention he enjoyed this evening might make Alecia jealous was in vain. She wasn't paying him and his beautiful companion any attention. Had she noticed Chandrelle's obvious seduction attempt? Had she seen the way Alique hung on his every word, or the interest in the eyes of Alia Kelsis? Even the older elven females had sought him out today and at this event.

Chandrelle hissed. "Even for a kingdom princess, she lacks decorum."

"I can't agree with you there, Lady Chandrelle." Vard knew adding the "lady", would discomfort her. In that, she was just like her sister Isiloe. "Princess Alecia has many aspects to her persona. I'd caution you not to underestimate her…in anything."

The beautiful elf's eyebrows rose. "Do I detect admiration from you, King's Blade?"

"There is much to admire." His eyes drifted back to Alecia, his heart quickening in anticipation of their meeting later. "Perhaps, now that you've agreed to travel with us, you'll have the opportunity to know her better."

"I have yet to meet the princess."

"Allow me to remedy that." Vard led her over to Alecia, Arelle, and Linnet.

He bowed. "Princess Alecia, ladies, I hope you're enjoying the party."

Alecia stood, as did Lin and Arelle.

"Hello, Vard," Alecia said. "We're having a lovely night. Who's your companion?"

He turned to Chandrelle. "This is Chandrelle, Rasalar's daughter and a gifted warrior." He sensed a spike of anger from his love. Perhaps she *had* seen the women flirting with him after all.

Chandrelle bowed gracefully. "It is my pleasure to meet you, Your Highness."

"Likewise," Alecia said. "You have a beautiful city here, one like none I've ever encountered."

Chandrelle nodded. "It is true that Selinore is unique. I shall miss it."

Vard's heart skipped a beat. He'd wanted to tell Alecia who was going with them himself.

"You'll miss Selinore? Why?"

"Has Lord Anton not told you? I am accompanying him to Brightcastle, and possibly to Wildecoast. I have rarely seen the ocean and think I would like to spend time there."

Alecia's eyes widened briefly, but she managed to hide her shock. Almost. "I see. Yes, you will surely miss the trees. Though perhaps you'll be far too busy in Wildecoast to enjoy the ocean?"

Chandrelle looked up at Vard and smiled. "I am never too busy for enjoyment." The way she said the words, Alecia could've been in no doubt of her meaning. The flash of her anger stabbed at Vard.

Luckily, Chandrelle spotted someone she wanted to introduce him to. They made their apologies and left the ladies.

* * *

Later that night, Alecia sought the meeting place Vard had suggested. It was reached by a narrow trail that led up the side of a hill and opened to a lookout. A wooden bench had been placed there so that one could look over the forest with the mountains as a backdrop. The moon cast a gentle light on the trees below. She took the seat and breathed deeply to allow the peace of the scene to settle her.

She felt Vard's presence before she heard or saw him. They'd been attuned to each other from the first meeting. She closed her eyes to gather her resolve.

"You look beautiful tonight." His sexy low voice never failed to make her nerve endings dance.

"Nice of you to notice. I thought you might've been too busy."

He sat beside her, not quite touching. "I'm never too busy to notice you, love."

Her eyes met his in the moonlight, and the gold chips of his irises sparkled. His pupils glowed faintly. Despite herself, Alecia shivered. Vard was as alien as the elves, sometimes.

She drew a deep breath. How to say this without angering him?

"You protest your love for me, and yet you allow Chandrelle to paw at you in public. What was that about?"

"I didn't notice. I only have eyes for you."

"Rubbish! And then to allow her to tell me she was coming with us!"

He huffed and stood, striding to the edge of the lookout and back. "It may surprise you, Alecia, but I don't control everything and everyone around me. Nor can I predict what a sly elven female will do."

"So, you admit she's sly!"

"As a race, the elves are certainly cunning. Even they would agree with that."

Alecia joined him and looked out over the forest. "It's quite beautiful with the moonlight on the tops of the trees," she said, her voice hushed.

Vard turned to her. "I didn't come here to fight. I'm sorry Chandrelle upset you. Always know I love you. You're the only woman for me."

She gazed up into his glowing eyes and wrapped her arms around his waist.

"How long will you wait for me?" she asked, her eyes on his lips.

"You're the mother of my daughter and the holder of my heart. I'll wait for you until the sun ceases to rise in the morning. We are one."

Alecia allowed the words to settle in her heart. When it was just the two of them, she could almost believe the world would allow them to be husband and wife one day. And it would, if only she could be queen. Deep in her heart and her gut, she believed that was what the Goddess had ordained—a new queen should rule Thorius. But would Vard wait for her?

"Are you sure? Is it fair to ask you to place your life on hold, to distance you from our daughter? What if we never find a time and place to be together?"

He drew her to the bench, and they sat. He placed his arm around her, and she rested her head on his shoulder.

"I know you, Alecia. I love and respect you. When you should've given up on me; when I left you more than once, no matter the reason, you'd have been within your right to turn your back. But you didn't. Our love can stand this test."

"Really? Is there still room for me in your life? You're hardly the same man who left me on Andra's farm."

"That man was desperate and frightened—almost mad. The man I am now is so much more. I can love and protect you—make you happy. I'm no longer a risk to your safety. That desperate soul has found his place. If you need to find yours, who am I to stand in your way?"

"It won't be easy, Vard." She reached for his hand and interlocked their fingers. "Even now, I long to melt into your arms and let you take me to Wildecoast. Is that a foolish dream? Would Uncle Beniel allow us to marry?"

Vard turned to face her, and she saw a desperate yearning in his gaze. It was gone in moments, replaced by his somber mask. "As to that, who can say? The king counts on my support, but as for marrying his niece—it might be a stretch to say he'd *support* us." He studied her. "But, my love, you have desires and plans to pursue. You wouldn't be happy to lay those aside. I'm content to watch you follow your path."

"But you don't think I can succeed. Why would you want me to pursue something you think I'll fail at?"

He kissed her. It was sweet and over far too soon.

"I love you and want you to be happy. I'd never stand in the way of something you truly desire. And you want to be queen with all your heart. As long as you don't try to depose King Beniel or undermine him, I'll support you."

She looked out at the moon. "If only this silly rule about females didn't exist, I'd be heir to the throne now. It can change. It only needs the king to nominate me as his heir, and I'll continue to urge him to do so. I won't have Piotr taking my place!"

"Alecia, for tonight, can we lay aside this problem and just be together? I know you don't wish to lie with me, but can we hold each other? May I kiss you?"

She gazed up at the man she loved more than life itself. "Kiss me, Vard."

CHAPTER FIVE

TEN days later, they arrived, weary and footsore, in Brightcastle. Alecia rode at the head of the party with her ladies, Vard, and Ruven Magbalar. She was astonished to see the royal household turned out to welcome them.

Ramón and Benae were the first to greet them. Standing with them was the king.

"You look much restored, Uncle Beniel," she said, dropping into a curtsy and then rising to hug her uncle. "How are you feeling?"

"Like a new man, Alecia. Benae has taken good care of me."

Alecia gritted her teeth, but smiled at Benae. "Thank you for all you've done. I trust our children are well too?"

Benae's smile was tight. "They're fighting fit, Alecia. Iona has missed you. She started crawling while you were away."

Alecia's heart cracked at the news. Late to reach this stage, she had nevertheless hoped Iona would wait to crawl until she returned. Would she miss more important milestones in her mission to rule Thorius?

She glanced at Vard and gulped at the sorrow in his eyes. He had missed *all* the milestones their daughter reached over the last year. And here she was, keeping him away from her.

She drew a deep breath and nodded. "I can't wait to see how she has changed. Is Solomon well?"

Benae's eyes danced at the mention of her son. "Solomon has been spending much time with King Beniel. They've become close."

Alecia knew a pang of envy. Of course, the king would make every attempt to form a bond with his heir.

Benae continued. "But Iona loves her great uncle as well. It was Beniel who first saw her crawl. He has become quite the babysitter in his time here." She lowered her voice. "It has kept him rested. Otherwise, I believe he would've found other ways to amuse himself."

Ramón bowed to her. "Princess Alecia, I welcome you back and trust you'll inform me before you run away next time."

She glared at him. "Do you really wish to discuss this here? There will be plenty of time to review my journey tomorrow. For now, it's time to rejoice in being reunited with our friends and loved ones."

"Indeed, Niece," King Beniel said. "I too will have something to say about your 'trip'."

Alecia attempted to smile at the king, but she failed miserably. Why must they treat her as a child? Even Vard did so at times. Well, they'd learn they must treat her as an equal. She moved on up the line, finding her way to Millie, who curtseyed, then gripped her hand. She had tears in her eyes.

"I was so worried, Princess. My stomach hasn't stopped churning since you left. I was fearful something terrible would happen, leaving little Iona motherless."

Alecia squeezed the woman's hand, feeling guilty. "Please be at ease. I must get outside Brightcastle sometimes. As a princess of the kingdom, I need to see my people." She added under her breath. "Even if there are those who would dismiss me."

Millie's face hadn't lost an ounce of the stress she must have endured while Alecia was away. A tear leaked from her eye as she nodded, and her lips trembled.

Alecia gripped her hands. "Be brave, Millie. This isn't the place to lose your composure." She nodded, and Alecia entered the castle, Millie following and sniffing.

She nodded to more servants in the entry and made her way to the palace nursery where Solomon and Iona were being minded. One good thing about her lowered status was that she didn't need to bother with finding accommodation for the many dignitaries they'd brought with them. Vard, Ramón, and Benae would see to that. It was no longer her castle to order.

She stepped into the nursery and froze, her hands going to her chest. The nanny drew Iona's attention to her presence and the ebony-haired child squealed and raised her hands into the air. Alecia crossed the room and picked her up, bringing the baby tight against her chest. She closed her eyes as Iona grabbed a fist of her hair and planted her lips on Alecia's cheek. She started sucking vigorously, and her free hand patted her mother's chest.

Alecia's heart cracked the rest of the way open, realizing that Iona wanted the breast, but she was now dry. She closed her eyes in a vain attempt to stop the tears. Iona's scent filled her nostrils, and all she wished for was to sit and nurse her child. The nanny quietly handed her a bottle of goat's milk.

"I'll leave you and check on Solomon," she said. "He's in the next room."

Alecia sat and adjusted Iona before placing the bottle to her lips. She fussed and cried out, her little forehead puckered in an adorable frown. But Alecia didn't smile, being too devastated that she couldn't give her daughter what she really wanted.

Finally, Iona settled and took the bottle. The gentle slurps of a feeding baby filled the room. Eventually, she fell asleep. Alecia relaxed back into the chair and closed her eyes. Her joyful return wasn't all she had imagined. How long would Iona's desire for the breast cause this intense guilt? She shouldn't have left her so early; should have made sure the baby was happily and gradually weaned before charging off to Amitania. More tears threatened as she struggled to get her ragged emotions under control. When she opened her eyes, Vard was there.

"What's the matter?" he asked.

She sighed. "Iona wanted the breast, and I'm dry now. I should never have left her so young."

He squatted before her and wiped a tear from the corner of her eye. "Don't be sad. You're an excellent mother. Iona is past twelve months old by my reckoning and, though she no doubt would find comfort in the breast, surely she no longer needs it?"

Alecia huffed. "Perhaps I underestimated how much *I* need the connection."

Vard smiled. "No doubt, but you can't go back in time. Your time away was important to you and Iona was in safe hands. Even if you fail in your quest, it's something you must do."

"You really know how to encourage a woman," she sniffed, quietly.

"I understand more than you think. Do you believe I ever wanted to leave you when I did? At any stage? I knew what I'd be giving up, what it would do to you—to us. But to remove the danger I posed to you and later to Iona, I had to make that sacrifice. I understand."

Alecia allowed his words to sink in. He *did* understand, and now she knew a little of what that sacrifice meant to him. He'd missed them; missed Iona growing up. She held out her hand to him, and he took it, gently squeezing her fingers.

He stood. "I must help settle our retinue. I just wanted to see Iona and make sure you were well. The news of her crawling hit you hard."

She nodded, unable to trust her voice.

"I'll see you later at the banquet." Vard left quietly, and Alecia stood and placed her sleeping daughter in her crib. She spoke to the nanny and left the nursery, glad to see the royal guard on duty in the hallway.

Back in her room, she shed her travel-stained clothes and stepped into the bath Millie ordered. The maid helped her wash her hair and chatted about castle gossip. Alecia allowed her voice to soothe away her worries. As Millie's fingers massaged her scalp, she concentrated on the glorious sensations, freeing her mind for a few precious minutes.

"I'll order early luncheon, Princess," Millie said, "and then you can have a quick nap before we prepare for the banquet."

Alecia sighed. "That sounds fine, Millie." Why must there always be a banquet before anything else? They could all do with a good night's sleep. Instead, they would eat and drink too much tonight before falling into their beds after midnight.

She sighed again. "This bath will ensure I really enjoy my nap. Thank you."

The maid helped Alecia into a simple shift for sleeping and left. She was glad of the chance to relax over the lunch that soon arrived. As she supped on fresh bread and creamy cheese, and fruit, she gazed out over the southern alps and wondered where she'd get her support from. It wasn't enough to have Gwaethe and Jacques in her corner.

She must speak with the nobility and guild leaders, gauge their feelings about Ramón and Benae, and even King Beniel. Despite giving her assurance to Vard that she wouldn't challenge the king while he lived, she couldn't just sit and wait, or events would overtake her. At the moment, no one thought her a serious contender for the throne, but she must correct that. Somehow, she would make it known that things must change in the kingdom.

But the men wouldn't take her seriously. If she could convince their wives of her suitability to rule, would that help? It couldn't hurt, that was for sure.

She finished her meal and retired to bed, asleep as soon as her head hit the pillow.

The ball was in full swing when Alecia made her way to the grand ballroom. Her satin lilac gown had a full skirt with gold thread worked in a leaf pattern over the bodice and running in vines down the skirt and sleeves. At the top of the stairs, she stopped and drew a deep breath, hoping to dispel the nerves battering her stomach. It reminded her of the night of her betrothal to Lord Finus. Thoughts of that time always left her uneasy.

Vard appeared at her side, resplendent in a dark gray brocade jacket and black breeches. She'd never seen him dressed thus, and he stole her breath.

"May I escort you to the ballroom, Princess?" he asked.

His voice sent shivers through her and banished her nerves. "Vard, I'd love that."

"You were remembering another night not so long ago, if I'm not mistaken."

She nodded, and they began their descent. "That night, everything went so horribly wrong in my life, except for you. But I came close to losing you as well."

He shrugged and Alecia wished she could be so nonchalant. "Everything changes. We make choices that seem correct. If I could go back, I'd change some things, but I'd *always* choose you. You've brought only good to my world."

She felt her face burn. "Hush. Someone will hear."

His gaze burned into her, its intensity firing the ache in her belly. "You only have to say the word, Alecia, and we'll be wed. I'll protect you until the end of time."

She went to reply, and he held up his hands. "I know what you wish for and am content to wait. I just wanted you to be in no doubt."

She smiled and squeezed his hand as they reached the bottom step and were announced. Alecia held onto Vard as they entered the ballroom. Honestly, she didn't wish to let go, but she must prove herself. Hanging off the King's Blade was not the way to do so.

"Save me a dance?" she asked.

"I'll find you. Go and enjoy yourself." He cast her a last, intense look, bowed, and left her. She watched him make his way through the crowd, trying to curb her jealous response to the women, young and old, who waylaid him.

"I won't look," she muttered to herself and turned to find Lin there.

"Talking to yourself, Princess?" she asked, a cheeky smirk on her lips. Lin looked gorgeous in a royal blue gown of simple cut that enhanced the willowy suppleness of her body. Her short curly red hair was unadorned, but someone had painted her face. A blue sapphire choker ringed her throat, and matching earrings hung from her earlobes.

Alecia beamed. "Countess, you're stunning!"

"I must thank you for the jewelry, Princess. And for this dress. I do indeed think I fit in well."

"You do," Alecia said, looping her arm through Lin's and steering her toward the food tables. "Now that we're back in Brightcastle, we must see to getting you a wardrobe and jewels fit for a countess. I don't have an unlimited supply of coin, but we'll manage. Where's Arelle?"

"She went to find Cretia and Kenna. I don't think she'll attend the ball. Does it matter?"

Alecia sighed. "It's always good to have support. These social functions can be like walking into a lion's den."

"Or the cave of a dragon. I can't believe we're looking for the beasts and elven lords who ride them. Are you certain Vard isn't completely insane?"

Alecia drew her friend over to a quiet corner. "Hush! This isn't common knowledge, and yes, I'm sure Vard is fully in control of his mind. You forget my dream, or do you think that's all rubbish as well?"

"Forgive me, but I only believe in what I see. When you can show me the dragon, then I'll believe."

Alecia folded her arms. "That's what the majority will say, I suspect. You may be correct, but the beasts did once exist—that's a fact. And if they *are* helping the *Sis Lenweri*, we must know."

"Forget them for now, I'm starving!" Lin led the way to the nearest table and piled her plate high with delicacies. Alecia followed her lead, then collected a goblet of mulled wine. As she raised the wine to her lips, Vard appeared beside her.

"A moment," he said, taking the goblet from her hand and raising it to his nose. He inhaled deeply and handed the wine back to her. Then he took Lin's and did the same. "Be sure to get me to check all wine before you consume it, ladies."

"What of the food, Lord Anton?" Lin asked.

Vard smiled at her. "It has already been checked, by me or a senior food taster, before being placed on the tables." He bowed and walked away.

Lin placed her hand on her stomach and sucked in a deep breath. "What has happened to Vard tonight? He just made my pulse race."

Alecia glared at her. "Not you too! I thought you were immune?"

"Clearly not!" Lin watched as Vard disappeared into the crowd, fanning her face.

Alecia put her concerns about Vard and other women aside and concentrated on how she was going to advance her position in court and with the elves. It wouldn't hurt to have as many friends as possible. And besides Gwaethe and Jacques, she must forge other connections within the elven community.

She spotted Isiloe standing alone and turned to Lin. "Can you find Chandrelle, and do your best to gain her trust?"

Lin stared at her. "What will *you* be doing?"

"I'm going to speak with Isiloe. She's alone over there. I wish to make her feel welcome. Please, do the same for Chandrelle."

Lin's eyebrows rose. "Right, I'll do my best." Her eyes flicked in Isiloe's direction. "Good luck with that one."

Alecia smiled. "I like a challenge." She left her goblet and food plate on a side table and headed toward Isiloe. The elven warrior reclined against a stone pillar, clothed in a cream version of her fighter's garb. It must be as close as she got to dressing up.

She stopped before Isiloe and the elven woman's piercing blue eyes swept over her. "Good evening, Princess."

Alecia smiled. "Good evening, Isiloe. Are you content with your accommodations?"

She raised one pale eyebrow. "As content as one can be in a human keep where all is stone, cold and dead. I do not know how you can live here. But the Guardian and his wife have done their best."

Now it was Alecia's turn to raise her brow. "Don't let Benae hear you call her the Guardian's wife. She's a princess now, having married my father. And she was given joint guardianship of Brightcastle by my uncle, the king."

Isiloe gave Alecia a flat look. "You are friendly with Benae?"

She frowned. "Not exactly, but we respect titles in my culture. To get along, you must understand this."

Isiloe shrugged. "I don't desire to get along in human society. I have enough difficulty in my own."

Alecia laughed. "As do I at times. Perhaps we have something in common."

Isiloe examined her again, especially her gown and hair. "Somehow I do not think you and I are alike."

Alecia would see if she could dispel that theory. "Come with me, and I'll introduce you to my daughter and Benae's son." She had heard that elves loved children and thought perhaps this would break through Isiloe's tough shell. "Then we can return and eat." She looped her arm through Isiloe's, and, although the elven woman tensed, she didn't fight the contact.

As they left the ballroom, Alecia spied several startled glances from elven guests. Chandrelle appeared positively ferocious at the sight of her sister disappearing with a human. She wondered if her objections were based on inter-racial barriers, or if she harbored hostility toward Alecia herself.

As they walked toward the royal nursery, she explained the paintings and tapestries on the walls. They were of Zialni monarchs and nobility, including her mother, Iona. Alecia stopped before her second favorite portrait of her mother. Seated upon a black mare, her hair was unbound, and her lilac eyes afire with life. Alecia lost herself in memories of this special woman.

"She is beautiful for a human," Isiloe said. "You look like her. What was she like?"

Alecia sighed. "Mother had much dignity, and she instilled in me the importance of being true to oneself. I think that's why…" Her voice trailed off as she realized she was about the say that's why she wouldn't give up on being queen. But she didn't know if she should mention that to Isiloe.

Isiloe's ice-blue gaze snapped to hers. "Why what? Do not stop now! Finally, I was learning something interesting about you humans."

Alecia giggled, but sobered as Isiloe glared at her. "I think that's what draws me to you, Isiloe. You're proud and don't suffer fools—or anyone really."

She turned back to her mother's portrait. Actually, this might be her favorite painting now. She wondered what had happened to the one that had been in her room before her year in exile. "I suppose there's no harm in telling you I wish to be the next queen of the kingdom."

A puzzled look crossed her guest's face. "But there are no ruling queens in the kingdom of men, just as there are none in my society."

Alecia continued up the stairs. "But there were. Let me show you." At the next landing, she stopped before a painting of a golden-haired woman, astride a chestnut stallion, sword raised and battle cloak billowing behind her. "This is Izebel, and she was a ruling queen of Thorius. Isn't she magnificent? Unlike my aunt and all who have gone since her, she rode into battle and was the supreme ruler of this kingdom."

"And you believe you can replicate that feat?" Isiloe's eyes were wide. "Why?"

"I thought you'd ask me how, and I wouldn't have been able to answer that. The why, I know." She touched her heart, and gut, and head. "It's in here, and here, and here. I have this deep awareness that my life is meant to be more. Our future shouldn't be based on our sex."

"Or our birth family, either," Isiloe said. "However, that is the way it is. Even I cannot change that." Her eyes bored into the painting of the warrior queen as if she rode with the monarch. Now *that* would have made an amazing picture.

"Isiloe," Alecia said, "don't you want to have the same opportunity as the males in your land? Don't you wish to lead and decide your fate?"

"I do not wish to be the queen of the elves, and neither does Gwaethe. As to being a leader, females can aspire to any other role, especially in our fighting force. Even though I am part of the ruling family, I have no desire to be drawn into that."

Alecia couldn't understand how someone as strong and feisty as Isiloe didn't have more ambition. She shook her head and ushered her guest up the final set of stairs and along to the royal nursery. A squeal of delight greeted her upon entering. Iona was across the room, on her hands and knees, crawling toward her.

Sheer delight suffused Alecia. Some days her entire world centered on this little girl. Others, she realized just how limiting being a mother was.

If her moment of weakness with Vard led to another child, it would be nigh impossible for her dreams to come true. But she'd know soon and, until then, must cast the worries from her mind.

She picked Iona up and hugged her close before presenting her to Isiloe. "This is my daughter, Iona. She has just learned to crawl and is very pleased with herself."

Isiloe smiled at Iona. "She is delightful, but I expected your child to have fair hair."

Alecia bit her lip, certain the elven woman hadn't missed a thing. Perhaps this visit hadn't been a good idea.

Isiloe cast Alecia a serious look. "Her eyes are extraordinary. The gold flecks hint at some as yet latent ability. Her father is Vard Anton, yes?"

Alecia drew a deep, steadying breath. "You're correct. We share this precious daughter and are yet to understand what her abilities will be."

"She has wisdom in her. To look into her eyes... I can't explain it, but some part of this child has been here before. She understands much without even knowing it."

Alecia laughed. "I don't mean to offend you, Isiloe. I completely agree she's special, but that's merely a proud parent talking."

Isiloe shook her head. "You are wrong. I feel it in Vard Anton too. Iona has inherited powers from her father. My uncle, Melandrach, has mysterious powers too. I know Lord Anton trained with him. The old powers and ancient creatures stir in readiness to face the evil our race has spawned."

"Isiloe, I tell you the truth when I say Iona hasn't shown her gifts yet. Part of me wishes any talents she has will stay latent. But powers need to be developed, or they can control you."

Isiloe nodded. "I vaguely remember Uncle Orionkael struggling mightily against something. Perhaps it was the power of the dragon lords surfacing." She sighed. "I wish he was still alive to lead our people. Although he rejected his magical power, he was a great king. We need him now."

"You don't think Kain Arenil can be a wise king of the elves?"

"He is half-human. He has inherited some of the family magic, but is it enough to convince our people? For his kingship to work, he should wed an elven woman, thus strengthening his line. But he will not do that. Even Gwaethe has thrown her lot in with a human. The elves cannot afford to dilute their blood this way. The Arenil line must stay strong."

Alecia was getting confused with the ins and outs of Isiloe's story. But she was correct when she said Kain couldn't afford to dilute his blood any further—not if he wished to keep the support of the elven nation and win the acceptance of the *Sis Lenweri*.

"A difficult situation, indeed, Isiloe," Alecia said, hugging her daughter tight to her. Iona squealed, breaking the tense moment. "Come, I'll show you Solomon."

They crossed into the adjacent room, where the cribs were situated, and found the golden-haired heir to the kingdom asleep, sucking his thumb. Alecia always experienced an intense surge of love for Solomon whenever she was with him. He was a most perfect child with his golden halo of hair, his flawless skin and sunny temperament. And she wasn't the only one who felt that way. All who knew him loved him, from the lowliest maid to King Beniel himself.

It also seemed Isiloe had fallen under his spell if her rapt face was anything to go by.

"How is it possible this child is so beautiful?" she asked, her hands clasped before her, eyes fixed on Solomon's face. "I thought our elven children exquisite, but this child is perfection. Does he ever cry?"

Alecia thought of all the times she'd been in his company. "Rarely. He has quite a placid outlook on the world. Everyone loves him."

"I can see why," Isiloe said, running her finger gently down Solomon's downy cheek. He opened his eyes, and, even though Isiloe was a stranger, he smiled and grabbed the finger she caressed him with.

"Strong grip!" She laughed, and so did Solomon. He then turned his attention on Alecia, his eyes turning serious for a split second before he smiled again.

Alecia's heart stopped. In that split second, she saw another face in the baby's. One that should not be there. It was Ramón's. She took a step back from the crib, struggling to get her bearings. She must hide her shock from Isiloe.

Suspecting Ramón of being Solomon's father was one thing, but being confronted with the clear reality was quite another. The ramifications of Solomon not being Jiseve's were serious, massive, destructive.

"Princess Alecia, are you well?" Isiloe's voice penetrated the fog of thoughts that consumed her. "You have gone quite pale." The elven woman took Iona from her and led her over to a chair by the window. She made her sit, then fetched a goblet of water.

"Drink this and take some deep breaths," she said, her eyes concerned. Iona started crying, her little arms reaching for Alecia. Isiloe placed the child in her lap, but stayed close.

Damn, she'd made a mess of trying to appear unaffected. How could she pass this moment off as something of no importance? She drank the water and breathed deeply, holding her breath and letting it escape her body slowly. Gradually, she felt more herself.

Isiloe's troubled face brightened. "That's better. You have some color. Can I fetch anyone for you?"

Alecia shook her head. "I feel quite well now. We should return to the ball."

She stood with Iona, and Isiloe stepped close so she could support her if needed.

"Thank you, but I'm well."

"What caused your malady, Princess? You looked like you'd seen a ghost."

"It was nothing. We should return before we're missed. I'll find a nanny." As if summoned by magic, a woman who cared for the royal progeny appeared. Alecia kissed Iona and handed her to the nanny. She braced for a tantrum, but her daughter smiled, then broke into a giggle as the nanny tickled her.

Alecia ushered Isiloe out of the crib area and through the sitting room, only to run into Benae as she reached the chamber door. Benae took in Alecia and Isiloe, and her eyes widened before a calm mask descended over her face.

"Princess, Lady Isiloe, is there something you need?" she asked.

Alecia raised her chin. "Only to see my daughter and… brother," she said. "I was giving Isiloe a tour of the castle, and our steps led us here. Solomon is well. The nanny is with him."

Benae took a deep breath and nodded before sweeping past them and into the nursery.

"Don't let us keep you," Alecia muttered under her breath. "Let's get back to the ball, Lady Isiloe."

Isiloe stopped in the hall. "I prefer no title besides Ramar, which means captain in elvish. Or you can just call me Isiloe as you are a princess and of higher standing."

"I'm sorry to offend. If you were human, being a member of the royal family, you would have the title of 'Lady'. I'm sure others have called you such."

"Yes, and it is getting wearying." She frowned. "You and Benae don't like each other? That must indeed be awkward."

"It's complicated. Benae married my father when I was in exile. Actually, it was more *because* I was in exile. He needed to shore up our family's claim to the throne. Benae competed for his hand with three princesses… and won."

Isiloe's eyes widened. "How common!"

"My thoughts exactly, but Solomon was the result, and I can hardly resent that little boy. I love him almost as much as I love my daughter." She fell silent as she reflected on her recent revelation. Ramón *was* Solomon's father. She was almost positive about that. But she couldn't be sure unless Benae or Ramón confessed it.

"He is miraculous. I can see kingly qualities in him already. All will love him."

Alecia was afraid Isiloe was correct in that. If an elven woman felt that way, how much more would Solomon's human subjects adore him? Unless Alecia revealed his ugly secret. Was he an imposter? Was he not her half-brother, but a child with no claim to the throne? What should she do? She took another measured breath. Tonight wasn't the time for making those decisions.

Isiloe was quiet, expecting an answer.

"I agree," Alecia said, "all will love him, but the next years will be precarious. My cousin Piotr would dearly love to get his hands on the throne of Thorius. Already he is suspected of attempting to kill the king, and he was perhaps involved in my father's death."

Alecia began walking toward the staircase that led down to the ballroom. Isiloe gently clutched her arm and stopped her.

"Princess, I wish to thank you for your kindness. I have enjoyed the tour of the castle and meeting your daughter and brother."

Alecia smiled and nodded. "You're most welcome. I'd like to spend more time with you, if that's something you would like as well. I think we can be friends. If there's one thing I've learned since being in exile and having Iona, it's that I was too alone before."

Isiloe bowed. "I am not sure where I will be based, but if it is here, I would enjoy your company. I believe you like to spar. Perhaps we can practice together."

They reached the double doors into the ballroom. "Yes, let's see what transpires. Where are you housed?"

"My sister and I have a chamber in the castle. It is small, but sufficient for our needs."

"Good," Alecia said, "it will be easier to find you that way. Enjoy the rest of the night, Ramar Isiloe."

As soon as Alecia took her leave of Isiloe, Lin approached. She beckoned Alecia to a quiet corner.

"How did your time with Chandrelle go?" Alecia asked.

"Better than I thought it would. We got along well, and I offered to show her around the city tomorrow. We may even train together. She seemed amused when she saw me in this gown." Lin smiled, mischief in her eyes. "Elven ladies in the fighting ranks have little choice when it comes to finery. It's that cream hooded gown she's wearing, or cream trousers and tunic such as Isiloe has on."

Alecia nodded. "While here, they can please themselves. It depends how traditional they are. The elves are quite strait-laced, at least in some things."

Lin lowered her voice. "You should see the looks she was giving the other ladies in their finery. Chandrelle *definitely* desires a kingdom styled wardrobe. I don't think it will be long before we see her in something like this." She fingered her blue satin skirt.

"What about Vard? Has she been speaking with him?"

"She tried several times, but he has been preoccupied with wine testing. Speaking of Vard, here he comes now." Lin left her, curtsying to Vard as she passed him.

He handed Alecia a goblet of mulled wine. "I thought you might be thirsty after spending time with Ramar Isiloe."

A warm glow lit Alecia's stomach that he would think of and watch out for her.

"I find Isiloe refreshing," she said, taking a sip of the delicious drink. "She says what she thinks. We could be friends."

"You seem to have collected a number of friends lately."

"You should be happy that I have," she said. "As I told Isiloe, I realized in exile how lonely my life had become. It's nice to have friends."

Vard smiled. "I suggest you get something to eat. I'll see you later." He bowed and left her. She wandered over to the banquet tables and loaded another plate with food. Perhaps this time she'd have a chance to eat it. Ramón found her there.

"Princess," he said, a muscle flicking along his jaw, "Benae told me she found you giving Lady Isiloe a guided tour of the nursery."

"That's correct, Ramón." She suspected Benae would go running to her husband to complain. She was protective of Solomon. Oh, how she'd like to confront Ramón with the accusation that Solomon was his son. But it was too soon. She must wait and consider how to play this to her best advantage.

"Do you believe that was wise?" he asked. "The elves are not to be trusted if the stories are true."

Alecia couldn't believe what she was hearing. She lowered her voice. "You believe the tales about elves stealing human children?"

"They could be true. As a race, they have few offspring, especially when you consider how long they live." He paused and frowned to himself. "Anyway, Benae is beside herself. She doesn't want Isiloe or any other elf near her son."

"I introduced her to Iona. There's no risk, Ramón. This time, Benae has gone too far."

"Alecia!" Ramón's voice rose, and some near them turned to look. He steered her to a quiet corner. "My wife is serious, and it's her right to control who goes near her son. If you can't obey the rules, we'll have to remove Iona from the royal nursery. Surely you see that the fewer visitors to those chambers, the smaller the risk to Solomon?"

Alecia gulped down an angry retort. She hated being taken to task by Ramón when this should be her home and under her control. Again, the urge to confront him with her suspicions rose. She battled it down.

"Alecia?" he said again. "Agree to this request of Benae's, or there will be serious consequences."

"Who do you think you are?" she hissed. "This is my home. You and Benae make me feel like a guest who has outstayed her welcome. Not only that, but you think you can order me about. Well, I won't be dictated to." She drew a deep breath to bring her anger in check. "However, I promise that in future I'll bring no visitors to Solomon that Benae or yourself haven't approved."

"Thank you." Ramón stalked off, and Alecia stood fuming. She took a great gulp of her wine and turned to walk away, only to run into Chandrelle. The elven woman was the picture of calm serenity and ethereal beauty. She gave a shallow bow, and her dark eyes regarded Alecia with thinly veiled hostility. She didn't know what she might have done to deserve that.

"Ramar Chandrelle," Alecia said, "I trust you've been made welcome."

Chandrelle's lips tightened. "Our accommodation is satisfactory, the wine acceptable, and the food not to my taste. But then, human food rarely appeals to our people. We are largely vegetarian, and you humans usually forget that."

"I'm sorry, Chandrelle," Alecia said. "I'll have a word with the Guardians and see if they can supply you a more agreeable diet." The elven woman nodded. "Have you been advised if you are to stay here in Brightcastle, or travel to Wildecoast?" Alecia kept her fingers crossed for Brightcastle, so that the elven warrior would be far from Vard. A small voice told her she could trust Vard to rebuff any advances, but distance couldn't hurt.

"I desire to see the ocean, so I will ask for Wildecoast. Many of our people yearn to visit the seaside."

"Yes, it's only natural, I suppose." Alecia was finding it difficult to keep her voice relaxed through the grinding of her teeth.

"I find your men intriguing, Princess," Chandrelle said, her voice dropping to a sexy throb. "Especially the King's Blade. I am told he is unmarried. Do you think he would welcome my advances? He seems so preoccupied with matters of war and politics. I think laughter would look well on his visage."

Alecia fought the green cloud of jealousy that descended. "You'd do well to stay away from Vard. He's a complicated man and takes his duties seriously. Stick to your own people. I'm sure your mother wouldn't condone a marriage with a human."

"Oh!" Chandrelle laughed. "I wasn't talking about marriage, but something far more enjoyable, guaranteed to put a smile on that handsome yet intimidating face. If there was ever a challenge, that man is one."

"Don't fool with Vard Anton," Alecia said through clenched teeth. She was sure someone would have hinted at the story of Vard and

Alecia. This wouldn't be happening if she'd accepted his marriage proposal. She must acknowledge that women would approach Vard and trust that he was loyal enough to wait for her.

"It seems there is no good reason not to, Princess, unless he is already spoken for. Word has it he recently proposed and was rejected. I know just the tonic to soothe his broken heart."

Oh, she knew about Alecia and Vard alright, but how had Chandrelle heard about the proposal? "Does he appear to be suffering from a broken heart?"

"I suspect, like all males, he is too proud to show his hurt and has buried it deep. Perhaps I will be the one to tend his wounds and tame the beast." Chandrelle smiled and left.

Alecia watched her go, trying to school her features to reflect peaceful enjoyment instead of fierce jealousy. That woman could *not* have Vard.

"That's a ferocious look on your face, Princess." The man himself stopped by her side and offered another goblet of mulled wine. He smiled at her, and her anger vanished. But then she remembered who was after him.

"Chandrelle is on the prowl, and her target is you."

"Now *there's* a problem I'm not sure how to solve. I can't have her hounding my steps. yet I can't afford to offend her." His troubled gaze fixed on something over her right shoulder.

"She knows you proposed to me, or at least to someone. She thinks she can mend your broken heart."

His eyes snapped back to hers. "I'm not interested in her, Alecia. And there's a way to fix this, if only you'd change your mind."

She chewed her lower lip. "I'm tempted to accept your proposal just to watch Chandrelle's response." Then she realized she'd spoken out loud.

Vard's face looked like thunder.

"I didn't mean that the way it sounded, Vard."

"I really hope you didn't." He took a deep breath, eyes on the ceiling, then breathed out as he focused back upon her. "My offer was genuine, and I've been patient, Alecia." He bowed and left her, stalking from the ballroom.

Alecia threw back the rest of her wine and went in search of Lin. She found her on the balcony with the son of a minor lord. The man bowed when Alecia approached, then left them.

Lin watched him leave with a gleam in her eye. "I may seek him out later. He's rather pretty."

"He's beneath you."

"Not yet, but he might be later." She laughed at the look on Alecia's face. "Sorry to shock you, Princess. That comment was a little common for my new station—which I'm already enjoying rather a lot. I didn't realize there were so many attractive men amongst the minor nobility."

"Never mind that now, Lin. I just upset Vard. He's been very patient with me, and now I'll be lucky if he speaks to me again before leaving for Wildecoast. Uncle Beniel is looking well, so he's bound to be returning home soon."

"That's if he can drag himself away from Solomon. He's quite smitten."

Alecia scowled, but she couldn't reveal her suspicions to Lin yet. "He won't allow that to distract him from running the kingdom. The *Sis Lenweri* are planning something, and we need to be prepared."

"What did you say to Vard that upset him so?"

"It doesn't matter," Alecia said. "Chandrelle annoyed me, and I … never mind. She's after Vard, and there's nothing I can do."

"You *could* marry him. I'm sure that offer still stands. You should see him when he thinks you aren't looking at him. It's quite tragic, really."

"Not you too! Chandrelle said she wanted to mend his broken heart or at least distract him. Does everyone know Vard has been rejected?"

"Only those who are watching closely."

"And that reminds me. How *does* Chandrelle know Vard proposed and was rejected? I only told you and Arelle."

Lin raised one brow. "I hope you aren't suggesting it could've been me who let it slip?"

Alecia frowned. "Not really."

"Well, it wasn't. I won't ever share what you tell me. But Arelle imbibed quite a deal of wine the night before we left Selinore. Perhaps she mentioned it. I'll have a word with her."

Alecia smiled. "Thank you, I appreciate your offer." She led Lin further along the balcony. "I must concentrate on gathering support, and you can help me. It occurred to me that I've been trying to approach the people at the very top of the power tree when I could do almost as well further down."

"What do you mean?"

Alecia leaned against the balustrade, her eyes on those in the ballroom. She didn't want to be overheard should someone approach unnoticed.

"There are many minor nobles and influential tradespeople in Brightcastle. Some know me well, or knew my father when he was alive. However, I haven't seen them lately. And then, there are the common people who've always been most in my heart. I feel I should concentrate on getting a groundswell of support rather than a few top-level nobles and generals."

Lin nodded, eyes narrowed as she took in Alecia's words. "That's how I heard about you. There's a whisper on the street that you tried to temper some of your father's activities when he was alive. I even heard you directly rescued people wrongly accused. Did you?"

Alecia's heart thumped at Lin's words. "Really? I thought I had covered my tracks well."

"Then it's true?"

Alecia frowned. "When did you hear this? How long ago?"

"Since you returned, not before. Someone out there is spreading the word of your deeds before you went into exile. Again, I ask—is it true?"

"Yes, I was quite reckless, and it caught up with me. After Mother died, Father changed. He did many things I abhorred. At the time, I blamed Lord Finus."

"Your betrothed?"

She shuddered. "Yes. But now I see that Father made most of those decisions himself. I'll never understand why."

"Then you *were* involved in those mercenary deaths and the rescues of prisoners. What about the mysterious coins that were distributed to the poor?"

"I did what I could," she said. "It wasn't enough. I came to realize I should've gone to Father and made him change his ways."

"Would that have worked?"

"I'll never know." She fell silent, wondering who was spreading this news. Could it be Hetty? She had many friends among the common people. "I need to get out more. Tomorrow, you and I will make a call on a friend I haven't seen for many weeks."

CHAPTER SIX

ALECIA and Lin gathered Arelle, Kenna, and Cretia, and rode into Brightcastle town mid-morning the next day. Silver was frisky, despite only having one night's rest. She was battle-trained and bred for stamina; not the best mount for a princess if a quiet ride was required.

Lin groaned. "Did we need to start so early? I had to leave my lordling before he woke. Some more fun might've been nice."

Cretia slapped her hands over her ears. "La la la... I don't wish to hear what you've been up to. Alecia, make her stop." Her brown gelding shook his head as if in agreement.

"Hush, Cretia," Lin said. "You'll not use her name in public. We're trying to get in and out without folk knowing who's in their midst."

"Sorry, but you shocked me with your reference to ... you know."

Alecia and Lin were dressed in modest gowns befitting noblewomen out on a ride, perhaps to the market. The other three women wore men's clothes, swords on display. Kenna led a pack horse suitable for carrying their purchases.

Alecia had agonized about how to appear and decided two noblewomen out shopping wouldn't attract much attention. Brightcastle wasn't a dangerous town for women, well-manned as it was with soldiers.

Indeed, as they rode and chatted, very few eyes noted their passing. After an uneventful journey through the streets, they arrived at Firedrake Alley and dismounted.

Lin gripped Alecia's arm. "Firedrake Alley! Aren't firedrakes small dragons? Everywhere we look, we see or hear about dragons."

"Yes, but it's only because we're thinking of them now."

Lin raised her brows. "Are you sure about that?"

"I'm going to speak with my friend. You take the girls and go shopping, leaving Kenna with me. She can stand watch outside."

Lin nodded and remounted, heading out of the alley with Cretia and Arelle.

"Keep your eyes sharp, Kenna," Alecia said. "Pound on the door if you need to alert me."

She knocked on Hetty's door, and, when nothing happened, she knocked again. As she raised her fist to pound once more, the door swung open. A dark figure stood in the hallway near the kitchen. Alecia's heart thumped as she stepped over the threshold. The outline of the person wasn't right for Hetty.

"Hetty?" Even to her own ears, her voice sounded frightened. Who was this in Hetty's house? Was it Katrine?

The figure stepped forward into the light, and Alecia gasped. "It *is* you, Hetty!"

"Come in and close the door, child." The familiar rasping voice settled the rest of her fears. She took two deep breaths as she closed the door behind her and was able to greet her friend with a semblance of composure.

What she saw stunned her.

Hetty's wild, gray hair sat in a neat bun at the nape, and she wore a silver gown. It was of an old-fashioned cut, but clearly of good quality. She looked like a member of the lower nobility. She'd tamed her wild eyebrows and applied a touch of makeup to her face. More than a touch, actually. Alecia saw a hint of the beautiful woman Hetty had once been.

"What's this, Hetty? You look wonderful."

"It would be nice if you could occasionally send warning of your visits, Princess. I was about to call on a friend."

Alecia froze. "A friend? I didn't know you had friends who required formal wear."

"You don't know much then. I have plenty of friends and acquaintances in Brightcastle. Lately I've been reconnecting with them. My brush with death showed me how vulnerable I am. I could be dead for days, and nobody would notice."

"That's never bothered you before."

"Well, now it does," she snapped. "Come in, and I'll make tea. It's an age since you visited."

"I know, and I'm sorry." Alecia followed Hetty up the hall to the kitchen. "I let my anger at your meddling damage our friendship."

Hetty sighed. "I truly don't believe my spell affected your father's heart. I'm sorry you lost him and weren't there to mourn properly. You know I'd do nothing to hurt you."

Alecia hugged her. "I know. We'll never know what caused his heart to fail. I've come to accept my father's faults. He didn't deserve to die, but he's gone, and I must make the best of my life." A tear escaped her eye despite the brave words.

She sat, and Hetty moved around the kitchen, preparing the tea and bread.

"Hetty, what are you really doing?" Alecia asked. "Your story doesn't have the ring of truth about it."

"I told you; catching up with old friends. You think I want to be alone for the rest of my life? I can't rely on you and Katrine to visit. You're both too busy. It's time for me to take back my place in society, now that I'm less likely to be persecuted."

"No one would even recognize you. Is this really about you feeling freer since my father died? I'm sorry his actions caused you such grief."

"Caused me grief?" Hetty snapped. "He tried to *kill* me! If not for you, I'd be bones and ashes!"

Hetty fell silent, and Alecia stared at her hands. They'd both lost so much. It was past time for them to reclaim their lives. Crippling shame rocked her. She had never thought how Hetty must feel, locked up in her own home, afraid to venture out for fear of being arrested.

She raised her eyes to her friend, who stood lost in thought. "I can see how bereft of joy your life must've been. I've been locked away, too, in more ways than I realized. It's one reason I'm here today."

Hetty frowned at her. "You need help?"

"I suspect you're already helping me. Someone has been creating a groundswell of support for me in Brightcastle; putting my name in the forefront of the minds of the common people." She paused, waiting for Hetty's response.

None came, but Hetty returned to preparing the tea and bread.

Alecia frowned at her friend's back. "When I saw you dressed as you are, I was certain my suspicions were correct. Are you trying to garner support for me in Brightcastle? You can tell me. I won't be angry."

Hetty whirled to face her. "Why would you be angry? I know your deepest desires, child. I know you long to be the next kingdom leader. I thought you'd appreciate any help you could get."

Alecia stood. "You still haven't answered. Yes, I want to be queen. But I'm tired of people acting on my behalf—like I'm still a child, incapable of ordering my own affairs." She lowered her voice and approached Hetty, placing an arm around her bony shoulders. "Please, just tell me if you've been acting for me. I need to know who's doing this so I can thank them."

Hetty peered up at her. "Alright, it's me. I got bored and thought I could do this small thing. I know I should've discussed it with you, but you were so angry last we spoke. Actions always speak louder than words. And here you are, so it worked."

Alecia heaved a great sigh. "Thank you for being honest. And thank you for advocating for me. It has taken me some time to realize that the common people may be my most staunch supporters. I'm their princess and have lived among them all my life. Benae and Ramón can't compete with that."

"And they know you'll do anything for them, even give up your life."

"Exactly, though with Iona to consider, I might not be so reckless in future. I've a lot to live for now."

"And the dark shifter? What of him? I've heard he has visited Brightcastle since your return."

"He has asked me to be his wife."

"How does that fit with your goal to be ruler?"

"It doesn't." She let go of Hetty and returned to her seat. "I'm confused. I love Vard and would marry him in a heartbeat, but I can't. He'd take me to Wildecoast, and that isn't the seat of my power. I'd never be queen if I moved there."

"I'm glad you understand that," Hetty said, pouring her a cup of tea, then slicing the bread.

To occupy her hands and eyes, Alecia added honey to her tea and buttered the bread.

Her friend continued. "He's not the one for you, Alecia. I feel it with everything in this old body."

Alecia laughed. "Don't be so dramatic. Vard's the father of my child, and he has full control of his gift." Her heart swelled. "You should see him now. He's a different man—confident, proud—everything I knew he could be. He's also the King's Blade."

"What's that?" Hetty asked, a scowl on her face.

"It's a new role created especially for him. Uncle Beniel has placed his trust in Vard, and I'm so proud. It would all be perfect if only I didn't long to rule my people. It's like Queen Izebel is inside me, pushing me to break out of this chrysalis and spread my wings. Does that sound insane?"

Hetty's eyes burned with what Alecia thought might be pride. "Of course not! You'd make a magnificent leader. You may have the authority from your father's side, but your mother gave you everything else you need for the job. I see so much of her in you."

Alecia sobered. "It all seems far away. And the *Sis Lenweri* are planning something big. We believe it will come sooner than we like. When I contemplate a war, it's overwhelming."

Hetty fixed her with her dark gaze. "You must find the right people to support you, and they'll make this chore easier. But Vard isn't one of them. You know that instinctively, or you would've married him. Instead, you have delayed, placing your trust in your intuition that you are destined to be leader. He doesn't support your ambition, does he?"

She sipped at her cup, putting off admitting this shame to Hetty. "He does not, and it hurts. He lacks the imagination to see me on the throne in my own right."

"I see there's no need to convince you," Hetty said. "Good. I thought I'd have a battle on my hands. Now we must only galvanize your support. The looming war with the *Sis Lenweri* is the perfect event to showcase your fitness for leadership. I'll do everything I can to support and advise you."

Alecia's heart lifted in hope. Could Hetty really help place her on the throne of Thorius? Perhaps not single-handedly, but she'd be a wonderful asset. Her wisdom and magic would be such a help.

"Who are you visiting today? This has to do with my ambition to be queen, doesn't it?"

Hetty drew a long breath. "It does. And so far, I've had more success than I imagined. Benae is seen as an imposter, and there are still whispers regarding her and Ramón Zorba. The kindest of them say they were intimate before your father died."

"And what do the less kind rumors say?" Alecia asked.

Hetty scowled. "That Zorba is Solomon's father." Hetty studied her reaction. "I see *that* comes as no surprise."

Alecia took a sip of her tea and placed the cup on the saucer. "I have my suspicions, but I'd rather have proof before I say anything."

"If Zorba is the father, Solomon has no claim to the throne. You're still the obvious choice as heir."

"Not while I'm female, Hetty. I've tried to convince my uncle, but he won't have it. Sometimes I think he'd rather Piotr inherit the throne than have a woman on it!"

"And Vard Anton? Despite his misgivings, would he stand up for you if you gathered enough support? Would he advocate on your behalf to the king?"

"I don't know, Hetty. He doesn't see me being queen as possible, so he doesn't countenance it at all. To Vard, my aspirations are just a whim.

"And are they?"

She held up her chin. "You know they're not. I've sacrificed much to reach this point. If I wasn't serious, I'd accept Vard's offer and make my life simple; though I don't believe my life will ever be easy."

Hetty stood to clear away the cups. "You could marry Piotr. I hear he's looking for a bride."

"Surely you jest! Piotr may be behind the attempts on the king's life."

"Nothing is proven, child. He could be your path to the throne. And, once you're there, you'll have more power."

"He's my cousin, Hetty." She fell silent, allowing the idea to settle in her mind. What if she *did* marry Piotr? It would benefit them both, but would it make her the queen she longed to be? Likely he'd try to control her too, just as her father and Finus had.

"Ha!" Hetty said. "You're seriously considering that!"

Alecia stood. "I like to keep an open mind. If it were the best thing for the kingdom, I'd certainly consider it. Piotr would have to be interested, and I don't see him knocking on my door."

Hetty smiled mysteriously. "We'll see." She patted her hair and stood with her hands folded before her. "I must keep my appointments. I'll tell you the outcome when next we meet."

It all sounded very formal. Not like Hetty at all. But Alecia couldn't be sad that her old friend had a new lease on life. She could use all the help Hetty could provide.

"Thanks for everything. I'll see you soon." She bent to kiss Hetty on her smooth cheek. It really was a revelation to see her primped and going out in society. "If you're to be my advisor, perhaps we should go shopping and get you some new clothes…"

Hetty's eyes flared at her words. "I'd really love that. I have my eye on some fabric."

"Then it's a date. I'll pick you up in my carriage the day after tomorrow. We should also see about getting you rooms at the castle, so I can more readily see you."

Hetty cackled. "I can imagine the look on Princess Benae's face when you tell her *that*."

Alecia scowled. "I don't care. I want Iona to meet you, and for you to be her grandmother. We can't do that when we live so far apart. And I'd rather not take her out in the town just yet."

Hetty patted her arm. "All in good time, my dear. Let's fix my wardrobe first."

Alecia grinned, already loving this new Hetty.

Alecia and her ladies escorted Hetty to her luncheon date, then returned to the castle. She made sure she reserved a coach for the shopping expedition she was planning in two days.

She dismissed her ladies and visited the royal dressmaker Benae had retained soon after her appointment as Guardian. Benae would have a fit if she discovered her dressmaker was making Hetty's clothes.

But Benae didn't have to find out until after the deed was done. Alecia would pay for the creations—as much as Hetty would allow.

The dressmaker was a petite woman, barely taller than Benae, with stunning black curls and limpid blue eyes. Her name was Isadore Bellemont, and she was about Alecia's age. She was amazed to find a woman so young in this position.

Isadore curtsied and welcomed Alecia into her domain. The apartment was beautifully appointed, with a separate bedroom and living area as well as the dressmaking room and a change room.

"This is splendid, Mistress Bellemont. I had no idea this apartment existed."

Isadore inclined her head. "Thank you, Princess. I love it and had input into the furnishing. Princess Benae is generous."

"Is it not tedious to sleep where you work?"

"Not at all. I love working with fabric. It's been my dream since I was a small child."

"Are you from Brightcastle?"

"No, Princess. I'm from Tylevia, from Princess Benae's estate. We used to play together as children."

"Oh, really. Then you're close?"

Isadore frowned. "Somewhat. Princess Benae promised she'd help my family before she left her estate. We were in deep trouble financially. Things got worse, but Prince Zialni looked after us once he became engaged to Benae."

Alecia drew a long breath. Of course, her father would've taken over the running of Benae's estate when they became engaged. It would've been part of the marriage pact.

"I hope I haven't upset you by speaking of your father, Princess."

Alecia snapped out of her pondering. "No, of course not. It's nice to hear Father took care of you. I imagine the estate is thriving now?"

"It's still dangerous, Princess. The dark elves are a constant menace. Lord Zorba has reinforced the town watch with soldiers, but the people must be vigilant nonetheless."

"I'll speak to the Guardians about what else they can do." Alecia said. "Now, to the purpose of my visit…"

She explained her plans for Hetty, leaving out her name and just calling her an aged friend and advisor. Isadore seemed content to accept the commission, and Alecia promised to deliver the fabric and bring her friend for a fitting in two days.

As she returned to her rooms, Alecia reflected on her own wardrobe. Though never one to dwell on clothes and fripperies, if she were to be taken seriously, she must present herself in the best possible light. As a battle queen, she'd need clothes comfortable for riding and fighting. Perhaps she could have Isadore modify the current Zialni uniform as had been done for Benae's female guards. And a warm but decorative cloak would be essential.

Yes, her wardrobe needed a dramatic overhaul. She only hoped Ramón didn't get wind of her plans, or he might try to stop her. On the other hand, if he believed she was merely playing at being a queen-in-waiting, he might humor her, thinking a focus on her wardrobe would keep her mind away from more serious matters. She must be cautious to hide the gravity of her intentions from now on.

Alecia reached her room and entered the bedchamber to find Millie giving Iona a bath. The little girl put her hands up to her mother, and Alecia bent and kissed her forehead. She got slapped on her cheek by a wet palm for her trouble. Laughing, she turned to Millie.

"Hello, Millie. I'm so pleased you have Iona here. I'll be able to feed her. I've missed her."

"And she has missed you, Princess. Sometimes, her little face looks so serious. I'm sure she's thinking of you. I'd love to know what's going on in that head of hers."

"You and me both, Millie." An idea occurred to her. "Is there any gossip that I should know?"

Millie frowned. "Let's see. I saw two of those elven ladies whispering in a corner earlier today. And Captain Anton… *Lord* Anton… has had a face like thunder all day." She paused and studied Alecia. "Has he asked for your hand in marriage, Princess?"

Alecia only barely stopped her exclamation. "Is that what people are saying?"

"Yes, Princess. The servants and even the nobles are taking bets on whether you'll stay in Brightcastle, or move to Wildecoast when Lord Anton departs. Perhaps that's what has him so angry?"

"Yes," Alecia said. "You could be correct in that assumption. Thank you, Millie. That will be all until dinner. I'll dine in my chamber as usual. Until then, I'll spend time with Iona."

Millie curtseyed and departed. Alecia could see the maid was dying to ask more questions, but, for once, she held her tongue. She lifted Iona from the bath and dried the baby while she mulled over Millie's gossip. While she detested being the subject of a bet, at least it kept her "front of mind". There would be nothing worse than not being spoken of.

She placed Iona before the fireplace and dressed the child before gathering her favorite toys. After a delightful hour spent teaching Iona the difference between cows, horses, and pigs, a maid delivered Iona's meal. Alecia fed her daughter and placed the sleepy child in her cot. By the time Iona was asleep, Alecia's own meal arrived.

After dismissing the maid, she poured herself a glass of red wine and relaxed in her chair at the dining table. Halfway through her meal, there was a knock at the door. Vard stood without, a tray in his hands.

"Good evening, Alecia. I wondered if I could share your table. I've brought my meal."

She smiled and let him in, clearing a space for his dishes and pouring him a glass of wine. Once she resumed her seat, Vard joined her at the table.

"This is a pleasant surprise," she said, taking a large sip of wine to calm her racing heart. Her thoughts touched on Hetty's words… *He's not the one for you.* Well, Hetty wasn't infallible, and she didn't know Vard as well as she thought she did. The two had had a rocky relationship since the start. It was understandable for her old friend to be suspicious of Vard.

"I wished to see you. It seems an age since we spoke at any length. What did you do today?"

Alecia took another sip of wine, wondering how much to tell him. "I went to see Hetty. I missed her while I was away."

"How is she?"

"You wouldn't believe how well she is. Better than I've seen her for years."

"Really? What has brought about this miracle?"

Alecia looked deep into his eyes. "A brush with death seems to have scared her into reconnecting with old friends. And, with my father gone, she doesn't fear persecution as she did."

"Meaning she is out and about more?"

She nodded. "It's wonderful to see her so fit and well. I've been contemplating moving her closer to me… so she can meet Iona and see her regularly."

Vard took a bite of bread. "And you wish to know what I think of that plan?"

She raised an eyebrow. "Well, Benae dislikes Hetty, and Ramón tends to agree with his wife. But why should I allow their feelings aboutHetty Hetty to dictate my decisions? I find myself in need of good advice on all matters."

Vard sat back in his chair and observed her, his expression guarded. "You'd have all the advice and support you needed in Wildecoast. And you could bring Hetty as well. I can't say I'm her biggest admirer, but I know you trust her. Won't you reconsider my offer?"

His words cut her, for each time he proposed, it was more difficult to deny him.

"You know why I can't. You're the king's greatest supporter, and you can't have a wife who aspires to the throne. Besides, *my* supporters are here—in Brightcastle."

"So, you haven't given up your ambition to be queen?"

"I'll never give up as long as there's breath in my body. The only promise I can make is that I'll do nothing to unseat my uncle. I'm his rightful heir; I don't care what you think."

Vard took a deep breath. "You know people are betting on your next move? Whether you'll stay here, or move to Wildecoast?"

"Is that what has made you scowl all day?"

His eyes widened. It was testimony to how comfortable he was in her presence. He never showed his emotions.

"How did you know that?"

"I have my sources. And I'm glad people are gossiping about me, but you know I'll be staying here, right? I can't marry you *now*. Not only does it not align with my short-term plans, but there's so much yet to do for both of us. It's not our time."

Vard stood and pulled Alecia from her chair. He held her by her upper arms, his gaze burning down at her. She recalled the first time he had looked at her thus—the first time she angered him. Now, as then, she was caught up in the magnetic force that he always evoked. She would do almost anything for this man, but she couldn't deny her people, even for him.

"We can *make* this our time, Alecia. This kingdom needs both of us, together and moving it forward. Our daughter needs us together, guiding her steps. King Beniel would be overjoyed to have you close, helping him shepherd his citizens."

He was so intense, so determined she almost believed him. How glorious it would be to live as a family; to have Vard in her bed each night, and to wake up to his love every morning. She could help her uncle and aunt with the running of the kingdom, raise Iona and have more children with Vard. She could guide her uncle gently to a more tolerant society that accepted magic and valued women for more than their beauty and child-bearing capacity.

That picture entranced her as it always had. But would she truly have more power if she took that step? Her heart urged her to make a family with the man she loved. But her head told her she needed to forge her own path, to take a step toward being a monarch in her own right. She felt it so strongly, she couldn't ignore it.

"I love you," she said, "but this is something I must do. If I don't follow my dreams, I'll have no power in this kingdom. I love my people too much to abandon them. I hope you can understand."

Pain scored his face, and he looked more miserable than she'd seen him since he last left her. Her heart cracked at what she was doing, and she teetered on the edge of changing her mind. But first and foremost, she must be true to herself and not wonder what might have been.

"You're walking away from me," he said, his throat moving with emotion. "Just as I've left you in the past."

Her heart fractured further, his words driving another wedge into the already fragile organ. "I'm not denying you to hurt you, Vard. This is me making a stand, drawing a line in the dirt of this kingdom I love.

If we're meant to be, then we can survive this. You must set me free to be the woman I know I can be."

He drew her closer. "Alecia, I know your potential. In your heart is all that's good and noble in this world. I just hope that's enough to sustain you when you're alone." He pulled her to him and kissed her with a searing heat that speared right to her toes. How could she live without his love? Her heart cried, the pain of her decision already weakening her resolve.

But he pulled back and carefully removed his hands from her arms, his gaze a palpable and painful accusation. He turned and left the chamber.

Alecia stood frozen, the feel of his blazing kiss branding her lips. She touched them gently and a zap on her fingers told of the intensity. It was as it had always been with Vard. Their relationship was fated, their connection unbreakable.

At least she hoped that was the case, for that kiss had felt an awful lot like goodbye.

CHAPTER SEVEN

VARD strode from Alecia's chambers, burning with the need to storm back there and make her see sense. She was so stubborn, and noble, and... He sighed. He loved her with everything he was, and now he could truly be her husband and protector, and father of their child. He was everything he'd ever wanted to be. But, without Alecia, it meant nothing. Now he knew how it felt to be abandoned—and hated it.

Reaching his chambers, he dismissed his man servant and began pacing across the room. All his plans were for naught. He must return to Wildecoast without her, without Iona. His heart flopped in his chest like a panicked toad. How could he leave them here to fend for themselves, possibly in danger? Why was she so determined to rule the kingdom? Vard felt pushed into a corner. How was he supposed to deal with this?

He closed his eyes and let a long, ragged breath escape. He took another breath and exhaled, trying to lose some of the pent-up frustration. Perhaps his father could help.

"She won't listen to me, Father." Vard sat on the edge of Lyam Anton's bed in a nearby inn. "I don't know what to do." He pulled his leather head band from his hair and ran it through his fingers.

"Why do you need to 'do' anything, Son?"

"I can't accept what she wants. I'm trying to understand this drive to lead her people, but I'm afraid I can't."

"I'd have thought that would be easy for you."

Vard shook his head.

"You've been a Defender a lot longer than I."

Vard frowned at his father, puzzled by the seemingly irrelevant statement. Then he froze. "You're saying Alecia's drive to be queen is as strong as our Defender drive to protect the innocent?"

"I don't know, but what if it is? Can you ignore those urges?"

Vard shook his head slowly. "I never thought of it that way."

"Then I suggest you do. It seems she has given you no choice but to leave her be for now. She loves you, but she also has a long-held ambition to be queen."

"Keep that to yourself, Father. I don't want it openly discussed."

"Of course. She hasn't denied you. Just as you leaving Alecia in the past wasn't a rejection of her."

Vard stood, his fists bunched at his sides. "I feel like we'll never be together."

Lyam stepped closer and poked a finger at his chest. "What does your heart tell you?"

He scowled. "That we'll never be one!"

"Look deeper, past the hurt."

Vard closed his eyes and calmed his thoughts. "That we'll *always* be one, even when apart."

Lyam held his finger up. "Trust that. I'll stay in Brightcastle and watch over Alecia and Iona. You return with the king to Wildecoast. There's a war to prepare for and not much time."

"You're right. I'll feel better knowing you're here, though I could continue your weapons training if you were with me. You're still vulnerable."

"Don't worry about me, Vard. I'm a survivor."

"You are at that." Vard hugged Lyam. "Look after yourself and keep in touch as you can."

"I will. Watch your back."

Vard returned to the castle. They'd leave for Wildecoast in two days, and there was plenty to accomplish before then.

* * *

Alecia cuddled Iona as Isadore took Hetty's measurements in the dressmaker's apartments. She gazed at her friend, thinking the older woman was nearly unrecognizable now. Still, she must avoid Ramón seeing her. He was the only one likely to recognize "Madame Henriette" as actually Hetty the witch.

"You are so slender, Madame. It will be a pleasure to create your wardrobe."

Hetty laughed. "And I'll save on fabric, too."

"You've chosen marvelous materials," Isadore said. "I particularly love this scarlet velvet." She held the fabric to her cheek. "And I know just the style that would suit it."

"I hope it's the latest fashion," Alecia said.

"A classic style that will stand the test of time, Princess," Isadore said, smiling.

Alecia smiled back. She enjoyed being around the dressmaker, who was always calm and friendly. She had a warmth that was balm for the soul. No wonder Benae had brought her here.

"You'll remember not to mention this to Princess Benae?" Alecia asked. "She'd insist on paying for the gown, and I won't have that."

"Of course, Princess. I'll be the soul of discretion. But you don't mind if she knows you're expanding *your* wardrobe?"

Alecia nodded. "That's correct. Benae has been at me to attend to my attire since I returned. She'll be overjoyed I've taken steps at last. I have no wish for her to be embarrassed by my appearance."

"I look forward to creating some magnificent gowns for you. I'll work night and day to make them in record time." Isadore took the last measurements from Hetty and wrote them in a small leather-bound book. She placed the notebook in the satchel she wore at her waist.

Alecia stood with Iona. "Please see to the cloaks first, Isadore. I wish to ensure I'm ready to appear in public in the Zialni colors, especially if we need to rally the populace."

Isadore's eyes widened. "Yes, Princess. You think war is imminent?"

"I hope not too soon, but it pays to be prepared for the worst. Don't worry, we'll be ready for the *Sis Lenweri* when they come."

Hetty cleared her throat. "Let us leave Mistress Isadore to her work, Princess."

Alecia thanked Isadore and left with Hetty. They returned to her chambers, and she rang for tea. Thankfully, the workrooms were in the same wing as Alecia's rooms, so there was no need to expose Hetty to an accidental encounter with Ramón.

They sat at tea while Millie bathed and fed Iona in the adjoining room.

"Our next task is to find you accommodation suitable for your station," Alecia said. "It's too risky to have you here, but there may be a small house close to the castle which will suffice. I've had Lin check that today."

"That sounds ideal." Hetty sipped from her fragile china cup and closed her eyes. "Mmm, I forgot how pleasant quality tea can be."

"And to think I nearly lost you." Alecia's eyes filled with tears at the thought of how close they'd come. "Have you heard from Katrine? Maybe we should summon her for a meeting?"

Hetty placed her cup back on its saucer. "Katrine is about her own business. She'll come when needed and inform me of anything that might pertain to the dragon." She lowered her voice at the last word.

"I think she's our best chance of finding the beast."

"Possibly," Hetty said, scowling.

"What's wrong?"

"She has taken up with a man, James Tomel. If I'm any judge, she's given him her heart. I want to make Kat my second, but I fear she won't want that if James proposes. A girl with her assets could have him on a string without tying a ball and chain to her ankle."

"Hetty!" Alecia exclaimed.

"What? It's true. Look at you. You have no man to tie you down and tell you what to do. You even have a child. I'm proud of you for standing your ground."

Alecia sighed. "Thank you, but this is only a temporary situation until I can resolve my future and that of the kingdom."

"What happens if Lord Anton finds another before then?"

"He won't. He'll wait for me. I know he will." She'd done the same for him, though it was easy to avoid attachments stuck out in the wilds with a newborn to care for. Vard was in Wildecoast with the queen and a bevy of beautiful women and elves surrounding him. And he was a Defender! Women couldn't resist him!

"You might do well to keep yourself free, even after you accomplish your goals," Hetty said, looking smug. "I'm living proof of that. It doesn't mean you can't enjoy male company from time to time."

Alecia's face heated. Hetty could be so inappropriate. "I have a daughter to think of, and I want more children. How would it look if I took men to my bed with no official attachments?"

"You shouldn't care how it looks, only about what makes you happy and keeps you free."

"This isn't the counsel I wanted when I made you my advisor, Hetty." Alecia rose to refill her cup. "I'd appreciate it if you restricted your advice to political matters. *I'll* make the romantic decisions for myself."

"I just don't wish for you to be tied down and trodden on by that shifter," Hetty hissed.

At a glare from Alecia, she sat up straight and pursed her lips. Alecia held up an index finger. "No more!"

There was a knock at the door. She looked at Hetty whose eyes were wide.

"Who can that be?" Alecia stood and collected Hetty's cup and saucer. She motioned for her friend to follow her into the bedroom where Millie was feeding Iona.

"Thank you, Millie. I'll take over from here." She took Iona from the maid. "Can you answer the door to whomever it is and ask them to wait in the sitting room? Don't mention I have company."

"Very well, Princess." Once Millie left the room, Alecia turned to Hetty.

"You stay in here while I get rid of whoever this is. Then we'll get you back home."

Hetty's brow wrinkled. "I could be stuck here for hours!"

"I'll make sure you're not. Now, quiet."

She returned with Iona to the sitting room to find Ramón standing beside the fireplace.

"This is a pleasant surprise, Ramón."

He nodded to her. "Princess."

Her spirits fell at his formality. She wondered if they could call each other "friend" anymore. "Would you like some tea? I have another clean cup."

"That won't be necessary." He approached and placed a gentle hand on Iona's cheek. The toddler reached out her arms, and Ramón took her from Alecia.

"She loves you." Alecia delighted that her daughter had a male role model close to hand.

"And I her." He held her close and breathed in deeply.

She studied his face while his eyes were closed for a few moments. Lines that hadn't been there before her father's death marked his face. Perhaps the responsibility of the principality dragged at him—or was it something else? *Guilt?*

Ramón opened his eyes and fixed her with his piercing blue gaze. "Vard Anton asked me to give you a message. Have things between you deteriorated so much that he doesn't even speak to you now?"

She drew her shoulders back and raised her chin. "We spoke before he left." He didn't have to know it was two days past. It hurt that Vard hadn't sought her out this morning before he departed at dawn. Still, there was really nothing more for either of them to say.

"He wanted me to give you and Iona a message—that he loves you, and you are always in his heart."

The words sounded awkward on Ramón's lips. A light blush climbed his cheeks.

"Thank you," she said. "As I mentioned, we spoke before he left, but it's nice to know we're in his thoughts."

Ramón stepped closer. "I don't like the man, but you two seem fated to be together. Wouldn't it be a sound idea to go to Wildecoast? He's Iona's father after all."

"I'm not about to discuss this with you, Ramón. It's not your business."

"Oh? I thought we were friends. I care for you."

"Better not let Benae hear you say that." She sat and sipped her tea. *Yuck!* It was cold. She stood, crossed to the bell, and rang for a maid.

"Benae is completely secure with our friendship. She knows I love her."

"Do we even have a friendship? I get a sense that you have many secrets from me."

"What secrets?"

She watched his jaw tighten and his fists clench. Ramón definitely hid something.

"I'll ferret out your little secrets if I stay. *That's* the real reason you wish for me to move to Wildecoast, isn't it—so you can get me out of the way?"

"No! I care for you and Iona, and I think you'd be happier with Vard."

There was a knock on the door, and a maid bustled in.

"Can I have fresh tea please?" Alecia motioned for the woman to take the old tea things. She left, and Alecia turned back to Ramón. "Thank you for the message. I appreciate you taking the time to deliver it. Now, please excuse me. I'd like to spend some time with Iona."

Ramón frowned, but gave Iona back to Alecia.

"*I* haven't given up on our friendship," he said, then turned and left the apartment.

Hetty appeared at the bedroom door. "I'd better go before someone else comes."

Alecia had been thinking about friendship and how it changed over time. "Of course. I'll take you out the side entrance, and the ladies will escort your carriage back. Soon, you won't be so far away. I'll send word when I have more news." She leaned over and kissed Hetty's cheek. "Be careful."

Hetty placed a gentle kiss on Iona's cheek, suspicious moisture in her eyes. "I will, and you look after this precious child."

Alecia nodded, and they left the chamber for the side entrance.

* * *

Vard was as jumpy as a wolf on hot stones by the time the convoy arrived back in Wildecoast. King Beniel had refused to ride inside a wagon or coach, and his figure drew unwanted attention. The effort of keeping watch had stretched Vard's nerves tight as a bow string. His friend and second, Samael Delacost, was almost as jumpy, which was saying much. Samael was the calmest man Vard had ever encountered.

The elven soldiers and nobles rode apart for much of the time, keeping to themselves and their own counsel. Vard was just as happy to leave it that way. He tired of watching his words even more than usual. It was so easy to say the wrong thing. He also tired of keeping one step ahead of Chandrelle and Alia Kelsis. It was as though the two worked together to corner him at every conceivable opportunity. If not for the ability to shift, they'd have trapped him more than once.

At least in Wildecoast, there were places he could escape where the elven ladies would be loath to follow.

There had been several small skirmishes with the *Sis Lenweri* on the way to Wildecoast. Vard had doubled the guard each night, leaving sleep in short supply for the soldiers and rangers. He himself felt he could sleep for days.

Samael rode up beside him. "I can't wait for a hot bath and a soft bed."

"And a hot meal," Vard said, the image of steaming beef and vegetable stew with warm buttery bread springing to mind. "I can't decide which order they should come in."

"Mmm," Sam said, rubbing his chin. "I think a long dip in the hot pools first, followed by a meal, and then bed!"

"It's a little early in the day for bed, isn't it?" Vard looked at the sun, which was only halfway to the horizon from its zenith.

"I've been known to sleep the day away, especially at sea after a hard night."

Vard snorted a laugh. "Spare me the details!"

Sam held up his hands. "Totally innocent, I assure you."

Vard shook his head, gazing at the crowds as they entered the city. "I'm afraid I'll have to report to the queen as soon as I get this lot squared away." He gestured at the convoy behind him, flinging his arm wide and catching Isiloe's eye. She scowled at him, and he nodded back.

"I can help with that," Sam said. "I'll get the soldiers and guides settled. You can have the elves and the nobles."

"Thanks very much. It was going to be your task anyway."

"Isn't it better that you have a second who anticipates your orders? How about we meet in two hours for a meal and some ale?" Sam named a respectable inn close to the keep.

Vard agreed and turned his attention to the people and buildings around him. It paid to keep a sharp eye out, even in familiar surroundings. Assassins could be anywhere. He approached the sergeant at the gate.

The man saluted. "Welcome home, King's Blade. We saw you coming, so summoned an escort. There's a carriage on the way for the king."

"Thanks Griff. Any news?"

"The admiral is ready to greet you, and the queen asks you attend her at your earliest convenience."

"Is that all?"

"Yes, My Lord. It's good to have you back."

"It's good to be home, Sergeant." Vard kicked his horse into the body of the convoy as it moved past, leaving Sam to head the procession. He detailed soldiers to ride up front to clear the path for the convoy, then rode to the king.

"Your Majesty, there's a carriage being sent for you."

Beniel frowned, but then sighed. "I'd like to protest, but to be honest, I'd welcome a break from the saddle. I'm feeling quite tired today."

"You'll be able to rest soon, Sire. Once you've greeted the admiral and Queen Adriana, perhaps you can bathe and rest."

"Next you'll be tucking me into bed and feeding me gruel," Beniel grumbled.

"If that's what it takes to keep you hale and hearty, I'd be happy to see to it, Your Majesty," Vard said, trying not to laugh.

The king's blue gaze met his. "I owe you much, Vard, and appreciate your support. If only Alecia had returned with us, I wouldn't need to worry about her and Iona. My niece is far too impetuous and stubborn."

"That may be true, Majesty, but I believe she'll be safe, as will our daughter. She has good people watching over her."

Beniel's eyebrow quirked. "Including your own father, Vard. He seems a good man."

"He'll see Alecia is safe and provide her with good counsel. I trust him with my life. And of course, the Guardians and Alecia's ladies will ensure my family is cared for. And there are elven friends in Brightcastle from Amitania."

The king took a deep breath. "Where will it all end? And will I be here to see it?"

Vard cast the king a sharp look, noting the grayish tone to his skin. He raised his arm and looked toward Lady Alique, where she rode beside Isiloe. She approached, and Vard dropped back to speak with her.

"He's exhausted, My Lady," Vard said, quietly. "Can you see he's cared for once we arrive at the keep? A carriage is on its way. I'd appreciate it if you could ride alongside the carriage to the castle, in case you're needed."

Alique nodded. "Of course."

"I never got to ask how your husband took the news that you were leaving with us," Vard said.

Alique's jaw tightened, and she swallowed hard. "He wasn't pleased. I miss him more than I can express. I know he worries about my health and safety. But I must be where I can be the most help."

"Let's hope you're reunited before too long." Vard bowed from his saddle and trotted his horse to the front of the line.

Apart from a brief stop when the carriage arrived, the trip to the castle was uneventful. King Beniel even climbed aboard the carriage with minimal grumbling. His lack of fuss worried Vard. He resolved to get the king into his rooms and under the eye of his doctor at the earliest opportunity.

The castle forecourt was abuzz by the time their retinue passed through the gates. Samael rounded up the soldiers and scouts, and hustled them off to the barracks.

"If there isn't room, find alternative accommodation for them," Vard called as his second rode away.

Sam raised his hand in response. Vard smiled at the casual reply. It was good to have someone he could depend on. He turned to find King Beniel, and his eyes met those of Nikolas Cosara.

"Admiral," Vard said, nodding. He dismounted and handed his reins to a groom, then strode to the king's carriage.

The admiral grasped Vard's arm as he made to walk past. "Anton."

Vard stopped and faced him, eyebrows raised.

"What's this I hear about the king's illness coming back?"

Vard huffed a deep breath. "It's been a hard trip from Brightcastle, that's all. His Majesty is tired." He lowered his voice. "And if you're bright, you'll downplay any other rumors. We need to get him into his chambers to rest."

Nikolas's eyes shot daggers, but he followed as Vard walked to the carriage and poked his head in.

"All clear, Your Majesty." Vard reached in and helped the king out of the conveyance.

King Beniel straightened as he alighted and waved to all those gathered in the forecourt. A loud cheer went up, and some of the staff and nobles came forward to welcome him home.

Vard stood by with Nikolas as their king greeted his subjects. This was the last thing Beniel needed, but it was critical he be seen before being whisked off to his rooms.

"Get him out of here," Nikolas whispered gruffly. "He's spent long enough with this lot."

Vard stepped up beside the king. "It's been a long journey, and King Beniel must take his leave to rest. He has a full day tomorrow." He turned Beniel around and walked beside him to the steps, praying there wouldn't be a stumble.

They traversed the short flight of steps and made their way into the reception hall adjacent to the foyer. He helped the king into a chair and sent a page to make sure Beniel's rooms were ready. Food and tea had been delivered, so he prepared a plate for the king and poured his tea. All the while, Beniel was quiet... too quiet. Had they undone all their progress during the grueling trip home?

"My love!" Queen Adriana bustled in, swathed in a golden gown with red embroidery over the bodice and on the small train. "I can't tell you how relieved I am to see you." She studied her husband. "You don't look as well as I had hoped." She plumped his cushion and sat in the chair opposite.

"Don't fuss, Adriana," Beniel said. "I'll be right as rain after a good night's rest."

The queen's eyes narrowed as she studied Beniel. She turned to Vard. "I trust you had an uneventful journey home?"

"Just the odd skirmish, My Queen," Vard said. "Nothing we couldn't handle."

"Any loss of life?"

"No, Your Majesty, nothing apart from the earlier battle before we arrived in Brightcastle."

"Good! We can hardly afford for something like that to occur again. Are you any closer to discovering how the scoundrels took you by surprise?"

"We have our theories, but nothing concrete."

The admiral joined them, pouring a tea for himself and taking a sweet biscuit from the tray. He raised his cup to Beniel. "Glad I am to see you returned, Your Majesty. You look somewhat better than when you left."

Beniel snorted. "Somewhat! I was at death's door. But the fine mountain air of Brightcastle, not to mention its healers, has cured me. I shall live to a ripe old age."

"Good to hear," Nikolas said.

The queen rose and rang for a steward. "Let us get you up to bed, so you can rest, my love. You'll feel much better in the morning. I shall see to your nursing myself."

Vard cleared his throat. "Lady Alique is here, Your Majesty. I asked her to attend the king."

Adriana smiled. "That *is* good news! And her husband?"

"He remains in Selinore to prepare for the *Sis Lenweri*."

"Best place for him," Adriana muttered. "It will be wonderful to have Alique around the castle again. I'll see she has rooms prepared that place her close to the king."

A steward arrived, and Adriana gave her orders. King Beniel was helped from the room. When they were alone, Adriana motioned for Vard and Nikolas to sit.

"Is it as grave a situation as we feared?"

Vard frowned. "If you speak of the king's health, I've been told his heart is failing. He has a potion which will extend his life but…" He studied the queen, who waved her hand at him to continue. "Eventually, his heart will give out. He may not have long."

The queen sat with her hands clenched in her lap. "It seems I must prepare both myself and the kingdom for a loss." She took a deep breath and looked at Vard. "What of the *Sis Lenweri*? Do we have any more intelligence on their intentions or movements?"

Vard hesitated. He'd sound like a crazy man if he told of his suspicions.

"Anton," Nikolas snapped. "What are you hiding?"

"I hesitate not to conceal anything but because I don't know how to tell you. We can't explain Gorin's escape or the ambush on the king. Both events were unusual in their own ways."

He took a sip of tea. "As yet, we've been unable to explain how the bars of the prison cell were removed without an explosion. It appears they were simply ripped out. If you discount the use of magic, which would be foolish, then one explanation is a creature strong enough to pull the bars from this elevated position."

Both the queen and Nikolas frowned as though he were speaking another language.

"I'm considering the possibility that a dragon was used to free Gorin."

Nikolas leapt to his feet; the queen sat ramrod straight.

"You're insane!" Nikolas said. "If there ever were dragons, they're long gone.'

Vard nodded. "Possibly."

"But you think not?" Adriana asked.

"I don't know, Your Majesty." Vard decided to elaborate on his theory. "A dragon could also have transported the *Sis Lenweri* to the scene of the ambush without our sentries and scouts detecting it. Perhaps there was more than one dragon."

"This is fanciful in the extreme," Nikolas said. "Have you considered the possibility that your sentries just weren't up to the job?"

"You insult me, Admiral." Vard growled. "May I remind you of my position?"

Nikolas raised his chin, his lips forming a thin line.

Vard went on. "Of course, I've looked at how both incidents could have occurred, but there is no logical answer for either of them."

"Suppose we consider the dragon theory for a moment," Adriana said. "Have the elves been able to shed any light on the beasts?"

Vard was quiet for a moment. He was reluctant to tell her the elves thought him as crazy as she did. "They think it unlikely."

"Typical!" Nikolas snapped from his position beside the window.

"The elves in Selinore—the elders—say that the lesser dragons were wiped out, but it's possible some greater dragons survived. It's also possible that Faenwelar has links to a line of elves called dragon lords. They could speak to the greater dragons, and they rode them. What's more, Princess Alecia dreamed of a dragon on our way to Selinore."

"Alecia went to Selinore?"

"Your niece is quite the adventuress, Your Majesty. I believe she also has dreams that are visions of the future? "

"Pretty flimsy evidence to base your theory on, Anton," Nikolas said. "You'll need to give me more than that."

Vard glared at the man. "Regardless, the *Lenweri* and our forces are adjusting our fighting strategy in case dragons come against us. Our best archers are training to shoot the eye from a dragon if necessary."

"You got High Prince Arenil to agree to this?" Nikolas asked.

Oh yes, he'd believe Kain, his best buddy.

"I did." Vard wouldn't give Nikolas any more ammunition.

Nikolas's brows rose halfway up his forehead. He looked at the queen and shrugged.

"Nikolas, install more large crossbows on your ships and recruit archers proficient in their use. Make it your top priority."

Nikolas bowed. "Your Majesty. I'll attend to it right away." He left the chamber without a backward look.

The queen allowed her gaze to rest on Vard. "You look well, Lord Anton. I've missed your presence in these halls, but it seems you've been busy."

Vard nodded. "Once the king was out of danger, I travelled to Selinore to meet with the elves. It was an enlightening trip. I hope I'm wrong about the dragons, by the way."

"But you don't think you are?"

He shook his head. "Alecia's dream seems to confirm the theory, unfortunately. I trust her premonitions, and she has had more training with the elven dreamers since this one. Hopefully, we can discover more before we join in battle with the *Sis Lenweri*."

"Where do you think the first attack will come?"

"I don't know. Kain Arenil thinks the enemy will start their campaign in Selinore, but they could choose Amitania. If they took that city, they'd be close to Brightcastle and Wildecoast."

"Or," Adriana said, "they could attack one of the kingdom cities first."

"I'm not sure that makes sense. We're fortified. That makes us a harder target. Even with dragons, they couldn't drop many soldiers within the walls; unless they have several of them, which I doubt is the case."

"No, but chaos could ensue for long enough to breech the walls and enter the city."

Vard contemplated the chaos theory. It could be successful. Dragons breathing fire, even one or two, would be enough to crack open the defenses of either Wildecoast or Brightcastle. He went cold as the pictures played themselves out in his mind. They were unprepared and split into four centers of population to defend. It looked grim, but, with good leadership, they could yet build a plan and save Thorius.

CHAPTER EIGHT

ALECIA sat up in her bed, heart pounding as the nightmare left her. She breathed deeply to bring her rampant fear under control. It had been so *real*; real as never before. The horrible images forced their way back in, but she pushed them away, not yet ready to examine them. First, she must seek the counsel of the elven dreamer who had stayed in Brightcastle. Thank the Goddess, Iona was still asleep. She had time.

She bounded from the bed and called for Millie, then dressed in her most comfortable gown and soft slippers.

Millie knocked quietly and entered. "Good morning, Princess. You're up early. Is the little one awake?"

"No, Millie. I need you to fetch the elven scholar I've been working with. She's in the forest room. Please tell her to come quickly."

"Are you well, Princess? You look —"

"Just do as I say, Millie." Alecia was instantly sorry for allowing her frustration and fear to show. "Please, just fetch the scholar."

She was forbidden to name the elven woman in the presence of a human, although, as a dreamer, Alecia herself could use the woman's name. Millie curtsied and left. She did so hate it when she lost her temper with her.

The trouble was that Millie could be a chatterbox and stepped over the line on occasion.

She paced the carpet as she waited for her guest. Another knock on the door brought Millie with a pot of tea and two cups.

"I'll arrange breakfast soon, Princess, but I thought you might like the tea. Your guest will be here shortly."

Millie deposited the tea things and hurried away—probably wishing to avoid Alecia's foul mood.

A gentle knock brought Alecia to the outer door, and she opened it to find a tall figure wrapped in a dark green cloak.

"Come in." Alecia stood back and ushered the elven woman to the fire. Then she brought the tea over to the small table before the fireplace. "Please, make yourself comfortable."

"What has occurred?" the scholar asked.

Alecia stilled her fidgeting fingers and met the woman's direct gaze. "I had a true dream. It was so real... more than any other. Does this training have that effect?"

The woman stared at her for a long moment. "Yes. Your premonitions will become as real as in life. It can be distressing. Perhaps you should sit and take tea while you tell me about it."

Alecia sat, and the woman followed her lead.

"I was amidst a battle, on horseback. I was terrified, but also exhilarated. My sword was like a magical weapon. I killed one, two, another... No one could stand against me. But they outnumbered us. Dark elves..." She faltered, knowing this could give offence.

"They are not my people, but Faenwelar's, Princess. Speak openly."

Alecia nodded. "Dark elves surrounded us. They had hate in their eyes, so I know they were *Sis Lenweri*." She swallowed hard. "Then a screech rent the air, louder than anything I've ever heard. I looked up and from the north came a giant beast with huge wings. A dragon. It exhaled vast gouts of flame as it banked and glided across the field of battle.

"As the sound died away, the *Sis Lenweri* attacked with renewed frenzy, but I couldn't take my eyes from the dragon. Another appeared, then a third, and a fourth. I turned my horse and charged toward the other end of the battle. Vard was there. I wasn't fleeing the beasts; I was desperate to get to Vard, so we could defend each other and our home."

"Did you see it in color, Princess?"

Alecia hesitated, thinking back to her nightmare. "Yes. There were colors—vivid, terrible. The four dragons each had scales of different hues. The first was…" She closed her eyes to recall. "Red, then black, a green one, and the last was golden."

The scholar sat back against her chair, a frown on her smooth forehead. She inhaled a deep breath. "I believe it *was* a true dream. In the texts of the great dragons, there were four that were colored as you describe. They had the most power, and elven lords rode them. Did you see riders?"

Alecia shook her head. "I didn't see any. Do you think these dragons are the same as those in the texts? That would make them ancient."

"The same, or descendants, Princess. Could you place the battle?"

"I believed it to be Brightcastle. The dragons came from the mountains and over the forests north of the city." Her voice broke. "How can we defend against that?"

The scholar rose. "Take heart, Princess. We are not yet defeated. Our alliance is powerful, and we fight for freedom and peace between our people. You must believe we will triumph over the *Sis Lenweri*."

The elven woman bowed and left Alecia sitting in front of the fire. She tried to rouse herself from her gloom, but all she could see were those four dragons coming for her.

* * *

Vard strode down the hallway leading from his rooms in the east tower, clad in the new uniform of the King's Blade. No more would he shirk everything that came with that title. Thorius needed him, and who was he to hide when called upon? The Goddess had a plan for him. For all of them.

From this day forward, he would do everything he could to prepare the kingdom, especially Wildecoast, for war against the *Sis Lenweri*. He only wished he knew where the enemy would attack. He didn't even know the size of the *Sis Lenweri* forces. Best to assume they at least were equal in number to the *Lenweri* and human forces combined, though how they could rival the size of the kingdom forces he didn't know.

A breakfast war council had been called. He entered the formal dining room where the meeting would be held. Queen Adriana was already there, along with King Beniel, looking much improved. Alique stood beside him as if to offer support. Vard greeted the monarchs and Alique, then stood before the window overlooking the forecourt. It was a hive of activity, with elves and human soldiers moving in and out of the castle precinct. He nodded in approval.

Admiral Cosara arrived with Sam. Both greeted the monarchs, then split—Sam to Vard, and Nikolas staying to chat with the king and queen.

"Good morning, King's Blade," Sam said, with a small bow. "I trust you've settled back into castle life?"

"I have, and you?"

Sam looked fit to burst. "I've had news! Esta and our son are due to arrive in Wildecoast!"

Vard clapped him on the back. "That's good news. What did you call him?"

Sam's grin widened. "Mika." His face fell a little. "I wish I could've been there for the birth. Imagine watching your child come into the world."

Vard's stomach squirmed with remembered fear. "I was there for Iona, but only just. Believe me, not being there might be preferable to fearing they would both die."

Sam's eyes widened. "Still, I feel I missed out." He smiled. "Oh well, perhaps I can help with the next one."

"I'm sorry our missions took you away from Esta in her time of need."

"We knew this could happen and agreed I must put the kingdom first." He paused for a moment. "And, every time I planned a visit, something came up. Until now, Esta hasn't wanted to travel with Mika, but he's almost three months old and a sturdy baby."

Vard shrugged. "Will they stay here?"

"Considering the coming conflict, I'm hoping Esta will agree to a prolonged visit. I hope my mother-in-law and parents are with her."

"That's a good idea," Vard said. "What are Esta's skills? I could have her trained to fulfill some role."

"She can sail a ship," Sam volunteered, then fell silent.

"Why do I sense there's a story there?" Vard asked, folding his arms.

Sam shook his head. "Her father taught her before he died, and she has a ship anchored at the harbor. You need only say the word, and *Dawn Lady* will sail in service to the kingdom."

Vard nodded. "That's good to know. Can you ask Lady Esta to ready the ship and have a crew on standby? We're having large crossbows built into the naval fleet, and I'll make sure *Dawn Lady* is included."

Sam stepped closer and lowered his voice. "So, you think the *Sis Lenweri* will attack here? Otherwise, the ships will be useless. Surely this will be a land-locked war?"

"We know nothing for sure. And, if there are dragons, ships with crossbows could come in handy."

Sam flinched. "Not sure I like the thought of my wife on a ship below a fire-breathing beast."

Vard frowned. "There'll be no guarantee of safety for *any* of us. As it is, I must decide if we should bring those in the southern coastal towns to Wildecoast for safety. It would have a dual purpose of more hands to fight and support."

"Many wouldn't come," Sam said. "They're an independent lot in the south. Might be worth a run down there though to gather the women and children and any able-bodied men who care to lend a hand here."

Vard nodded. "Good plan. I'll send Lady Esta south on that mission. If she'll agree to it."

Sam nodded. "She'd be willing. I'll see if Katrine will go with her."

The mention of the witch caught Vard's attention. He needed to speak with her to see if she had information garnered through the night hounds. "Where *is* Lady Katrine?"

"I'm not sure. Lately, she has spent time in Costa and on the Aranati estate. There's something going on between her and James Tomel, the master jeweler."

"Well, if you see Lady Katrine, tell her I'd like to speak with her. And let me know when your wife arrives." Vard glanced up as someone else entered. "Ah, General Formosa is here. Now the fun begins."

Isiloe, Chandrelle, and Ruven entered soon after Josef Formosa. Vard went to greet them.

He bowed to the three elves. "Good morning. I hope you found your housing suitable?" The elven members of the nobility were housed in a large mansion near the inner keep walls, within an easy walk to the palace.

Isiloe cast him a hard look. "It is very comfortable, King's Blade. Even the food is to our liking."

Vard barely stopped his brows from rising in surprise at Isiloe's agreeable remark. "I'm glad. The queen will be pleased too. She evicted a distant family member so you could move in."

Isiloe's eyes widened slightly. "Really?"

"It's true. Although the family member has moved into the castle for the time being, so they're not so much put out. This is much better use of available dwellings, and we hoped you'd feel more comfortable in the mansion."

"Are you sure it is not *you* who feel more comfortable with the elves away from the keep, Vard Anton?" Isiloe fixed him with her icy blue stare.

"My only goal is the comfort of your people, Ramar Isiloe," Vard said, proud of himself for maintaining his composure. Perhaps he *might* make a diplomat someday. Alecia would laugh. Then the thought of his love, far away in Brightcastle, sobered him.

Chandrelle laughed. "Don't mind Isiloe, Lord Anton. She is merely teasing you, aren't you, sister?"

"If you say so, *sister*," Isiloe said, sharing that icy smile with Chandrelle. Vard wondered how the two women *really* got on, but that wasn't his concern.

He turned his attention to Ruven. At least here was an elven leader with a forthright disposition. "And what of you, Ruven? How are you enjoying your accommodations?"

"I like them very much, Vard, but then I need little for comfort." He slid his eyes sideways at the women and quirked one brow.

Isiloe shot him daggers with her gaze. Vard suppressed a smile.

Luckily, Alique joined them. She approached Isiloe and kissed both her cheeks, then did the same to Chandrelle, murmuring words of greeting. To Ruven, she simply nodded politely. Soon, Vard found himself the subject of Alique's attention.

"Lord Anton, I hope you've recovered from the journey. I must admit to being a little weary this morning."

Vard bowed to her. "I'm fit and ready to organize a war, My Lady." He turned to the elves. "Would you excuse us?" Vard guided Alique to a quiet corner. "How is His Majesty this morning?"

Alique frowned. "A little restored, but it dismayed me he didn't cope with travel better. How will his body deal with a campaign?"

"Exactly my thoughts."

"We must hope the *Sis Lenweri* attack doesn't come too soon."

Vard nodded. "We need time to plan our campaign." He'd begun to think attacking the enemy first might be the best form of defense, but the king would want to be involved. Vard sighed, the enthusiasm of just moments ago draining from him.

King Beniel took a seat at the center of the table with the queen on his right. He motioned Vard to take the seat on his left. Vard ignored the scowl that Josef Formosa gave him. The rest of the guests were left to find their own places.

"Please serve yourselves from the platters, and we will begin this council as we eat."

The queen served her husband, then prepared her own plate. Vard poured the king a cup of tea and a goblet of mulled wine before he prepared his own breakfast. His gut tightened as he contemplated the inevitable arguments to come.

"I will ask the King's Blade to recount our travels," King Beniel said, waving Vard to his feet.

Vard recounted the ambush on their approach to Brightcastle and the journey to Selinore. He drew a breath and explained his theory about the dragons.

Josef Formosa leapt to his feet. "Preposterous! If dragons ever existed, they're long extinct." He glared at Vard. "You'll have us jumping at shadows!"

The king cleared his throat. "I know it's a stretch, General, but you remember that this very keep once housed more than one dragon, or so the legends say."

"Your Majesty! It sounds like you're entertaining this theory," Formosa said. "I say we forget fairytales and mount a large force to attack the scoundrel Faenwelar where he lives."

"That would be venturing into enemy territory," Nikolas Cosara said quietly, "attacking the elves where they're strongest. I'm not sure it's a viable option."

"Better than waiting here for them to ambush us," Formosa snapped. "A bold move would catch them by surprise."

"Have you forgotten the slaughter that occurred when my father was taken, Josef?" Alique asked. "The elves fight well in the forests."

Ruven stood. "The lady is correct, General. An open plain would give your longbow men an advantage."

Formosa barely stopped himself from sneering. "Since when do we listen to females?"

Ruven's brows shot up amid gasps from around the table.

The queen cleared her throat. "Perhaps you have forgotten I am present, General. I think you'll find I have an excellent grasp of battle strategy, as do our elven guests, and Lady Alique is married to the former general of Brightcastle."

"Him!" Formosa snorted. "Where is *he* now? Up in the forest licking his wounds."

Vard stood. "General, keep a civil tongue in your head. This is a war council, not a tavern brawl."

Formosa spluttered. "King Beniel! Will you allow this man to insult me?"

The king stood. "I'm afraid I agree with Lord Anton. Be polite and constructive, or you can leave." The king fixed his general with sharp eyes. "Your idea of attack has merit. Let us give that further thought."

Formosa appeared somewhat mollified that the king was entertaining his suggestion, but he glared at Vard as he took his seat. And the day had begun so well...

They debated the plan of locating Faenwelar and attacking his stronghold, thought to be high in the mountainous forests north of Amitania. Nikolas Cosara recounted a recent expedition to Ravenskeep, so named because of the birds the town used to communicate with the outside world. The occupants of the northern border town were suspicious of outsiders and kept a close watch on their local lands and beyond.

Nikolas had had a hard time getting their cooperation, but finally established access through Ravenskeep to the forests west of the town. Some locals guided Nikolas and his men through the outer edge of the forest, and they had seen evidence of the passage of many soldiers. None were actually seen, but the trackers agreed the paths were worn down by humans or elves.

Formosa stood, interrupting Nikolas. "So, we could take ships north to Ravenskeep and then strike west to find and flush out Faenwelar and his forces. I say we prepare now. Admiral, do you have ships ready to sail?"

Nikolas fixed Formosa with a cold, aqua gaze. "My ships are *always* on standby, General, but I think it unwise to make hasty decisions. If we deploy our forces to Ravenskeep and beyond, we leave ourselves weakened in Wildecoast. Faenwelar could send a force south and overrun us before we could turn and defend our cities."

There was a general murmur of agreement around the table. Formosa frowned.

Vard mulled over the idea nonetheless. "I like the concept of knowing more about our enemy. We have no count of Faenwelar's forces, or of how many strongholds he has."

The queen cleared her throat. "General Magbalar, surely you know something of the *Sis Lenweri* forces? Can you enlighten us?"

Formosa sat with a scowl as the former *Sis Lenweri* stood. "I wish I could fully detail the extent of Faenwelar's forces, Your Majesty. I will tell you what I know, but remember, Princess Gwaethe Arenil discovered me in the same prison she was sent to. Faenwelar and his underlings must have sensed my lack of support for his practices."

He took a breath and squared his shoulders. "As far as I know, Faenwelar has soldiers spread through the northern forests from Ravenskeep to the borders of Selinore. He holds more territory than the *Lenweri* do. As for soldiers, *Sis Lenweri* females don't fight, but they have been prolific in producing young to bolster the ranks of the army. The high prince has training camps like the one that was in Amitania all through the rugged forests of the northern alps."

Ruven paused, looking around the table at his companions. Vard did the same, gauging the mood of those in the meeting. A jumble of scents assailed him, including fear, frustration, and anger.

"The battles the *Sis Lenweri* have fought against us have hurt their numbers," Ruven said, "but not enough to make them weak. Faenwelar has been building his army for decades. He has hundreds of trained elven soldiers and hundreds more young cadets ready to step into the breach."

He sighed. "I don't think we can win against Faenwelar on his territory. He will have superior numbers, warriors trained in forest warfare, caches of supplies and weapons, traps and tunnels through the mountains… do I need to go on?"

King Beniel had gone pale. "We should have been more aware of this threat."

"My Liege," Vard said, "there's no value in looking backward. We'll learn from our inattention and move forward. I suggest we send a small force into the mountains west and north of Ravenskeep and take a survey of the terrain and the *Sis Lenweri* encampments."

"And you have someone in mind for this?" Formosa asked. "You perhaps?"

Vard quirked a brow at the general. "A small force of rangers and some elves should be able to accomplish the task, and, yes, I have a leader in mind. As soon as we complete this council, I'll organize the mission." He met the king's eye. "It won't be without risk, Your Majesty. I'd normally ask for volunteers, but for this task, only the best rangers and most talented scouts will do."

The king inclined his head. "Of course. Now, let us resume this meeting."

Formosa snorted and lapsed into a brooding silence, his arms crossed and eyes narrowed. Kain had warned Vard about this man and the trouble he'd caused in past battles with the *Sis Lenweri*. He was a loose cannon who must be watched and managed. A pity Kain wasn't still in charge of the kingdom army, but the scandal over his half-elven heritage had brought an end to his promising military career.

Vard thoughts tuned back into the meeting as they returned to the discussion of dragons.

"I don't wish to give this theory more time than it warrants," the king was saying, "but we cannot discount any possibility, however foolish it may seem."

Vard felt the heat of Beniel's scrutiny, as well as that of the others who sat around the table. He'd expected disbelief, and that was what he got. He kept his head high and met the eyes of all those seated with him.

"I've enlisted the help of elven scholars to track the greater dragons and dragon lords through the texts. I have two working in Brightcastle and Wildecoast as well as those in Selinore. The elven dreamers say something dark that hasn't been present before blocks them." He paused, trying to find his words. "They think Faenwelar is preventing them from seeing his plans."

The king raised one brow. "Elven dreamers? What manner of magic is this?"

Vard took a deep breath. "Their dreams show coming events, Your Majesty. As I understand it, they can predict the future, but they must train in the art before it can be used accurately."

"Preposterous!" The king stood and strode about the room, his eyes darting around his guests. He found Ruven. "What say you, Ruven Magbalar? Do these elven witches exist, and, if so, can we trust them?"

Ruven stood. "The dreamers are not sorcerers, Your Majesty. They simply go to sleep or put themselves into a trance, and pictures and experiences come to them. They cannot 'make' things happen. The dreamers are a conduit, enabling the waking world to see events which are to come."

The king scowled and shook his head. "I don't like it. Witchcraft is outlawed in this kingdom. We can't be seen to partake in it to aid our cause."

Vard cleared his throat. "There's no need for you to have any involvement, Sire."

"That's not the point!" The king leapt to his feet. "I simply won't allow Thorius to become a den of evil and sorcery." The monarch was red in the face and blowing hard.

"King Beniel," Vard said, his voice firm, "we can't ignore that which may help us. You've made me your advisor, the King's Blade. Allow me to keep you remote from issues which are distasteful to you."

Formosa snorted and shook his head.

Nikolas Cosara stood. "King Beniel, My Queen, I think Vard Anton's advice is sound. I'll work with him to spare you the taint of magic. But we need to use these so-called dreamers if they can give us warning."

Now Formosa flew to his feet. "They could tell us *anything*. They could lead us into a trap!"

Vard quelled the urge to punch the man. He looked at Cosara.

"If you'll allow me to finish, General?" Nikolas said, his jaw tightening. Formosa sat, and Nikolas continued. "I was about to say, I'll guarantee we won't walk into any traps because of the information provided by the dreamers." He looked at Adriana. "Cousin, I know you trust me. Give me this duty—to oversee the validity of any magical processes used during this conflict."

Vard's feelings on the matter were mixed. He was relieved Cosara had stepped in, but the last thing he wished for was to work in close cooperation with a man who detested him.

The king and queen removed themselves to the corner of the room to converse, Adriana whispering fervently into the king's ear while Beniel shook his head. Finally, they returned and seated themselves at the table.

"Very well," Beniel said, "I agree that the admiral can be our representative on the matter of magical interference in this war. My queen has reminded me that the elven people have foreign ways, including the use of dream interpretation, by which they interact with the world and each other." He paused, casting his gaze around the table. "But do *not* assume this gives magic practitioners permission to openly practice their arts, nor does it condone the use of magic in the kingdom of Thorius."

Beniel sat down, looking tired and pale. Adriana patted his hand.

Vard stood. "I think that's all for now. Thank you for attending. We'll meet again in two days."

They all bid the king and queen farewell and filed out. Vard found himself beside the admiral.

"Just as well the king doesn't have any knowledge of your special talents, Anton."

Vard's stomach flipped. The bastard would reveal all Vard's secrets in a heartbeat if he thought it was advantageous. That he hadn't must mean he wasn't threatened by what he'd seen that day in Vard's chambers.

He stepped into a side corridor, beckoning Nikolas to follow him.

"Why don't you spell out what you want instead of making threats? We're all on the same side here."

The admiral's brow rose. "Are we? I haven't decided yet. You pursued my wife. It was innocent on her part, but I don't believe for a minute you were just teaching her riding and weapons."

Vard blew out a breath. "That's all it was, and the longer you refuse to believe that, the more damage you'll do to your marriage. We have more important things to do than fight amongst ourselves."

Cosara relaxed back on his heels and folded his arms, studying Vard, his aqua gaze disconcerting. "Unfortunately, you're right. Now's the time to put aside our differences and work together. But I'll be watching you—like a *hawk*. You may have the king and my brother fooled, but I see what you really are."

"You see what you want to see, Cosara," Vard ground out. "I doubt you'll be able to work with me without your prejudice coloring your decisions."

"We'll see about that!" Nikolas turned and strode up the hall.

Vard's eyes met Sam's. The ex-pirate leaned against the wall across the hall, his brows raised. As usual, he appeared completely relaxed.

"He's in a good mood this morning," Sam said sarcastically.

Vard joined him, huffing out a breath. "He refuses to believe I have no designs on his wife. Doesn't he see I have enough on my plate without trying to conduct a clandestine affair with a noblewoman?"

Sam patted his back. "He doesn't think like that, my friend. All he sees is Merielle, and how isolated she is most of the time. He believes she's lonely and that men will take advantage of her open heart."

"Perhaps he should take her with him sometimes. Then *he* could teach her riding and weapons."

Sam sighed. "That would make far too much sense. Anyway, Esta arrives today, so she'll help keep Merielle occupied." He got a faraway look. "I can't wait to see Esta and Mika. Despite the times, I have so much to be grateful for."

Vard smiled. "I feel that way, too. When you've been through a rough patch and life evens out, you appreciate the good times even more. Which is another reason I don't understand your brother. From what I can tell, he's lost so much. I'd have thought he'd treasure the peace and love that his wife brings to him."

"Hmmm," Sam said, "Niko loves Meri, but he's afraid of losing her too. In part, that's why he reacted to you so badly. She does have some strange ways, though."

"I've noticed," Vard said. "She's fond of raw seafood and is inordinately strong for her size and sex."

Sam shook his head. "A mysterious lady indeed."

"Anyway, we don't have time to uncover the secrets of the Cosaras. We must locate the leader of the mission to Ravenskeep and help him select his team."

CHAPTER NINE

VARD and Vortek Cruzen circled each other, a ring of rangers watching. The man moved with fluid grace and appeared completely relaxed, even though Vard knew that wasn't the case. Only another fighter could pick the small signs of tension in his body. Vard watched for an indication that his opponent was about the strike while he planned his attack. They fought without weapons, a definite advantage for Vortek, who was a master of unarmed combat.

Hoping to gain the element of surprise, Vard aimed a kick at Vortek's head. The man slid out of the way and, spinning, drove his own boot at Vard. The kick slammed into the side of Vard's knee and pain shot down his leg. Desperate to control his fall, Vard rolled and gained his feet again, instantly looking for Vortek. The other Defender had followed him and launched a chin jab. The shot connected, but Vard jerked his head back and spun away.

Vortek was good—better than good. The glancing blow to his chin stung as though the skin had been split. He eye-balled the other man, noting the glowing golden irises. Hoping Vortek had enough control over his temper to prevent transformation, Vard launched at him, punching him in the sternum then using the edge of his hand to strike the other man, first on one side of the head, on each collar bone, and then on the other side of the head.

His opponent reeled back, spinning and stomp-kicking Vard's other knee. They were both breathing heavily now, and the fight had moved into dangerous territory. As Vortek completed his spin, Vard again moved in, grabbing a handful of dirt and hurling it into Vortek's face. While the man was blinded, Vard seized him from behind, his arm across his opponent's throat.

Vortek tensed, ready to release his explosive power in a move that might easily kill.

"Steady, man," Vard growled. "We wouldn't want to hurt each other."

"That last was a dirty trick, King's Blade," Vortek hissed, but his body relaxed a little.

"Can I let you go without risk to my person?" Vard asked.

Vortek nodded and Vard slowly release his hold, stepping clear just in case.

Those watching clapped and cheered, moving forward to clap Vortek on the back. Someone offered the Defender a cloth to wipe his face.

Vard joined Sam, who stood against the side of the barracks.

"I thought you were in trouble there," Sam said, handing Vard a clean cloth. He dabbed at his chin and the towel came away bloody.

"I was. The man's seriously good. His only error was to believe I was an honorable man."

Sam laughed. "He won't make that mistake again."

They turned to listen to Vortek address the group of men who were to travel with him to Ravenscroft. The eight rangers and guides, including two elven trackers, had been selected by Vard and Sam earlier that day.

Along with his unarmed combat skills, Vortek could shift into wolf, owl, and bear. He had trained with Melandrach, along with Lyam, and was the other Defender Vard discovered after his first trip to Brightcastle to recruit rangers; the same occasion when he had been reunited with Alecia and Iona.

Vard and Sam were teaching him the sword and bow. Though proficient in the weapons, he'd be vulnerable in battle. However, his hands and feet were lethal to any stupid enough to come within reach. He wasn't a large man, not as tall as the elven people, but wiry like they were.

Vortek's ability to disarm almost any opponent who came against him had earned him great respect amongst the men and women. And so, when a man was required to lead this mission, Vard immediately thought of the Defender. He wished he knew more about the man's past, but was prepared to allow a fellow Defender his privacy. Lyam had vouched for him, as had Melandrach.

As Vortek dismissed his team, Sam clapped Vard on the shoulder.

"I need to clean up. Esta and Mika should be here by now." He studied Vard's face. "Perhaps you should get that chin looked at."

Vard nodded. "Enjoy your reunion and meeting your son."

Sam grinned. "Oh, I will, you can be in no doubt of that."

Vard watched as Sam jogged away, trying not to feel envious of his friend.

* * *

As a man with a shady past, Sam had been given a tiny room in the lower reaches of the keep. And even that was only because he'd kept his nose clean since being handed to Nikolas to watch over. His room had a small, shuttered window high in the east wall which allowed a chink of natural light in. However, Sam spent little time there, preferring to be out training the men. Now, he was here to change into fresh clothes after a trip to the cavern baths. Nikolas had been there, washing away the stink of the day before seeing Merielle.

Niko had still been in a grump and refused to discuss the morning's meeting. All he said was "thank you for spending time with Anton, so I don't have to". Sam shook his head. Vard Anton was a man of talent and ethics who was a good support to King Beniel. He didn't seem to be out for his own profit.

Sam prided himself on being an excellent judge of character and was confident he had assessed Vard accurately.

So what if Vard held magical talents of his own? He itched to ask his friend about the shapeshifting, but years of piracy had given him a deep appreciation for secrecy. Vard would reveal all when he was ready, and Sam respected that.

But he was careful not to praise Vard in front of Niko. It wasn't worth the grief he'd get. Let the man work out his anger at the world and at Vard, and hope he didn't self-sabotage in the meantime.

Finished dressing, he hurried to the upper stories and found the room Esta had been assigned. It was the chamber with the golden oak door. He straightened his shirt and breeches, which had become uncomfortably tight on the journey up, then knocked. Esta's aunt, Paurella, answered.

"Samael! Come in, boy. Esta is just having a fitting for her new gowns." The older lady ushered him into the sitting room of the chamber, and Sam froze at the sight of his love.

Esta stood, swathed in gold satin and lace, her hand over her mouth and tears in her eyes. He took two steps to reach her and folded her against him while their hearts pounded their own greeting. Then he kissed her.

He never wanted the kiss to end. It was full of all he hadn't been able to tell her over the last weeks—all the love, regret, longing, fear and desire he contained, he breathed into her body. A throat cleared behind them, and they broke the connection, still looking into each other's eyes. Her caramel gaze warmed his heart and stoked his desire.

"I'm almost finished," Aunt Paurella said, "and then you can kiss all you like."

Sam kissed Esta's hand and turned to Paurella. "I'm sorry, Aunt. I apologize for my unseemly behavior."

Paurella flicked her fingers. "Pah! I was young once and would've been just as unseemly."

"Paurella!" Esta said, eyes wide and a smile on her luscious and very-kissed lips. Sam couldn't take his eyes off them. He wanted more.

Paurella ignored her niece's protest and bustled around, pinning here and there until she was satisfied. "There. Take the gown off, and I'll be back for a last fitting tomorrow."

Esta did as asked, and soon they were alone. She closed the door behind her aunt and leant against it.

"I've missed you." Her voice sounded breathy, needy.

Sam strode to her and took her in his arms. "You don't know how I've longed for this moment." She undid his tunic and shirt while he played with her breasts through the fabric of her gown.

She groaned. "I need you inside me *now*, Sam."

Her words frayed his tenuous control. He undid the lacings of his breeches and freed himself before hoisting Esta's skirts to her waist. She wore no pantaloons! He groaned as she lifted one of her legs and curled it around his waist. That was all the invitation he needed to guide his rod to her slick entrance and thrust it to the hilt. Home! He hoisted her a little, both legs wrapped around him, and thrust with the door behind her.

Esta moaned. "Harder!" Her words gripped him with a frantic need to lose himself in her tight heat. "I love you," he grunted, each thrust more powerful than the last, each squeeze of her muscles taking him closer to the edge.

"Come for me, love," he said, feeling her close to climax. He ground against her sensitive nub, and she tightened around him, screaming her completion. Two powerful thrusts more, and he joined her, emptying his seed into her for what seemed an eternity.

They stood like that against the door, she in his arms, legs wrapped around him, him buried inside her, their breathing slowly returning to normal. When he could do so, Sam walked with her to the wide chaise lounge and lay down, ready to continue their lovemaking. An angry cry rent the air.

Esta giggled. "Mika! He's due for a feed."

Their son had excellent timing. But Sam was eager to see his child, too.

He got up, gave Esta a moistened cloth to clean herself, then tidied himself up. They both entered the bedroom to indignant cries and frantic infant limbs jutting above the crib. When their faces appeared, Mika's eyes went wide for a split second before he reached for them. Sam wondered if he instinctively knew his father.

He picked the infant up and held him to his chest, inhaling the first scent of his son. Mika had the auburn hair of his mother, but the green eyes of his father. Sam hoped he inherited Esta's integrity, too. He didn't want his son to be forever tarnished by his own murky reputation. Mika was quiet for a few seconds, then wailed and began thrashing his arms about.

"He wants feeding." Esta took the child and sat on the rocking chair. Sam handed her a pillow to lay Mika upon, and she undid her dress and placed her son at her breast. A contented slurping filled the room. Sam sat on the bed, watching his son feed. He'd never tire of this.

"Has he been well?"

Esta sighed as she watched Mika. "So well! He seems to grow as I watch." She saw the bleak look on Sam's face and reached for his hand. "Don't be sad. You must do this, especially now that the kingdom is under threat. You're helping to keep us safe."

Sam wondered if he should tell Esta that the king might need *her* help. But he decided to wait, having no wish for the war to intrude on their family time; not this soon, anyway.

"The elves are wondrous, my love. Did you know they have people called dreamers who can see the future?"

She smiled. "I didn't know that. It could come in handy."

"That's what we think, though it seems to be a rather fickle gift."

"You can't just tell yourself what you need to know and dream the answer?"

"It seems not."

"How is Nikolas? And Merielle?"

"Nikolas is his same cranky self. Merielle, I've seen little of, but she's due to arrive today."

"It all seems rather real when we start leaving our estates. Mother and your parents wouldn't come with us. I talked to them until I was hoarse, but they wouldn't budge. Your father has become quite adept at managing the estate and wants to stay to oversee it. Since your mother wouldn't leave him, and our mothers are inseparable, they all stayed." She chewed her lip. "I made them promise to evacuate if there were signs of trouble, and that if soldiers asked them to leave, they'd comply."

Sam nodded. "I'm not surprised. Father's a stubborn man, and he has already left his home in Costa. He wouldn't wish to move again so soon."

"He has taken to farming life like a duck to water. He tells me he grew up on a farm, but his father made him study to be a carpenter."

Sam nodded. "Father's garden was always the best in Costa. I often saw a sad look in his eye that I could never explain. Perhaps it was his longing for another life?"

Esta smiled. "He's truly happy now. No wonder he won't leave. Do you think they're safe?"

"For now, they are. The king has patrols in the area, and I'll speak to Vard about what else we can do."

"He will be *so* grateful to have another chore to see to!"

There was a knock at the door. When Sam opened it, Katrine greeted him. He gave her an awkward hug and bade her enter. They'd never really accepted each other, but he lived in hope.

Katrine went with Sam to the bedroom and stood before Esta, gazing down at Mika as he fed. "He has grown so much!"

"He has. How are you, Sister? And James?"

"I'm managing." She drew a deep breath. "James and I are… married! I couldn't deny him any longer. I must hope he can accept me as I am. He says he loves me, so that's all that matters."

Esta's eyes widened. "That's just the news I needed. I'm so happy for you. And I can't even hug you with the baby attached!"

Katrine bent over Mika to receive her sister's kiss, and then Sam kissed her on each cheek.

"Congratulations, Katrine," Sam said. "I hope you'll be very happy."

She looked up at him. "But you don't think James is the man for me?"

He frowned. "I didn't say that, nor did I mean it."

James Tomel was a quiet and complex man who Sam didn't yet know well. After his reaction when they last met, he had little hope *their* relationship would be a close one. But if he made Kat happy, Sam was all for the union.

"Where is the bridegroom?" Sam asked.

"He had a meeting with the king, so I said I'd take my dinner with my sister and her family." She gave Sam a hard look, as if challenging him to send her away.

Esta finished feeding Mika, who had fallen asleep at the breast. She placed him in his crib and hugged Katrine.

"Now you're married, I suppose we'll see little of you at the estate, Sister."

Katrine frowned. "James and I stopped on the way through and spent time with Mother. She was beside herself with joy to have me off her hands." She fixed Esta with her penetrating blue eyes. "You know, I must be about my business. And now I have a husband to care for."

Esta rang the bell for dinner, then sat before the fire, patting the seat beside her. Katrine sat, and Sam took the armchair. "Exactly what *is* your business?"

"The less you know, the better, but it involves keeping my finger on the pulse of the kingdom. I have other magic practitioners I communicate with, including elven sorcerers."

"I hope they are all on the *Lenweri* side, not Faenwelar's," Sam growled.

"What do you take me for?" Katrine asked. "But I must say I look forward to the time when the elves are united. The *Sis Lenweri* may well have their own brand of elven magic, and I'd like to study with them."

Esta scowled. "Why can't you be a normal person? You'll get us all in trouble with your magic!"

"Or I might just save us all! Really! My magic is a part of me, and it's about time you accepted that."

"Just don't go drawing attention to yourself, Katrine," Sam said.

The silver specks in her eyes flared at his words. "You're a fine one to talk, pirate! Your wicked ways almost ruined this family. How can you advise me on how to behave?"

Esta shot to her feet. "That's enough! We've both made plenty of mistakes, Sam and I, and now that I've made him part of this family, I expect you to welcome him with open arms."

Sam stood and moved to Esta, pulling her into a hug. "I can take care of myself, love," he murmured into her ear. "Don't make me a cause of strife between you and your sister."

He held Esta until her trembling subsided, then turned to Katrine. "If you have anything to say to me, let's keep it private. But I'd like us to get along."

Katrine stared up at him, her eyes flinty, the silver sparkles in them swirling with her agitation. She sighed. "I suppose you're right. We can get along for Esta and Mika's sake. Who knows? One day we might be friends."

Sam smiled, relieved he had sidestepped another fight with his sister-in-law.

Dinner arrived, and they enjoyed a sumptuous feast, just the three of them. Sam relaxed over several goblets of wine, and even Katrine sipped on some. By the end of the meal, the ladies were giggling over Sam's jokes, and he was looking forward to having Esta all to himself.

Katrine stood up from the table. "I must bid you good night. I have business to be about and a husband to find."

Esta scowled. "I wish you'd tell me properly what this so-called business is. I worry about you."

"I'm a grown woman. I'll visit you for breakfast tomorrow and bring James." She bent to kiss her sister on the cheek. "Good night. And you, Sam."

Sam bowed as Katrine left them. He approached Esta and pulled her up against him. "Now that we're alone, I have some business of my own to attend to, my love." He claimed her lips, crushing her body against his, so she could be in no doubt how much he needed her.

"I like the way you think," she murmured against his lips.

"I hope you aren't tired, wife. This might take some time."

Sam picked Esta up, and she giggled all the way to the bedchamber.

* * *

Vard found the witch in the queen's flower garden. He halted at the archway into the sanctuary and allowed his senses to tune into his surroundings. The perfume of late season roses drifted to his nose, along with that of leaves and earth redolent with the smell of horse manure that had been turned into the soil of the flower beds. No danger presented itself, except for the genuine threat this sorceress could pose.

"Come," she said, and Vard smiled. She was like Hetty, impossible to fool.

He approached her where she stood amongst the leaves of a wisteria vine.

"We must stop meeting like this," he said, and she quirked a brow.

"We do make a habit of clandestine meetings, Lord Anton. This is our third if I'm not mistaken."

Vard smiled. "It's the nature of the work we do, Mistress. Thank you for meeting me."

She sighed. "I'm tired. Tell me what you want, so I can find my bed."

"Last time we met, you warned of a looming darkness. Do you have any sense of what that is?"

Her eyes darted around the garden, then rested upon him. "I'm not sure, but I think it's a dragon. I didn't tell you before, but I've seen one in the flesh."

Triumph coursed through Vard, and he took a step toward her. "You've *seen* one?"

She nodded. "Several weeks ago. It attacked James and one of his servants in Costa. The hounds warned me, and I got there in time. I chased the beast off with fire."

"What was a dragon doing in Costa? It makes no sense."

"You don't seem surprised at the mention of dragons. Why?"

"I've had my suspicions we could be dealing with the beasts, but I've not been able to convince many that I'm sane. The presence of a dragon would explain Gorin's escape from Wildecoast and also the ambush on the king's party."

She nodded. "I've been undertaking research and have discovered the *Sis Lenweri* have links to the greater dragons."

"You could help convince the king and his advisors, Lady Star."

She put her hands up, palms facing him. "No. I must stay in the shadows. You know how the king feels about magic."

Vard shook his head and began pacing.

"Try to draw me into this and you'll be sorry, Lord Anton. If I'm exposed and arrested, the hounds will have no one to guide them."

Vard met her eye. "Is that the only reason I'll be sorry?"

"Believe me, you don't want to find out."

"Don't worry. Your secrets are safe with me. You don't need to threaten me to keep me silent."

She had the grace to look embarrassed. "I don't trust easily. You learn to depend on yourself when your secrets could get you killed."

"I understand. I'll find another way to convince the king we need to take dragons seriously. Just knowing you've seen one helps me. Now I can be certain my plans are valid."

She nodded. "If there's any way I can help, I will. My hounds are at your disposal."

"Thank you, however, to use them you may have to reveal yourself. What if they're needed in daylight?"

"I'll cross that ditch when I come to it." She folded her arms under her breasts.

"Where are you staying in Wildecoast?" he asked.

"I'll be close. If you need me, give Esta a message, and she'll arrange it. If I need *you*, I'll leave a note with your man as I did this time."

"Stay safe, Lady Star. I have a feeling you're an important link in our success against the *Sis Lenweri*."

She inclined her head, and Vard bowed. When he straightened, she was but a shadow through the archway. He returned to his rooms, shaking his head.

* * *

Nikolas paced the gold and silver patterned rug that lay on the floor of his sitting room. He'd been told that Merielle had arrived, but she was nowhere to be found so far. If his information was correct, she'd been present for the last two hours. *Damn it*! He must know she was safe; know she still loved him. He might have threatened his marriage with his jealous reaction to Vard Anton's presence on the Cosara Estate.

And damn the man for interfering with his wife! If Meri wanted training, she could ask him, her husband, for it. He ignored the voice that reminded him she'd been asking him to teach her to ride for months. There was never enough time in the day. How was it possible that Anton had the time when he had an equally busy role in the kingdom?

Hah! Well might he ask! The man could shift into the form of a hawk and fly wherever he wanted. He had a good mind to reveal all of Anton's secrets. But the king trusted the shifter, and Anton appeared to be doing a good job. He certainly had Sam fooled.

The door opened, and Merielle bustled in, her lush figure wrapped in shimmery aqua fabric. She was a vision, her bright red hair arranged in intricate braids over her skull.

She squealed when she saw him, then froze, composing her features and attitude.

"Hello, Nikolas." Her brilliant green eyes swept his face and body as if taking inventory. "I hope you haven't waited long?"

Nikolas flinched at her formal tone. Her unease was his fault. He strode to her and kissed her on each cheek before pulling her into a hug. She tensed and then relaxed against him, wrapping her arms around his body, and burying her face in his neck.

"Oh, my love," she said on a sob. "How I have missed the feel of you in my arms."

"And I've missed *you*." He pulled away to look into her eyes. "I don't want this distance between us. We've been through too much to lose what we have. I shouldn't have accused you of being unfaithful." He paused and kissed her, long and lingeringly. "Please say you forgive me."

Tears pooled in her eyes. She was so beautiful, and she was his. He must remember that.

"Nikolas! Of course, I forgive you. You are everything to me, especially since we likely will never have children. We must always hold each other close. Never believe I will be unfaithful."

He pulled her near again, and they stood, eyes closed, her heart pounding against his chest.

She pulled back a little to gaze up at him. "You must understand I need to have a life, too. I cannot just sit on the estate and be a prim and proper lady. That is why I turned to Vard. I wish to have the skills to be a fitting partner for you in love, life, and war."

Her words set his heart pounding. He swallowed hard at the thought of Meri amid battle, in danger, his entire world at risk.

He pulled her close, eyes locked tight against the fearful tears that threatened. "I want your happiness." He gathered the strength required to speak the next words, battling down terror at exposing her. It was what she craved. "I'll see to your training."

She squealed and spun him around, then flung herself back into his arms and kissed him with a passion that he'd only known from his precious wife. Her love gave him the courage to put her at risk. He couldn't imprison her on their estate any longer. He'd been wrong to isolate her to protect her. But how to keep her safe now?

She pulled away and gazed up into his eyes. "You are the best husband I could ever wish for. Thank you for agreeing to this. When can I start?"

He took a deep breath and worked muscles in his neck and shoulders that were suddenly tense. "Show me your skills on the morrow, and I'll gauge from that where your training should take place and with whom."

She jumped up and down, clapping her hands. "I cannot wait! You will see I am quite proficient, my love."

Nikolas growled at the thought of who had taught her, and she giggled, a mischievous glint in her eyes. She wrapped her arms around him. "I love you, Nikolas."

"I love you, too." He pulled away. "Now we must go to dinner if we're not to be late. King Beniel and my cousin are expecting us."

* * *

The next day dawned, overcast and blustery. Vard hunkered down beneath his cloak as he observed the training ground from behind a row of trees. Lady Cosara and her husband occupied the ground, amongst his rangers, male and female.

They used practice swords, and Vard grinned as Cosara struggled to fight off an agile and ferocious first attack from his flame-haired wife. He adjusted and wasn't taken by surprise at the next assault.

Merielle had learned her lessons well. The admiral wouldn't be able to fault her proficiency, and she was as strong as most men. Vard wondered again where her power came from.

She attacked again, and Nikolas was hard-pressed to fend her off. He went on the offensive, pushing Merielle into the far corner. She was too quick for him and escaped when Vard thought Nikolas had the upper hand.

"I thought I might find you here." Sam's deep voice startled him.

Vard just avoided spinning into an attack against his friend. "You want to watch yourself, sneaking up on me."

"I never get near you, ordinarily. What has you so distracted?"

"Your brother and sister-in-law."

"Ah," Sam said. "Meri fights well. You must be a good teacher."

"She's a quick study, with strength and agility—a useful combination."

"A rare combination," murmured Sam. "She moves like... I don't know what she reminds me of." They watched as the two fought, Meri with the advantage at least half the time. "She looks like a seasoned fighter. How long have you been her instructor?"

"A few weeks. And stop talking about it. I'm sure Cosara doesn't wish to be reminded of the fact that his wife has been spending time with me."

Sam snickered. "You whipped him good when he challenged you. That's what stung the most. It's good to see him on the back foot with someone."

"Tell your brother that. He'd challenge me again in a heartbeat. He's just waiting for a chance to make my life difficult."

"I guess jealousy will do that."

"It's a little more complicated, but I'm just going to stay out of his way if I can."

"Hmmm. Good luck with that. Now that we're on battle alert, we'll be under each other's armpits even more."

Vard pulled a face. "Sounds delightful."

"Any idea of what our next move is? What are my orders?"

"We have another council after luncheon, which I expect you to attend. You'll know more after that. For now, I'd like you to put the rangers through their paces. Make sure you challenge them. And they need to work on their stamina. I want them training in their battle armor, chain mail, and whatever body protection they'll wear in battle. And see that Merielle gets protective clothing."

Sam thumped his fist on his chest in salute. "Yes, King's Blade. It shall be as you say." He grinned and strode away.

Vard shook his head. Sam was bold, but a good man to have in his corner and guaranteed to lighten a grim mood when required. His eyes sought Merielle and Nikolas again as they moved to the hand-to-hand combat phase. *This* would be interesting.

CHAPTER TEN

VARD made sure Lady Esta was present for the council, even though a few eyebrows rose when she entered the audience chamber. Merielle and Nikolas arrived together, still covered with the dust of the practice yard. Meri's eyes glowed with excitement, her cheeks rosy, hair askew. Esta approached and hugged her, not seeming to mind the dust and sweat. They were soon laughing together in a corner of the room.

Nikolas approached as Vard stood talking with Sam by the hearth. He nodded at the admiral, who wore a scowl on his tired features.

"Admiral," Vard said.

Nikolas fixed him with a look that would cow most men. "King's Blade." His eyes narrowed, and Vard wondered what was next. Sam interrupted whatever was coming.

"Merielle gave an excellent account of herself this morning, Brother. I didn't see anyone beat her."

Nikolas almost smiled. "Indeed." His gaze flicked back to Vard. "It pains me to admit that you taught her well."

Vard smiled. "She was an outstanding student with extraordinary strength, but also suppleness. One rarely sees such levels of both those elements. Does she have a background in acrobatics or dance?"

Nikolas cleared his throat. "She was a proficient swimmer before we married. Perhaps that has helped." His jaw tensed.

"Whatever it is, I've seen nothing like it before." Vard watched Nikolas closely. There was something about Merielle and her abilities which seemed to make her husband uncomfortable. Perhaps it was merely that he disliked discussing his wife with other men, especially Vard. That was understandable.

"She's certainly very fit." Sam crossed his arms and leaned back to examine his brother. "You, on the other hand, Niko, seem exhausted."

"Nice of you to notice, *Brother.*" Nikolas stalked off and collected his wife before sitting near the front.

The king arrived and clapped his hands for attention. "Please be seated, friends." He sat on one of the thrones at the front of the room, Queen Adriana gliding to his side.

The queen locked eyes with Vard and smiled at him. The look spoke of long kisses and more. He hoped no one else saw.

In his role as moderator, Vard sat on the king's other side, but on a plain chair. When everyone was seated, Vard stood.

"Thank you for attending. I have details of the mission to Ravenskeep. I selected Vortek Cruzen to lead a party of eight rangers and elves. They left at first light and will send word when they can." There was general muttering.

Formosa stood. "What do we know about this Vortek? What's his background? And don't tell me of his proficiency in hand-to-hand combat. I already know that."

"Cruzen spent some time in the Tylevian army," Vard said. "Since leaving, he's spent several years guarding caravans both within Thorius and in neighboring kingdoms. Most recently, he trained with the elves, the *Lenweri*. I consider his skills in unarmed combat and in tracking, as well as his army background, made him most suitable to lead this mission. He has the respect of his party. The force is small enough to enter and move about in the mountains without drawing attention."

"You had that little speech ready, didn't you, Anton?" Formosa sneered.

The king cleared his throat. "General, please be respectful and make positive contributions to this discussion."

Formosa bowed, but remained standing. "Of course, Your Majesty."

"You have something else to say, General?" Vard fixed Formosa with a look guaranteed to intimidate. Formosa squirmed a little.

"I don't like sending an unknown on such an important mission."

"You'll have to trust my judgement on that," Vard said, his voice almost a growl.

The king flapped his hands at the general. "Yes, Formosa. If Lord Anton says Cruzen is suitable, then he is. Let us move onto the next item on our list."

"Well," Formosa said. "I've loaded wagons with supplies and weapons, so we can be ready to move at short notice. I don't want to be caught on the hop if the *Sis Lenweri* attack, nor take needless time to prepare if it's decided we'll make the first move."

"Very good, General," King Beniel said, a frown on his brow.

Vard ground his teeth. but kept his silence. He had given that very order as soon as he arrived back in Wildecoast... But let Formosa think he was giving the orders—it would keep the man busy and out of *his* way. "Thank you, General."

This time, Formosa sat, and Vard continued. "We plan to fetch those who wish to seek shelter in Wildecoast from the southern coastal villages. We'll deploy several ships to Shawmere, and they'll work their way up the coast, putting in at each town to collect those who wish to flee their homes." He stopped to judge the response of those present. Most were nodding.

"However, we don't wish to use naval ships in case those are required to defend against the *Sis Lenweri*. That's why we shall commandeer private vessels of a size sufficient to carry up to one hundred passengers."

Lady Esta stood. "If I may, Lord Anton?"

Vard nodded.

"I have a ship I'd like to make available to the cause. I sailed her here, and she lies anchored in the harbor."

Vard smiled. "A most generous offer, My Lady." He found Sam and raised his brows. Sam nodded. "Lady Esta, we wondered if you'd consent to lead the mission to collect our southern citizens?"

Her eyes widened, and her hand flew to her throat. "Me?"

"I know it's asking much, but we need all the help we can get. You leading the mission means we can spare another captain for our naval vessels and more dangerous operations. I'm not saying there is no danger in the southern trip, and you'll be sent with armed men, but we feel this is the best use of our forces. I'll enlist another two or three ships to accompany you and they will be sailed by experienced captains."

"My child?"

"That would be your decision, My Lady. Your son could stay here or travel with you, whatever you decided was best."

Vard glanced to Sam, who appeared stricken at his words. The child was too young to be separated from his mother ordinarily, and taking an infant to sea was not to be undertaken lightly. He turned back to Esta.

"Are you interested in leading this mission, Lady Esta?"

Esta's eyes glowed with excitement, but she clutched her hands in front of her. "I am, Lord Anton. When would I leave?"

"Within the next day, two days at the latest. The weather is favorable, but I fear the storm season is close."

She swallowed hard and squared her shoulders. "I'll see to a crew and provisions today. May I leave?"

"Just a moment, My Lady," Vard said. "Please be seated."

Esta sat, and Vard continued.

"Lady Cosara, would you stand please?" Vard asked.

Merielle stood, as did her husband.

"What's this about?" Nikolas asked.

"All in good time, Admiral," Vard said. "Lady Cosara, the king would ask a favor of you. He requests that you travel with Lady Esta to bring our citizens home."

"Out of the question!" Nikolas snapped. "You have a hide, Anton!"

Merielle placed her hand on her husband's arm and whispered in his ear. He shook his head and cast his stony gaze at Vard.

"Merielle will not be setting sail for the southern coast," Nikolas said. "I absolutely forbid it."

Merielle cleared her throat and stepped forward. "Lord Anton, I thank you and His Majesty for the opportunity. I will discuss this with my husband and speak with you again later today."

Vard nodded, and Merielle left the room with Esta, the two whispering together as soon as they neared the exit. Vard almost laughed out loud at the look on the admiral's face. He was clearly torn between staying for the meeting and following his wife. Sam appeared similarly conflicted.

When Vard turned back to the gathering, Ruven Magbalar was on his feet.

"I hope you will forgive my interruption, but I have been giving more thought to an offensive on the *Sis Lenweri* stronghold—that is assuming we locate it."

The king nodded his permission for Ruven to continue.

"I know the general favors this approach, but I think it is fraught with problems. The humans would fight at a disadvantage on ground that is unfamiliar even to we *Lenweri*. The enemy may have constructed traps and other obstacles which they can deploy to slow us down. Even if we know where to attack, they may get wind of our intentions and circle around, thus both attacking our flanks and entering our cities."

"I still favor that approach," General Formosa said, hooking his thumbs in his belt.

"General," Ruven said, "you don't know the elves as I do. They will not *act* as you would or *think* like you do."

"That's where you come in, Magbalar," Formosa said. "You give us the intelligence to predict what the enemy will do."

Ruven placed his hands on his hips, his brows stormy. "If I were Faenwelar, I would already have spies in every kingdom city and town, and also in Amitania and Selinore. You must assume he knows every movement you will make."

"He can't be that well informed!"

"It's safer to assume he is," Vard said, looking at Ruven. "Isn't that what you're saying?"

Ruven nodded. "Assume he knows of our mission to the north to discover his stronghold, that he is aware of every preparation we make, of all our numbers, both elven and human."

"Preposterous!" Formosa said.

"No," Vard growled. "Magbalar is right. The *Sis Lenweri* are shrouded in mystery while we're open. It wouldn't be difficult to discover all our plans and numbers." He recalled his fight with the strange hawk shifter, the identity of the intruder still unexplained. "Meanwhile, we don't even know where Faenwelar's forces are placed, or how many they are. All we do know is that they fight in a traditional sense with short bows and swords suited to forest battlegrounds. However, I know they've recently trained with the long sword and bow. It's what they were doing in Amitania."

"We should have followed them north from Amitania when we took back the city," Formosa cried.

"I wasn't involved then, General," Vard said, "but I heard your force was only small, merely enough to drive the elves from Amitania and rescue Princess Gwaethe. It wouldn't have been wise to push on into enemy territory."

"No!" Formosa said. "You weren't around then, were you, King's Blade? And yet you lecture me!"

"General Formosa!" the king said, standing. "I urge you to maintain decorum."

The general sat, his face stormy.

Vard drew a long breath and observed others do the same. "It will do us no service to fight amongst ourselves. All here want the same thing—for the kingdom to be strong and free; for peace in this realm."

All present nodded, their gazes strong, determined, even Formosa. Privately, Vard believed the general cared more for his own advancement than the kingdom. However, that motivation could still serve well enough. The elven enemy must be neutralized, and Vard would forge a way forward, bringing the others along.

"Then we must trust each other. I know we come from different paths, and we have varied skills. However, we can form a powerful alliance with a common purpose. To overcome the threat Faenwelar poses, we must put aside our differences." He fixed his gaze on Nikolas. "We must put personal enmity aside." He swung to the general. "*And* personal gain." He looked at Ruven and the king. "Not to mention fear of the future."

He strode across the room, feeling all eyes upon him. "Now is the time to use our skills and purpose to defeat Faenwelar and forge a peaceful and prosperous kingdom. I believe the future will then take care of itself." A future in which his daughter could thrive.

Sam stood and clapped. "Bravo, well said, King's Blade."

The king and queen were next to rise. Others joined them until all in the hall were on their feet clapping, even Nikolas. The admiral didn't appear pleased to have joined the approval of Vard's speech, but Vard nodded to him, anyway. Nikolas's jaw tightened.

Vard strode back to the middle of the room and raised his hands. Those assembled resumed their seats.

"I believe we also need to be flexible in our plans. We don't know where the first attack will come from, or the form it will take. I've devised several strategies with the army leaders in consultation with the king and admiral. These strategies cover attacks on Brightcastle, Wildecoast, and Amitania. I think Amitania is least likely. Meanwhile, Kain Arenil is fortifying Selinore, preparing for an attack there." He paused to allow his words to sink in then continued.

"I think it unlikely the *Sis Lenweri* will attack in more than two places, but we also must prepare for multiple theatres of war. Depending on the size of the *Sis Lenweri* force, they may have enough soldiers to stage more than one or two battles. We must be ready for them.

"Now, I have duties to hand out. Admiral, you are to continue your preparation of our ships. They must be ready to ferry soldiers to defend the coast. Since your fighting force is unlikely to engage the enemy by ship, I'd like you to select skeleton crews to man your ships and fire your crossbows. The rest will continue their weapons training on the field north of the city."

Nikolas nodded, bowed to the king and queen, and left.

"General Formosa," Vard said, "you'll see to sharpening your soldiers for battle, both foot soldiers and mounted. Especially, I want your archers to practice shooting small targets at over one hundred yards."

"In case of dragon attack?" Formosa said, smirking.

Vard fixed the general with a stern gaze. "Yes. I want to see them practicing just as I described. Only your best archers. And I want all skills being fine-tuned—short and long swords, short and long bows, hand-to-hand and knives. Those who are skilled at one form of combat can train others. The men will know who they are."

"I know my men, Anton. I don't need their help to select the best warriors."

"Ask them anyway," Vard said.

Formosa bowed to the monarchs and left, a scowl on his face.

"Ruven, you're in charge of the elven soldiers and the rangers. The elves are already good forest fighters, so get them into longbow and long sword practice. Most of the rangers are gifted in one or both disciplines. Use them as trainers. Sam will help you. And stay well away from Formosa."

Ruven nodded and left, but Sam stayed.

Vard approached King Beniel. "Your Majesty, do you have further orders?"

He rose from his throne. "No, Lord Anton. I am content with what I have heard, except for the talk of dragons. I just cannot believe we will face the beasts."

"But Majesty," Vard said, "your own niece has dreams of them."

"That's merely a young woman's fancy."

"Alecia has true dreams, Sire. Her skill is erratic, but with all that's happening, I can't ignore what she has seen. I hope I'm wrong."

"Let them prepare for dragons, Husband," Adriana said. "It cannot hurt. At the very least, it will hone their marksmanship. And if the beasts appear, our soldiers will be prepared." She fixed Vard with a hard look, every ounce a ruler at war. "Will you advise the soldiers of what they may face?"

"I've not yet decided, My Queen. Perhaps some of their leaders will be told. I don't wish to panic them and affect morale."

Alique approached. "What of the horses? Won't they panic if a dragon appears?"

"It's likely any who aren't battle-trained will try to bolt. That's why I've enlisted your father to buy any battle-trained mounts he can find, both from this kingdom and neighboring ones."

Admiration lit her gaze. "How did you come to select my father?"

"It was Queen Adriana's idea." He glanced at the lady in question and found her studying him. "A stroke of pure genius, if you ask me. Lord Zorba will put the horses through an intensive training program, including replicating dragon noises and wings as well as fire. Of course, there is only so much he can do, but the horses he trains will be well prepared."

"If I know Father," Alique said, "he'll have selected his stock well." She paused. "You haven't given me a task."

"You'll oversee medicines, Lady Alique. While the rangers and I have been out in the forest over the last weeks and months, we've collected many plants useful for creating medicines. They've been hung for drying, and they're now ready for grinding and making tinctures."

"Lord Anton, you astound me!" Lady Alique said. "Is there anything you've overlooked?"

"Again, it was the queen who suggested I collect the plants as I trained the rangers and scouts. She has also gathered a band of young women to help you in preparing medicines, cutting and rolling bandages, and collecting bottles for holding powders and liquids."

Alique's eyes were wide. "I thought I'd have to start from scratch when I arrived, and here I find I have supplies and my own army to help me!"

"There is still much to do, Alique," Queen Adriana said. "You must get to work. Please let me know if there is anything you need.

Currently, I'm scouring the city for bottles and baskets as well as linen for bandages. You should have a steady stream coming to you. I've made the feast kitchen available for compounding, and there is an adjoining staff dining room you can use."

"Thank you, Your Majesty." Alique curtseyed.

"It is the kingdom who should thank you, Alique. You almost gave your life in the past, and, certainly, you are still recovering. That you would be prepared to give your all again is appreciated."

Alique nodded and left, her steps eager. Vard marveled at the talent at his command. He only wished Alecia could have shared this with him.

"Now you must be about your work, Vard," King Beniel said. "We are most happy with your preparations. Let us know of any developments."

"There is one, Your Majesty." He hesitated to tell the monarchs, but it was too big a tale to keep to himself. He could almost feel Sam's ears prick.

"Well, out with it," King Beniel said, seating himself again.

"I have reports of a kingdom citizen seeing a dragon. It was a credible report, Your Majesty."

"And just who is this citizen?"

"They don't wish to be identified. There were actually three people involved, and this occurred in Costa some weeks ago."

"And you are only just telling us?"

"I only learned of it last night."

"I don't know what to believe, Vard," King Beniel said. "It seems fanciful to believe dragons ever existed, let alone that they may play a part in this war."

"Your Majesty, the elven people are firm in their belief, and those who study the lore tell me, that once there were what they call lesser and greater dragons. The lesser were small and aggressive, feeding upon elves and humans alike. Elves and the greater dragons worked together to hunt the lesser dragons who were wiped from the face of the world. The belief is strongest among the *Sis Lenweri*. Faenwelar's people are the most closely linked to the dragons. If any survive, the *Sis Lenweri* will know of them. It's not much of a leap to imagine the beasts aiding them in the war against us."

The king spluttered. "It is a mighty leap as far as I can see. I would need to see one with my own eyes to believe they existed."

"Are you saying I can't plan a defense for them?" Vard asked.

The king fell silent, his brow drawn down, his hands clenched. "Bring me someone who has seen a dragon, and I will listen to them and decide."

Vard strode from the hall with Sam on his heels. Of all the things he must do today, tracking down a witness to a dragon attack was not high on his list. However, if he could convince the king, it would give him greater credibility.

"Are you mad, man?" Sam asked, grabbing his arm. "Who the hell saw the beast? Or are you making it up?"

Vard spun on him, jerking his arm free. "I don't make things up. And I can't tell you who saw the dragon until I speak to them. If I were you, I'd get on with your assigned tasks and leave me to the rest."

Sam's eyebrows shot up. "Fine! I'll leave you in peace." He turned and stalked off, his boots striking sharp snaps off the stone floor.

Vard sighed. He'd have to apologize to Sam later, but he hadn't expected to have his integrity questioned by a friend. He shouldn't be so touchy. It was just having his word examined at every turn and having to validate each decision and suggestion that wore him down.

The meeting had gone very well, in fact. His campaign had begun smoothly, and all he must do now was ensure his orders were followed.

He was pretty sure Formosa was the only one likely to defy his instructions, but Nikolas would also have to be watched. He hoped the admiral was too professional to step far away from his brief. The king and queen were valuable allies in dealing with both men. A niggling voice in his head asked what the outcome would be if Nikolas told the monarchs of his special talents.

He shook his head. Nikolas wouldn't want to disrupt the war preparation by undermining the king's trust in him. The admiral was likely to keep quiet unless he gave him reason to think the king or kingdom was in danger from him. And *that* wouldn't happen.

He turned his efforts to locating Katrine.

It proved more difficult than he had hoped. After finding Lady Esta and leaving a message with her for Katrine, Vard heard nothing more all that day. By mid-morning the following day, he was still wondering when he could speak to her. In the meantime, he'd been perusing intelligence from the king's spy network and trying to piece together the most likely location of the first *Sis Lenweri* attack.

To get his mind off the fact that he was getting nowhere fast, he sought the practice grounds outside the city. He trotted the perimeter on horseback, observing all the elements of his forces, including the naval soldiers who were practicing their horseback skills. The crack archers appeared to be hitting their targets at the required distance. Small groups of soldiers, elves, and rangers sparred around the perimeter of the large field.

If the *Sis Lenweri* spied on them, they should be quaking in their boots. He decided to survey the action from above and cantered up the hill toward the forest. Entering beneath the thick canopy of firs and pines, he located a small clearing he'd used before. He dismounted and tied his horse to a tree, but just as he was about to shift, the hairs on the back of his neck stood up.

"Show yourself," he said, drawing his sword from the scabbard.

Nothing happened for long moments, then, one by one, shadowy forms appeared between the trees. His heart kicked up a notch when he recognized the night hounds. Perhaps the bear was called for if these beasts were here to attack. Even then, he'd be hard pressed to fight that many and survive.

"Be at ease, Lord Anton," a cool female voice said. "I'm merely here at your request, and where I go, *they* follow."

Vard relaxed at the sound of Katrine's voice and replaced his sword in its scabbard.

"It's about time you showed up," he growled.

She appeared from the trees wearing leather breeches and a dark green cloak. The silver sparkles in her eyes drew his attention, as did the purple paint on her nails. She lowered the cloak's hood.

"I'm not at your beck and call, King's Blade."

"Regardless, you have offered your help. The king wishes to speak to someone who has seen a dragon."

Her gaze pinned him. "You told him!"

"Stand down! I told him I had spoken to a witness, and he has demanded to do the same."

"I can't reveal myself. The king can't be trusted to deal with magic practitioners in a fair manner."

"You said James and a servant were the target of the attack?"

She chewed her bottom lip. "Yes."

"Then ask the servant to testify."

"I don't think the king would listen to a servant's account." Katrine looked off into the trees. "James might speak up."

"Then ask him and organize it," Vard demanded.

The closest hound growled, and Katrine placed her hand on its head. He knew he was pushing his luck with the witch, but dammit—*he* was the one who had stuck his neck out talking of dragons. This was his chance to prove he wasn't crazy.

Her eyes snapped to his, the silver sparkles swirling wildly. "You have no power over me, King's Blade. I come and go as I please, and I do as I wish."

Vard stepped closer, partly phasing into the bear to intimidate the hounds. They whined. Katrine's eyes widened.

"I have the authority of the king, and that means I could have you arrested if I chose. Your secrets are safe with me as long as you're not a threat to the security of Thorius. Don't think you have all the power, Lady Star, because you don't."

She wasn't cowed, but he could see his warning gave her pause. She suspected what he was, but not everything he could do. The same could be said for him. He knew enough of the sorceress to have her arrested. He wouldn't hesitate to put her away if she threatened his plans.

She swallowed. "Very well. I'll speak to James. But he'll be taking a risk if he agrees to speak out."

Vard nodded, letting go of the bear. "Do so with haste. I don't know how long we have to prepare. Lately I've felt an urgency that we're running out of time."

"The hounds are restless, too. Each night when I lay my head on the pillow, they invade my dreams." She shivered. "They're always urging me to run with them, showing me horrible things—dark wings and fire."

"Dragons?"

She nodded. "I don't know how much of it I can trust, but perhaps they feel the same urgency you do. Maybe when we finally begin this campaign, I can get some peace." She raised haunted eyes to his, and he felt sorry for his earlier anger.

"Go now," he said. "Leave a note with your sister to let me know the outcome."

She nodded and walked into the trees, the hounds following her on soundless paws.

Vard waited until they vanished and started forming the hawk in his mind.

* * *

'Lady Henrietta' turned from the mirror in Alecia's sitting room, twirling before the princess.

Alecia clapped her hands, and Iona mimicked her. "You look marvelous! No one will ever remember you as you were."

"Are you sure? This is quite a risk we're taking."

"Granted, Ramón is sharp, but it's months since he last saw you, and then only once. Even I wouldn't recognize you if I didn't know."

157

She approached and grasped Hetty's hands. "It's time to introduce my advisor. I want to be taken seriously by those two usurpers."

"Alecia!" Hetty said. "The king has placed them in their roles. You can't call them that."

"The king doesn't know the full truth, otherwise he wouldn't have done what he did. Ramón ingratiated himself by saving Uncle Beniel's life, and then Benae lied about Solomon's parentage. I'm almost positive Ramón is the boy's father, which means they betrayed *my* father. If the king knew that, I hate to think what he'd do."

Hetty scowled. "What will *you* do?"

She chewed her lip. "I haven't decided yet. How goes it with the nobles and merchants? Will they support me?"

Hetty took a seat before the fire and placed her hands in her lap.

"Hetty?"

"Don't call me that, even when we're alone. I still don't know if this is such a good idea… exposing me to the Guardians."

"I've told you. I want you by my side to advise me. For that, I need you to be accepted by Ramón and Benae."

"Yes," Hetty said slowly. "As your advisor, I can be present for functions and meetings. I'm just concerned I'll be recognized."

"And what if you are? They can't tell me who I can consort with. If they try to have you arrested for witchcraft, I'll accuse Benae. Her healing is far too effective for it not to be magic wrought."

Hetty frowned. "No. It will be your word against theirs."

"You didn't answer my earlier question."

Hetty squared her shoulders and lifted her chin as well as one now-sculptured brow. Alecia marveled at her friend's transformation and forgot to be intimidated.

"I've spoken to almost all the merchants and nobles in Brightcastle. Assuming King Beniel dies or abdicates, you'd have their support over the Guardians until Solomon comes of age. Some of them even expressed the desire to support you ahead of Solomon as you're the oldest issue of Prince Zialni."

"Really?"

Hetty nodded. "And if it was confirmed that Solomon is Zorba's son, you'd be the logical choice."

"What about Piotr?"

"The rumors he was behind the attempt on the king's life at his brother's funeral still circulate, and many feel they could be true. I've done nothing to dispel them."

"Well, someone wanted Uncle Beniel out of the way," Alecia said, "and Piotr had the most to gain. We can use that rumor to our advantage. But I struggle to believe the people will welcome me so easily after all this time without a queen."

Hetty grinned. "They love you, my dear. They know you're their champion. If you continue to do good works, you'll only grow in their estimation. The orphanage has already used the money you donated to buy clothes and place new pillows on the beds. Not only are the children and their carers happy, but the merchants who supplied the materials are singing your praises. Of course, I let it be known that you're using your own funds to achieve this."

"That reminds me, I'm almost out of coin. I need to ask Ramón for more."

"You could do that, Princess, or…" Hetty reached into her skirt pocket and pulled out a bag. It jingled as she handed it over. "From the nobles I saw this week. I told them what you were doing, and some donated gold to your cause. The merchants who benefitted from your generosity have also donated a percentage of their earnings. They even had suggestions about how they wished it to be used."

Alecia gasped and covered her mouth with her hands. Tears pooled in her eyes. "This is everything I wished for, Het — *Lady Henrietta*. All those years when I fought against Father's ill treatment of my people, I could've been doing this."

Hetty shook her head. "You had to learn the hard way, girl. Besides, it's not always about gold. Not everything can be bought. Now, let's go visit the Guardians. I hope you're right, and they don't recognize me."

She muttered the words of the spell which would smooth her voice from its customary gravelly rasp and joined Alecia at the door.

Alecia's insides writhed like a pile of maggots by the time she and Hetty arrived at the audience chamber. She held Iona to her so tightly the child squirmed and shrieked.

"Sorry, my darling," she said, giving the little girl some breathing room.

The footman announced them, and they entered to find Benae and Ramón already seated and sipping their tea. Ramón came forward to take Iona and greet them.

"My little Iona," he said, his grin taking over his face. Alecia felt remorse for deceiving him. But hadn't *he* lied to her? "Alecia, welcome." His gaze slid to Hetty.

She hurried to introduce her advisor. "Ramón Zorba, this is Lady Henrietta Guiote."

Ramón bowed. "It's a pleasure to meet you, Lady Henrietta."

Alecia watched closely for any sign of recognition, but saw not a flicker.

"Lord Zorba, you have a beautiful home." Hetty's voice was smooth, thank the Goddess.

"Well, My Lady, we are merely trustees of the castle, but I thank you. Please, won't you sit and take tea?"

Hetty took his arm and was introduced to Benae, who had only seen the witch when she was gravely ill. She welcomed Hetty and took Iona from Ramón, balancing the little girl on her lap. Again, Alecia felt guilty. They did so love Iona, as much as she loved Solomon.

"Lady Henrietta," Benae said, her warm voice soothing Alecia's unease. "I hear you've taken a position as the princess's advisor."

"That's correct. Princess Alecia and I have known each other for years. When I heard she'd been orphaned, I sent a message offering my help and advice."

Benae nodded. "I think that's wise of you to accept help, Alecia."

Alecia ground her teeth, wondering what Benae really meant by that statement. She schooled her features to calm and smiled. "Often of late, I've felt the need for someone to talk to. Lady Henrietta has been like a mother to me in the past. I hope for that again."

Benae's face folded into sadness. "A mother is a precious gift. You and I have both lost ours. We must take consolation and advice wherever it is generously and selflessly offered." She placed Iona on the rug and busied herself pouring tea for her guests.

Again, Alecia wondered what Benae meant by her words. At least she didn't appear to recognize Hetty, and neither did Ramón.

Ramón cleared his throat. "I assume we won't see a repeat of the impulsive and dangerous behavior you've recently displayed, Alecia?"

"Ramón!" Benae gasped.

Alecia's brows shot up her forehead. "I beg your pardon? Impulsive and dangerous? I only acted in the best interests of the kingdom of Thorius and its people, especially my people of Brightcastle."

"Oh, come on!" Ramón said. "A princess, not to mention a mother, doesn't hare all over the countryside getting into fights and making trouble for those who are trying to help her."

She boiled inside. He was so pompous! With difficulty, she pulled her anger back under control. "I appreciate your efforts of the past year when you never lost faith in me, Ramón. And I won't forget the risk you took finding Vard and bringing him to me." When she recalled his efforts, maybe she *was* being a little ungrateful. "Perhaps I *have* been impulsive in the past. But no more. Lady Henrietta is here to advise me now. I intend to act only as a princess would. Already I've made steps to that end."

Ramón nodded. "I've heard of your efforts. Please let me know if you need more funds. I believe you've been using your allowance."

Alecia paused, stunned at his offer when she had so recently caused him grief. But Ramón had always been caring and generous. It was difficult being on the opposing side to him.

"Thank you, Ramón. I'd welcome more financial help." She decided to keep the donations a secret for now. Perhaps she could save her allowance and use the donations for her good works.

He nodded. "Then you shall have it. I'll speak to the treasury and have a small portion of the war funds diverted to your causes. You can send me a report of the disbursements each month."

"You're very generous."

He stood. "Now, if you'll excuse me, I must leave you in Benae's hands."

He bowed to them and left the room.

Benae's smooth voice interrupted her thoughts. "You're surprised by his generosity, Alecia."

She met the woman's intelligent emerald gaze. "I am, though I shouldn't be. Ramón has always been a generous friend."

"Your recent attitude hurts him. He seeks only to care for you as your father would have."

"I don't need a father figure. Wouldn't you be happier if he ignored me?"

"I admit his regard for you threatened me at first. But I'm long over that. I know Ramón loves me totally and completely, and I see you regard him as a friend—and sometimes as a nuisance."

Alecia grimaced. "That's an accurate assessment, unfortunately. Let me assure you I've never had a romantic interest in Ramón. I always encouraged him to find the right woman when he thought he loved me. However, I've always valued his friendship. That's why it hurts so much when he tells me untruths."

Benae didn't quite hide the gasp at her words. "What makes you think Ramón has lied to you?"

"You're *both* lying to me, but the truth will come out. Let me assure you, I wish Solomon no harm, and I'll do nothing to challenge Uncle Beniel. He's our rightful king and deserves our support and respect." She stood. "Thank you for the tea."

Benae also rose, a frown on her brow. "Please, Alecia, explain yourself," she said, hands clasped before her. "What do you mean by not harming Solomon?"

"Just as it sounds. I love the boy as if he were my child. In case you imagined I'd try to remove him to give myself a better chance at the throne of Thorius, let me reassure you—I'd lay down my life for him."

Benae's eyes were wide as she took in Alecia's words. She nodded. "So, you still wish to be heir to the kingdom? You know that isn't possible?"

Alecia met her eyes. "Perhaps you're right; perhaps not." She caught Hetty's eye. "And now, Benae, I must leave you." She retrieved Iona, who was playing with a teaspoon and gestured for Hetty to follow.

Benae hadn't lost her frown. "Yes, of course."

"It was lovely meeting you, Princess," Hetty said, curtseying.

Benae nodded, and they left.

Alecia couldn't wipe the smile from her face on the way back to her chambers. They hadn't recognized Hetty, and she had slipped a thorn under Benae's saddle. Now she had more work to do in endearing herself to the people before she ran out of time.

CHAPTER ELEVEN

KAIN stood on the balcony of his forest home in Selinore, gazing out over the tops of the trees to the north. Word had reached him from Vard Anton that morning. The King's Blade had sent a mission into the far northern mountains and found evidence of Faenwelar's forces in three vast encampments, each numbering hundreds of elven soldiers. There could be more if he knew Faenwelar. There was also evidence of regular movements by elves into the giant mountains further north.

He sighed. If there were dragons, the mountains were where they'd be.

Elora was working with the elven dreamers and lore holders, both in the *Lenweri* and *Sis Lenweri* tradition, and concluded that the continued existence of the great dragons was possible. And Vard's message this morning contained code confirming *his* belief in the creatures. They must prepare for the beasts—as best they could.

His mind drifted to Alique, who he missed with a nagging ache that wouldn't cease. She was well and sent her love, according to the note. He gave thanks that Vard had thought to include that piece of information. He swallowed hard, wondering when he'd see her again. *If* he would see her again. He longed to hold her in his arms and make love to her like it was their first time. Did she yearn for him, too? Did she realize how much he loved her? They'd both been busy since moving to Selinore, with little time to devote to each other besides coupling, and that was often interrupted.

He wondered what she was doing in Wildecoast and then snorted at his stupid musing. Alique would be in the thick of medical issues, organizing medicines and hospital beds, herbs and poultices, and training orderlies. There would be great need for her if… *when* the war began. He should send a message back, including one to Alique letting her know Julli and Tuthariel were coping well. The hospital here was in excellent hands. Not that they had much to do except care for the last few of the *Sis Lenweri* females to give birth. That was another story. With their leader, Alia Kelsis, gone to Wildecoast, some of the other *Sis Lenweri* women had become uncooperative, petitioning Kain to allow them to leave Selinore and return home to see if their males had survived the battle of Amitania.

Although he originally said they could leave if their children remained, some females had no children to tie them to Selinore. He couldn't risk them handing valuable information to Faenwelar. It was getting harder to keep them under control, and several had been imprisoned to remove their damaging influence on the others.

He was in daily contact with his half-sister, Gwaethe Arenil, in Amitania. Through his bracelet and her ring, they could mind speak. At first, it had spooked him, but now he was used to her voice in his head. Earlier that day, she had popped in to update him on their latest reports. Her elven scouts were on edge and advised the forest "felt wrong". There was a brooding silence, as if it waited for something. She assured him they were as prepared as they could be for an assault on the city.

Kain sent his senses out to the trees, noting their unsettled rustling. That was another phenomenon he'd adjusted to. As the elven leader, the trees recognized him and the magic he held. They called him "forest mage" and bowed to him, literally. This evening, there were whispers in the leaves, but he was having difficulty making out the words.

He sensed a presence behind him and turned to find Elora, the previous king's widow, at the door to the balcony. The stately elven female had been a rock of support for him since arriving in Selinore.

He smiled. "Elora! I was just talking to the trees and not understanding much."

She nodded. "Orionkael took years to understand them. Sometimes they chatter so much it is difficult to make out individual words."

"They're unsettled today. And Gwaethe says the forest north of them has her scouts jumpy. I'm concerned Faenwelar may be on the move."

Elora bowed her head. "Perhaps he is. I shall gather my elders and see what we can glean from them and the dreamers. In the meantime, keep talking to your trees."

He bowed to her. "I'm going to warn Wildecoast. They can get a message to Brightcastle. I'll set the old people and children on the road to Amitania. There's no shelter here if an attack occurs."

"That is wise, Kain Arenil. I shall return when I have met with the elders."

Kain sent a mind message to Gwaethe advising her to look out for their people within the next week. He then went in search of his Uncle Melandrach, who had shifted his home from the forest into Selinore. Kain pondered the mysterious elder, brother to Orionkael and to Rasalar, the army command trainer. Kain still didn't understand the full extent of Melandrach's powers. One thing he was certain of, though—his uncle would be useful in the coming war with the *Sis Lenweri* and must be kept close.

He found Melandrach in the company of the elves he was training. When he saw Kain, he left his companions and joined his nephew.

"High Prince," he said, his voice a deep rumble, "you have news?"

"Of sorts, Uncle. There are murmurs in the forest over a great distance between Amitania and Selinore. Gwaethe's elven scouts are jumpy, and so are the trees here. I can't make head nor tail of their whispering, but I think it's time to move the vulnerable."

Melandrach nodded, not a trace of fear discernible. "As you wish. I will see they are on the move within the hour."

Kain blew out the breath he'd been holding, relieved his uncle hadn't asked him to validate his decision. "Thank you, Uncle. Will you go with them?"

He scowled. "As if I would! Do you think me an old fool in my dotage?"

Kain held out his hands, palms to Melandrach. "I meant no disrespect, Uncle. I was merely making sure you had no intention of leaving me. I have a feeling I'll need you in this coming war."

Melandrach looked down his nose at Kain from his slightly superior height and raised one brow. "And you shall have my help."

The old man turned, cloak swirling, and stalked away, clicking his fingers to bring his companions along with him. Kain grimaced, stunned at how his uncle had fired up. He'd never witnessed such anger from the man. Perhaps he, too, was on edge.

Shaking his head, Kain returned to his balcony, determined to translate the whispers of the leaves. He sat on the wooden deck and quietened his thoughts, making the image of a flame and feeding all his turbulent feelings and worries into it. Once his mind was still, he allowed the murmurs of the trees to penetrate, listening to each voice one by one. After some ten minutes, he heard words... *darkness... sweeping... burning... fear.*

His eyes snapped open. Burning! It was his greatest worry, living in Selinore with trees all around. There were fire breaks, but they couldn't afford to lose the great trees. He must protect them at all costs, and the forest tracks, though wide, wouldn't be enough to save the trees from leaping flames. He cast his gaze again to the north, in time to see a ripple moving out from Selinore in all directions. The trees were spreading their message of dread throughout the forest. He must prepare!

Kain charged down through the trunk of the tree and out into the town center, running for the great tree where the council met. He flew up the stairs, barely acknowledging the attendant responsible for preventing interruptions, and barged in amongst Elora and the elders.

"We need to act now! I've interpreted what the trees are saying. They're frightened of fire. Our mages need to create the fire protection spell and settle it over the great trees, so we don't lose them. We also need a path out of here protected against fire."

Elora rose from her seat, appearing completely calm. "We will attend to it at once. Come friends. Gather your strongest mages. It will be a long night." She squeezed Kain's arm as she passed him. "We need you, High Prince Arenil. As the forest mage, though your magic isn't developed, it will be the lynch pin upon which we build our protective spell."

He nodded and followed them from the tree, his mind listing all the things that needed doing before the threat arrived.

* * *

Gwaethe jogged through the corridors of her palace in Amitania. It was a far cry from the grandeur of Wildecoast castle, but it had begun to feel like home. That was if a structure of stone could be home to an elven princess more used to soft forest greens. But stone was beautiful and natural, and it spoke to her in its own way.

Kain's last words froze her heart. An attack was likely in Selinore and, therefore, possible in Amitania as well. This city had already endured one battle with the *Sis Lenweri* and been the home for the enemy during their training. Gwaethe vowed they would never hold it again. She growled as she thought of the hurt done to her in this place by Gorin and Faenwelar.

"There you are!" she said, as Jacques appeared from a meeting room with Theoden Leovaris, one of the *Sis Lenweri* she had rescued during the battle of Amitania. He had now come to the *Lenweri* side. She had made the elf captain of her guard and trusted him completely.

"Gwaethe!" Jacques said. "What has you so agitated?" He pulled her to his side and kissed her mouth, despite Theo's presence. The elven captain averted his gaze.

Gwaethe allowed her husband's lips to linger for a moment before breaking the contact.

"Kain has been in contact this afternoon," Gwaethe said, her face still warm from Jacque's public display of affection. "He is sending his old people and children to us, believing attack by the *Sis Lenweri* is imminent."

"What has happened?" Jacques asked.

Gwaethe looked around and motioned them into the room they had just left. She crossed to the window and turned back to Jacques and Theo.

"The trees have spoken to my brother," she said. "They murmur of fire and darkness. Their distress has convinced him the *Sis Lenweri* plan an attack soon. He also thinks the fire may indicate dragons."

"Or it may not," Jacques said, ever the practical army leader.

Gwaethe shook her head. "I would agree, except he heard from Wildecoast today and a witness has come forward speaking of a dragon attack in Costa around two months ago."

"And we are just hearing of this?" Jacques said. "I'd like to know why!"

"I can't answer that. Perhaps the witness didn't think they would be believed or didn't understand the significance of it."

Theo interrupted. "That is not important now. Confirmation of a dragon loose in the kingdom is. The question is what significance does the dragon have for the war with the *Sis Lenweri?* Is Vard Anton correct in thinking our enemy will use this beast or others in the war? Does the dragon even have a link to Faenwelar?"

Jacques paced back and forth between the window and the hearth. "We'd be foolish to rule that out. Too much has happened of late that appears to tie the *Sis Lenweri* with dragons. What I wish to know is if we have done enough to prepare for a war in which the beasts may play a part." He paused. "No wonder Kain is sending us the vulnerable. Imagine what would happen to them should the forest and the great trees burn."

Gwaethe swallowed a sudden burst of fear. Her mother, brother, uncle, and aunt were in Selinore, not to mention many others dear to her. She squared her shoulders and met first the eyes of her beloved and then of her captain.

"We will make sure we do everything to prepare," she said. "I will make room for those Kain is sending. Theo, see that the archers are ready to shoot the eyes of any dragon they come up against. Jacques, brief the rest of the soldiers for war, human and elf." Mind working to grasp all that was required, she continued. "I will see that stores of both food and weapons are ready for imminent war. Also, we must ensure all the city's fountains are functional and have maximum water storage. Each home must have a drum of water at their disposal."

Theo thumped his fist on his chest, bowed, and left the room.

Gwaethe turned to Jacques. "I only hope we can be ready in time."

"Whatever we can do, it must be enough, my love."

* * *

Alecia sat up in bed, heart pounding from the nightmare she had just woken from. It felt like one of her true dreams. Everything was so clear, as her dreams had been since she began her training. Elves were moving through the forest, their eyes filled with a hatred and thirst for power that made her blood freeze. The shrieks of dragons filled the sky and their huge wings blotted out the moon.

She got out of bed and rang for Millie. Outside the window, dawn was just breaking. A rooster crowed from the castle yard, and the small sounds of a new day floated to her from below. She checked her daughter, who slept with her arms flung above her head, lips moving in a sucking motion.

Opening the door of her wardrobe, she debated what to wear. Today would be one for decisions and persuasion; one of the most important days of her life. She'd wear the red velvet with the silver and black piping. The Zialni colors were warranted.

Millie knocked and entered. "You're up early, Highness. I ordered your breakfast before I came up. It should be here soon."

"Thank you, Millie. Please help me dress."

Millie did as requested. Once dressed, Alecia stood, assessing her appearance.

"That gown is perfect, Princess. You look like a queen in it."

"Just the effect I'm looking for, Millie," she said. "Now, please send a message to Lady Henrietta to attend me as soon as she can. Also, as you'll be busy with Iona, I need a maid to do my hair."

Millie curtsied and departed. Alecia marveled at the woman's unusual brevity of words, but was grateful for it. She sat at her dressing table and applied her makeup, taking advantage of the time she had before Iona would awaken.

Her breakfast and the maid for her hair arrived together, so she nibbled on her rolls and honey while her hair was dressed. She chose an elaborate plaited arrangement with pearls wound through her braids. Pleased with the effect, Alecia felt prepared to take on anything.

Millie arrived with Hetty. The two were chatting like old friends as they entered her chambers. The maid hushed immediately and went to check Iona.

"Good morning, Lady Henrietta," Alecia said.

Hetty curtsied. "Good morning, Your Highness. What a fine day it is, though a little early for one as old as I."

Alecia drew Hetty over to a chair by the fire and had the maid ring for more tea and sweet buns. "I had another dream," she said, her voice low. "I think it indicates imminent war in Brightcastle. There is much to do today if we are to prepare in time."

Hetty's eyes widened. "That's fell news indeed."

"You believe me?"

She nodded. "I was in contact with Katrine last night. Her hounds have been unsettled for weeks. The poor girl is beside herself, struggling to make out what they're trying to tell her. She thinks it wise to assume there will be an attack by the *Sis Lenweri* soon; perhaps this week."

Alecia stood and paced back and forth before the unlit fire. Hetty mumbled a few words and flames sprang up. Alecia added more wood and resumed her pacing.

"I don't want to alarm the populace, but Brightcastle must be prepared for war. The Guardians aren't ready as far as I can see. Thank the Goddess Gwaethe sent us two hundred soldiers. They could mean the difference between victory and defeat."

She turned to Hetty. "What needs doing first? I think Ramón has summoned all the outlying villagers and farmers into Brightcastle in order to train suitable men and women to fight. They started arriving a week ago. Training proceeds, both of the army and the new recruits."

Hetty snorted. "I've heard there's unrest amongst the recruits. They say they're being forced to fight against their will."

Alecia gasped. "Don't they realize we'll lose everything if they don't fight? That we can't do this without them?"

"I think your father is to blame, Princess. It was a practice of his to take young men from their families to feed his army and not to give anything but threats in return. The people are resentful."

Alecia bit her bottom lip. "What of the nobles you've spoken to?"

"As requested by Zorba, they've been training their fighting men in preparation for war. But they are resentful too. They see this request as using their private funds for defense of the kingdom. They say it is the king's responsibility."

Alecia rolled her eyes. "It's money well spent! However, I wonder how good a job of training they are doing. Doesn't Ramón understand that he needs to oversee the instruction of his forces? Even if they are employees of a noble estate?"

"Perhaps Lord Zorba needs help to achieve this, Princess."

"He has left me out of his war meetings, thinking to spare me worry. Or perhaps he thinks I have nothing to contribute or doesn't want to encourage my aspirations to be queen." She considered. "Most likely the latter."

"Then you need to make an impression somehow, Alecia. Also, you must warn Vard Anton about your latest vision. He must prepare Wildecoast for war."

Alecia nodded. "I'll send several messages by raven this morning. At least some will reach him." Thoughts of her love distracted her. "I hope he is well."

Hetty huffed. "You just worry about yourself, my dear. You have enough to be getting on with."

Alecia sighed. "You're right, of course, Lady Hen, but I can't help fretting about the task that he's taken on."

The tea arrived, and the maid set the pot and cups on the table before the fire.

"Now," Hetty said. "Drink your tea and eat some more breakfast. You'll need it for the day ahead."

After Alecia arranged for the ravens to Wildecoast, Amitania, and Selinore, she returned to her chambers where Hetty was playing with Iona.

Alecia had never seen her friend so happy as she was with her daughter. She allowed herself a moment to enjoy the carefree interplay of the two, sending a prayer to the Goddess that they'd be safe in the coming conflict.

"This looks like fun!" she said. "Can I join in?"

Iona squealed and flung her arms up. Alecia picked her up and whirled her around, then cuddled the little girl close. She closed her eyes and inhaled the precious perfume of her child. A tear escaped despite her best efforts to control her fears.

Hetty joined her. "She'll be well, Princess."

Alecia sighed. "I wish I could be sure. Everything is so uncertain."

Hetty smiled. "Uncertainty is the spice of life. Nothing in this world can be taken for granted. Admittedly, it would be good to know when the elves will attack and where. It would also be beneficial to know if they have dragons on their side."

"You're so right. The thought that those people could be in charge here is monstrous. They won't want any of the royal line surviving to rally the humans."

"Stop it!" Hetty said. "This thinking won't help you win, and it won't give you courage."

"What won't give Alecia courage?" a male voice said from the door.

Alecia turned to find Ramón in the doorway. "You wanted to speak with me, Alecia?" His eyes ran over her, and he frowned. "I must say, you look regal today." He bowed to her and nodded to Hetty. "Lady Henrietta."

She straightened and squared her shoulders. "Good morning, Ramón. This is a big day, and so I dressed accordingly."

"Oh?" he said. "I wish you'd get to the point. I have a strategy meeting to get to."

"That's exactly why I wanted to talk," she said. "I think the signs point to imminent invasion by the *Sis Lenweri*. I wish to know how you're progressing with Brightcastle's preparations."

His eyebrows climbed his forehead. He closed the door and joined them.

"What signs?" he asked.

"For some time now, my dreams have shown dragons."

Ramón looked at the ceiling. "Not this again."

"Hear her out, Guardian," Hetty said.

Ramón folded his arms and sighed. "Go ahead."

Alecia tried to ignore his attitude. It wouldn't help for her to lose her temper.

"As much as you don't wish to believe it, I have dreams that foretell the future. Lately, I've dreamed of dragons. At first, they were vague, but since the elven dreamers have trained me, they're more vivid and detailed."

Ramón frowned. "You actually believe there are dragons in the kingdom?"

She nodded. "And I do believe they'll be used against us in the coming war."

"Alecia, I'm sorry, but I can't enter into your fantasies. I've seen no sign of imminent invasion by the *Sis Lenweri* and nothing to indicate dragons even exist. I knew it was a mistake allowing you to train with the elves."

She bristled. "What do you mean 'allowing'? You had no say in that."

Ramón remained silent, his arms crossed over his impressive chest.

"I demand to be allowed to address your meeting."

He shook his head immediately. "You'd make a fool of yourself. And that would make me appear foolish as well."

"And we can't have that!" Alecia's blood boiled as she desperately sought to convince him. "What harm can there be in hearing me out?"

"I just told you," he snapped. "It's been difficult enough to maintain order over the nobles and the army leaders. If I go in there asking them to listen to a woman who has dreamed of dragons..." He trailed off and shuddered.

She sighed. "When you put it like that, I can see your point." She stepped closer to him. This was Ramón, and he was her friend. "I *know* something terrible is coming. Don't you think it wise to prepare for the worst? Please, allow me to help!"

He eyed her, a scowl on his face. "I don't know. Perhaps if you tell me more about your dream, it will help."

Alecia led him over to a chair and bade him sit, then poured him a cup of tea, good and strong as he liked it.

"In my first dream, Brightcastle was under attack from the *Sis Lenweri*. You and the other leaders can't decide where the first attack will come. I think it will come here."

Ramón shook his head. "You can't know that."

"Perhaps not, but, in my gut, I'm sure. Anyway, amidst the battle, hideous shrieks rang out. Four dragons of differing colors came appeared from the north. My elven scholar says they are the colors of the four greater dragons of legend."

Ramón appeared uncomfortable at the news. "It means nothing but that you have an overactive imagination, Alecia."

She huffed. "Tell me there aren't things you can't explain in this world. As much as you'd like to deny it, magic is real. Your own wife wields healing magic." She threw her hands up when Ramón shot to his feet in alarm. "Don't worry!" she said. "Benae's secret is safe with me. Even though I don't like her, I wouldn't expose her special talent."

He looked sourly at her. "You shouldn't even mention it." His eyes flicked to Hetty. "Lady Henrietta, swear what you just heard will never leave this room."

Hetty raised one brow. "You don't need to fear my loose tongue, Lord Zorba."

He nodded his thanks. He lifted his eyes to the ceiling and shook his head. "You said that was the *first* dream."

She nodded. "This morning I had another, and it was so vivid. Something dark and evil was moving through the northern mountains on wings that blotted out the moon. And the elves traveled below in the forest... their eyes, Ramón... it was pure hate."

His eyes narrowed as he listened. Finally, Alecia had hope he'd accept her interpretation of the visions.

"Even if I believe you, how am I supposed to make the others listen?"

She sucked in an excited breath. "You think I'm telling the truth?"

"It doesn't matter what I think, Alecia. What matters is what I can convince the others of—the nobles, the city leaders, the army commanders."

She seized his forearms. "We *must* make them act. Let me speak to them. I know I can convince enough of them, and then you won't look silly."

He frowned. "I don't know. It seems so stupid to be talking of dragons."

"Then make up a story." She stalked across the room as she thought. "We know the *Sis Lenweri* are intending to attack, right?"

He nodded. "No one can deny that. It's a matter of when and where."

"You've already begun preparations?"

"Of course. The king set that in motion when he arrived in Brightcastle. The outlying farmers have been arriving for weeks. We've put them to work, the older in war preparation and the younger in the army."

"We could construct a note, apparently from Amitania... say from Lord Vorasava... telling of *Sis Lenweri* movements in the northern forests and heading south. We don't need to mention the dragons, only to be ready for them. But please, Ramón, we need to prepare for imminent war."

There was a knock at the door, and Millie answered. She took something from the person outside and approached Ramón, handing him a slip of paper.

"This just arrived, Guardian Zorba," Millie said, curtsying and returning to the bedroom.

He unrolled the parchment and shot Alecia a sharp look. "It's a message by raven from Wildecoast telling of suspicious activity in the far northern forests. It warns us to be on alert."

Alecia strode up to him. "*There*! You see! And this comes on the same day I have a true dream! We must act, Ramón, and we must prepare for dragons. Don't tell your advisors. I'll speak to the elven leaders Gwaethe sent with me from Amitania. I'll see that they're ready for fighting the beasts."

Ramón shook his head. "You aren't in charge, Alecia. It's not your place to be throwing orders around."

She wrapped herself in the command of a Thorian princess. "Ramón, my uncle is the king. I'm a princess of Brightcastle. I have at least as much right to be involved as Benae. If you stand in my way, I'll go behind your back. You may as well work with me."

He studied her face. Alecia had no difficulty keeping her mask of calm command. He knew what she was capable of, how stubborn she was, and he had never bested her. She saw defeat in his gaze and smiled, but he threw up one finger.

"If you make me regret this, I'll never trust your judgement again."

The war meeting began within the hour. Alecia's insides buzzed with excitement at finally being involved. Hetty sat on her right and Lin on her left. None of the army commanders or nobles would be able to fault her. She thanked the Goddess for the note from Wildecoast. At least she and Ramón hadn't lied to those attending.

Ramón and Benae sat on their thrones, the chairs of the attendees drawn up in a semicircle before them. Alecia and her two advisors sat on the far right. The lieutenant of the Amitanian forces sat on the extreme left with Aemon Reese, the highest-ranking elven soldier from the city. In the center was Captain Jules Estevot, current leader of the Brightcastle armed forces.

Also present was Lady Stenmore, whom Alecia had been told was a widow and part of the city's intelligence network. With her was another spy, Master Goldsmith Cal Delcore. The rest of the attendees were nobles, all of whom Hetty had approached to aid Alecia's cause. The buffeting moths in her belly settled to quivering butterflies.

Ramón stood, and the hall quietened. "Thank you all for your attendance. This may be our most important meeting to date. This morning, I received news from Wildecoast of elven movements in the northern mountains. It seems the *Sis Lenweri* have mobilized."

The announcement produced a buzz amongst those gathered.

Ramón cleared his throat. "Captain Estevot will brief you on preparations made so far."

The captain came forward and stood beside the Guardians. "I'd like to reassure you that this warning comes as no surprise, nor do I feel we're under prepared."

Alecia stifled the snort that battled its way out. Lin's boot hit her ankle and Hetty's lips tightened.

Estevot continued. "However, we'll ramp up the speed of our preparations, assuming the elves will attack within the week."

Ramar Reese stood. "Can I request we call the enemy *Sis Lenweri* or Faenwelar's followers rather than elven? Your language is unlikely to endear you to your allies."

Estevot nodded. "I apologize, Ramar. I meant no disrespect."

"Of course, you didn't, Captain," Lady Stenmore said. "Some of us are perhaps a little thin-skinned?"

Benae interrupted. "I have no issue with being reminded of our manners, My Lady."

The lady in question nodded, but remained silent, a deep frown on her forehead. Alecia made a note to learn more about her.

Ramar Reese bowed and seated himself.

"To continue," Estevot said, "we are stepping up the movement of outlying residents into Brightcastle, where they can be safe and of use to the war effort. Food is coming with them, and water storage has been enhanced. Our scout numbers have been doubled and armed forces boosted by our country cousins."

Alecia spoke up. "I hear there's discontent in the ranks of the new soldiers, Captain. How are you combatting this?"

"There will always be conscripted soldiers who don't wish to fight, Princess," Estevot said, smiling.

Alecia refused to be put off by his patronizing attitude. "If ever there was a time to convince a man of the importance of defending Thorius, it's now. It can't be that difficult."

Lady Stenmore again interrupted. "Perhaps if Prince Zialni hadn't been so harsh in his treatment of the people, we wouldn't be having these issues, Princess."

Alecia turned her attention to the woman, who regarded her with a challenging smirk, and stood.

"I'll be the first to agree my father wasn't always fair in his dealings. However, that's water under the bridge, and we must all work together to make our kingdom safe."

"That's easy for you to say from the comfort of your castle," Lady Stenmore said.

Lin gasped and went to rise, but Alecia shook her head.

"I think, Lady Stenmore, that if you do a little more research, you'll find I'm not shy of throwing my support and body behind my people."

A few of the attendees clapped.

Ramón stood. "I'm sure Lady Stenmore meant no disrespect by her words, Princess." He stared at the lady until she met his gaze.

Lady Stenmore shook her head. "I only meant it's more complicated than just expecting the peasants to fall in with our plans."

Alecia couldn't help her gasp at the woman's words. *Peasants!* No wonder they were having such difficulties getting drafted soldiers to cooperate! And she accused Prince Zialni of causing all the resentment? *Honestly!*

Alecia sat down, shaking her head in disgust. Hopefully, those present would see the woman for what she was and wouldn't agree with her.

Ramón continued. "Estevot, please go on with your report."

The captain nodded. "Those who are causing trouble are brought to me, and I certainly explain the dire situation to them. But, if they still refuse, they can be charged with treason."

Alecia stood again. "How does that help? Can't you find another way they can assist the war effort?"

"It's just not that simple, Your Highness!" Estevot snapped.

"I didn't say it was simple, Captain," Alecia said. "Please send dissenting draftees to me. I'll talk to them."

"It's not your place, Your Highness!" Estevot's eyes were wide as if she had suggested she ride into battle herself. She smiled at the thought. Imagine his face when she did that!

"Then what *is* my place, Captain? Darning socks and hosting tea parties? Would you rather me be just a decoration rather than a real and useful human being? I have several programs running in this city, and I'm sure I can think of ways all citizens can be useful to the war effort, not just as soldiers."

Estevot frowned and looked at Ramón.

"The princess has offered her help," Ramon said, "and is to be utilized where possible. She has a good relationship with the people and may gain cooperation where you will not, Captain. If she's guarded, I don't believe it will hurt for her to speak to dissenters."

Alecia battled against rolling her eyes. Ramón was so frustrating. *Guarded indeed!*

"Thank you, Lord Zorba," she said. "As soon as this meeting finishes, I'd like to speak with anyone who hasn't shown cooperation with your requests. I'll have my ladies attend with me, so I'll be more than safe."

Estevot opened his mouth to speak, but Ramón intervened.

"Very good, Princess. I'm content with that. Captain?"

He nodded and continued. "Further to organization, our smiths have been working around the clock for weeks, forging weapons and arrows and ensuring all horses are shod. We have sufficient chain mail and partial armor for half our force."

"Half?" Ramón asked.

"Yes, Lord Zorba. The call has gone out for more smiths and metal. I hope to increase that to three quarters within two weeks."

Alecia stood again. "That may be too little too late, Estevot."

"Then you may help, Princess, since you're so determined to do so."

She fired him a frigid look. "I'll be happy to assist. Where are the new smiths to be sent?"

"I've set aside room in two of the city squares, one to the east, and one to the west, Princess. All volunteer smiths will gather there to be assessed and put to work." He approached and handed her a parchment. "The locations are marked here."

Alecia was impressed. It seemed Estevot wasn't the dunce she imagined.

"Training proceeds as usual with a focus on longbow, mounted warfare, and sword. Many of the new men are being trained as pikemen. It's just too difficult to train them to fight on horseback. Most have no weapons skills at all. Any who've had army exposure are under the tutelage of the weapons master." Estevot paused and faced Ramón. "Are we to use the trained women, My Lord?"

Alecia froze. This would indicate how successful her role in the war effort would really be.

Ramón glanced in her direction, and she narrowed her eyes at him. He wouldn't sideline the women; he just would not! He swallowed and looked back at Estevot.

"I know it goes against the grain, Captain, but we can't afford to dismiss anyone, especially those who are weapons trained." He paused and looked down at Benae. She nodded.

"Women who wish to be part of the pike wall should be allowed," Alecia said. "The rest can be used in other roles unless they have children to mind. However, I'd prefer the older women to be minding children while their daughters support the provision of food and water, and tend to wounds."

Benae stood. "Princess Alecia, anyone you think appropriate, please send to me for training in bandaging and wound care. I'll also need orderlies to attend the field and bring in the wounded. I intend to set up makeshift hospitals just inside the city wall entrances. Today I begin moving families out of the chosen houses and setting up my hospitals. Those displaced will be taken in by other families."

"I know you won't allow anyone to be made homeless, my dear," Ramón said. "However, there may be trouble when you ask them to leave, however temporary the arrangement."

Alecia had no desire to work with Benae, but she gritted her teeth and spoke up. "If I can be of any help in persuading the families to relocate, please ask."

Benae quirked one dark brow, but nodded her acceptance. After their recent words, she could expect nothing more friendly.

Ramón nodded, looking pleased. "I think that covers most items. One thing has me concerned, though. Captain Estevot, you appear to be taking on too much responsibility. I'd like you to delegate some of those tasks you listed to others. Some of them could be taken over by non-military. Lady Stenmore, could I task you with gaining support from the nobility? They can use some of their vast resources in stockpiling food and water, and rounding up weapons from their outlying estates. Please see that none of them have overlooked this."

The lady in question nodded. "I will see to it today, My Lord."

"Master Delcore," Ramon said, "can I ask you to speak with the other heads of guilds and secure donations for the war effort. Anything else the trades can contribute will be greatly appreciated."

Cal Delcore smiled. "Consider it done, Guardian. I know there will be great benefits for us after the war."

Ramon frowned, perhaps imagining the guilds calling in their debt once Thorius was secure. He sighed and continued.

"I don't wish to place them at risk, but communication could be aided by using the older children as runners. There are plenty of speedy ponies in the city they could use as well."

"Are you sure, Ramón?" Benae's eyes were wide with concern.

"No, my dear, but we can't spare soldiers for that task. Much of it will be within the city streets. We have horns for messages on the field. There'll be risk, but it can be minimized."

She nodded, but seemed far from happy. Alecia thought again that Benae had a soft heart where children were concerned.

"I think we can be about our tasks now," Ramón said. "We'll meet here at the same time tomorrow unless something changes."

He approached Alecia. "That went better than expected. What I said about Estevot applies to you too. I want you to delegate. And, before you assume too much, you won't be taking any part in the fighting."

"What? Of course, I'll be fighting. I can wield a sword and shoot an arrow as well as a man, as can my ladies. I won't have people fighting for me while I stay safe behind castle walls."

He shook his head. "We'll have this conversation later. Just remember what I said about delegating. You always bite off more than you can chew." He bowed and escorted Benae from the hall.

Alecia watched him go, her emotions a mix of relief and annoyance. "He really frustrates me," she said, glaring at his retreating back. "For some reason, he thinks he can order me about."

Lin laughed, but bit her lip at Alecia's sharp glance in her direction. "He's not so bad, Alecia. I think he truly cares for you."

"I don't need him 'caring' for me," she said. "His brand of care is stifling. Honestly, I think it was easier to tolerate when he thought he was in love with me."

Lin's eyes widened. "Do tell! I didn't know that!"

"Water under the bridge," Alecia said, reaching for some hair to yank and finding none. *Damn my "up do" this morning.* "It was a long time ago, and we're both well past it."

"Are you sure *he* is?" Lin asked.

Alecia scowled at her. "Very sure. Now stop trying to cause trouble. I have enough difficulty dealing with Benae as it is without her thinking her husband has unresolved feelings for me."

"Will you youngsters stop flapping your gums?" Hetty said. "We have work to do if we're to be ready for the *Sis Lenweri*."

"Yes, Lady Henrietta," Lin said, wiping the grin off her face. "Where are we headed first?"

Alecia raised her brow at Hetty, unsure her friend's attitude was appropriate toward a princess. "First stop is to find these army objectors and gain their cooperation."

Alecia and her ladies, along with Hetty, visited the chief army barracks where conscripted soldiers were being interviewed. Dressed in breeches and tunic, except for Hetty who was clad in a riding gown, she hoped they would draw little attention. She stood back, observing the process as men were sorted by their fighting ability.

Some appeared happy to cooperate, taking their uniforms and moving off in groups led by officers. Others stood by, muttering amongst themselves. She was impressed by the efficiency of the process. The sergeant in charge had processed twenty men in the half hour she had been present.

However, a similar number had been sent to a corner of the yard, surly looks on their faces. Two armed soldiers stood by, watching the recalcitrant candidates carefully.

"Looks like those men have been sent to the 'naughty corner'," Alecia said.

Her ladies snickered but Hetty peered at her with shrewd dark eyes. "What are you going to do?"

"Nothing dangerous," Alecia said, still observing the men. She returned to her mare and removed the bag of coin that Hetty had collected from her supporters. Then she started toward the men in the corner of the yard. "Follow me."

Alecia stopped before one of the soldiers. "I wish to speak with these men. I have the permission of the Guardians. Can you tell me who amongst them is the leader of this group?"

The soldier frowned and his jaw tightened. He cast his eye to her ladies and then over the men. "As for a leader, I can't say, having little knowledge of most of them. However, that one there... " He pointed to a dark-haired, bearded man who stood taller than most... "I grew up with him. He was always the ringleader if trouble was afoot. Got me into more than one scrape, I can tell you."

"Name?" Alecia asked.

"Soma Nuran."

"Thank you for your service, Corporal."

Alecia walked past the soldier, her ladies close to her, Kenna and Arelle with short swords drawn. She stopped at the edge of the group.

"I wish to speak with Soma Nuran," she called.

At her words, their muttering increased, and some turned toward her, expressions varying from suspicion to outright hostility.

"Who's asking?"

Alecia didn't see who had asked the question.

"Princess Alecia Zialni," Lin said.

Alecia felt their interest prick and a shiver ran up her spine. This could be a brilliant move or a very foolish one.

The dark-bearded man pushed forward through the crowd. "I'm Soma Nuran, Princess and I can't imagine what you have to say that would interest me."

She peered up at Soma who was even taller than she expected. Straggly black hair fell over eyes that were a disconcerting pale grey. His broad chest was clad in a leather jerkin reinforced with metal discs. To Alecia, he had the appearance of a mercenary, without an ounce of good in his soul. Perhaps this would be more difficult than she had imagined.

Swallowing down her nerves, she took a step toward the brute.

"Master Nuran, am I correct in assuming that you are reluctant to fight in defense of the kingdom?"

He folded his arms across his chest and spat into the dirt beside her. "Indeed, you are, Your Highness. Why should I put my life at risk for the measly pittance the kingdom pays its soldiers?"

"Measly pittance? It seems many don't share your distaste and find honor in the life of a soldier. Surely there's value in defending Thorius against those who would steal it from us? Do you think the *Sis Lenweri* would be more generous?"

He tilted his head to the side. "Perhaps. If a soldier has such value, the kingdom can pay the bill. I've lived the life of a fighter for hire for years. Why can the king not pay fairly for my services?" His eyes took in the bag that Lin now held. "Or are you here to buy us?"

Alecia studied the men before her. They were a ratty bunch, many with the desperate look of mercenaries, others who appeared to be thieves and pick pockets. All would be a nuisance in the army. Perhaps Estevot had been right to condemn them. But could they be used in some way? Most appeared sound and many were trained fighters.

She drew in a deep breath. "Do you know these men?" Her arm swept across the group.

Soma nodded. "Most of them."

"Are they loyal kingdom men?"

"Some of them," Soma sneered.

Alecia pushed down her frustration. Dealing with this man was like trying to catch smoke.

"Would they be loyal kingdom men for double army pay?

An angry snort came from behind and she turned to find the corporal glaring at her. *Oops!*

Her words had caused one of Soma's brows to arch. "Double you say? Take home, with food and bed included? "

Alecia scowled at him. "You drive a hard bargain. I would need your absolute guarantee of loyalty and discretion."

He looked long and hard at her as if trying to judge if she could be trusted. Alecia stood her ground and met his eye, unblinking. It cost her but she did it.

Finally, he nodded. "What do you have in mind?"

She held up one finger to him. "Just a moment." Alecia walked back to the corporal, pulling out a gold coin as she approached him.

"Corporal, I have a solution for these men who are causing you concern. However, I need you to forget everything you just heard." She held out the coin. "For your trouble, you may take this." She reached for his hand and placed the gold coin upon it.

The soldier closed his hand on the coin, his brows drawn down. "All I have to do is forget? This could buy a year of forgetfulness."

Alecia smiled up at him. "Just until the war is won, Corporal. And I'll take away this nuisance. Do you agree?"

He swallowed hard. "I guess so." Drawing in a breath, he straightened his shoulders. "As long as it doesn't get me in trouble, I'll forget, Your Highness."

Alecia nodded. "I promise no trouble will befall you. Deal?"

The corporal slapped his breast in a salute. "Deal!"

Alecia returned to Soma and drew him aside.

"Master Nuran," she said, "if you join the kingdom army, I'll guarantee you and your men double the salary of the regular soldiers, from now until the war is won. You may call on me at the palace once a week to collect your extra wages."

He nodded. "I would need to be reimbursed for my trouble. It seems as though I would be organizing the payroll."

"I'm sure you'll appoint an assistant in that role, but regardless, I'll see you get compensated." She hesitated. "Please understand, your task is not just to manage these men." Her eye swept the small gathering. "You must convince every man who refuses the army to join under my rules." She held up two fingers. "Also, you must swear that your approach will come *after* their refusal of Captain Estevot's offer. My coffers are not bottomless. *And,* any you deem unsuitable for soldiering must be sent to me to be interviewed for other roles in the war effort. As an experienced fighter, I'm sure I don't need to list those other roles."

Soma scowled but nodded. "You drive a hard bargain, Princess."

Alecia made a quick count of the men and handed over enough coin for the first week. "See you distribute that. I'll stay until I witness you sign up and receive your uniforms—all of you. I will also clear it with Captain Estevot that he is to send for you, daily if necessary, to speak with any recalcitrant recruits. You are to keep my name out of this. Do you understand?"

Soma nodded and returned to the gathered men, drawing them with him. Alecia and her ladies retreated to the barracks entrance where they observed Soma, and the others, sign on as Thorian soldiers.

Alecia heaved a sigh of relief as she turned and left the barracks precinct.

"I hope you haven't set the cat amongst the pigeons, Princess," Hetty said. "Those men have trouble written all over them, especially Soma."

Alecia waved her hand at her advisor. "All will be well. I'll keep an eye on him."

Lin shook her head. "I think you bamboozled him good and proper. He didn't know what hit him."

Cretia laughed. "I'll bet he sits down tonight and wonders how she got him to agree to such a thing."

As she mounted Silver, Alecia blocked their chatter. It might fail spectacularly, but she was pleased with the morning's work. Not only had she solved the problem of the conscripted soldiers, but she had delegated it to Soma. And if the war came and went quickly, it would cost her only a few week's coin—well worth it, she thought.

CHAPTER TWELVE

"**W**ELCOME, Master Tomel," Vard said. "It's good to see you again." Vard shook James Tomel's hand in the antechamber of the formal audience hall. The king and queen were within, ready to meet with Tomel, who'd been the victim of a dragon attack some months prior.

He had met the man soon after Alecia returned from her exile. He'd been escorting Katrine to Brightcastle, and the two hadn't seen eye to eye. Tomel had thought Vard was still a wanted man and been openly hostile. They had spoken again when he and Sam traveled to Costa recently. The relationship was still frosty.

The master jeweler's grip was firm and callused, not what he would have expected of an artisan. He also appeared extremely fit, considering he must spend many hours each day crouched over a bench. Vard had tried to discover as much as he could about the man before this meeting, but even Sam, who was now James's brother-in-law, had little to say of him.

"Thank you for attending today," Vard said.

"I must say you've had a miraculous rise to your current position, Lord Anton."

"I'm gratified I can help the king in this time of great threat. He needs people around him he can count on."

"Yes, he does." Tomel's tone stopped just short of outright hostility.

"It means a lot to me personally that you're willing to come forward and tell your story."

Tomel's dark brows lifted. "Why personally?"

"Let's just say I've had a theory for some time, and you might be the man to give it credence. Tell me of your experience."

"Lord Anton, if you don't mind, I'd rather just tell the king and queen, and you, in one go. That way, you all hear the same thing, and there can be no confusion."

The man really was paranoid. There was more to him than his role as a simple craftsman, however skilled. King Beniel had been stunned when Vard told him who was to attend the meeting. He was yet to learn why it was so surprising.

"Whatever you wish, Master Tomel."

The door opened, and a footman ushered them in.

Vard went first, with Tomel trailing behind. He stopped before the king and queen.

"Good morning, Your Majesties." Vard bowed and stepped aside to reveal the master jeweler. "May I present James Tomel, Master Jeweler of Wildecoast, lately of Costa."

Tomel stepped forward and swept a bow, then approached the queen. "Queen Adriana, you're as beautiful as ever." He kissed her ring.

Queen Adriana smiled. "Thank you, James, you are too kind. When will my next piece be ready?"

"Stop fussing, Adriana," King Beniel said. "The man isn't here for an update on your blasted jewels."

"King Beniel," James said, "it's good to see you again. I hope you're well."

"Tomel," the king said, "stop the fancy greetings and get to the point. When Vard said it was *you* who witnessed the dragon attack, I was shocked."

Vard stiffened at the king's angry retort. What was going on here?

"I do apologize, Your Majesty," Master Tomel said. "I should've come forward earlier."

"Why didn't you?"

"I didn't think you'd believe me, My Liege. I feared it would destroy my credibility if I told you I was the victim of a dragon attack in my backyard."

The king frowned, considering his words. "Tell me what happened."

Tomel drew a deep breath and began. "Late one evening, I went outside into my backyard to perform a last check before I locked up. Something wasn't right. The hens were making a fuss, and my dog, Lamb, was missing. I heard a grinding noise and realized it was coming from a massive dark lump perched on my roof. The lump took off, knocking me off my feet and dropping Lamb's head beside me."

The queen gasped.

King Beniel hushed her. "What happened then?"

"I recovered my footing, picked up the pole and lantern I had dropped, then searched for what had swooped at me. The moon came out from behind a cloud, and I saw a monstrous dragon sitting on the roof of my neighbor's house. The beast attacked. I would've made it back inside except my worker appeared from an outbuilding. I couldn't let him face it alone."

Vard listened, spellbound, as the nightmare came to life in his imagination. One thing was certain. Tomel was a brave man.

"You defended yourself with a pole and a lantern?" the king asked.

"There was no time to get anything else, My Liege. My man ran to help with a rake, and together we tried to fend it off before I flung the lantern at it and the flames took hold of its wing. It flew off, thank the Goddess."

The king stared at Tomel. "You expect me to believe you fought a dragon, let alone were successful in chasing it off?"

"It's true, Your Majesty." James said, hand over heart. "I'm sorry I didn't come forward sooner, but I was trying to determine exactly how I'd convince you without risking your ire."

"Oh, don't worry, Tomel. You *have* incurred my anger."

Vard was still confused. "If I may ask, Your Majesty, why is his not coming forward such an issue?"

King Beniel glared at Vard. "It's an issue, King's Blade, because this man is the *head* of my intelligence service."

Vard left the chamber without Tomel. He'd been dismissed soon after the revelation about James's secret kingdom position. He still couldn't believe the man hadn't come straight to the king with news of the incident. Perhaps he'd been trying to protect Katrine? He had certainly not mentioned her, and she had told Vard she had seen the beast, even helped chase it off.

Exiting through the servant's side door, he started toward the practice yard, then detoured to enter the stables. He should check on his mount and speak to the stable master about preparing the horses for battle. He wanted to alter their feed to boost their energy reserves. The man would gripe about it, as it would make the horses difficult to handle.

He said hello to Trax and issued orders to the stable master, then left the building, bound for the weapons practice yard. Katrine, clad in breeches, tunic, and cloak, called to him from the shelter of a small stand of trees outside the stable.

"Lady Star! Should you be here, dressed as you are?" Vard whispered.

She hissed at him. "I was attending to other business this morning and came straight here when I saw you enter the stable. What happened?"

He shook his head. "The king detained your husband. I'm not sure what will happen next, but suspect he will be imprisoned."

Her eyes widened. "I knew it was unwise to do as you requested. James has said his position was precarious." Her mouth snapped shut as though she was afraid she'd said too much.

"I know about his spying," Vard said. "Walk with me, and we'll find somewhere less conspicuous to talk."

They left the castle forecourt via the gate and moved into the city. A short walk later, they entered a tavern which was a popular drinking hole for soldiers and sailors.

"This is less conspicuous?" Katrine asked, looking around. Plenty of interest was being paid to the attractive, dark-haired woman. But few would recognize her as Katrine Aranati, and Vard wasn't out of place here.

"It will be of no concern, Lady Star. Have a seat, and we'll talk." He raised his hand and summoned a serving girl whose eyes slid over him appreciatively. The woman's gaze flicked to Katrine, and she frowned as if the beautiful witch were her competition. "Two ales and two plates of stew and fresh bread, please."

She sauntered off, and Vard turned to Katrine. "Tell me everything about that night. Your husband didn't mention you to the king, yet I know you were there."

"He's trying to protect me. I fought off the dragon with my fire balls. James can hardly mention my part in chasing off the beast. Best that my name stays out of it." She fixed her sparkling blue eyes on Vard. "I can't be exposed. It would spell disaster for my family."

"I understand, Lady Star. I thought he cleverly avoided mentioning you. However, he said a worker of his was involved."

"Probably to add credence to the story that he was able to fight the beast off," she said. "You know he was badly wounded?"

"He didn't mention it."

She sat back in her chair, looking dispirited. "James told me about his other life, even though he wasn't meant to. If the king believes he's disloyal, he could face treason charges. The penalty is death." Tears filled her eyes. "I can't lose him."

"Lady, we're far from that, though the king was astonished James and his worker vanquished a dragon."

She groaned. "It all sounds so far-fetched." Her angry eyes speared him. "This is *your* fault. I should never have talked him into it."

"It would've come out, eventually. It's best we sort it out now. Tell me the real story."

She sighed. "The hounds were unsettled, and they sent me messages in my dreams about a great threat. It felt related to James. So I traveled to Costa that night and arrived to find James in the clutches of a dragon. It was so huge it could barely land in his yard."

"Color?" Vard asked.

Katrine thought for a time. "Dark, perhaps black or green?"

"He was trying to battle the thing with a knife while it had him by the shoulder and knee." Pride laced her words. "He didn't give up and risked his life to save Dant, his servant."

"What happened then?"

"I hurled two fireballs at the thing. They hit its side and then the wing. It dropped James and flapped off, just clearing the rooftops. It set fire to the house next door as it screamed in pain. Dant and I got James inside and while I tended to his wounds, Dant raced next door to save the house."

"Quite a night, then," Vard said. "Do you think the beast targeted James, or was he just unlucky?"

She shrugged. "I don't know, and neither does he. I still can't believe what happened that night. It was a week before I could leave him to care for himself." She grasped Vard's sleeve. "Don't tell the king about the wounds he sustained. If he sees the scars, he'll never believe James fought it off."

"Don't worry about James, Lady Star. The king is stubborn, but he *will* listen to reason. I'll speak to him and see what I can do. Also, Queen Adriana won't want her master jeweler languishing in jail."

Rather than reducing her fears, Vard's words brought tears to the tough lady's eyes. "You started all this with your dragon theories needing to be proven." She fixed him with an accusing eye. "I wish I'd never said a thing to you."

"You don't mean that."

"I most certainly do. James might pay the ultimate price for your credibility."

"Lady Star," Vard said, his voice firm. "This kingdom is at war. Only the truth about the enemy will help us win. If we go against them, and they have dragon aid, without preparation we'll be slaughtered."

She stood and leaned forward with her fists on the table. "That's easy for you to say when your lover isn't rotting in some dungeon. You free him… or I will." She stalked out of the tavern, and Vard blew out a long breath of frustration.

Had he just lost one of his most powerful allies?

Vard headed for the practice yard, hoping to blow off steam and check on the progress of his rangers and new recruits. He took a class in hand-to-hand combat that Vortek would've overseen if he'd been present. The shifter should be back soon unless something held him up. Vard was satisfied that the trainee rangers and others who'd been sent to the course were progressing well. He was taking a breather and having a drink when Sam arrived.

"Time for lunch?" Sam asked, pushing sweaty hair off his forehead.

Vard quirked a brow at him. "What've you been up to?"

"Supervising the archery practice, though I think you'd be better suited to it. Can you come over after lunch and give some pointers? We're working on our longest-range accuracy. But I can't make an arrow hit the bullseye at 350 paces like you can."

Vard smiled. "I'll come over. Make sure they practice the short bow over close distances with small targets too."

"Right, like the size of a dragon's eye?"

Vard held up his palm. "I estimate the target should be about this big."

Sam shook his head. "I hope you're sure about this." He studied Vard for a few moments. "What's the matter?"

Vard grimaced. "Nothing. I'll sort it out."

"Tell me."

Vard blew out a long breath. "A witness to a dragon attack came forward to speak with King Beniel. He's now in the dungeon."

"What?! Because he said he saw a dragon?"

Vard shook his head. "No, because he should've come forward sooner. He's involved in kingdom intelligence, and His Majesty would like to know why this critical information wasn't divulged."

Sam cocked his head. "When you put it like that, why *didn't* he come forward?"

Vard fixed his gaze on Sam. "His wife has magical talents."

Sam's eyes widened. "Are you saying it's *James* in prison?"

Vard nodded. "Unfortunately, the king didn't take the news well. Tomel left out the part about Katrine helping to chase the dragon away, and Beniel thinks it unlikely that two mere men could beat a dragon. Also, he's royally mad that the man didn't come to him immediately with the report since he's his chief spy. I guess he's doubting his loyalty to the throne."

"Wait, James is the king's *spymaster*?" Sam's eyes were round as he struggled to accept the news about his brother-in-law. "I guess I can see the king's point."

"Tomel was in a no-win situation," Vard said. "At least now, King Beniel must admit dragons exist."

Sam narrowed his eyes. "You're right. And not a moment too soon for our defense plans." He fell quiet for a moment. "Why did James stay quiet? Besides protecting Katrine?"

"Is that not a good enough reason?" Vard asked.

Sam shrugged. "Sounds like only part of the reason. Perhaps he didn't think he'd be believed. A man has his pride." He eyed Vard. "Except for you, who spouts dragon theories with no proof. You don't care at all."

Vard shook his head. "I can't afford to dismiss the hunches I get. But I feel responsible for Tomel's situation. I convinced Katrine to ask him to come forward. I still think I did the right thing. Would Nikolas speak on his behalf to Beniel?"

Sam smiled. "Why don't *you* ask him?"

"I think it would be better coming from you, somehow."

Sam nodded. "I'll track him down after luncheon and see what I can do. See you at the archery range later?"

Vard nodded and returned to his combat lesson while Sam went into lunch.

* * *

Katrine paced the floor of the modest room she and James had shared until today. Her link with the hounds, though distant as they were out of the city, vibrated with shared fear and anger. They felt her distress, but didn't know the cause. She'd have to go to them and calm them, but she must see James first. *Damn Vard Anton.* Things had been perfectly fine before *his* interference. Now her husband's life was threatened, and she had no power to stop it without revealing herself. She'd do that for him, but there was no coming back if she took that step.

If only Esta was here, she might be able to help. But she'd left on her ship for the southern coast, taking Mika and Merielle with her.

She changed into a modest gown and wrapped a shawl around her shoulders. After a short walk to the castle precinct, she arrived at the prison. Drawing a deep breath, she stepped within the imposing stone walls of the jail. A soldier stopped her.

"You can't come in here, Miss."

"My husband is being held here, and I wish to speak with him. I *must* speak with him."

"What's his name?"

"James Tomel. He came in this morning."

"Oh, yes," the soldier said, "the traitor."

Katrine glared. "My husband is no traitor."

"You *would* say that, Madam."

"Just please ask your superior if I can have five minutes."

The man sighed and left the guard's office. Katrine spent the next fifteen minutes pacing and trying to calm her hounds via their bond. The trouble was she was so distressed that all they wanted to do was come into the city to rescue her.

The soldier returned with a guard sergeant. "Can I help you?" He examined her gown and added, "My Lady."

"You're holding my husband, James Tomel. I wish to see him."

"No visitors allowed, My Lady," the sergeant said, folding his arms over his chest.

She drew a deep breath, forcing down panic. "Please. I just need five minutes. I promise I won't cause any trouble."

The man laughed. "As if you could cause trouble. I'm more concerned about getting myself into hot water with my superiors. The king has decreed that no one is to go near the prisoner."

Katrine's heart battered against her ribs, and she felt the hounds howl in terror. She must settle herself down. "Sergeant, I'm known to the King's Blade. He wouldn't mind me seeing my husband."

The man himself materialized as if by magic.

"Sergeant? What's going on here?" The gold chips in Vard's irises caught her attention. "Lady?"

She took a step closer to him. "I need to see James."

"Step this way, My Lady," Vard said, escorting her back toward the entrance.

She hissed at him. "Why can't I see James? The sergeant said His Majesty ordered it."

"Short-term prisoners don't receive visitors unless it's their legal representative. Family isn't normally allowed."

"Poppycock! Esta visited Sam in this very prison several times."

Vard's face hardened. "Things have changed. The king tightened security after a breakout and again after Gorin escaped."

She pushed her face up toward his, so the guards wouldn't hear. "Well, if you don't want my hounds terrorizing the streets, think of an excuse to get me in. They can feel my fear and are chomping to come and rescue me."

"That sounds like a threat," he ground out.

"Oh, believe me, it's not a threat, but sheer reality if I don't get in there."

Vard gazed down at her for long moments while she battled her fear and tried to reassure the hounds.

"Very well." He led her back to the sergeant. "Lady Katrine may have a short visit with her husband. I'll escort her down myself."

The men thumped their chests, and the sergeant accompanied Vard and Katrine below to the dungeons and along to James's cell. He unlocked the door and gave the keys to Vard. "Lock up when you're done." He stomped back up the hall.

Vard pulled the door open and stepped into the cell, followed by Katrine. She spotted James in the gloom near the far wall and approached him.

"Katrine, why did you come? I don't want you to see me like this."

She hugged him, gasping when she saw the manacles on his wrists and ankles. "Are these necessary?" she asked, glaring at Vard.

He had the grace to look ashamed. "It's merely protocol for one charged with treason."

"I haven't been so charged, Anton," James spat, "not yet, anyway. Last time I ever do *you* a favor."

Vard stepped forward. "Don't blame *me*. I didn't know you held a senior position in security. And you should have come forward about the dragon sooner."

James looked down. "I just never got around to reporting it. I didn't know how to make anyone believe my story and I couldn't bring Katrine into it for obvious reasons. The king would persecute her if he knew of her magic. Better that only *I* draw his ire."

Vard huffed and walked back and forth across the cell. "What a mess!"

Katrine grabbed his arm. "You *must* get him out!"

Vard met her gaze. "I've spoken with His Majesty since you and I talked and, truthfully, I don't know if I can. King Beniel has dug his heels in. Perhaps it's best if I appeal to the queen. She may convince him to back down." He looked at James. "Is there anything besides Katrine's powers and the dragon attack that you're hiding?"

James shook his head. "I swear I've passed on everything else. What do you think the consequences will be?"

"If I can get you released, the best outcome you could hope for would be banishment from the kingdom."

"What?" Katrine said. "No! We have family here. James is a respected craftsman."

Vard held up his hands. "I'm truly sorry. I'll try to get the queen to speak on your behalf. Perhaps I'm wrong, and you'll escape with a warning."

Katrine met James's gaze. Her brave husband had tears in his eyes, but still carried himself proudly. Knowing him, the tears were for her.

"Don't worry, my darling," she said. "I'll get you out of here if I have to break you out myself." She kissed him passionately. Her body shuddered as the chains brushed against it.

James broke the kiss. "Don't do anything silly, Kat. Allow the proper processes to run their course. I'm sure the king will see sense."

"You're right, of course. And Lord Anton here will have a plan, I'm sure."

Vard escorted her from the cell and locked the door.

They made their way to the guardroom and handed the keys to the sergeant, then stepped into the cool day outside. Katrine pulled her shawl around her tightly.

"I can't lose him, Vard. I just found him. He's everything to me." She gazed up at him, recalling the melancholy that had been such a part of life before James.

Vard grasped her hands. "I'll do all I can. Sam will speak to the admiral on James's behalf, and I'll approach the queen. Just keep those hounds under control."

She nodded. "Now I've seen James, I'll take them for a hunt."

"Be careful," Vard said.

She pulled her hands from his and walked off down the street.

* * *

Vard had convened a meeting with the king and queen, and Nikolas Cosara. James Tomel was the topic. The trouble was Vard didn't know how he was going to achieve the master jeweler's release. King Beniel could be inflexible, especially when his pride was wounded. He had dug his heels in about magic, outlawing it in Thorius. And dragons were a little too close to magic for King Beniel's comfort. Add to that his being kept in the dark about the dragon attack by a man who was supposed to report to him, and...

Vard blew out a breath as he paused before the door into the audience chamber. He must try, or Katrine would be difficult to control. She and her hounds were important to the war cause. A nagging thought poked at his conscience. He hadn't revealed the existence of the night hounds to the king before the attack by the *Sis Lenweri* on the way to Wildecoast. Obviously, King Beniel knew of them now, but Vard had known long before that. Was he just as guilty as James Tomel—of keeping secrets from the king?

The footman announced him, and he entered the anteroom. Queen Adriana came to greet him. The monarch was dressed in a gray gown with silver thread decorations and was wearing her silver chain mail choker with the emeralds. Tomel had made the piece. Was that a sign of support for him?

"It's lovely to see you, Vard, though I wish it were under different circumstances. We must have dinner again soon."

Vard bowed over her hand and kissed the large emerald ring she wore. When he straightened, he spied a *desperate* longing in her eyes, which she quickly hid. What was wrong with her? He hadn't seen *that* look before; the predatory lioness was her usual expression when she gazed at him.

"Of course, Your Majesty. You only have to ask, and I'll attend you."

Her eyes flared at his remark. "I love it when you *attend* me, Vard," she whispered. "There is just not enough of it." She beckoned him into the audience room and offered him tea and light refreshments.

The admiral cast him a disdainful glance. "King's Blade," he said, nodding.

"Admiral."

Vard crossed to the king and bowed. "Your Majesty, I hope you're well."

Beniel's eyes narrowed. "I wish everyone wouldn't keep referring to my health. I am quite well and have the best of care. It's not your job to nursemaid me, Lord Anton."

"I stand chastened and corrected, my Liege." Vard glanced to Cosara and caught a momentary startled look on his face. Was he surprised Vard could be a courtier when required? Good; he wanted to keep the grouchy admiral on his back foot.

"Let's get down to business," King Beniel said. "Master James Tomel, Royal Jeweler and spymaster, has incurred my wrath, and, in case you were wondering, I am not inclined to be lenient."

Vard grimaced. As he had warned Katrine, the king might make an example of her husband.

"I feel somewhat responsible for the man's plight, My Liege," Vard said. "I convinced him to come forward."

"And a good thing you did," King Beniel said. "Otherwise, I would never have known my spymaster was corrupt."

Nikolas interjected. "I think that's a bit of a stretch. He withheld information which he didn't think was relevant or would be believed, surely?"

The queen gave her cousin a sharp look. Nikolas's words wouldn't be tolerated by most men. It was why Vard had asked for him to be there—because of his close relationship with the queen. But he must still step carefully.

The king stood and approached Nikolas. "I don't know why he withheld the information, but it is not his place to do so."

"Surely there's much that comes to him as spymaster which is of no concern to the kingdom?" Nikolas said. "James must have to weed through what's important and what's not."

The king frowned. "Yes…"

"And," Nikolas continued, "if he had come to you with word of a dragon attack, what would you have done?"

The king considered. "I would have found it difficult to believe."

"There you go!" Nikolas slapped his thigh.

"But," King Beniel said, "I would have taken him on his word and looked for more evidence that the beasts existed. After all, there *are* legends involving them."

Vard interrupted. "Excuse me, Your Majesty, but when I proposed dragons as an explanation for Gorin's escape and the ambush on your caravan, you scoffed at *me*."

"Yes, Lord Anton," Beniel said, "but had I been told of the dragon attack before, I would have more readily considered your theory, and we could have saved much time."

Vard nodded. "I can't deny that. So what should we do with Master Tomel?"

"He is married to a noblewoman," the queen said. "She is Esta Aranati's sister, Katrine."

"Oh yes, the woman with the strange eyes," King Beniel said. "I don't trust her either."

"You can't distrust someone because they have unusual eyes, Your Majesty," Vard said. "Otherwise, you wouldn't have made me King's Blade."

The king scowled. "Stop making so much sense, Anton!"

"Husband," Queen Adriana said, "I do not wish any hurt to befall my jeweler. Additionally, you cannot sentence to death a man with links to the nobility without serious consequences."

"But what he has done is *treasonous*!" King Beniel started pacing the room, and Vard feared he had worked himself into an unhealthy state.

"James Tomel loves Thorius," the queen said. "His intention was not to be disloyal. I know him better than any of you. Can you not just dismiss him from your intelligence service?"

"He knows too much! No one leaves that service alive," the king growled.

Adriana paled. "Then we have a problem."

"We can't sentence him to death, and we can't let him leave the spy service alive," Nikolas said. "I'd say that's a real quandary." He looked at Vard. "Any ideas, King's Blade?"

Vard returned Cosara's stare, and an idea came to him. "Your Majesty, what if someone you trusted could ensure Master Tomel posed no threat to security, at least until this war with the *Sis Lenweri* is over?"

The king quirked an eyebrow. "You mean someone should take the man under their wing and watch him like a hawk, thus minimizing any threat he poses?"

Vard nodded.

Nikolas threw his hands up. "Don't look at me. I've already done that with Samael, and I don't intend to put myself through it again."

The queen laughed. "But you have grown so close to your brother in that time. And look at the fine job you did. You have reformed a pirate into a trusted member of our war effort."

"I'm not certain I did such a fine job," Nikolas growled. "*And* he was a royal pain in my ass."

The king flung up his hands for silence. "Then, if not Nikolas, who would be suitable?"

"Vard, of course," the queen said. "He would be the *perfect* man for the task."

Vard had already thought of himself. He was ready to take on the role, but remained silent. This must be King Beniel's decision for it to resonate well with him.

The king considered, holding Vard's gaze as he did so. "Would you take the man on, Vard? You're already busy with the war effort. However, I can't think of a man I would trust more. It would set my mind at rest."

"I appreciate your faith in me, Your Majesty," Vard said. "I'll see that James Tomel brings no harm to the kingdom and put him to good use."

"How so? My wife will insist the man still makes her jewelry. He can't do that while running around after you."

"I believe Master Tomel must sacrifice his craft for the time being," Vard said. "He'll be stood down from the spy service and another appointed from within the group to take his place. I also suggest you brief me on this organization, so I can oversee its effectiveness and security. I'm surprised you haven't done so already."

Adriana cut in. "The king has been unwell, and I did not want to overstep by exposing his spy network, Lord Anton. He has always operated that himself. It *is* his prerogative."

Vard nodded. "I look forward to my briefing."

The king frowned deeply, but finally nodded also. "You must stay after this meeting, and I will update you."

"Thank you, Your Majesty," Vard said. "I have one more thing to discuss. The night hounds. You know they rescued us during the attack on your convoy by the enemy. They're under the control of a person known to me, however, I can't reveal their identity at the moment. I wanted you to know that."

The king stiffened. Would this be an affront to him, as James's failure had been?

"Why can't I know who this person is?" King Beniel asked.

"The hounds are on our side. If I must reveal the identity of the hounds' handler, I believe they'd leave this kingdom, and we'd lose the help of the beasts in the coming war.," Vard said.

The king slumped back into his throne. "So, we have dragons reportedly against us and night hounds on our side. Somehow, I'd rather it be the other way."

"Your answer, My Liege?" Vard asked. "

"Those hounds are damned terrifying," King Beniel said. "Oh well, you may handle this matter as you see fit for now, Vard."

"And you will release James Tomel into my custody?" Vard asked.

The king nodded. "Before you leave here, I'll write you an order to have him released. Now—on to matters of war."

They spent the next hour discussing the defense of Wildecoast and incorporating dragons and night hounds into their plans. As Vard was leaving the chamber, Nikolas caught up to him.

"Wait up, Anton," the admiral said. "I want to talk to you."

"Make it snappy, Cosara. I have a man to free from prison."

"Nicely done, by the way."

"You did most of the work to convince the king," Vard said.

"I beg to differ. However, that's not what I wanted to discuss. I saw what you did back there."

"Oh?"

"You informed the king of the night hounds and neatly dodged the fact that you've been withholding information on them. It's exactly what Tomel has done and yet you end up being trusted, and Tomel is a pariah."

Vard shrugged. "I've worked closely with the king for some time now, and I saved his niece. Let's just say I wanted to clear the air on the night hounds. I don't want him thinking he can't trust me."

Nikolas pushed his face into Vard's. "If he knew what I know, he wouldn't want you anywhere near him or his niece."

Vard fixed the admiral with the look he reserved for intimidating criminals and bullies. It didn't seem to affect Cosara as far as he could see. "And yet, you've chosen to keep my secret, Admiral, so you're withholding information from the king too. Is that perhaps because you have something yourself to hide? Something the king would never accept?"

"Don't you worry about why I act as I do. Just watch your back. If I even think you pose a threat to the king or Thorius, I'll spill my guts to Beniel so fast it will take your breath away." Cosara stalked off down the hall, his boots marking an angry staccato on the stone floor.

CHAPTER THIRTEEN

THE trees screamed, and Kain woke in a cold sweat. He knew instantly what caused the dread in his heart. His beloved forest was under attack. He threw off the covers and bounded from the bed, seizing his sword, bow, and arrows, and the pack he had prepared ten days ago. He grabbed the horn that hung on a hook by the door to his small balcony and stepped into the open air.

Kain blew three short blasts, then three longer ones. He waited and replies came from four quarters. Good, no one would be caught by surprise. When the horn echoes died away, Kain tried to grasp what had alerted the trees. Did a faint scent of smoke hang in the air, or was it his imagination? He scanned the tops of the trees he could see from this height and came up blank.

Charging down the staircase, he burst from the base of his great tree and took the path to the lookout closest to him. All seemed quiet in the forest he jogged through. Was this a false alarm? Had his tree friends spent too long on high alert? It didn't seem likely that they'd be wrong. He rubbed his amulet and spoke to his sister.

Gwaethe, something is happening here. The trees are going crazy, and I think I smell smoke. I've sounded the alarm and am trying to find the source of the threat. Stand by.

He arrived at the lookout, and still the odor of smoke came to him. Was it stronger here? He cast his gaze out over the trees and spied a tendril of smoke weaving a lazy path out of the forest canopy. Damn! No false alarm. That was the start of a forest fire. And over further was another. And another. To the north of Selinore, the forest was under attack. Kain shut out the sounds of the trees, so he could function without their terror intruding.

Brother! What is it? Gwaethe's commanding voice sounded in his mind.

The forest is on fire in several places to the north. There's very little wind, so it will be slow moving. Be on alert. If we're under attack, then you might be too. Did my people arrive?

They came yesterday, very much the worse for wear. Some of the elderly died on the trail. The children are well, but traumatized. We have housed them in the center of Amitania where they will be safe.

He sent his gratitude down the bond and felt Gwaethe leave. She needed to prepare her city for war. He had a brief thought of Brightcastle and Wildecoast, but there might not be time to send a raven or pigeon. Ravens would be better, as they were tough and smart.

He turned and made his way back down the lookout path, mindless of the roots and rocks in his path. He made it safely and was almost back at his tree when a shadow with a short sword appeared in front of him.

The shadow hissed, and the glint of steel slid toward his throat. Kain ducked, and his momentum carried him past. He kicked his assailant as he went, and the enemy crashed to the ground. Another took his place, this time brandishing a long sword.

"Prepare to die, false prince!"

The words confirmed he was indeed under assault by the *Sis Lenweri*. Kain attacked before his assailant had a chance to, sending a deadly flurry of blade strokes in a matter of a few seconds. His opponent fended them off, but barely. In the blink of an eye, another elf joined the first, and a third appeared.

"To me!" Kain shouted. "Prince's Guard to me!" Then he launched himself at his three attackers. He could handle them, but it was tricky in the half-light.

Several close calls later, one of his guards arrived to aid him, and they dispatched the three attackers as well as the first elf whom he had kicked. Kain stood sucking in breaths, trying to ready himself for the next assault.

"How many of them are there?" he gasped.

"They have us surrounded, High Prince," the guard said.

The smell of smoke was now overwhelming, and, as dawn approached, smoky mist shrouded the city of Selinore.

"We can't allow them to kill the trees," Kain said, his breathing returning to normal. He looked around. "Where are the rest of my guard?"

"They are defending the elders as they protect the great trees."

Another of his guards arrived from the northeastern side of the city. "Come quickly, Kain Arenil! We are being overrun!" The elf led the way, and they came upon a fierce battle being fought for possession of the hut where the elders staged their defense of the trees. Kain felt the waves of their magic pulsing from the structure.

"Get them out of there!" He shouted to the elves with him, and hurled himself into the battle. *His* elves wore white headbands, easy to spot in the poor light. He joined three *Lenweri* who fought at least twice that number. They held their own until his two guards returned from clearing the hut of elders.

Once the guards rejoined them, they dispatched the *Sis Lenweri* fighters, though Kain received a deep cut to his upper sword arm. The wind picked up, and so did the smoke. He and his group went from tree to tree, and cottage to cottage, checking for survivors and the enemy.

Eventually, they gathered all the defenders in the city square. It seemed that, for now, the *Sis Lenweri* had fallen back into the forest.

Kain called his army leaders together. "Reports please."

"I've lost twenty percent of my fighters," one sergeant said.

The rest had suffered losses from ten to thirty percent of their force. Tuthariel and Julli moved through the defenders, checking their wounds and suturing them, including Kain's.

"What injuries, Julli?"

"Half of the wounded won't be able to fight," Julli said, her shoulders already slumped with fatigue.

Rasalar approached, wearing a bandage around her forehead. Kain's heart bled that the elder must fight at all. She should be enjoying her retirement and training the young fighters, not risking her life. But she had insisted on being a part of the defense, and he could ill afford to decline.

"It was a small advance party that attacked us, Kain Arenil," she reported. "They will return in larger numbers. I think we should retreat while we can."

"Where's Melandrach?" Kain asked.

"He is with the elders, helping them find a safe place to protect the trees," Rasalar said. "He insists on guarding us and, for once, I am glad of my brother's meddling."

A shrill cry came from the north. The defenders searched the skies.

"What was that?" Kain asked, though in his heart, he knew.

Rasalar's eyes met his. "I have never heard such a call, but I suspect it issues from the mouth of one of the greater dragons."

Kain grabbed her arm and started running for shelter, calling to all around. "Take cover! Find shelter! Dragon!" He dragged Rasalar along behind him, and they reached the overhang of one of the stone cottages. The sun had crested the tips of the trees.

The shriek came again, this time louder. Elora appeared beside him.

"The protection is in place, Prince Arenil," she said. "The great trees will be safe for the time being. What do you suggest we do now?"

"We should retreat, Elora," Rasalar said. "I do not think we can fight fire, dragons, *and* the *Sis Lenweri*. But it depends on how many they are. That was just a scouting mission."

"I don't think we can defend Selinore," Kain said. "But I don't want to risk losing the great trees."

"The trees are here to serve the elves, Kain," Elora said. "Not the other way. We have done all we can for them. Perhaps their best chance is for us to leave. Faenwelar may not linger here to destroy our home if he can chase us all the way to Amitania."

"And the *Sis Lenweri are* elves at heart," Rasalar said. "They love the forest too. I don't think they want to wipe out the great trees."

"But that is exactly why they have set fire to the forest!" Elora snapped, glaring at her sister-in-law.

Rasalar shrugged. "My advice still stands. If we retreat, we may survive to fight another day. If we wait, we fight them again, and more of us die, and the trees are lost anyway. No. *This* was never likely to be the place that humans and elves made their last stand."

"I've decided we retreat." Kain pulled the horn from his belt and blew three long blasts. He waited and repeated the call.

A shrill cry came from the north again, and a huge black dragon swept over the forest. Kain saw two riders on its back, both with arrows nocked to their bows. It was too far away to be a threat, but on the next sweep, it would cross over the most northern part of Selinore. They must be gone by then.

"Move out!" Kain blasted three more notes on his horn and sent the women toward the route out of the city to the south. "Stay under cover until you get to the forest. Whatever you do, keep moving as fast as you can."

They nodded and hurried away between the buildings. Kain turned in the opposite direction, hustling those he met and gaining a rear guard as well. He selected all the best archers to stay with him. It gratified him to see most of the evacuees had packs on their shoulders. Soon horses and ponies were being led past, as well as cows and goats. He didn't like to think what would become of them if left to the invaders.

"Hurry now," he said, stopping to speak to some artisans. "Stay under cover. When you reach the southern trail, move as fast as you can. Don't wait for us." Many carried their tools, which Kain was also glad to see.

He stationed his archers along the path out of Selinore at strategic intervals. Before he reached the tail end of his departing populace, the dragon was upon them. It flew across the tops of the great trees in the city's north, a gout of flame blasting through the smaller neighboring trees and setting them on fire. The elves on its back shot their arrows at fleeing citizens, devastatingly accurate in their aim. Four *Lenweri* dropped before the rest could take cover.

Kain kept running for the stragglers. Those in the center must take care of themselves. The dragon blasted another row of trees, and more *Lenweri* fell to the enemy arrows. Kain was careful to stay under cover. One of those with him wasn't so lucky.

"Pick him up and bring him!" Kain shouted. "That's everyone! Retreat!"

The soldiers with the wounded elf turned and bolted for the southern trail, zig-zagging when they must run in the open.

Kain ran with them, keeping an eye out for stragglers and the enemy. He had six of his best archers with him. "Keep your eyes open!" he shouted, though it was nigh impossible to do that with the smoke getting thicker. However, the smoke cover helped as much as it hindered.

A dragon shriek sounded so close the ground shook. The black beast flew overhead, and Kain saw its red-rimmed eye. He already had an arrow nocked, so took aim and released. The arrow bounced off the boney upper rim of the beast's left eye and the monster turned and blasted fire at him.

Kain ducked behind a stone building just in time, but his clothing was still singed. The beast flew on, and Kain charged out to check one of his soldiers who had fallen. The elf had an arrow through his heart and never stood a chance. He closed the dead eyes and ushered his troop on.

Some soldiers stationed along the evacuation route had remained in case they were needed. Kain took them along with him as he edged closer to the path out of the city. The burning trees were shrieking in his head, and he was too fatigued to block them out. Those with him were tiring. He signaled to them and ducked between a stone cottage and one of the great trees.

He leaned against the cottage wall and took a long pull on his water bag. Closing his eyes, he focused on blocking out the pain from the trees. Finally, as his breathing settled and his heart rate returned to normal, he was able to do so.

"One last push, friends, and we'll be in the forest. It will be harder for them to harass us."

Kain and those with him took the path out. The dragon flew back and forth over the city, torching anything not made of stone. He had a brief hope that Alique's hospital was safe. It was stationed between two great trees so the spell might protect it, and it seemed the dragon was avoiding the great trees with its fire.

The beast loomed over them again as they prepared to make a last dash for the forest. Kain felt a warning stab from the trees and pulled his men into shelter just in time. The building behind them went up in flames, but Kain avoided shooting at the beast. He didn't want to draw its attention and lose more soldiers.

They gained the trees, heading south, and ran until their strength faltered. Kain ran far longer than his body wanted to. Finally, they came upon the first stragglers, comprised of those injured from the earlier battle and soldiers protecting them.

Julli was with them, as well as Tuthariel. They had grabbed horses and ponies and used them to transport the injured. Some who were too ill to ride were dragged on stretchers made from blankets and tree branches.

Kain caught up with Julli. "Alique would be proud."

She smiled and brushed hair off her forehead with a dusty hand. "How's your arm?"

"I hadn't thought about it until now," he said. "So, I guess it's better than I expected."

"How many more did we lose?"

"A few," he said. "But there was no other attack except by the dragon. Perhaps they wanted to herd us out of the city." He stopped a soldier who was striding by. "Get one of our best runners and spread the word to watch out for ambush. No, make that *ten* of our best runners."

The elf saluted and ran off.

"Are we to be harassed all the way to Amitania?" Julli asked.

"We should assume so," he said. "Don't you worry about that. Your task is to care for the wounded. Let me see to the rest."

She smiled again and let out a long sigh. "Thanks for the reminder. It's hard enough tending to the wounded without worrying about the fighting."

"Just stay as quiet as possible. At night, minimal fires, and those must be shielded."

Julli nodded, and Kain moved on up the line, keeping his senses alert for attack from above and at the flanks.

* * *

Gwaethe poked Jacques awake. "Hurry and get up. Selinore is under attack."

Jacques sat up, instantly awake, his tired eyes finding her in the half light. "Have you heard from Kain?"

"Yes," she said, drawing on her forest garb and throwing a cloak around her shoulders. She stalked to the balcony and surveyed the city before her. All was quiet. Jacques appeared behind her, hurriedly half-dressed. She turned in his arms. "I'm itching to know what's going on, but Kain is silent."

"Speak to him then."

"I don't want to distract him in case he is fighting. I can wait until he has a moment to call out to me. In the meantime, I must trust he is well. Finish getting dressed and join me in the dining room. We'll need food before we start the day."

Gwaethe hustled out, more worried about Kain than she was willing to admit. Also, her mother, aunt, and uncle were in Selinore, not to mention childhood friends and elders. She wanted to be sure they were all well.

She stuck her head in the kitchen door. The cooks were already baking. She cleared her throat.

"Good day to you. Please have breakfast delivered to the dining hall as soon as possible. And be on high alert. The *Sis Lenweri* may be on the move."

She left the alarmed kitchen staff, and found the table already laid in the dining room, but no food there yet. She poured herself a cup of herbal tea and stood before the fire, sipping it to calm her fears. Mentally, she went through the various preparations and defenses they'd put in place in the preceding weeks. It *must* be enough.

The food arrived, and she prepared her breakfast and Jacques's. Army and administrative staff entered to partake of the meal, and Gwaethe informed them of the attack on Selinore and quizzed them about the preparations to defend Amitania. Most of them grabbed their food and hurried out at her warnings. The army officers would assess any imminent threat and ensure their troops were on high alert. The administrative staff would see to further preparing food, water, medicine, clothing, and transport.

When Jacques arrived, she went to him and wrapped her arms around his waist. Eyes closed, she breathed in his masculine scent; it never failed to calm her. "We have so much to lose," she said.

"And a lot to gain, my love. Come." He led her over to the table and poured her another cup of tea. She sat and watched the steam rise from the cup. Jacques grasped her hand. "We will prevail. We've known this day would come. No one is going to take our home, least of all Faenwelar."

"I wish I could be so sure."

He placed his fingers under her chin and raised her gaze to his.

"You must be sure. *You* are our leader. And there isn't a better person for that task. Think of what you've accomplished here. We won't just hand it back to the *Sis Lenweri*."

She straightened her back, remembering how Gorin, Faenwelar's son, had treated her. She had vowed to make him pay—and she would. "No, we won't hand *anything* back to them but their deaths."

"That's more like it. Now eat up. We prepare for battle."

Gwaethe couldn't help ducking as the dark green dragon swooped low over Amitania. Her eyes followed the beast and the two elves perched on its back. One of them looked suspiciously like Prince Gorin. She shivered at her first sight of the magnificent creature. What she wouldn't give to master it and ride through the skies. She recalled the legends Uncle Melandrach had told her as a child. Until now, she had thought that the dragons might only be the product of the elders' imagination.

The beast screeched its warning, and it was only rigid discipline that prevented her from clapping her hands over her ears. It flew back and forth over her city, occasionally belching flame, arrows flying from the bows carried by its riders. Smoke and fire rose from several spots around Amitania, and she hoped those in charge of controlling it had enough water.

She, Jacques, Theoden Leovaris, and several human commanders had deployed to different segments of the city to respond to the attacks mounted by Faenwelar's force.

The alarm had been sounded across Amitania not long after breakfast as the dragon appeared overhead and attempts were made to break through the walls to the north, northeast, northwest, southeast, and southwest. As well as concerted efforts in these areas, the dragon had dropped small companies of enemy soldiers inside the walls, their aim to cause as much confusion and damage as possible.

Their tactics worked to a degree, and, had the Amitanians not expected dragons to be used in the war, they would have been severely compromised.

Apparently, it had been Vard Anton who guessed about the beasts. He had been determined to discover the truth of their continued existence. She smiled grimly and nodded to herself. Princess Alecia had a good man there.

A group of her human soldiers appeared around a corner, running toward her, chased by a larger troop of *Sis Lenweri*. The enemy screamed their defiance at the humans, and Gwaethe gritted her teeth. They sounded like animals.

She signaled to her elves, and, just as the humans bolted past, her group dashed into the alley from a small side street. Gwaethe's sword rang with the rhythm of cut and thrust.

Most of the *Sis Lenweri* were dead or disabled before the humans even had time to turn around. When they returned to the battle, all that was needed was to round up the prisoners and remove the injured and dead.

Gwaethe spoke to the man in charge. "I'll leave the tidying up to you and your men, Sergeant," she said, signaling to her squad to get moving. "Injured to the closest hospital. Prisoners to the central square. We need to follow that dragon."

"Right you are, Princess." The man saluted and turned away, his men efficiently dividing into smaller groups to carry out Gwaethe's orders.

Gwaethe's second in command, Syndra Ilirie, jogged beside her as they followed the path of the dragon across Amitania.

"The humans respect you, Princess. I thought never to see that day." Despite the recent battle with the *Sis Lenweri*, Syndra seemed not out of breath. In contrast, Gwaethe felt the need for a rest. She knew she should have prepared harder physically for this war. Being married had made her soft.

"It's a respect that has been hard won, Syndra. This is not the first battle I have fought alongside the humans. And being married to one has its advantages."

Gwaethe followed the tail of the dragon until she lost sight of it and pinpointed the location. Shouts came from behind them. At a flick of her fingers, her troop melted into the side streets. Syndra peered back up the street from their alley.

"It's *Sis Lenweri* being pursued, Princess," she hissed. "Humans herding them. We can box them in."

Gwaethe nodded, and Syndra signaled to those across the street. As the enemy approached, Gwaethe's soldiers emerged and blocked their retreat, brandishing short swords. Faenwelar's soldiers skidded to a halt, momentarily surprised, then formed up, ready to fight.

Gwaethe didn't hesitate. She charged into the pack, laying about with her sword like a demon, too quick for anyone to defend. She may have been lax in her fitness training, but she had fine-tuned her skills with both short and long sword. Jacques said she was approaching the level of blade master.

She plastered a grim smile on her face as she fought. Perhaps she *would* be a blade master, but she must drive this scum from her kingdom first.

This troop of *Sis Lenweri* were more skilled fighters than the others had been, but they still lost the skirmish. It merely took longer to defeat them. They all lay dead. Two of Gwaethe's elves were injured, and four of the human soldiers were either dead or wouldn't fight again in this war. She called their corporal over, recognizing him. He'd been Jacques's aide before they settled in Amitania.

"Exmund, isn't it?"

The young soldier smiled at her. "Yes, Princess."

"You fought bravely. Since your sergeant is wounded, I promote you to sergeant and leader of these soldiers. Convey the injured to hospital."

He saluted. "Yes, Princess, thank you, Princess." He turned and detailed men to carry out the task. "If you don't mind me saying, I'd like to stay with you."

Gwaethe frowned at him. Though young, he *was* sensible and might be an asset. She knew he also had basic medic skills.

"You and your remaining men may join us, Sergeant," Gwaethe said. "But see that you keep up!"

She turned to see a stunned look on Syndra's face. "Do you have something to add, Gir Ilirie?"

"Is he not too young for this position, Princess? I don't wish to babysit any soldier, let alone a human."

Exmund must have heard, for he scowled at her.

Gwaethe moved closer. "It's called a field promotion, Syndra. I know this man. Don't presume to judge him or me."

Syndra wilted beneath her words, and she glanced at Exmund. He wiped the smug look off his face when Gwaethe called him over. "Sergeant Exmund, this is Gir Syndra Ilirie, my second-in-command today. You will learn much from her." She fixed Syndra with a stern look. "Gir Ilirie, this is Sergeant Exmund. I expect you to work with him and protect his back."

She nodded, and the two shook hands.

"Congratulations on your field promotion, *Sergeant.*" Syndra turned abruptly and gathered her soldiers with hand gestures, then jogged up the street.

"Don't allow them to get too far ahead, Exmund," Gwaethe said before following.

CHAPTER FOURTEEN

WILDECOAST had seen better times. As he hurried to the king's meeting, Vard wondered what had possessed him to accept the position he now found himself in. Word had come of the attack on Selinore, and the far northern forests were burning. Selinore had been evacuated, and Kain and his people were on the run.

James Tomel strode alongside him. That was another thing he'd readily change. Since being released from the dungeon into Vard's custody, the jeweler had barely left his sight. At night, James inhabited a guarded room close to Vard's. During the day, James was with Vard or under the supervision of a senior ranger. To say the man was unimpressed was an understatement.

Anyway, they would *both* have to make the best of it, though Vard was yet to see how *that* would happen. Even Katrine was furious with the arrangement. It seemed she still blamed Vard for the whole sorry mess and was unhappy that she and James couldn't cohabit. It should be the least of his worries, but Vard didn't need the extra aggravation.

He and James were ushered into the meeting room, and James moved to the corner, where he was pointedly ignored by the king. Also present were the queen, Alique, Nikolas Cosara, Josef Formosa, Ruven Magbalar, Isiloe, Chandrelle, and the various leaders of the army units. He wished Sam could be there as a friendly face, but Esta had just returned from the south, and they were enjoying a family reunion. He shoved down a flash of envy.

"Ah, Lord Anton," Beniel said. "At last. What detained you?"

"I came as quickly as I could, Your Majesty." Vard said.

General Formosa muttered something, but it seemed only Vard heard.

"Please update us, then." The king, face pale, leaned forward on his throne.

"The *Sis Lenweri* have attacked Selinore, My Liege." There was a general murmur of distress in the room, though most would've heard the news. "The northern forests are on fire."

"The great trees?" Isiloe asked.

"I can't be sure, Ramar Isiloe," Vard said. "There were reports of an enchantment to protect them from fire."

The king stood. "Must we speak of this now? I want to hear the reports. Facts, not fairytales."

Isiloe and Chandrelle cast the king dark looks. Vard interrupted before they could speak.

"Yes, Your Majesty. I'll speak with our elven friends later." He raised his brows at Isiloe, and she nodded.

"Rather than wait and be cut off, Prince Arenil withdrew his troops and evacuated the city while there was a lull after the initial attack. Selinore has been abandoned." He paused as the elves in the room gasped their dismay.

"I knew he couldn't be trusted to defend our home."

"The great trees will be no more!"

Ruven held up his hand. "Prince Arenil would have consulted with the elders, especially Rasalar and Elora. I think we should reserve judgement until we speak with eyewitnesses."

Vard nodded at the elven leader.

Isiloe and her sister fell silent, arms folded across their chests. It seemed there was no love lost between the elven women and the former *Sis Lenweri*. Not to mention a deep distrust of Kain Arenil.

"As we speak, Kain and his people are on their way to Amitania. Some of them were already evacuated there—the old and sick, and the children. As far as I know, this first group arrived safely. However, I fear for the more recent evacuees. It won't be easy fleeing and fighting." He kept the worst fact for last.

"There was a dragon involved."

It was news to all but the king, who glared hard at James Tomel.

"Oh, come now," Formosa snapped. "I won't believe in dragons until I see one with my own eyes."

Vard pinned him with his wolfish irises. "You may indeed get your chance."

"*May! May!* You just said there *was* a dragon! Your Majesty, how can you trust these lies? Please, get rid of this imbecile and give me the role of King's Blade. I'll attack Faenwelar and wipe all elven scum from the face of this kingdom."

Three elven knives were at Formosa's throat before he drew another breath.

Ruven's was one of them. "Forgive me for drawing steel in your chamber, Your Majesty," he said, his eyes burning into Formosa's. "But I think your general's words need clarification. Surely he does not refer to *all* elves?"

Formosa did well. He swallowed hard, but held his gaze on Ruven and stayed silent.

"Well, General?" King Beniel said. "Will you confirm you were not referring to our allies? That you meant the *Sis Lenweri*?"

The three knives were still at Formosa's throat. He cleared it. "I meant the *Sis Lenweri*, Sire."

The knives disappeared in a flash.

"Good," Beniel said. "Now we can stop this nonsense and finish the report. What of Amitania?"

"Kain Arenil feared an attack there as well, Your Majesty," Vard said. "He has a means of contacting his sister, Princess Gwaethe Arenil, and she had indicated enemy elven movements in the north. I've had no recent word from them."

There was a knock on the door, and the footman entered, giving Vard a slip of paper. The room was silent as he read it.

He looked up at those gathered. "Amitania is under attack by the *Sis Lenweri*. They have assaulted the walls in five places—and a dragon is involved."

He looked at Formosa. "Still need to see the beast for yourself, General?"

Formosa straightened. "I always like to see things firsthand, Anton."

Vard shook his head and returned to the task at hand. The general was a persistent thorn in his side. "According to this, the enemy used the beast to drop soldiers within the city. The dragon has two mounted enemy who fire arrows from it. It's breathing fire into anything flammable."

One lieutenant spoke up. "How are we to combat that, Lord Anton? I mean, we must surely expect the same tactics to be deployed here?"

Vard nodded. "It seems Faenwelar will attack on many fronts, and I can't see why he would spare Wildecoast. I want our best archers deployed on all towers. Do you agree, General?"

Formosa nodded, as if there were any question he'd fall in with the plan. But Vard needed to be seen consulting the "experts".

"We'll have daily briefings until this war is over," Vard said. "For now, we stick to our organizational plans and beef up the preparation against dragons. Questions?"

None came forward, so Vard dismissed the group except for the elves. Alique remained, too. The queen accompanied King Beniel from the chamber.

Vard turned to his companions. "I understand these are worrying times."

"You understand nothing, King's Blade," Isiloe hissed. Alique placed her hand on Isiloe's arm, and she calmed a little. "I am concerned for my relatives and for the great trees. Alique's husband is pursued by the enemy. Can you not offer more than platitudes?"

"I promise I'll bring you any news I have, Ramar Isiloe," Vard said. "However, it travels slowly, and what we get is usually at least a day late."

"What *do* you know?" Chandrelle asked, her hands clutched together before her.

"There were casualties among the warrior elves, including deaths. Kain wanted to prevent a slaughter of his people and knew if he tried to fight on, he'd lose the opportunity to retreat. The elders consulted with him and agreed to pull out after the first skirmish. He describes a black dragon."

Isiloe's eyes flared at the mention of the beast. "Tell me all you know of it."

"The note was brief. It merely confirmed the existence of a dragon, and its color. Now we know there are at least two. The elders described greater dragons of differing colors. I got word from Brightcastle this morning as well. Alecia has dreamed of four of the beasts—black, green, crimson and golden."

"Can we trust her visions?" Alique asked.

"She's strong in her dreaming," Vard said. "I have faith in her."

"If four dragons come together, it will sorely challenge us," Isiloe said. "We must try to destroy them one at a time."

"Is there no other way but to kill them?" Chandrelle asked. "The dragons have survived for hundreds of years and been no danger to us in that time. It seems a shame to kill such magnificent beasts."

Vard thought the same thing, but as control of the beasts rested with their enemies, the only way he could see around killing them was to convince one of the so-called dragon lords to switch sides. Even then, there was no guarantee all the beasts would be thus neutralized.

"That's a problem for another day, Chandrelle," Isiloe said. "I wish to know more about our loved ones and the great trees."

"Kain mentioned Rasalar, Elora and Melandrach as having been with him when he abandoned Selinore." Vard looked at Alique. "He also said Julli is making you proud."

Alique smiled and nodded. "Julli helped me establish the hospital. Though I suppose that's in ruins now."

Vard took her hand. "Let's not imagine the worst, Lady Alique. It seems we have much to be grateful for regarding Selinore. Many lives have been spared."

"But what about the great trees?" Isiloe asked. "Do you know anything of these protection spells?"

"Only what Kain Arenil said. That the elders and dreamers cast protection spells over the great trees to shield them from burning. Wouldn't the *Sis Lenweri* have as great an attachment to the trees as you do?"

Isiloe's pale eyes flared. "Who would know? I fear the worst after seeing their behavior in Amitania against our people. It is to be hoped they have more regard for the trees than they do for their brethren."

Vard nodded. He could only agree after hearing of the appalling treatment of the *Lenweri* prisoners in the last battle. They'd flogged Princess Gwaethe near to death.

"If that's all, my friends," Vard said, "we have tasks to complete. I'm off to order extra scouts. We must have enough notice of impending invasion."

They nodded and left. That was when he remembered James Tomel, still standing in the corner.

"James," he said.

"You had forgotten I was here, King's Blade," the jeweler said. "It's understandable. I think we both want to forget this."

Vard shrugged. "None of this is ideal, but it was the best outcome I could achieve. I plan to leave you with Vortek for the rest of the day. You'll like him. He's a master of unarmed combat."

James lifted one brow. "I guess I should be grateful I'm still breathing. It just grates that I'm minded like a naughty puppy."

Vard clapped James on the shoulder as they left the room. "Hopefully, it won't last long. Cover yourself in glory during the coming war, and I'll see what I can do afterwards."

After leaving Tomel with Vortek, Vard rode to the edge of the northern forest and shifted into the hawk. He climbed high on the wind currents, higher than an arrow could fly. As usual, he was wary in this form.

The hawk headed north as fast as it could fly and took advantage of the updrafts whenever it could. Conserving energy was essential. When it had flown as far north as it dared, the bird turned and drifted southward, its sharp eye trained on the forest below. Far to the west, smoke cloaked the mountainous forests, but the trees below were clear. Nothing appeared to move, except, here and there, a rabbit or deer.

The forest creatures didn't appear skittish at all. Then the hawk noticed the movement of a clump of branches. What the hawk thought were small pines and spruce were moving across the ground. Its heart beat faster at the sight of the unfamiliar.

As the foliage moved, it left footprints. The hawk let out a shrill cry and swooped lower, careful to remain out of range. An arrow flew at him, but fell short.

He climbed several wing strokes higher and turned to the east and west, examining the northern forests, and spied the same moving trees that sent arrows shooting at him. Abandoning his surveillance, the hawk hastened south toward the keep and relative safety.

Vard morphed back into his human form and walked to his horse. Trax nickered at his appearance. This brave creature had lost its inherent fear of the wolf and bear within him. For that, Vard was grateful. In the past, though compliant, he couldn't have said his mounts had been glad of his company. Trax was not only battle trained, but he had successfully desensitized the stallion to his animal essence.

He smiled and patted the black and white giant, who snorted as an errant feather fluttered to the ground.

"Not much into birds, Trax?" Vard asked as he soothed the horse. "Calm now. We must return to the keep and warn the king of impending invasion." He mounted and trotted off through the trees, reaching the grassy planes north of the city as the sun was three hours past the zenith. Soldiers and trench diggers were hard at work, placing the finishing touches to the defenses.

At the north gate, he spoke to the gate sergeant. Grif had little time for him, thanks to the man's deep admiration for Nikolas Cosara. He saluted and fixed Vard with a hard eye.

"Send word to the king, Sergeant," Vard said. "We'll see action here within the next day and a half, perhaps a little longer. I'll meet him as soon as I speak to the general and my rangers."

"Action, you say, Lord Anton?" the sergeant said. "Looks pretty quiet up there to me. Seems we should be on the road heading to Brightcastle to help with their defense. The elves are closer there than here."

Vard gritted his teeth. "Just send word. Thanks for your input."

As he trotted through the gate and turned for the keep, Vard spied Sam, mounted and in company with Tomel. He beckoned them over.

"Sam, what's James doing with *you?*" He nodded a greeting to the jeweler.

"Vortek had something he needed to do, and Niko said it was fine for me to keep James company."

Oh, did he now? What the hell was Cosara trying to do to him?

"Fine," he said, making a mental note to speak with Vortek about what had been so important as to change his duties without consultation. "He can come with me now. You find Nikolas and tell him to prepare for invasion inside the next two days. We must finish any urgent tasks within a day. Tell him to put all available resources into those assignments. We need to halt training now and get the men to rest up and eat while they can."

Sam saluted and cantered off, leaving Tomel with Vard.

"With me," Vard said, trotting up the street. He could feel the man's angry presence like a dark thundercloud at his right shoulder.

He pulled up at a respectable inn and dismounted. "Come inside with me."

"This is Kat's lodgings."

"Correct. I must speak with her."

The two men entered, and Vard spoke to the innkeeper. He sent one of the serving girls upstairs, and Vard thanked the Goddess that the sorceress was in.

In mere minutes, Katrine arrived in the public room, went straight to her husband, and wrapped her arms around him. Vard averted his gaze, studying the few occupants of the room. They observed the couple with interest. When he looked back, the couple were locked in a passionate kiss.

He cleared his throat. "Take a seat, Katrine, we need to talk."

She sent him a withering look and gave her husband one last kiss. He pulled out a chair for her and seated himself. Vard followed their example. The two held hands as they looked at him.

"The *Sis Lenweri* are in the northern forest, less than two days away."

Katrine gasped and looked at James. "That's why the hounds were howling last night. They were in the forest to hunt and wouldn't stop snarling. They caught nothing either, which is strange."

"The forest is unusually quiet," Vard said. "Perhaps the *Sis Lenweri* have scared the prey off."

"More likely the…" Katrine lowered her voice, "… dragon."

"That's possible. I need you to speak with Hetty as soon as you can. Let her know we're under threat here. She must tell Alecia. Also, if Brightcastle has word from Amitania or the refugees from Selinore, I'd like intelligence from there."

James stiffened. "I have a whole spy network that will only report to me. Allow me to contact my web and see what I can find."

Vard shook his head. "The king will have other networks."

"Not like mine. Please. I can help."

Vard imagined the king's displeasure if he ever found out James was using his network. He hesitated, loathe to use James, but needing information.

"I guarantee His Majesty will never know!"

"You can't possibly say that with any surety," Vard said. "Secrets have a way of coming out." *Especially with Nikolas Cosara sniffing around.*

"Can you afford to dismiss my help?" James fixed Vard with an implacable look. The man could certainly be stubborn.

Vard sighed. The king trusted him to do the right thing and protect Thorius. Trouble was, His Majesty was prejudiced against magic, and anything linked to it.

That was the crux of why James was in this situation. But Vard couldn't allow the king's bias to interfere with the war effort. He just hoped King Beniel never discovered what he was about to do.

"Do you have a second who can move freely and give your orders?" he asked.

James thought for a moment, then nodded. "I have one I was training to step into my shoes. She should be suitable."

Vard nodded. "Good. We'll go now and send word to your second. Where is she?"

"Brightcastle."

Katrine cleared her throat. "I was hoping James and I could spend some time together."

Vard shook his head. "I'm sorry, my lady. That won't be possible."

Her eyes hardened. "This is your fault. I'm sorry I ever clapped eyes on you, *my lord.*"

"Kat," James said, "you know that's not true. It's not Anton's fault that we're embroiled in this mess. I decided not to reveal the dragon attack, and part of the reason was to protect you. If any fault is to be laid, it's on me. And I could have refused to come forward when asked."

"I should never have suggested it," Katrine said, tears welling in her eyes.

James reached for her hand. "This will pass, and the kingdom will again be peaceful. You'll see."

Katrine looked at Vard. "I'm sorry. I don't truly blame you. It's merely my frustration talking." She appeared to want to continue, but shut her mouth and shook her head.

"Thank you for your apology, Katrine," Vard said. "I've done my best on your behalf, and I truly appreciate what you're doing for the kingdom."

He reflected on where he was at this moment, on his responsibilities and concerns. It was a far cry from his life when he first came to Thorius. If King Beniel knew how low he had sunk in the past, *he'd* be the one clapped in irons and thrown in the dungeon.

"We should go," he said, rising from the table.

The couple followed suit, Katrine hugging James and giving him a last kiss. She turned and made her way up the stairs without a backward glance. James watched her until she passed from sight, then accompanied Vard from the inn.

"Your wife is an impressive woman, James," Vard said.

The jeweler drew a deep breath. "We're so different, she and I. I truly don't know how we fell in love. But it works, and I'd do anything for her."

"I think the feeling is mutual," Vard said, mounting his horse.

The unofficially reappointed spymaster smiled. "Let's get to work."

CHAPTER FIFTEEN

ALECIA and Hetty walked together toward the small audience chamber where most of the war councils took place. It was approaching midnight, and Alecia yawned at the thought. But the information Hetty brought was too important to wait until the morning. Katrine had contacted Hetty after dinner tonight to report that Wildecoast was preparing for an attack by the *Sis Lenweri*. They were in the forest to the north of the city.

She sent a quick prayer to the Goddess to protect Vard and turned her thoughts to the matter at hand.

She had asked Ramón to call an emergency war meeting, but how was she going to relay the information without giving away Hetty's involvement?

All she had come up with so far was to say that she or one of the elves had dreamed of it.

The elves might be more believable, but Alecia longed to present the information as coming from her. Then when the note came from Wildecoast, it would prove the accuracy of her premonitions.

More importantly, that would raise her credibility. She was to be queen and queens needed the respect of their supporters. She pulled Hetty over to the first alcove they came to.

"I'm going to say the information came to me in a dream, Lady Henrietta," she whispered. "I know I risk not being believed. But I can use that to my advantage."

Hetty nodded. "You must use all the weapons in your arsenal."

"Just follow my lead," Alecia said and ushered her friend back into the hallway.

They reached the audience hall and entered unannounced. It was too late for footmen to be in attendance. Ramón looked up from a discussion he was having with Estevot and excused himself.

He bowed to Alecia and nodded at Hetty.

"What's this all about, Princess?" He was dressed, but his hair was rumpled as if he had crawled from his bed.

"I've had another premonition."

He groaned quietly. "Not this again. What's happened this time?"

Alecia curbed her anger at his attitude. "Wildecoast is under threat of imminent invasion."

He swallowed and then seemed to gather himself. "Wildecoast? Why would the *Sis Lenweri* attack there? What did you see in this dream?"

Alecia drew in a long breath through her nose. "The elves have disguised themselves under tree branches and are moving through the forest north of the city. They're about a day's march away."

He drew them away from the gathering. "And you're sure of your details?" He shook his head. "Listen to me! How can you be sure of this mumbo jumbo? So far none of your dreams have come true."

"Present this as my premonition, Ramón. I don't care if I look silly. If it's true, you'll be getting a missive from Wildecoast soon." She was about to add more, but Hetty shook her head.

He frowned. "And if I allow you to appear silly, what do we gain by discussing this now?"

"We need to keep moving with our preparations. Get the men back to the trenches, and the smiths to their smithies. Work needs to be occurring around the clock. Focus must shift from training to making sure our supplies and communications are in place."

He nodded. "And there's no loss if it doesn't come true. We'll be better prepared." He led the way back to the assembled guests.

"Thank you all for being here. I know the hour is late, but I believe we have urgent information that can't wait until the morrow." He looked to Alecia. "Princess?"

Alecia joined Ramón at the front of the chamber. She looked at each of the army leaders and organizers. To keep her hands from trembling, she folded them before her. Finally, she took a deep breath and let it slowly out. *Here goes nothing.*

"Some of you know I have dreams that show future events." She paused as her audience muttered and looked at each other. "These have become more frequent lately." *Don't mention the dragons, Alecia.* "This evening, I dreamed of a pending attack on Wildecoast by the *Sis Lenweri*."

She paused again for another wave of angry muttering and sent a quick prayer to the Goddess that this wouldn't fail. "I know most of you won't place any credence in my dreams, but I don't think we can afford to ignore them. The *Sis Lenweri* have attacked Selinore and Amitania. We must not wait a moment longer to complete our preparations."

Alecia allowed those assembled to expend their disgruntlement and disbelief at her words.

"As I said," she continued, "I don't expect you to take my dreams as truth. However, I believe it would be wise to switch our preparation from training and complete our defense plans. I also believe we need to work around the clock to achieve this."

Estevot stepped forward. "With all due respect Princess, My Lord Guardian, we must have more concrete evidence to base our plans on. This kingdom has outlawed magic, and yet the princess asks us to believe that her dreams reveal the future, and that we should act on them." He paused and drew a breath. "Well. I won't do it. That's my final word."

He stepped back and folded his arms across his chest, his jaw set and eyes hard.

Ramón cleared his throat. "Is that how you all feel?"

They talked among themselves, then Estevot stepped forward. "It is, My Lord."

"At the least, we should hasten our preparations," Alecia said. "What harm can it do to finish our trenches and get our supplies into place ahead of time?"

Estevot fixed his skeptical blue eyes on her. "Princess, you may think it can do no harm to work our people around the clock, but we can't afford to exhaust our soldiers and support staff right before an attack. It's still a no."

Ramón dismissed the assembled military, and, when they were alone, he turned to Alecia. "I hate to say it, but I tried to tell you this was a bad idea. Now those men will associate me with your 'strange visions'."

"You'll be fine, Ramón," she said. "I'm certain we'll be hearing from Wildecoast by morning. Then they'll have to eat their words and apologize."

"In the meantime, we've achieved nothing," he said, "except generate rumors of your questionable sanity, and my support of you."

Alecia sighed. "All will be well, you'll see." She frowned. "I suppose there's nothing to be done this night. We must hope that losing a night of preparations doesn't hurt our cause in the long run. Good night, Ramón." She turned and left the chamber, Hetty beside her.

Alecia was out of sorts and tired the next morning when she arrived at the daily council meeting. Hetty had slept with her overnight, and she, too, seemed weary. Both in low spirits, they took seats at the front and nodded to Ramón and Benae as they settled in their chairs. Alecia felt hostile stares from the military leaders, even though she hadn't caught anyone's eye.

Had she done the correct thing last night? Perhaps the people didn't wish for their leaders and royals to exhibit supernatural skills or to mention their belief in them. In fact, she was certain they didn't. The military dealt in hard facts, not dreams and fancies. Even if word came from Wildecoast today that the city prepared for attack, would it change their opinion of her? She suppressed a sigh and tried to settle in her chair. Her gaze met Benae's, and the woman nodded to her. Alecia returned the gesture. What a mess they were in.

As Ramón stood to begin the meeting, two elves entered. One was Alecia's scholar elf, and the other was Ramar Reese, the head of the elven unit in Brightcastle. They sat behind Alecia and Hetty. Ramón raised his brows, but nodded to them in welcome. Who had invited them? Alecia hadn't asked them. She had advised her elven unit that she would keep them up to date with the military effort and preparations. Ramar Reese had seemed happy with that.

Ramón spoke. "Welcome to all and thank you for your attendance. We'll begin with the reports. Estevot?"

Captain Estevot stood and gave a detailed account of the training of his men and women, and the progress of the smiths in weapons and munitions. Alecia was impressed with the man, but he gave her a frosty look as he returned to his seat. Next came two of the sergeants who oversaw logistics and communication. They had almost completed their preparations and incorporated young teenagers into their systems.

Benae explained what had been achieved for the care of the wounded and the creation of medicines. She needed more women and girls to help with medication and bandages. Alecia agreed to recruit more.

Soon it was Alecia's turn to stand before the assemblage and speak. Even though she was proud of what she had accomplished, it didn't help her confidence. How could she be queen if she couldn't even stand before this small group and deliver a speech? She squared her shoulders and began.

"My duties have been varied. I've been liaising with the elven soldiers from Amitania and advising on any additional training they need."

One sergeant sniggered. "Training in how to shoot a dragon in the eye, I suppose," he said. This raised a general laugh from those seated near him.

Alecia felt her face heat. *I must keep my composure.*

Ramar Reese stood and pinned the sergeant with his dark gaze. "We have reports of dragons both in Selinore and Amitania. Should we ignore the threat they pose? Do you wish to wait until one carries you away to believe in their existence?"

Even though Alecia was grateful for his support, she didn't wish for conflict.

The sergeant shot to his feet. "I'd rather believe my own eyes than those of the elves," he snapped, hand on his sword hilt.

Ramón stood. "Please be seated, and remember you're fighting on the same side." His voice was dignified, and Alecia noted how he had matured. Benae's gaze held pride in her husband.

Once Ramar Reese and the sergeant sat, Alecia continued. "As you mentioned, Sergeant, we have been training at archery both with the short bow and the long. Short bow practice has been aimed at small targets, suited to hitting a dragon eye. The elves are proficient now and will be stationed in small groups around the battlefield and on the battlements. Some human soldiers have also volunteered for the training. It has become something of a competition."

"My efforts with the conscripted soldiers have been fruitful. More than half of the dissenters have joined the army and signed contracts. The rest have agreed to help in other areas, such as with the medical units or in the smithy. There are plenty of ways they can help the war effort. Some of them have undertaken basic arms training as part of their paramilitary duties. I've seen to their training myself."

Again, there was a snicker from some attendees. She sighed. Perhaps she didn't need to add that last detail. "And," she went on, getting to the last topic on her report, "we have relocated all the families who were living in the buildings needed for the hospitals and first aid stations. They are living with family, in previously vacant buildings, or nobles have taken them in."

That last statement caused the biggest buzz of all. Her connections with the Brightcastle nobility had proven beneficial in many ways. They possessed resources that could be deployed for the war effort and had dozens of spare rooms going unused—until now. Alecia smiled at Hetty, who nodded. Her friend's eyes held warmth and pride.

She walked back to her chair, breathing a sigh of relief as she sat. Thank the Goddess she could finish on a high note that nobody could laugh at. Hetty patted her hand.

"Well done."

There was a knock at the door, and a footman entered with a note. Alecia's insides jiggled with nerves. Could this be the missive from Wildecoast?

Ramón read it, and his gaze met hers. He turned to his guests.

"I have just received fell news. Wildecoast expects attack today or, at the latest, by dawn tomorrow. The *Sis Lenweri* have been sighted in the northern forests, moving toward the city and trying to cover their presence with foliage. The city is locked down and making its last emergency preparations."

The announcement sent a buzz through the military leaders, most of whom had been there at midnight. More than one looked at her, speculation in their eyes. Oh yes, they were in two minds about her ability now, false though it was on this occasion. Had she done the correct thing in exposing herself? It had achieved nothing last night, and now the influential military men might think her a witch.

She gripped Hetty's hand. "I don't know if I should've announced my dreams last night," she whispered.

Estevot stood. "Is there any mention of dragon sightings, My Lord?"

Ramón shook his head. "Nothing yet. I'm stunned Faenwelar has the numbers to attack on three fronts."

Ramar Reese stood. "No doubt the dragons have helped with that, My Lord."

All heads whipped around to stare at the elven leader with expressions varying from amusement to speculation.

Reese continued. "*I* trust my *Lenweri* leaders when they report dragons," he said, his gaze scanning those gathered. "I urge you to make allowances for the beasts in your preparations. And I advise we push ahead with all haste in securing this city." He sat amid a low buzz of discussion.

Alecia made a mental note to give more responsibility to Reese. He appeared a capable and determined fellow. Ramón clapped his hands.

"We all know what we must do now. We'll meet tomorrow morning if we're able, otherwise I'll use our communication channels to get updates to you."

The meeting broke up, and Alecia stood with Hetty, Ramón, and Benae as the military leaders filed past. Estevot stopped to speak to her.

"I feel an apology is in order, Princess. I was unwilling to believe you last night, but with the recent news from Wildecoast, perhaps it's time to open my mind to things I don't understand."

Alecia nodded. "Like dragons, Captain?"

"Perhaps." He bowed and departed.

Ramar Reese also stopped. "Forgive me, Princess, but I did not hear an apology from the good Captain." His lips curved in the ghost of a smile.

Alecia grinned back. "It doesn't matter, Ramar. It won't be easy for the military to acknowledge their mistakes and change their beliefs. I thank you for your support, though. I appreciate your words about the dragons."

"It makes sense for me to be the one to remind them about dragons. I'm in contact with the other theatres of war, and the beasts *have* been used. It is a fact that can't be denied."

"Well, I'm glad you spoke up. I'd appreciate it if you could be one of my advisors," Alecia said.

Reese bowed. "I would gladly agree to that." He looked like he wanted to say more.

"Is there something else, Ramar?" Alecia asked.

He still hesitated. "Forgive me, Princess, but I got the feeling you had no desire for council from the elves in Brightcastle. You have been somewhat dismissive of us."

Alecia's stomach plummeted. She cast a look at Hetty, who stepped forward.

"Ramar Reese, the princess is open to advice from all areas. If she has given any other impression, she is sorry."

Alecia recovered. "Yes, Lady Henrietta is correct. I'll certainly be more inclusive in future." She smiled at Reese, and he bowed and departed.

Ramón frowned at the elf as he left. "He has a cheek, speaking to you like that."

Alecia was surprised he was offended on her behalf. "Thank you, Ramón."

"On the other hand," he said, "you shouldn't allow Lady Henrietta to speak for you. Surely *you* could've put Reese in his place?"

She should have known his support wouldn't last long. No— perhaps that was unfair. Ramón had always been in her corner, even if sometimes his idea of support annoyed her.

She frowned at him, then bid farewell to Benae, and swept from the room, Hetty in close pursuit. When would this leadership thing ever get easier? Either she was too dismissive, listening to advice too much, letting others speak for her, or taking too much on herself. She shook her head at it all.

Hetty chuckled. "Don't allow them to get under your skin, Princess. You're doing just fine. I shouldn't have stepped in just then, but you looked so lost when you turned to me. I just jumped to your defense. In future, I'll give you more time to answer."

"Thank you, Lady Henrietta," Alecia said.

CHAPTER SIXTEEN

AMITANIA was in chaos. Gwaethe took a moment to rest in the shelter of the western wall. From her refuge, she saw a dragon in the distance, blasting fire into the city. Her heart blazed at the assault. She had never expected to feel so attached to the city after what happened to her here. But the months since her torture and imprisonment had changed this place, made it one where elves and men could live happily.

She sighed. Where was Jacques? If she could only see him for one moment, she could take strength and comfort from that. The attack had begun yesterday at dawn, and it seemed like days had passed instead of only thirty-six hours. The trouble was the fighting continued through the night. Dragons obviously had excellent night vision, as did the elves. However, their human allies struggled during the dark hours.

Gwaethe had fought for half of the night, and Jacques for the other half. They saw each other for a mere twenty minutes to report before assuming command. She closed her eyes, remembering the tenderness of his caress and the love in his eyes. This war could not be the end for them. In her heart, she knew her place was beside this human man, creating a world where all races were valued.

She started, waking suddenly. Had she fallen asleep? *I cannot afford to close my eyes!* She pushed herself up and looked around for the rest of her troop. The area was silent. Off to the east, the clash of swords alerted her to a battle, and she moved down the street, heading in that direction. She felt disoriented after her cat nap and tried to shake herself out of the stupor. Somehow, she must discover where the battle stood.

Suddenly unnerved, she stopped and listened, wondering what had set off her warning bells.

"Well, well, if it isn't the princess herself," a hated voice said.

Gwaethe spun to find Prince Gorin several paces away, sword in hand. He, too, was alone. She peered around for anyone who could assist, but the street was deserted except for the two of them.

She drew her sword, thanking the gods she brandished her long sword, which matched her enemy's weapon. "I've been waiting for this day."

"I doubt that very much, Princess," Gorin said, his lip curling.

"Prepare to die," she said. "You deserve that and much more for what you did to my people."

"Your people?" he said. "What about what I did to you? How did it feel to be whipped in public? I imagine you never thought that would happen to you, the high and mighty Princess Gwaethe Arenil."

Gwaethe lifted her chin and stared him down. The warrior in her would not allow Gorin to see any fear. She held her sword before her, the tip facing her enemy. It did not waver. She held his gaze, determined to be the victor of this fight.

Hoping to surprise him, she attacked with a flurry of blows which he easily deflected. She danced out of reach, feeling for the balance of her sword, and seeking the quiet center of her being. Gorin was good, but she was better. Better, faster, and more agile. She attacked again, this time targeting his armpit. Her opponent deflected her strike and launched one of his own, which she only just escaped.

Gorin laughed as he gathered himself. "This is like fighting a child."

His words, designed to anger her, slid off without hitting their mark. She was a gifted sword fighter, one of the best in the *Lenweri*. Gwaethe attacked in a vicious flurry of strikes, at Gorin's arms, legs and head.

She *was* quicker than him, even though he was stronger. He deflected each attack only just in time. Was he playing with her, or did she truly have his measure? She couldn't afford to underestimate him.

The next attack came from her opponent before she had time to catch her breath. She blocked a strike to the head and one to the legs, but the third clashed against her sword with such force that the weapon flew from her hands.

She hustled away, drawing her dagger, shuffling toward where her sword lay. If she could only reach it, she might pick it up before he was upon her.

"Ha, Princess! I knew you could never hope to match me. Perhaps I will keep you alive and have some fun. It might be entertaining to peel the skin from your body one strip at a time."

Gwaethe shuddered, despite herself, and took another step closer to her sword. Gorin attacked, aiming a vicious blow at her head and chasing her from her own blade. She threw her knife up, and his sword slid down it to the guard. Gwaethe gritted her teeth, her strength ebbing as the seconds ticked by.

"Save yourself, Princess!" Gorin sneered as he shoved her away.

Taken by surprise, Gwaethe fell on her backside, the knife held before her. Gorin stepped closer, his sword at her throat. She forced her gaze up to his and saw her death there.

"What will it be, Princess?" he asked. "Will you change your mind and be my wife? I may be able to talk Father around, even though he wishes your demise."

"I already have a husband," she said through gritted teeth.

"Then prepare to die..."

In a blink of the eye, a knife thudded in Gorin's shoulder. The man staggered back, allowing Gwaethe to roll over and scramble for her sword. She jumped up, ready to fend him off—but he had vanished.

She looked around and saw Exmund, Syndra, and a handful of elves approaching.

Exmund ran to her. "Are you unharmed, Princess?"

"Yes, but who threw that knife?"

Exmund blushed. "We were too far away to save you, so I did the only thing I could. A pity my aim wasn't better. It looked like Gorin."

"It *was* Gorin," Gwaethe growled. "He would have killed me but for you, Sergeant. Thank you."

Exmund nodded. "I only did what had to be done, Princess. You would've found a way to escape the situation."

"Where did he go?" Gwaethe asked.

Syndra pointed at the sky. Gwaethe turned to see a dragon clear the houses two streets over, an elf hanging from a rope underneath it. As she watched, she could have sworn the figure saluted her.

Gwaethe growled. "He is going to wish he had let me kill him this day."

"Princess?" Exmund said. "I think we should continue our patrol along the western wall."

Gwaethe shook herself out of her contemplation. She had come so close to death just now. Jacques would be furious if he knew how foolish she had been. She must be better prepared and keep her troop close by.

"Let us keep this little debacle to ourselves, agreed?" she asked the others. "Lord Vorasava need not be told what happened here today. I am well and will make sure I am always supported in the future."

Syndra and the other elves nodded. Exmund looked troubled.

"I don't like to keep things from Lord Vorasava, Princess."

"Then consider it an order, Exmund." Gwaethe turned and trotted away along the western wall.

* * *

The *Sis Lenweri* had harried Kain and his people since leaving Selinore. And now Gwaethe had confirmed that Amitania was under attack. She had spoken to him last night and reported there were two dragons menacing the city. His sister was never far from his thoughts, not that he had many of them to spare with trying to keep his people safe during repeated attacks from the enemy and their dragon.

He felt like a failure. If he had somewhere to defend, he could turn and fight, perhaps even win. But at present, his soldiers were strung out along the path trying to defend the elders, who were maintaining protection of the surrounding forest. The dragon blasted its fire into the trees all along their flight path, and their magicians were their only hope of surviving an inferno. In the meantime, Kain created strategy on the run, his ears straining for fresh signs of enemy attack, his senses on alert for the next dragon strike.

They were still days away from the safety of Amitania. He'd been trying to take the dragon out of action, but their efforts had been dismal failures. What they needed was respite from battle for even half a day. Then he could gather his soldiers together and form a decent strategy. He was comfortable with strategy on the run, but this was ridiculous. He was exhausted, as was his entire force.

During a brief respite as dark fell at the end of the second day, Kain sat against a tree trunk, eyes closed, trying to clear his mind of thought. The trees intruded, still panicked over the dragon fire. He sent out calming thoughts to them, but it made little difference. To protect his sanity, he shut the tree chatter away and thought of Alique.

"Kain Arenil," Elora's voice forced his eyes open. She and Rasalar stood before him.

"Yes," he said, pushing himself upright. "What is it?"

Elora smiled. "You are tired and dispirited. We thought we might lend you strength." Rasalar nodded.

Kain tried to smile but couldn't. "Thank you, but I'm quite well. We will prevail."

Elora's brow rose. "We need rest from this constant attack, Kain." It was a testimony to her concern that she used his first name only. That was rare amongst elves that weren't related. "We thought it might help to discuss tactics."

He walked off down the fighting lines and bade them follow. "We do need a break. I just don't know how to achieve it. I thought to incapacitate the dragon, but so far have been unable to do that."

Rasalar nodded. "That would certainly help. Our archers will achieve it, eventually."

Kain huffed. "We've already lost two of our best. The longer it takes, the less chance there is." He stopped and closed his eyes, gathering his thoughts, his courage. "I've sent scouts into the forest ahead to find somewhere we can defend. A small hill or ridge would be ideal. There is such a spot closer to Amitania, but I don't think we can wait that long."

"You are correct, Kain Arenil," Rasalar said, her face grave, "we must make a stand within the next day if we are to prevail. We also need shelter for the injured."

"The scouts will continue to search into the night," Kain said. "Perhaps by dawn, we will have an answer."

The elders nodded and left, Rasalar toward the tail and Elora the front. The women must have been ready to drop, but the straight carriage of their shoulders didn't show their fatigue. At the sight, he straightened himself and lifted his chin. He'd follow their example. The dragon flapped overhead, shrieking so loudly the earth trembled. He felt the sound through his body. If only they could disable that thing, they'd have a chance!

Kain moved toward the back of the line, lending help and encouraging words where he could. Before he reached the end, his shoulders ached from swinging his sword and firing his short bow. They were under constant attack, but the enemy's numbers, though troublesome, weren't enough to decimate them. However, over time, they'd wear Kain's elves down. They needed somewhere protected to make a stand.

After a ferocious attack on their tail by the *Sis Lenweri*, the enemy fell back into the forest, and Kain urged his people into a jog toward the middle of their group. They bunched up and kept running, even though they all felt like falling over. The elves were a hardy race and weren't easily daunted, thank the Goddess.

An hour later, near midnight, there still had been no new attack on their convoy. But they kept moving, not daring to rest. A scout appeared on the track before him, and Kain halted, motioning those behind him to keep walking.

"What news?" he asked.

The elf's dark eyes gleamed. "We have found what you seek, Prince Arenil."

"Really?" Kain couldn't believe they might be so fortunate.

"Yes, it is ideal, but we must reach it before the *Sis Lenweri* find it." The elf squatted and drew in the dirt. Kain could barely see in the scant moonlight. "It lies to the north and east of here; a short ridgeline pushed up from the forest floor. It is not high but tall enough. There are caves near the top where the injured can rest. The trees on top are sparse. There may be more chance of hitting the dragon."

More chance of it picking us off one by one, Kain thought.

"How long to reach it?"

"If we hurry, we may be there by dawn. There is a stream between us and the ridge where we can fill the water containers."

"Can we cut straight through the forest from here?"

The scout nodded. "There are two other scouts with me. I will send one each to the tail and the front line to spread the word. Then I will guide you to the game trail that leads to the ridge."

Kain nodded. "Urge extreme quiet."

The scout spoke to his friends and motioned Kain to follow him. After a brief journey along the direction of their flight, the elf leading him stepped onto a narrow game trail that would barely allow the horses to pass. Kain followed and motioned for those closest to accompany him. They moved quickly but quietly into the forest as only elves could. Unfortunately, the *Sis Lenweri* possessed equally excellent sight and hearing. He sighed. It must be enough, whatever they could achieve.

When they were around halfway to the ridge, the dragon shrieked above them. Weary muscles that had screamed in protest got a new energy as they pushed on harder. Kain stepped to the side and urged the elders and wounded past to find shelter on the ridge. He pulled soldiers and archers into fighting ranks to protect the injured and guard their flanks, and sent an advance party to prepare the ridge. His best remaining archers, he sent to the top of the ridge, their goal to seek cover and shoot the dragon.

Kain estimated around half of their force occupied the ridge when the first attack occurred. He'd been about to climb to the summit when shouts and the clash of swords sounded from behind him. Rasalar was at the tail, stubbornly refusing to seek the ridge despite his orders. The forest blazed with dragon fire and the blood-curdling screams of the *Sis Lenweri*. He ran back down the line, hacking at attackers and urging those he freed from battle to flee and take up position on the ridge. As he moved to the tail, he collected a personal guard of perhaps twenty elves. Finally, they made it to the end where Rasalar, protected by her own rag-tag guard, was battling to keep the forest from being torched. She couldn't do it on her own.

"Tell me what to do," Kain said, as his protectors went to work on the enemy.

"You are not skilled, Kain," she said, casting a wild look in his direction as she faced the blaze, palms outstretched.

"Just let me try!"

Kain watched a ripple extend from her fingertips into the trees, and the blaze ebbed, only to gain renewed strength when a wind swept toward them.

"Keep your eyes open," she said. "Open your mind to the trees."

Kain did as directed, also watching for threats from the enemy.

"Ask the trees to provide water. It will gather on their leaves. You must imagine it being swept up and then settling over the flames." Rasalar demonstrated, and Kain saw the wave spread from her hands and settle over the trees.

He opened his mind to the trees and called them to attention.

"Forest Mage!" The call came from all directions. "Save us!"

You must help me save you.

He was swamped with feelings of fear, anger, and worse.

"You are the mage, protect us!"

He shook his head. You have the power within. Release your water. Send it to your leaves. Spread it through the forest.

He felt some of them respond. Gathering his will, he imagined the water droplets lifting and spreading through the forest. He cast his palms outward and saw a ripple as he did so.

Rasalar's eyes widened. "Very good, Kain Arenil. Keep it up."

So, this was what it meant to be a forest mage. He tapped into the trees again and commanded them as before. *You can do more. Release more water and cast it further. Draw water from the earth and send it to your leaves.*

Kain again imagined waves of energy spreading from his fingers and into the trees. This time he saw a mist of rain force its way through the flames. The flames sputtered and died. The trees cheered in his mind.

"Forest mage, forest mage, forest mage!"

Be on your guard. You can protect yourselves. Gather the water and release it if there is smoke. Make your delivery powerful!

At least he hoped the trees could protect themselves. They'd soon see. He turned to Rasalar and found her slumped amongst her guard. Kain helped finish the last few attackers and knelt beside Rasalar. Her eyes fluttered open.

"Kain Arenil, you did very well."

"I had an excellent teacher. What happened to you?"

"A sword glanced my skull. My head is pounding. I am sorry to burden you."

Kain helped her up, but she swayed, and another elf stepped in to help.

"You aren't a burden and never will be." Kain looked at her guard. "Help Elder Rasalar to safety, then half of you form a guard for her. The others report to me on the ridge." He met Rasalar's gaze. "Be well."

Kain turned and jogged with his guard toward the ridge, which, he was pleased to see, had no flames apparent. Smoke hung heavy in the forest. He coughed as he sucked in a deep breath. His group reached the ridge, and he made a quick inspection of the base. A double ring of soldiers guarded it. They had done well.

Melandrach prowled the base of the ridge, his normally dark eyes glowing golden, grey-streaked black hair tangled with sticks and leaves. The elder appeared half wild.

"Are you well, Uncle?" Kain asked, gripping the older man's shoulder.

Melandrach almost snarled at him, his lip lifting to show yellowed teeth. "Of course I am, young pup. You take care of that dragon, and I will see that no enemy reaches the summit."

The older man's eyes blazed with something Kain couldn't name. Something had possessed him. This wasn't his uncle—the calm and sober elder. Melandrach whirled and leapt into the pre-dawn gloom, a cry that became a wolf's howl echoing back at Kain.

Kain stood frozen for a moment, seized by the desire to plunge after his uncle, but then he shook off the spell. He was tired, that was all. Uncle Mel had been taken over by battle rage, not the spirit of a wolf or demon.

He started the climb to the summit, stopping to speak with groups of soldiers and archers stationed in various places. Reaching the two-thirds point, he found the caves where the injured lay. Soldiers guarded them. They performed double duty as protection for the wounded and to prevent the enemy from getting to the summit. Rasalar rested in one cave along with nine others. Julli was tending to her. He pulled her aside.

"How is she?" he asked.

Julli shrugged. "She's still capable of ordering others around, but I think she is deteriorating. I've done the tests Alique taught me several times and…"

He gripped her shoulder. "Just do your best, Julli. No one expects you to perform miracles. I'll find Tuthariel and send him to you."

She nodded and returned to Rasalar while Kain continued to check the rest of the caves at that level. Tuthariel was tending to soldiers who suffered burns in the last attack, so Kain passed on Julli's concerns regarding Rasalar. The old elf nodded, and Kain proceeded to the summit. What he found there surprised him.

The ridge had a flat top with a rock wall running around its edges. Many of the large rocks in the wall had fallen out and tumbled down the ridge, creating dangerous drop offs, but also places where soldiers could see below.

Those who arrived before him had laid canvas or timber across the spaces, forming a shelter from aerial attack. They would be the perfect places from which to fire arrows at the dragon. Several firepits had been lit along the ridge and lookouts were spaced every ten paces around the rim.

The commander was Ramar Lyari Morlynn, one of the stockiest elves Kain had seen. He was shorter than average, with long dark hair braided across his scalp and bird feathers tied to the ends. The elf jogged up to Kain and saluted.

"Ramar Morlynn," Kain said. "Are you responsible for the setup here?"

"Yes, Prince Arenil. Do you approve?"

"Very much so, Ramar. Do you have more suggestions? How will you defend against the dragon when it comes?"

The elf pointed to several spots along the nearby wall. "We have shields which we have placed along the wall. They will help block the flames, though they are small. We intend to disable the dragon before it can do much damage."

Kain admired his optimism. "I hope you're able to do so, Morlynn. What bows are your archers using?"

"A mix of short and long, Your Highness, depending on individual aptitude. Personally, I think the short bows will give us the best chance, but I have always believed in a soldier using the tools he is most comfortable with." "As do I, Ramar. Where do you want me?"

"In the center of the western side, Your Highness. I expect the attack to come from there. Where is your personal guard?"

Kain motioned his soldiers forward, and they occupied the center ground, peering out over the forest as the sun rose behind them. He closed his eyes and opened himself to the trees. They vibrated with a desperate force, not unlike the energy of battle.

"Forest mage, we listen to you. Protect us."

Be on your guard. The dragon will return. You can make it difficult for the beast. Stretch your tallest branches to hinder it.

Kain felt he was a father teaching his children to save themselves. But these ancient trees were older and should be wiser than he.

"Dragon!" The leader of his guard pointed out across the trees to the north, and Kain spied the beast making straight for them.

"Shields or take cover!" Kain shouted. He raised his long bow and took aim, even though the sun had barely poked its head over the horizon. He placed all his thought and focus on the dragon's right eye, not even blinking as the beast loomed closer. The creature's shriek exploded across the ridge, and Kain knew that next would be a blast of deadly fire.

He drew the arrow back to its full extent and released, watching the dart fly true and straight. At the last second, the dragon dipped, and the arrow struck a glancing blow between its eyes. Dark blood sprayed, and the beast shrieked and swerved away to the east, its tail slicing through the air above them. Kain's guard cheered as some of the higher branches seemed to flail against the creature's soft abdomen. It flapped hard and rose to clear the reaching forest.

The dragon shrieked louder, and it sounded like a challenge to Kain. If the beast wasn't angry before, it certainly was now.

"It's coming around for a second sweep, Prince Arenil," Morlynn said. "You will have your chance again."

Kain tracked the beast as it circled to the north and turned south for the ridge. He thought of dipping the arrow tip in oil and setting it aflame, but a burning arrow would be easier for the dragon to see and dodge.

"He's damned agile for his size," Kain muttered, taking his position, and centering himself again. *This is our battle, my friends*, he said to the trees and felt the brush of their consciousness on his mind.

"Forest Mage, we will help this time. Your battle tactics are new to us, but we learn." The trees' words made little sense to Kain, but it didn't matter. This time, he'd hit the dragon's eye. He must, or they'd lose this battle.

The dragon bore down on the ridge, and Kain imagined it trained its eye on him and only him. A worm of fear tried to rise in his gut, but he squashed it with single-minded purpose, nocked an arrow, and drew the string to his ear. He sucked a deep breath as he took aim at the dragon's right eye. In that moment, he felt the beast tap into his soul and a myriad of images rose in his mind. He saw himself mounted on a golden dragon, sword in the air, screaming a challenge at his enemy. The image confused and distracted him.

"Forest mage!" The trees shattered the image, and, as Kain prepared to release the arrow, a fine mist shot skyward, creating a crystalline curtain that caught the rays of the morning sun. Kain could still see the dragon, but the beast slowed and drew its head back. The elf on its withers pointed his sword in Kain's direction and spoke foreign words.

"Saleh ral elrie."

Kain couldn't have cared less what the rider said, but the meaning was clear— attack! He took advantage of the dragon's hesitation and released his arrow. It flew true and straight this time, directly into the beast's eye. Dark blood sprayed, and the dragon screamed in pain. It twisted to the right, then left, and the rider fell to the ridge to be surrounded by *Lenweri*.

Once he saw the rider restrained, his gaze snapped back to the beast he had disabled. It appeared to have lost control of its coordination, its wings and tail carrying it closer to the trees with every flap and sweep. As he watched, the dragon crashed into the forest just east of the ridge. Birds flew squawking. Leaves and branches sprayed up as it carved a path to the forest floor. After a few seconds of twigs crackling, the forest fell silent.

A roar went up from all those on the ridge and many on the ground. Kain moved toward the captured elf, shouting commands as he went.

"Look to the north and east! We still have an enemy to defeat!"

Those around him snapped to attention and drew their weapons, taking their positions on the wall.

The dragon rider was on the ground, being held down by members of Kain's guard. He looked much the worse for wear. Blood poured from a cut on his brow, and it appeared he'd broken the arm and leg on his right side.

"You will pay for this!" he spat. "That beast was one of the most ancient and revered creatures to roam this kingdom."

Kain stood with his hands on his hips and fixed the rider with a stony stare. "Then it's you who'll pay for bringing the dragon against us. Just as the *Sis Lenweri* will pay for killing my father, Orionkael, and disrupting the peace and security of this world."

"You are *weak*, Elrie. Your human blood undermines you. You are unworthy to lead your people or mine. I will see you dead." A half dozen arrows were suddenly trained on the rider's chest.

Kain smiled. "I don't think you're in any condition to make threats. What's your name?"

"Alen Nevarth Pettris," he said, his dark gaze burning into Kain's. "Dragon lord of the *Sis Lenweri*." He laughed. "But that last is unnecessary as you don't have any dragon lords, do you, Elrie?"

"What's this Elrie you call me?" Kain asked.

Ramar Morlynn, slapped his hand on his chest. "It is a derogatory term meaning half-blood, Prince Arenil."

Kain carefully kept his face from displaying emotion. "Names won't hurt me, Alen Pettris. I'm honored to meet a dragon lord." He bowed to his prisoner.

Pettris sneered. "Your honor does not impress me, and neither do the pretty titles your people give you. The only true king of the elves, *Lenweri* and *Sis Lenweri*, is Faenwelar. Soon you will bow before him, but I do not think you will impress him, either." He paused, his eyes narrowed. "He most especially will be furious that you have killed Nugoriem. His name means 'eternal fire', and you have extinguished it."

The dragon lord's words sent guilt rocketing through Kain. He felt the loss of the great dragon keenly, but it had been self-defense. He turned away from the elven lord.

"Take him to the prison cave and guard him closely." He stalked away across the ridge top, trying to block out the elf's accusing words. Morlynn joined him.

"You had no choice, Kain Arenil. Do not take his words to heart."

"My heart is heavy at the loss of a beast which has existed for hundreds of years. They are sentient beings after all."

Morlynn nodded. "Where will you fight?"

"Gather my guard. We'll make our home in the center of this ridge, on the eastern side."

As Kain took his position, a cry rose from below, along with a wolf's howl and the mournful note of a horn. Four long blasts announced the *Sis Lenweri* attack, and the clash of swords followed soon after. Kain thanked the Goddess they had made it to the ridge in time.

"Archers, ready your bows," he called, preparing his own. Soldiers jogged along the line, placing spare arrows behind the bowmen.

The enemy were visible through the trees below. Some had already engaged with the *Lenweri* at the base of the ridge.

"We must reduce the numbers attacking our forces," Kain said. "Shoot the enemy if they're in range, before they engage us. Take out any who make it to the ridge and begin the climb. No enemy will gain this staging ground."

Kain looked at his forces and was content with the steely determination he saw there.

"I repeat," he said, "no enemy will gain this ground."

All on the ridge slapped their chests and turned their attention outward.

Kain joined them, nocked an arrow, drew, and fired.

CHAPTER SEVENTEEN

ALIQUE ground the herbal powder in her mortar as though her life depended on it. Anything to take her mind off what was happening to Kain; to distract her from what Wildecoast was facing. If only she could be sure her husband was alive and well. Surely if anything happened to him, word would be sent. He was an important cog in the wheel of power in the kingdom. Or was he?

As potential king of the *Lenweri*, he was critical to the elves, but what if the kingdom fell to the *Sis Lenweri*? Kain's position, and therefore hers, was precarious until they defeated Faenwelar's forces. And that was by no means a certainty. She shuddered at the thought of dragons coming against them. Dragons! Alique couldn't believe she was contemplating such a thing.

But Vard was certain of their existence, and reports from Selinore and Amitania confirmed they had already seen the beasts in combat. How was Kain supposed to defeat the *Sis Lenweri and* a dragon without even a safe staging ground to protect his troops? She was no soldier, but even she realized it would be difficult to fight while fleeing Selinore.

She swore as the pestle slipped and jammed her finger against the stone of the mortar. As she sucked on her bruised digit, Alique sighed. This was doing her no good, to be giving into her fears like this!

Kain was strong and resourceful, and he'd see his people through, including Julli, her assistant. Alique knew one thing for certain. She should never have fled Selinore. There was no use denying the fact that she had run away. If anything happened to loved ones she left behind, she'd never forgive herself.

Someone stopped in the doorway of the spare kitchen she was using and cleared their throat. Alique turned to find the queen, resplendent in a Zialni crimson, black, and white gown, smiling at her. Alique dipped into a deep curtsey as Adriana approached.

"How goes it, Alique?" The monarch's eyes studied her, seeming not to miss a detail. "You are tired."

Alique smiled. "We're all tired, Your Majesty. There's little time to rest, now that the enemy is on our doorstep."

"If you fall down from exhaustion, how does that help?"

She shrugged. "I'm finding it difficult to sleep."

"Ah…" The queen smiled and nodded. "You are concerned for your husband. That is understandable. You also wish you were with him, but what would that achieve?"

"It would be better than not knowing."

"We will know soon enough. I am worried about my Beniel. It is why I have come to find you. Would you examine him? He looks even grayer than usual today."

"Certainly, I will. And I'll get the doctor to see him, too."

"Mosard has already seen him early this morning. He nods, and shakes his head, and says nothing that makes any sense." She fell silent for a few moments. "I wish Benae were here. I'm sure there is something special about her healing. Have you seen her at work?"

Alique nodded. "I have. She's gifted, and her attention definitely helped the king last time."

"Do you think she's a sorceress?"

Alique had her suspicions about Benae's healing, but she certainly wouldn't call the woman a witch. "Definitely not, Your Majesty. Princess Benae merely has a deep understanding of herbs and of the body systems."

Adriana's eyes narrowed. "Oh really? Then why don't you learn at her side? Then you could be just as talented."

Alique flinched internally. That hurt. She squared her shoulders and faced the queen. "I'm still learning and still recovering from my own serious illness. I don't think I'll ever be hale and healthy again." She clenched her jaw to stop angrier words from spilling forth.

It gratified her to see the queen's gaze drop for a second. "I meant no harm by my comment. It has truly been a difficult time for you. I would deeply appreciate your attention to the king." Adriana turned and left the kitchen.

Alique stared after the monarch, trying to drag her spirits back from the darkness. After all her working and striving to learn medicine, and her struggles to create new remedies to fight the corruption of wounds and the fouling of the lungs, still she must fight for recognition. No, not even that, but defend herself to the queen. Why was she not as talented as Benae? Really? Alique shook her head. She should have stayed with Kain where she was appreciated.

She reflected on all she had learned in the last nine months since moving to Selinore. Yes, it was difficult being isolated and with people she didn't know or understand. But she was beginning to realize that the *Lenweri* had welcomed her and made a place for her in their midst. And she hadn't seen it or been grateful.

She leant on the table, both hands on the wooden edge, her head slumped between her shoulders. Would she get the chance to make right her mistakes?

"Alique Arenil? Are you well?" Isiloe's voice interrupted her self-pity.

She pushed herself erect and turned to face her friend. "I'm well, just regretting a few things."

Isiloe approached, her cool blue eyes assessing. "I worried you would regret leaving your husband. However, it is now too late for misgivings. You cannot return to Selinore. Even if you could, the *Sis Lenweri* will have us boxed in here for some time."

Alique shook her head. "It's not only leaving Kain I regret, though I'm worried about his safety." She had a thought. "Have you heard from Rasalar or Elora?"

Isiloe frowned. "Not a word. All I know is they are somewhere between Selinore and Amitania, and fighting the *Sis Lenweri* as they go. It is a perilous situation. We have heard nothing for over a day."

Alique clutched Isiloe's hands, and the elven woman stiffened. "They must survive, Isiloe. I couldn't live without Kain. He's everything to me, but now he probably thinks he doesn't matter."

Isiloe squeezed Alique's fingers. "Kain Arenil knows you love him, and he knows you have struggled with the move to Selinore. I should not have to tell this to you. There will be nothing to forgive, and you will meet again."

Alique's heart lifted a little at her words. "Thank you. That's very generous, considering how worried you must be about your kin. And here I am, moaning to you!"

Isiloe shrugged. "I am concerned, but there is nothing I can do for now. However, Vard Anton has sent me to ask you to assess King Beniel's health. I don't know why I am suddenly his messenger, but I agreed because I wanted to check on you."

Alique laughed. "And there was no need. The queen was just here asking the same thing. I'll go now."

Isiloe nodded and turned to leave.

"Wait, Isiloe," Alique said, "I'll walk with you for a way." She gathered her basket of herbs and tonics, looped her arm through Isiloe's, and they left the kitchen.

Feeling buoyed by Isiloe's visit, Alique knocked on the door of the king's chamber. It surprised her when Vard answered.

"Lady Alique, I'm relieved you came so quickly."

She entered the antechamber and turned to face Vard as he closed the door. "What has happened?"

"His Majesty has been coughing all night. I fear he needs something extra. I hoped you might help. Benae said you'd have more of the heart strengthening brew she gave him."

Alique nodded. "I have something similar, but I've been working on a new medication for failing hearts. It's something the elven scholars taught me."

Vard's eyes gleamed. There was something about the man that stole her breath and made her lean toward him, even though she was a happily married woman! She'd seen his influence on other female members of court and even amongst the elves.

"That's perfect timing, My Lady. Is it ready to trial on the king?"

"I'd rather not take this gamble, but if I examine him and think it would help, I'll prescribe it if he rests. We must make this clear to him." She fixed Vard with her stern look, and he nodded.

"I'll tell him, but with the *Sis Lenweri* on our doorstep, I don't know if he'll listen. "

"Then make him listen! This is important."

He nodded again and escorted her into the king's bedchamber. Beniel was sitting up in bed at least, but he was deathly pale, and his breathing labored. He opened his eyes and smiled at her.

"Lady Alique! You are a welcome sight! They've told you I am dying, I suppose?"

Alique curtseyed and approached. "I've been told no such thing, Your Majesty. May I examine you?"

Beniel nodded and then started coughing, his body wracked by great spasms that left him weaker. It pleased Alique that no blood appeared on the cloth he coughed into, but quite a deal of frothy fluid came up.

She bent over and placed her listening tube to his chest, then over his lungs. She also checked the color of his gums and felt his pulse, which was weak and fast. Upon completing her examination, she stood back, hands clasped before her. Should she try this new medicine which might give the monarch better quality of life in his last days?

"Well, my dear," the king said, "spit it out, so to speak."

She sighed. "Your heart is failing, My King. The medicine Princess Benae prescribed can help no more."

The king's eyes widened. "But I *can't* be incapacitated. I must be able to ride to battle, to lead the troops. Is there nothing you can give me?"

Alique bit her lower lip. "Your Majesty, you have little time left. It may be measured in days, perhaps weeks. I want you to understand that."

He nodded. "I have come to terms with that fact. By the Goddess, I have. I am fortunate to have had these past weeks, thanks to Princess Benae."

She clasped Beniel's hand. It was forward of her, but seemed right. "I may extend your life a little. I have developed a new medicine in cooperation with the *Lenweri* scholars. They had knowledge of a plant which I've used to formulate a powder. It can make the heart beat more effectively, but it's much stronger medicine than you've had before."

The king's eyes brightened. "Then let's have at it!"

Alique tightened her grip on his fingers to gain his attention. "If we use this medicine, and you respond, you'll feel well for a time. The cough will go, and more energy will return."

"That's exactly what we want!" Beniel said.

Vard interjected. "There's a 'but' coming, I take it."

Alique shot a look sideways at him and nodded.

"You're trying my patience, My Lady," the king snapped, then laid back on his pillows, alarmingly pale.

She huffed out a breath. "The medicine may help, but it will also allow you to exert yourself, and, if you overdo it, your heart could fail completely."

The king closed his eyes, and his throat spasmed as he swallowed.

"I'm sorry, Your Majesty," Alique said. "This can't be easy to hear."

Beniel fixed her with his blue eyes. "I desire to see this kingdom safe before I go. I must take this medicine you have made. The Goddess sent you to me just for this purpose, Lady Alique. Please, prepare it, and I'll be as calm as I can be."

Alique nodded and fetched her basket, removing a stoppered glass bottle. She fetched a teaspoon and filled it with the medicine, then gave it to the king.

"I want you to rest," she said. "I'll be back this evening to supervise your second dose." She curtseyed and left the room, followed by Vard.

"Thank you," he said as he opened the outer door for her. "You saw how much this means to him."

She nodded. "See that he always has a maid with him. Call me if anything changes."

* * *

Vard faced King Beniel after Alique left, appalled at the rapid deterioration of the monarch, but trying not to show his concern.

Beniel broke the silence first. "This is a fine pickle we are in, my friend."

Vard swallowed hard at his last words, "my friend". That Beniel Zialni should consider Vard his friend was one of the highest honors he'd ever received. He pushed the emotion aside.

"We will prevail, My Liege."

"Stop it, Vard. You can see, and I can feel the changes in my body. My heart *is* failing, and I may have only days. We need to speak plainly."

Vard inhaled sharply, then nodded. "Of what would you speak, Majesty?"

The king closed his eyes as if preparing himself, then brought his sharp gaze to rest on Vard. "You love my niece. I need to know—before I depart this world—that you will protect her, along with my great niece."

"That goes without saying, My King. Alecia is more precious to me than my own life. She'd be at my side now, except for her stubbornness."

Beniel nodded. "She *is* that. Tell me, does she still hold the desire to rule this kingdom?"

Vard didn't know if he should honestly reply to that question. Alecia could be charged with treason. And she claimed she'd never move to gain control while Beniel was on the throne.

"Spit it out, man! She's my niece, and I'm dying. I must know where things stand."

"Yes, Alecia still wants to be queen."

"That can never happen," Beniel snapped. "The people won't stand for it. The kingdom is not ready for a ruling queen."

"Even one that comes from the Zialni line?"

"Even that. I'm telling you, Vard—dissuade my niece from this foolish plan. She always was too impulsive for her own good. I know there has been some ugliness about her involvement in revenge killings of mercenaries in Brightcastle. I choose not to believe them as is my prerogative."

Vard remained carefully quiet. How he was to prevent Alecia from pursuing her most heartfelt dream, he had no idea.

"I need your assurances, Vard."

"I'd like to give them to you, My King, but I've already tried to steer her away from her dream. So far, I've been unsuccessful. It's the reason she won't accept my marriage proposal."

The king's eyes widened. "I hadn't heard that! I see you've been more proactive than I realized." He fell silent. "What to do?"

Vard cleared his throat. "Your Majesty, with your health so precarious, I wonder what your plans are for the succession? It seems to me you've boxed yourself into a corner with only one option unless you wish Piotr to step into your shoes."

"I don't wish *that*. He was responsible for the attack at Jiseve's funeral. I know he was. I won't reward that! And where has he been lately? Sneaking around court and avoiding me. If he truly cared, he would be here now."

"Perhaps he thinks he wouldn't be welcome," Vard said.

"He got that right!" The king sent Vard a furtive glance. "What do you think of my great nephew's Guardians? Can they do the job until he is old enough?"

Vard's jaw clenched. "Zorba is untried as a leader. Princess Benae has run only an estate prior to her position in Brightcastle."

"Yes, I know all that. Do you think they are up to running the kingdom?"

"Frankly—no," Vard said, his words clipped. He really didn't wish to undermine Benae and Ramón, but, asked outright, he must give his blunt assessment.

Beniel nodded. "It is the impression I have formed over the last year. Guardian Zorba is a fine man and has a good heart, but I can't see him administering a kingdom. And Princess Benae is a mother. The two of them could care for Brightcastle on behalf of my nephew, but the entire kingdom? No, that will not be wise."

Vard frowned. Not Alecia, not Piotr, and not the Brightcastle Guardians… "Who do you have in mind, My Liege? The queen? I think she'd do an admirable job."

"She would indeed and is perhaps the obvious choice, but, again, she is a woman, and the people will not accept her."

"Then who?" Vard asked. "Again, we seem to be at an impasse, unless you have a son you've been hiding."

The cunning look Beniel gave Vard sent a shiver up his spine. He tapped into his wolf senses, but all that came to him was illness and an aloof musing. Beniel was hiding *something*, that was certain.

"I have no sons that I am aware of, but perhaps someone may be found. Think on the problem for me, please. I depend on you more than you know. You have been loyal in your service. I do not know what I would have done without your stalwart support these last months."

Vard bowed, touched by the king's words, but also unnerved. If Beniel died soon without a smooth transition of leadership, he'd leave Thorius vulnerable.

A power struggle was guaranteed, as Piotr would think himself more suitable to rule than the Guardians. Piotr might also be more capable than Ramón and Benae. He might even demand to raise Solomon, which would leave the child exposed to danger if Piotr was as ruthless as Beniel believed.

A maid arrived. Deep in thought about the state of the Monarchy, Vard left the king to her care. What did Beniel mean by his words, "someone may be found"? If he did have a son hidden away, he'd better find him quickly.

Even that wouldn't solve the problem, however, as an unskilled king could create havoc. Vard shook his head. This wasn't the time for contemplating Beniel's replacement. They had a war to win.

However, all he could see was trouble ahead if the king died with no clear successor.

CHAPTER EIGHTEEN

ALECIA rode with her ladies along the new trenches outside Brightcastle. The forest encroached close to the city walls, so they didn't have the luxury of rows and rows of ditches as Wildecoast would have. However, their barriers were well constructed and deep. The outer row contained sharpened stakes in its base, was wider than a man could jump, and was covered with calico, dirt, and grass.

This first defense was disguised so the enemy would think they were running over flat ground until the calico gave way, and they were impaled on the wooden stakes. Alecia flinched just thinking about such a gruesome death. With difficulty, she shook the unwanted images from her mind and bent her thoughts to more useful ones. Twenty paces separated each trench from the next, and there were narrow spaces where you could enter without having to walk the entire length.

"Well. *I* approve of the design," Arelle said from the back of her black elven mount. "I can't wait for the battle to start. Just our luck Brightcastle has missed out so far."

Kenna nodded. "My thoughts exactly."

Alecia looked over to spy Kenna's foot jiggling in the stirrup. She frowned and turned her head away from her companions. Looking out across the space between the forest and Brightcastle's city wall, she tried to imagine it as it had appeared in many of her dreams. Blood, death, and screams dominated those nightmares, but, on this peaceful, sunny morning, it was difficult to believe it could be so transformed.

"Perhaps the *Sis Lenweri* won't attack Brightcastle," she said, twirling Silver's reins in her hand. The other women went quiet, and she turned to face them.

All four stared at her in disbelief.

"What?"

"You've been urging your involvement for months, and now you say that," Lin said.

Alecia bit into her lower lip. "I was just imagining the slaughter. It makes it even more real when you see the trenches and imagine the fighting. People will die and be maimed, changed forever."

"Princess," Cretia said, "it's too late for thoughts like that now. You've killed men and elves. I thought you'd have been more prepared."

Alecia was taken aback. "Perhaps it's that very fact that has me thinking like this. I've seen men die at my own hands. They were wicked men, but still it hurt something in me. Don't tell me you weren't affected by killing the elves who attacked us on the way to Amitania."

Cretia's eyes dropped, and so did Kenna's and Arelle's. Lin was the only one able to meet her gaze, but she was made of stern stuff and wouldn't back down easily.

"There's no point dwelling on how killing affects one," Lin said. "I just block it out and try not to think about it."

Alecia's eyes snapped to hers. "And you think that will work forever? Let me tell you, it won't. Yes, block those feelings during battle, but, when the fight is over, you must deal with them. If you don't, they'll create a deep pit of despair, and it will consume you."

Cretia laughed, but the sound was hollow. "Oh, Alecia, you're so dramatic at times."

She frowned at the younger girl. "If you think I'm being dramatic, you're wrong." She fixed each of her ladies with a penetrating look. They met her gaze, but only Lin appeared comfortable. *Uncompromising.*

Their talk was halted by Captain Estevot, who rode toward them in the company of Ramón and Ramar Reese.

"Now there's a sight for sore eyes," Lin purred.

Alecia examined the three, wondering whom Lin referred to.

"I'll say," Kenna said. "I'd have any of them any day." She seemed to reconsider. "Perhaps all three at once." Her tongue flicked out to moisten her lips.

Alecia stifled a gasp. "Kenna! Mind your words," she whispered. "There'll be no foursomes, especially not with Ramón."

"Ooh, Princess," Kenna said, "saving him for yourself? That's fine. I'll settle for just the two then. Benae doesn't seem the type to share, anyway."

"Princess Benae to you, Kenna," Lin said. "Now, mind your manners—here they come."

Alecia's face burned as the men rode up. She couldn't help but imagine Kenna in bed with them. No matter how she tried, she couldn't banish the images. *Great!* she thought sarcastically.

Ramón addressed them. "Ladies, Princess." He bowed from his saddle. "Good morning." His gaze flicked to Alecia. "Are you well, Princess? You appear to have taken too much sun. Your cheeks are quite flushed."

To her extreme embarrassment, the others giggled. She glared at them and turned back to Ramón.

"I'm quite fine, My Lord. It's a little warm out here, don't you think?"

He raised a brow. *Fabulous...* He knew she was deceiving him. Somehow, he *always* knew! Time to change the subject.

"We were just inspecting the trenches," Alecia said. "I'm impressed with what I see."

Estevot nodded. "Thank you, Your Highness. I'm so pleased they meet with your approval."

She studied the captain, hearing more than a hint of sarcasm, but finding no disrespect on his face. She nodded. "Please convey my thanks to those who dug the trenches and to the designers."

Estevot's brow shot up. "*I* designed them, Your Highness. And I'm sure it's not necessary to thank the builders. They're merely doing their jobs."

Alecia's spine stiffened. "Thank them anyway. I find workers are always happier when graced with words of appreciation."

Estevot appeared bemused, but nodded, pressing his lips together as though forcibly preventing any more conversation. Likely he didn't agree with her, but he'd find a need to adjust when she was queen. She smiled to herself and caught Ramón's eye. He positively scowled at her.

"And Ramar Reese," she said, "how go *your* preparations?"

Reese bowed his head. "Very well, Princess. All is in readiness for the *Sis Lenweri* and whatever they bring against us." He fixed her with a glance that spoke volumes, and she was grateful he hadn't mentioned the dragons. It had been his task to prepare the archers for dragon attack, but there was no need to refer to it again in front of the doubtful Estevot.

Ramón turned to his companions. "You go ahead, gentlemen. I'll escort the ladies for the rest of their inspection."

Estevot and Reese rode off with polite nods to the ladies. Alecia kicked Silver forward, and Ramón trotted up beside her, leaving the other ladies behind.

"What are you up to?" he muttered.

She turned to him with wide eyes. "Can't I inspect the work of our soldiers, Ramón? I need to see our preparations, so I can determine if they're adequate. From there I can help with adjustments to battle strategies."

Ramón rolled his eyes. "You're not responsible for strategic planning. When are you going to understand that?"

"When will *you* understand that this is my home, and my family is the ruling family? I should be heir to the throne, not Solomon." She hurried on. "Not that I begrudge him being heir, but he's an infant, decades from being able to rule." Actually, if the child was Ramón's, Alecia *did* begrudge him being heir, but she'd hold that card close to her chest for later.

"That's where Benae and I come in. How many times does it need to be said? King Beniel made us Guardians of Brightcastle."

Alecia jumped on that. "So—you'll follow the instructions of the king?"

"Of course."

"And what if something should happen to Uncle Beniel? He's not well. Are you ready to rule the kingdom for at least eighteen years until Solomon comes of age?"

Ramón nodded. "If necessary. You know all this, Alecia."

"You're wrong. You and Benae are Guardians of Solomon and Brightcastle, but ruling an entire kingdom is a very different matter."

Ramón huffed. "That's why one has advisors." He paused, his tight jaw gradually relaxing. "Listen, Alecia, don't worry. All will be well."

She pursed her lips and released a frustrated breath. "I'm not a child who needs to be reassured. It's you who must defend yourself if anything happens to Uncle Beniel. Prepare for opposition." She snapped her mouth shut to stop more hasty words from leaking out. Talk about giving Ramón fair warning!

He pulled his horse up and grabbed her reins to stop her. The ladies behind stopped, too. "What do you mean by opposition? You? Do you have plans to remove your uncle?"

"I'd never move against my uncle! I hope he lives a long and healthy life." *Especially if you and Benae are the alternative rulers!* "However, I'll not be your only opposition if my uncle's heart fails, or he dies in battle. With the inheritance of the kingdom so precarious, you may find several challengers stepping up." She fixed him with a determined look. "And believe me—I *will* be one of them."

Ramón's blue eyes turned icy, and his fists bunched in the reins. "At least I know where you stand."

Alecia held his stare, but spoke to her ladies. "I think we've seen enough of the preparations. Let's return to see if Princess Benae needs any help." She raised her eyebrow at Ramón, pulled her horse around, and galloped off, her ladies hot on her heels.

"Why did you antagonize the Guardian?" Lin asked, as they entered Brightcastle and turned toward the field hospitals. "I thought you were trying to lull him into a false sense of security?"

Alecia sighed. "He made me angry. I'm sick of being treated by men as though I'm useful for nothing. Did you see Estevot? He could barely hold in his mocking smirk. And Ramón… well, I can't come to terms with him ruling Brightcastle, let alone Thorius. It's not right!"

"Right or not, King Beniel appointed him and Benae as Guardians for Brightcastle, and Solomon, his heir. I think you should at least hold your tongue. It does no good to fight with them."

Alecia raised her chin. She would not be lectured! Even though Lin was one of her advisors, she didn't have all the information. More and more Alecia felt Ramón and Benae were usurpers, especially if Solomon wasn't Jiseve's son. At best, they should be advisors or administrators. She shook her head, trying to disperse the mist of anger that settled on her. Silver tossed her head, too. She smiled at the mare.

"I see your point and thank you for your advice," she said through clenched teeth, and Lin knew it if her raised brow was anything to go by.

Wisely, her second only nodded. "Let's do as you suggested and see if Princess Benae needs anything for her hospitals."

They dismounted outside the first infirmary and sought the princess, finding her three buildings away, supervising the preparation of medications and bandages. Despite her feelings for Benae, her organization of the medical facilities impressed Alecia. Neat rows of pallets were housed in each building which had formerly been houses. Alecia had helped rehouse the occupants of the seized buildings and smoothed over the upset tenants. Some of her supporters amongst the nobility had taken in families and given them work.

"You've done wonders, Benae," she said, taking a tentative sniff at the contents of a bowl.

Benae paused and wiped her hands on her apron. "Thank you, Alecia. This has always been my passion, so it's easy to find motivation. These homes have been ideal for the purpose."

"I saw the surgery. Do you have surgical skills?"

Benae grimaced. "Some. I have several field surgeons helping me. And even some of the town dentists have volunteered their services.

Many of the displaced mothers have come for nurse training. I think they wish to see that we look after their homes."

Alecia smiled. "Thank you for allowing them to do that. Is there anything else you need?"

"I don't think we have enough stretcher bearers. If you could send me two dozen more men and strong women, that would be helpful. They should have weapons training as they could face attack while bringing injured in."

Alecia nodded. "Of course."

Kenna stepped forward. "If you don't mind the suggestion, Princess," she said to Alecia. "I can organize the bearers. I have an idea where I can find them."

Alecia agreed, and Benae smiled in thanks. The Guardian drew Alecia away from the other ladies.

"I wanted to thank you for all you've done," Benae said, hands clasped before her.

"There's no need. These are my people."

"There *is* a need. You could've blocked my attempts to help."

Alecia shook her head. "Why would I do that? This is war. We must put aside all disagreements for the good of the kingdom." She fixed Benae with a stern gaze. "I haven't forgotten my animosity, merely set it aside for a later time."

"You can do that?"

"I'll do anything for Brightcastle and Thorius." She could've said more, but had learned from her earlier encounter with Ramón.

Benae nodded. "I'll let you know if there's anything else I need." She returned to her medication preparation, and Alecia ushered her ladies out.

As they exited the building and retraced their steps to their mounts, a handsome blonde noblewoman, dressed all in black, stepped in front of Alecia.

"Please excuse me, Princess. I need to speak with you." She pressed a small square of parchment into Alecia's palm. "Can you meet me here immediately?" Turning abruptly, she strode across the street and between two buildings.

"What was that about?" Lin asked.

"She asked to meet me at The Dancing Lion." Alecia showed Lin the note.

"You aren't going?"

"It was a strange encounter, don't you think?" Alecia asked. "I need to find out what Lady Stenmore wants. I got a funny feeling when she was near."

Cretia gasped. "All the more reason to ignore her request!"

Alecia shook her head. "I'm going, and you all need to come with me."

"The Dancing Lion is frequented by mercenaries and other unsavory types, Princess," Lin said. "We'll stick out like roses in a weedy garden."

They reached their mounts, and Alecia climbed onto Silver.

"Let's go. The sooner we meet her, the sooner we'll find out what she wants." Amidst grumbles from her ladies, Alecia led the way to The Dancing Lion.

Kenna eyed the rendezvous venue doubtfully as she tied her cream mare to the hitching rail.

"How did you know where to find this place?"

Alecia returned her a mysterious smile. "I know many things a princess isn't supposed to know." She turned to Lin. "Are you familiar with Melanis Stenmore?"

Lin nodded. "She was widowed over two years ago and is still in mourning, though I heard she enjoyed a liaison with the master jeweler from Wildecoast recently. There was word that the two almost married."

"Indeed!" Alecia said. "James Tomel?"

"I believe so."

"Is there anything else I should know?"

Lin shook her head.

"Let's go and find her then."

Kenna and Arelle led the way, with Alecia behind them, and Cretia and Lin behind her. The five women stepped through the doors to the establishment and paused just inside. The room went quiet as all the occupants eyed them.

As Alecia looked for Lady Stenmore, the innkeeper approached Kenna and Arelle.

"This isn't the place to bring your mistress," the man said.

"We've been asked to meet a noblewoman here," Kenna said firmly, arms folded across her chest. "Have you seen her? She's dressed in black."

"Oh…" The man stepped closer. "She arrived a little while ago. She's in the private dining room. Follow me."

Kenna turned to Alecia, brows raised, and Alecia nodded. The five of them followed the barkeep down the hall to a door on the left. He knocked and stuck his head in, then pushed the door open for the ladies.

"I'll bring you mulled wine and something for luncheon."

"Just the wine, Innkeeper," Alecia said. "We won't be staying long."

Alecia gulped at the state of the so-called "private dining room". Stains marred the whitewash on the walls, and the floor hadn't known fresh reeds in months. A cockroach almost the size of a mouse scuttled away as she took a step toward the table in the center of the room.

Melanis Stenmore sat at the table, hands clasped in her lap. Alecia advanced to join the young widow while the other ladies stood by the door.

"What do you want?" Alecia asked, flinching at the abruptness of her tone.

Lady Stenmore's brow rose, and her eyes widened just a touch. "Information. I thought you may know of the whereabouts of James Tomel?"

"Why would I know that, Lady Stenmore?"

She shrugged. "Just a hunch I had."

Alecia scowled. "Well, I have no idea. Why all the subterfuge? You could've asked me those questions outside the field hospital."

"There are subjects you don't discuss in public."

"Like?"

Lady Stenmore took a deep breath through her nose. "Spying. James Tomel is a spymaster for the king, but, over the last few days, he's gone quiet. And today, someone I rarely hear from contacted me to advise I was now in charge of Tomel's network."

Though security of the spy network *was* important, Alecia really didn't see the significance of this when they were at war with *Sis Lenweri*.

She shuddered at the thought of the grimy world of espionage. She had suspected that James Tomel was responsible for intelligence gathering, but not that he was the master. It was just luck that she knew of the man, having met him by chance at the castle when Hetty was ill. He'd been far too interested in Vard for her liking. He was also linked to Katrine Aranati.

"I'm afraid I can't help at this time. If I learn anything, how can I contact you?"

Melanis reached into her reticule and withdrew another sheet of parchment, handing it to Alecia. Her eyes flickered to the ladies near the door. "This stays between you and me. I'm taking a risk even speaking to you, so the fewer people who know what we discussed, the better. I just hoped you might know what happened to James."

Alecia nodded as she tucked the note into her bodice. "I'll let you know if I discover anything." She paused as an idea came to her. "Are you helping with the war effort, Lady Stenmore?"

The woman frowned and raised her chin. "I've taken in a family that was displaced to cater for the field hospitals. I've also donated food and fuel from my household stores and estates."

Alecia nodded. "Very good. Thank you for your help. I'll let you know if I think of anything else you can do."

She turned and gathered her ladies, leaving the inn in quick time. As they emerged into the street, Alecia felt like a weight lifted from her shoulders. She felt grubby just entering under the roof and couldn't help remembering the night when she had killed "The Devil". It felt like another life.

Lin squeezed her shoulder. "Are you well?"

She took a deep breath. "I will be when we escape this place. It has terrible memories for me."

"What did Lady Stenmore want?" Lin asked.

"I'd rather not tell you yet," Alecia said. "She asked me to be discreet, and I agreed for now."

Lin's eyes widened. "That's not a good idea. You shouldn't keep secrets from us."

"She wanted to know if I knew the whereabouts of the king's spymaster."

"And do you?"

Alecia huffed. "Of course not!"

Lin fell quiet as they mounted their horses. Alecia was glad her second didn't ask further questions. Such as who that spymaster was. She didn't know how Lady Stenmore's involvement was important. Perhaps it wasn't. Perhaps the woman only wished to check on the health of her friend or ensure she wasn't giving the wrong person information.

As she returned to the castle, Alecia mused on the missing spymaster and the role Melanis Stenmore now occupied in the realm of intelligence gathering.

CHAPTER NINETEEN

J ACQUES ran a *Sis Lenweri* soldier through with his sword, then spun to engage another enemy fighter. "To me! To me!" He called to his guards and was relieved to see them respond after disengaging from their various battles. They couldn't win, fragmented as they were.

He caught the eye of his second in command. "Where are all the blighters coming from, Dodlan?" It was a comfort to have the stalwart sergeant guarding his back.

"Don't know, My Lord, but we must be close to victory by the savagery of their attack."

Jacques returned a wicked grin. "A good way of looking at it." He engaged another enemy elf, who sneered at him with maniacal glee and attacked with insane ferocity. Jacques was hard pressed for a time until he learned the enemy's weakness. He spotted an opening and ended the fight, wiping his blade on his adversary's shirt.

He looked up and found his guard finishing the last two *Sis Lenweri*. Casting around the immediate area, he saw Dodlan slumped over an elven body.

Jacques hurried to his second, heart in his mouth.

"Dodlan?" He placed his hand on the man's shoulder but got no response. Pulling Dodlan up from his slumped position, he saw the man's hands grasped a bloody gash in his belly. Lifeless eyes looked up from a pale face. He was dead.

Shock and dismay washed over Jacques. He rolled the man on his back and closed his eyes. "Know your sacrifice was not in vain, my friend—we will win," he whispered sorrowfully.

"Jacques!"

"My Lord!"

Two familiar voices broke him from his observance. Gwaethe had found him! And Exmund.

He stood to greet them and gave Gwaethe a brief hug. Exmund knelt beside Dodlan, checking for signs of life.

"No need, Corporal. He's dead."

Exmund nodded. "He was a good man, the best. I'm sorry, Sir." He rose and motioned for those present to gather the dead and wounded.

Jacques looked at Gwaethe and raised his brows.

"I gave Exmund a field promotion. He is now Sergeant." Her gaze bathed him with regret. "I'm sorry, my love," she whispered. "I know Dodlan was your friend."

Jacques squeezed her hands and nodded. "He was. Damn this war, and damn Faenwelar. We're going to kill that bastard if it's the last thing we do."

"And Gorin," Gwaethe said. "Don't forget him."

He examined her closer. "Are you well? You seem…jittery." Gwaethe was rarely unsettled, but something had upset her more than usual.

"I will tell you after we win, Husband, and not before."

A horn sounded from the east, followed by another from the south.

Jacques examined the surrounding area, as well as the sky. He spotted the red dragon flying south over the eastern part of Amitania.

"I think they're retreating," he said, pointing. "Where's the other beast? Or did one of our archers succeed in downing it?"

Exmund pointed to the south. "No Sir, there's the green."

"No!" Gwaethe said, "stay and fight, you cowards!" She stood watching the dragons leave, and then turned and ran into the city.

"Follow me," Jacques said to his men. "Exmund, you stay with your team and sort this out, then find us."

Exmund nodded and turned away while Jacques jogged after Gwaethe, trying to keep her in his sights. At least twenty of their combined guards were with him. He sent some elven members forward. "See if you can keep up with her."

They encountered two pockets of the enemy as they followed Gwaethe. Jacques engaged them, even though he was desperate to catch his love. He fought like a demon, as did his guard, and they lost another two members with several injured. In their desperation, they left the bodies of the fallen unattended.

When Jacques finally caught up with Gwaethe, she was at the top of the tallest tower in Amitania, her arms resting on the ledge of one of the south-facing windows. He came up behind her and circled his arms around her belly, resting his chin on her right shoulder.

"Thank the Goddess, you're safe," he said.

She leaned her head against his. "I'm sorry I ran." She pointed. "The *Sis Lenweri* forces are headed south. The cowards didn't even finish their fight here. Looks like they will attack Brightcastle next."

"Yes, they have more soldiers than we ever thought," Jacques said. "But not enough to win. I believe Faenwelar has badly miscalculated, and that's why he has abandoned Amitania. His plan seemed to be to neutralize Selinore and Amitania before attacking the human capitals."

Gwaethe turned to face him. "We need to marshal our forces and follow them as soon as we can. We'll leave a small force here to protect the citizens. I'll contact Kain and get him to detour to Brightcastle." She kissed him and went to leave, but he held her for a moment longer, kissing her lingeringly.

When they parted, Jacques brushed her cheek with the backs of his fingers. "You contact Kain, I'll set about gathering those who can march with us."

She nodded and dashed down the stairs while he followed at a more human pace. What he needed was a day of rest, but it appeared he wasn't getting that anytime soon.

* * *

Kain sagged against the rock ringing the ridge where they'd made their stand. He was beyond exhausted. He closed his eyes, turning his thoughts inward to check on the trees.

"Kain Arenil!" A voice roused him, and he realized he had fallen asleep. Berating himself for his weakness, he climbed to his feet and greeted the commander of the lower forces. If Kain was tired, this elf must be even more so, but his eyes were bright despite the dirt and blood that caked his face.

"Yes, Ramar, what is it?"

The elven leader clapped a hand on his chest, and Kain returned the salute. "We have won the day. The enemy has sounded the retreat. Do you wish for us to harry and finish them?"

Kain stared, unable to believe it was over for now. "Were any of the *Sis Lenweri* nobility among them?"

"No, the only one of importance I have seen is the dragon lord already in our custody."

"How many do you estimate remain of the attacking force?"

"It is difficult to be accurate, but I would say less than fifty. And many of them are injured. They made their retreat in desperation to save themselves, not to reorganize and press back."

"Then we'll let them go. Tell the soldiers to stand down. You did well, Ramar."

The elf nodded. "As did you. Without the cover from above, we would never have prevailed. This ridge was fortuitous. It was a gift to have the wall at our backs, and you above us."

Morlynn jogged up and saluted. He appeared to be none the worse for wear.

"Kain Arenil, are you well?"

"Yes, of course. Congratulations. We won the day, and you let no enemy on this ridge, apart from the injured flier. That doesn't count."

Morlynn nodded. "Thank you. When I saw you with eyes closed, I worried you had been hit."

Kain grimaced. "Don't forget I'm half-human. I was merely resting my eyes." *Hah, resting his eyes, indeed.*

Morlynn grinned, but the base commander frowned. Kain addressed the base leader.

"Have as many of our dead buried as possible. We can't spare the time to deal with the bodies of our enemies, even though I know you'd like to." He added the last as he saw Morlynn open his mouth. "Any of ours we can't bury, we'll take with us and honor on the march. At each rest, we'll detail a burial squad. Hopefully, we can have them all farewelled within the day."

The two leaders nodded.

Morlynn looked out across the forest. "There are plentiful rocks. Instead of burying, we can lay the bodies out and cover them with the rocks. It will be quicker."

Kain looked at the other commander, who nodded.

"I'm happy with that," Kain said, "as long as it meets with the elders' approval."

"All will be well." Morlynn and the other leader saluted and left to see to their duties.

Kain sent those on the ridge to gather the injured and take them to the healers.

Two elves arrived from below to stoke the fire and make a meal for their group. Kain could smell the cooking food from other campfires below.

He smiled at the small piece of normality that had returned to their lives after the fear of battle.

A little while later, Elora joined him, and they sat on a rock eating the simple, yet delicious meal.

"How is Rasalar?" he asked.

Her sad eyes met his. "I do not think she will recover. Her head has been too damaged. But there is always hope."

"Have faith the healers will bring her back. We need her wisdom."

"Perhaps she has completed her task, Kain," Elora said. "Perhaps playing her part in allowing us to reach this ridge and defend it was the task for which she was born. We have much to thank her for."

"Perhaps. However, I like to think that we are born to achieve more than one task, Elora."

She cocked her head to the side and regarded him as if he were a strange bird, then returned to her dinner. They ate in companionable silence until the meal was over, then Elora rose. Kain also stood.

"I will leave you now, Kain Arenil. You have much to attend to, as have I." She bowed her head, and he returned the gesture. "I assume we march at first light?"

"Yes, Elora. I thought we could enjoy a night's rest before setting out. To tell the truth, we all need more, but we can't risk the delay." A buzzing popped into his head, and then a voice.

Kain! We must talk!

He excused himself and walked away to a more private place, seating himself on a rock.

What is it? Are you well?

Her voice sounded irritated. *Yes! We are leaving Amitania, following the scum who attacked us. It appears they march on Brightcastle or Wildecoast. How fare you?*

Kain closed his eyes and inhaled a leisurely breath. Good question.

Our battle is over, and most of the enemy dead. The rest fled into the forest with no leadership. I can't spare the soldiers to pursue them, as much as it hurts. We downed a dragon and have its rider in custody.

The dragon is dead? You must check for signs of life. I have heard they can place themselves into suspended animation to lower their needs for sustenance and can magically heal.

I'll check it out, but I shot it through the eye, so I'm confident it won't be a threat.

Just check! When do you march?

At dawn.

Head to Brightcastle and bring the injured with you. They may heal and be useful. I hope we may meet soon.

I agree with your plan, Sister. Do nothing foolish.

An angry spike came through his amulet before her presence vanished. Kain smiled.

As much as he had resisted Gwaethe and her relationship to him at the start, he'd now come to appreciate her in his life. She brought a richness of experience he never would've enjoyed if he hadn't embraced his elven heritage. Now all he must do was to convince Alique of that.

Kain did the rounds of the camp to ensure the assigned tasks were proceeding. At the base of the ridge, he found Melandrach seated by a fire.

A wave of relief swamped Kain as he observed his uncle had returned to relative normality. His hair was still wild but the eyes he lifted to Kain were without the gold he had witnessed that morning.

"My congratulations, High Prince." Melandrach's dark eyes flicked away and then returned to Kain. "I apologize if my earlier behavior disconcerted you. Sometimes the battle rage hits hard."

Kain had witnessed battle rage and he didn't think his uncle had been suffering from it. Also, there was the howl of the wolf but Kain didn't want to think what it might mean.

"All is well, Uncle. I'm glad you are more yourself. Thank you for your efforts this day. We leave at first light."

He went in search of the dragon, using the walk to rid himself of the mental picture of Melandrach, overcome by madness. Having memorized the trajectory of the dragon's fall from the sky, Kain soon found the beast. He approached cautiously, hearing Gwaethe's warning in his head.

The magnificent creature had crashed into a relatively open patch of woodland. It was massive, the body easily the size of a modest house. Its black scales glistened in the late afternoon sun. They were iridescent, reflecting all the colors of the rainbow. Kain was struck by sadness he hadn't expected to feel. Nugoriem had existed for centuries, and he had ended the proud dragon's life. He appeared to have sustained minimal damage in the fall, including the wings which were folded against his back.

He walked up to the head, which was almost as tall as he was, and tentatively laid his hand over one nostril. "I'm sorry, Nugoriem, even if your master has cursed me for killing you."

He jumped as a deep, gravelly voice rumbled in his head.

Typical human!

Kain swallowed hard. Am I going insane now? Perhaps I'm more tired than I think.

He looked up at the wound he had caused and flinched. The arrow protruded from the socket and flies buzzed around a blob of gore that clung to the lower lid.

Kain made his way around the beast, walking past the right shoulder to the ribcage and carefully laying his ear against the chest wall. He should be able to hear the heartbeat if Nugoriem was still alive. He heard nothing. Continuing down the right side, he stepped across the tail, where it was narrow enough to do so, and made his way up the left side. Again, he heard no heartbeat.

When he had finished his inspection, Kain stood several paces in front of the nose of the beast and looked up again at the killing wound. He inhaled a sharp breath at the sight.

The arrow has vanished. Where there had been blood and gore, a partially healed wound remained. He rubbed his eyes and looked again.

Oh, I really am tired. I can't be seeing what I think I am.

The gravelly voice filled his head again. *The magic you carry has augmented my healing, human.*

He looked up at the dragon's undamaged eye. It remained closed. He scratched the side of his face as his heartbeat kicked up several notches. Tentatively, he reached for his mind speak and sent it out. *Nugoriem?*

No response. Next, he closed his eyes and sent his senses into the dragon as he would if he were speaking to the trees. He hit a wall there. Time was wasting. His body called for rest and concentrating had leached what little energy he had left. But something strange was occurring here. A dead body couldn't heal, not if it followed the laws of nature. Even a magical being that was dead wouldn't heal.

So, either this beast was dead, and he was hallucinating, or there was life and magic at work. He'd check again in the morning. For now, it was time to curl up in his cloak and shut his eyes.

Kain turned away. He had taken two steps when the voice sounded again.

Thank you for your healing, Elrie. When I am whole, you and I shall meet again.

He spun back, but the body of the dragon lay just as it had upon his arrival. The wound was sealed, and no blood dripped, but nothing else had changed. He rubbed his eyes and forehead, and shook his head, trying to dispel the lethargy that cloaked him. It was no good. He was spent, too tired to solve this puzzle.

He tentatively sent out his mind speak. *If you can hear me, Nugoriem, know that what I did was in self-defense. I bear you no ill will. Rest easy.*

As Kain walked away, a laugh like a distant echo shook his body. He kept walking, determined to return to camp and take the next step in their defeat of the *Sis Lenweri*.

CHAPTER TWENTY

THE *Sis Lenweri* would attack Wildecoast at dawn. Kingdom troops had moved into place under the cover of darkness and were now spread across the grassy field to the north of the city. The front-line troops would form a shield wall when the enemy charged and attack the *Sis Lenweri* through gaps in the wall.

Reserve soldiers gathered in three groups, in the center and on each flank. Archers accompanied them, and the foot soldiers had three functions: to attack the enemy, defend the archers, and take the place of fallen front line troops.

Vard's hawk had flown over the enemy encampment north of the city during the evening hours and noted their preparations. All was in readiness for them in Wildecoast.

The king had risen from his sick bed, declaring he felt better than he had in years. He had donned his armor, determined to take part in the fighting. That was what made Vard most nervous. They couldn't risk the king in this battle.

Shaking off fears of losing their leader, Vard strode the length of the north-facing battlements, partly transforming into the hawk to take advantage of the bird's vision. There! Movement in the deep shadows under the trees told of enemy preparations nearing completion. Sam appeared at his side.

"All is in readiness, Vard. The archers are in place, including your special dragon defense force. Backup troops are in the middle three lines of trenches and all provisions are in place in the back ditches, including medicines and arrows. The front two trenches are covered and disguised as bare ground."

Vard grimaced as he imagined the enemy falling onto the sharpened stakes in those trenches. It would make for a grisly end. The first ditch was within shooting distance of the walls, so any who avoided the stakes would succumb to missiles from the kingdom archers.

"Good," he said. "I hope we haven't missed anything. There's been so much consultation regarding preparations. I think we have everything covered."

"Well, I've never prepared for a war, but I imagine there are always things you forget." Sam raised one brow.

Vard blew out a breath. "Undoubtedly."

At that moment, the city gates opened, and the cavalry cantered out. They split to the left and right of the field of battle and would wait at the end of the infantry lines. Their purpose was to fill any gaps and disrupt the lines of the enemy. They could also pinch at either end of the field of battle. Two distinct groups of cavalry were gathered on the right, one led by Nikolas Cosara and the other by Formosa. Vard spotted the general's white charger. The man was many things, but he wasn't a coward.

Most generals would be on the wall, as Vard was, watching from a distance. He snorted.

"What's so funny?" Sam asked.

"Nothing. I was just thinking Formosa has courage for a…"

"Complete ass?" Sam offered.

"Something like that. How's Esta?"

"I'm pretty sure she and Merielle are cooking up a plan, which makes me nervous."

"I'd believe it of Merielle," Vard said, "but Esta is a rather different personality from the admiral's wife."

"You didn't know her back in the day."

Vard was sure Sam was going to expand on his statement, but no more was forthcoming. "I don't know what we can do about that. Our ladies will want to help with the war effort. That's who they are. I should've given them safer tasks to keep them occupied."

"It wouldn't have made any difference," Sam said. "I heard the queen offer that to Esta, and she declined. She explained she already had her duties, but she wouldn't say what, even when I questioned her."

"Speaking of duties, what are yours for this day?"

"I'm about to ride out and take my place on the left flank. That way I can be wherever I'm needed. Nikolas will be on the other flank, and the general and his cronies have chosen the center. Just like him to hog all the glory."

Vard shrugged. "We all have our roles to play. Watch your back today."

"You'll be in the center?" Sam asked.

Vard grinned. "Yes, I'll be in the center with the glory hogs. The king has chosen to fight from there. I'll stick to him and try to keep him safe."

Sam grimaced. "Good luck. You've a lot of backs to watch."

Sam bowed and walked away. Vard took one more look over the battlefield preparations and followed his friend.

* * *

Esta and Merielle met Alique in the field hospital, housed in a temple near the northern outer wall of Wildecoast. Esta gulped as she saw the medicines and instruments laid out on the benches and the rows upon rows of pallets and blankets. A cool breeze swept through the building. She pulled her cloak tighter. This was becoming very real. Soon there would be soldiers lying and dying on those pallets.

Merielle hooked her arm through Esta's and drew her toward Alique, who was giving instructions to a group of women. They stood at the back and listened.

"You all know what you need to do," Alique said. "Report to your stations and stay safe. For those who leave the city walls, make sure you always have a guard with you."

The women murmured agreement, bowed, and moved away, many with wide eyes and trembling hands. Esta knew how they felt.

"Good morning, ladies," Alique said. "Thank you for your service."

Merielle clapped her hands together, as if relishing the moment of truth. "I can't wait to feel useful. Nikolas thinks I am rolling bandages and grinding potions. But after my recent training, I know I am ready for this."

Esta gulped. Nikolas would be furious when he discovered what his wife was actually doing.

Alique frowned. "I'm not sure it's best to deceive your husband, Merielle. I have no desire to be the recipient of his wrath when he finds out."

Merielle flapped her hands dismissively. "Oh, have no fear. I will tell him you and Esta had nothing to do with me being on the battlefield. And I won't be fighting unless our carriers are threatened. If the men do their jobs, that won't happen."

Esta shook her head. She loved Merielle like a sister, but sometimes felt she didn't understand the woman at all. Merielle had no fear, and that could be dangerous.

Alique turned to Esta. "You're in triage, which means you must assess those whose injuries are the most serious, but may live, and have them attended to first. You must also evaluate those who can't be saved, but need pain management."

Esta nodded. "And those who can obey commands and aren't bleeding badly or in respiratory distress can join the 'wait an hour' group. The walking wounded will see a nurse, and then a healer when one is available, unless they deteriorate." She paused. "Where are we placing the dead?"

"Our dead who make it to this center will be taken down into the tombs below this church. Enemy dead shall be placed in carts and taken to a morgue outside the city walls." She paused and fixed Esta with a serious expression. "Don't confuse our *Lenweri* friends with the *Sis Lenweri*. That wouldn't be wise."

Merielle jumped in at that advice. "Our allies will wear a white headband of cloth with the Zialni crest embroidered on it, yes?"

Alique nodded. "That's correct. If you find a headband that doesn't have the embroidery, that elf is likely an imposter. If in doubt, ask one of the elven guards stationed around the hospital."

Esta drew in a deep breath. What she needed was a cup of tea to calm her nerves. She walked to the kitchen, took the kettle from the fire, and made a pot of tea. She took it and several cups back to the other ladies.

"I thought we could all do with a brew," she said, setting the pot and cups down.

Alique smiled. "Yes, please pour for us. Now, before the fighting begins, take this list and check that all our provisions are in place in sufficient quantities." She handed two parchments to Merielle. "Merielle, you check the surgery room, and Esta can work in the dispensary."

Merielle handed the second list to Esta. "I am getting to work right away. I don't need tea." She hurried toward the surgery.

Alique cast her surprised smile to Esta. "Merielle seems rather keen to get started."

Esta sighed. "She's easily bored, and it sometimes gets her into trouble. I trust this isn't one of those times."

Alique frowned. "So do I. I hope she appreciates the seriousness of this situation. I don't want her falling to pieces when things get tough."

"Oh, she won't, believe me. I'm more worried about her running off and doing what *she* thinks needs to be done. You see how eager she is."

"I'll watch her closely. It seems I've chosen the right person in you to see to the triage."

"I only hope I can live up to your expectations." Esta hesitated, not sure she should ask her next question.

"Go on," Alique said. "What's the matter?"

"I wondered who'll take over from me when I need a break. At some stage, I'll have to feed my baby boy. But I can be here all day and feed him at dinner time."

Alique grasped her hand. "Of course, you must feed your son. Your hours of work will be from six am to six pm. Then you can return to the keep. The queen has found able women to do the night shift. Even I will snatch a few hours here and there."

Esta was certain Alique wouldn't get much rest while the battle was on. "As long as you *do* rest, Alique. We can't have you returning to Kain a burnt-out shell."

Alique's smile dimmed, and Esta felt like kicking herself for mentioning the elven prince. "He'll be safe, Alique. Have you heard any news?"

"The last I heard, Kain and his people were being chased through the forest as they tried to flee Selinore. Perhaps more news will come today. In the meantime, I try to keep busy."

Esta squeezed Alique's fingers. "Have faith. All will be well with Kain and in the war. We have many good people on our side."

"I assume that's what the *Sis Lenweri* think as well," Alique said. "But you're right."

Esta nodded and turned to start her check of their medical supplies.

* * *

Dawn came and still there was no assault by the *Sis Lenweri*. They had formed into fighting ranks just south of the forest, spread out across the field in a concave line that looked to be twenty elves deep. That meant the kingdom forces, who were arranged three hundred paces in front of their trenches, were outnumbered by two to one.

Vard didn't understand how that could be the case, considering this was the third theater of war for the enemy. They had underestimated the *Sis Lenweri* in the numbers of soldiers they could bring to the fight.

However, in his opinion, this tactic of theirs, to strike on several fronts simultaneously, was a mistake. Dividing your force was never a wise move, especially if there was another choice. But if your numbers were far superior to your enemy, it would be less of an issue. So just how many *Sis Lenweri* were there?

"Why don't the bastards charge?" King Beniel said, his eyes glued to the enemy forces. "They just sit there and stare. Are they hoping to spook us?"

Vard cast his gaze along the enemy lines. "I think that's exactly what they're trying to do." He focused on an elf on a black charger in the center of the line. "That must be Faenwelar." He pointed and employed his hawk vision. "Yes, that's him. Finally, we come against the leader."

"Leave him to me, Vard," the king growled. "I've been anticipating this for many months."

Vard sighed. "My Liege, I don't think that's wise. Allow one of us to fight on your behalf."

The king's head whipped around. "What? You don't think me capable of vanquishing Faenwelar? I'm fit as a bull, and I won't take 'no' for an answer."

Vard sought General Formosa and found the man frowning at the king. Formosa rode his horse closer.

"My Liege," he said. "I'd be honored to fight the elven scum. I too have longed for this moment since he kidnapped my uncle. Please grant me this."

Vard doubted Formosa could beat Faenwelar, but at least losing the general wouldn't be as giant a blow as losing the king.

"No!" King Beniel huffed. "Faenwelar is mine. And, by the Goddess, I'm sick of this waiting!"

As the first rays of the sun lit the ocean, a horn sounded from the elven forces arrayed against them, and, with a roar, the *Sis Lenweri* charged. The leading line screamed like enraged stallions as they ran toward the kingdom men. Vard saw his front line hesitate and sway backward at the inhuman sound rolling down at them.

"Hold the line!" he cried. "Advance! Advance at a walk. Shields up!" He raised his hand to Sam on the left and Nikolas on the right flank, and received a flag wave back. They trotted their cavalry units forward, ready to charge inward and disrupt the enemy lines.

"Finally!" King Beniel said, and trotted his horse forward.

Vard signaled to the king's guard to stay with him. He had chosen the best soldiers and rangers to stick close to their leader.

With a sickening crunch, the two forces met, shrieks of pain ripping through the eerie cries of the *Sis Lenweri*. The kingdom shield wall held, and the foot soldiers thrust pikes and swords to stab their enemies through the gaps. Many of the elves in the leading row fell and were trampled. Vard kept his eye on Faenwelar, fearing he'd want to strike an early blow to kingdom forces. That meant taking out the king or one of his generals.

The *Sis Lenweri* horn sounded again, and the front row of elves was augmented by the second line of troops.

The *Sis Lenweri* soldiers hit the shield wall again, which had thinned with the death of some of the kingdom fighters. The wall buckled, and they fell back under the weight of the enemy lines.

Formosa called for reinforcements to the shield wall, and they jogged into place. The reinforced wall held, but the *Sis Lenweri* attacked with ferocity. Their greater reach, leant by their superior height, meant they could inflict damage without getting too close to the kingdom soldiers.

This must be stopped. Vard signaled to the cavalry on the wings to enter the field, and Formosa did the same for the central cavalry unit. A kingdom horn sounded, indicating the foot soldiers in front should step to either side to allow the horses through.

A narrow corridor formed, and, while the cavalry on the wings charged into the fray, the central group trotted into place. The *Sis Lenweri* had held back their small, mounted force, but Vard suspected they didn't have long before it entered the field. He signaled to the king's guard to box him in, so he couldn't enter the fray, and Beniel roared with fury.

"Get out of my way, you dolts!"

"Await your chance, My Liege," Vard shouted. "It's not safe at this stage for you to challenge Faenwelar." Faenwelar sat upon his dark horse amidst *his* personal guard, observing the battle from relative safety. Vard pointed this out to Beniel, and he nodded.

In the meantime, the once orderly front lines were in disarray. The shield wall still held in places, and pockets of cavalry had ridden in from the sides and center to engage the *Sis Lenweri* foot soldiers. Screams of horses spiked with elven swords, and the shrill cries of *Sis Lenweri* deaths dominated. Vard swept his gaze over the battle, trying to determine his next step. It appeared they were on top, and they must stay there; they had to maintain their superior position.

It was time for their elven forces to enter the fray. Vard blew a whistle, and their mounted elven allies, led by Isiloe and Ruven Magbalar, charged forth from the city gate, splitting once they passed the trenches and circling around to come at the battle from either side as the kingdom cavalry had done. He raised his arm to the archers on the walls of the city, and his signal was repeated to the archers on the keep battlements. They were to look out for dragons which were so far absent.

Isiloe's forces took the left flank, and Ruven's the right, augmenting the cavalry units already engaged. The elven mounted force pushed their way across the field from either side, cutting off the forward *Sis Lenweri* from retreat. Vard's eyes snapped to Faenwelar, who had whirled his horse to take in the scene behind him. He raised something to his mouth, and a horn blast screamed across the field.

Across the trees from the north came a huge beast, the rays of the late morning sun reflecting from its brilliant gold scales. Its wings spanned fifty paces and giant hind legs sported taloned feet that hung below its body. The creature's head was straight out of a nightmare. It was large enough to engulf a destrier, and it swept from side to side as if searching for something. Partially morphing into the hawk, Vard spied two figures on its back.

"Dragon!" The cries rang across the kingdom lines and horns blasted from all quarters. The front line of kingdom soldiers retreated as well as they could, forming an uneven line and raising their shields overhead in case of fire. Faenwelar blew on his horn again, and the *Sis Lenweri* who were still fighting, disengaged and ran for the forest.

The kingdom and *Lenweri* cavalry gave chase, taking down many of those fleeing. The dragon turned and flew toward the east, lining itself up with the kingdom forces as it turned and flew due west. Vard pulled his longbow from its clip and nocked an arrow, all while urging the king's guard to get him to safety. The whistle in his mouth warned of danger with short sharp blasts which were echoed across the field.

Retreat, retreat, retreat!

The dragon, though cumbersome, changed its course quickly toward the retreating kingdom forces. The cavalry harrying the *Sis Lenweri* were somewhat saved in that they were too close now to the enemy forces for the dragon to attack them without endangering its own. Vard stored that morsel of information away as he took aim on the dragon. It loomed closer, its left eye in Vard's sights.

At that moment, a volley of arrows launched from the walls of the city, flying straight toward the golden beast. As the first arrows hit their target, the dragon changed course to the northeast to avoid the darts that slammed into its body. Vard swore as his aim was spoiled by the last-minute change in direction. His arrow glanced across the beast's boney nose ridge, causing naught but superficial damage.

The dragon shrieked, releasing a massive blast of flame that flew harmlessly across the now empty battle scene. At least they had escaped dragon burns this time. A horn blew from the direction of the cavalry, and all the mounted forces galloped toward the city, injured riders being towed on their horses or riding behind able-bodied soldiers.

Vard watched as the dragon and its riders soared high and disappeared over the forest to the north. His attention switched to the northern part of the battlefield, which was empty except for *Sis Lenweri* collecting their dead and injured. He joined the king and his guard as they retreated.

"Damned good show, King's Blade," Beniel said, slapping Vard on the shoulder. "Only issue I have is no confrontation with Faenwelar. We should have attacked him when we had the chance."

Vard tilted his head to the side. "You don't think he'll take part in the battle again?"

Beniel snorted. "He didn't take part this time. Perhaps he will again join us. One thing is for sure. He won't avoid me. I can tell you that."

The king's words concerned Vard, but he shelved the worry for a later time. For the moment, they needed a battle council. Sam trotted up.

"Ask all the leaders to meet in the battle headquarters for a debrief, Sam," Vard said.

Sam saluted and cantered off. They had organized an efficient line of communication for the commanders. Sam must only contact four leaders: Nikolas Cosara, General Formosa, Ruven Magbalar, and one of the highest-ranking lords. These leaders had their own chain of communication to spread orders and requests to their teams. They each would decide who needed to be at the battle debriefing.

The battle headquarters was in a cramped room within the northern wall of the city. The king took a seat at the table and reached for the watered wine that an attendant offered. He drained the cup and had it refilled. The monarch's face was pale and sweaty. Vard hoped it was the exertion and not his heart that caused him to look so worn. He pulled out a flask of Alique's potion and tipped some into Beniel's cup. The king raised the cup in thanks before downing that one, too.

Vard turned and asked the attendant to have Lady Alique visit at her earliest convenience. He wouldn't have the king suffer for lack of care. Gradually, the other leaders filed in, including Isiloe, several lords, and some lower-ranking officers. By the time everyone was in attendance, there was standing room only, and very little of that.

Vard stood behind the king's chair and a little to his right. He raised his left hand to bring the meeting to order, and the company gradually quietened. Formosa wore his usual scowl, and Nikolas's eyes were cold, but that was to be expected.

"I wish to congratulate you on how your respective teams conducted themselves in this morning's battle," Vard said.

"Hear, hear!" King Beniel said.

There were nods all round.

"I think we can safely say we won that clash," Vard said. "But we know they'll come against us again, and the dragon will be featured. The next battle will be very different."

"You are correct, Vard Anton," Ruven said. "We were lucky they did not employ the dragon earlier, though Faenwelar was clearly reluctant to endanger his own soldiers with its fire. I am surprised by this. The *Sis Lenweri* high prince is not known for his mercy."

"Even he can't afford to lose soldiers for no reason, surely?" Nikolas said.

Ruven nodded. "He has a finite force, and, now that he has made his move, will want to do everything he can to conserve his soldiers."

"Considering he has been fighting a war on three fronts so far," Isiloe said, "he cannot afford to sacrifice his elves to the dragon."

Vard nodded. "I agree. We can use that to our advantage. The cavalry engaging the *Sis Lenweri* as they fled served two purposes—causing more enemy casualties and preventing the dragon from using its fire. It must have been hard for Faenwelar to make that call though when our mounted units were causing chaos with his retreat. We can't assume our involvement with *Sis Lenweri* units will always deter the dragon."

"We cannot," Ruven said.

"Where is he?" The queen's voice floated into the meeting room from beyond the door, soon followed by her royal presence. The fear on Adriana's face shocked Vard. Once she saw Beniel alive and well, she smoothed her features into composure.

Her eyes latched onto the king's, but all he did was nod. Adriana smiled, and the tight lines around her lips relaxed. Nikolas made his way to her, and she clutched his hand before allowing herself to be led from the chamber.

Vard glanced around the room at the other attendees, noting their frowns. None dared comment on the queen's interruption, but all seemed unsettled by it.

He cleared his throat. "As we were saying, we can't assume Faenwelar will always spare his troops, so we must make plans for defending ourselves against the dragon—perhaps against more than one."

"This is clearly not the same beast that was menacing Selinore and Amitania," Isiloe said. "It is golden where the others were black, green, and crimson. Is there any word on the other beasts?"

Vard shook his head. "Not yet. I had hoped for word from Kain Arenil today, but I assume he's busy fighting his own battle." His eyes met Isiloe's, and he could see how troubled she was.

"Congratulations to all leaders on their performance this morning," Vard said. "I don't wish to be premature, but I believe we managed the first battle well. Can I get everyone's feelings on what may occur this afternoon?"

As always, Formosa was eager to voice his thoughts. "I'm not sure there *will* be another attack this afternoon. If I were the *Sis Lenweri*, I'd regroup and come at us again in the morning, or perhaps stage a night attack. They have much better vision than us, after all."

Vard took on board his thoughts. They couldn't be easily dismissed. Faenwelar wouldn't be keen for a repeat of that morning. "If an attack does come this afternoon," he said, "I believe the dragon will be involved."

Formosa's eyes struck his. "What of a night raid? We could stage one ourselves."

"We could," Vard said, "but our *Lenweri* would have to be involved. Don't forget we'd be fighting in the forest in the dark. Not ideal for human soldiers." He remembered the night hounds, and wondered if they could be used.

Most of the leaders around the table nodded.

Ruven stood. "I agree with General Formosa. An attack on the *Sis Lenweri* tonight has great merit. And even though the fight may be in the forest, at least the dragon would be disadvantaged."

"Except that it can set the forest on fire!" Isiloe said.

Ruven rounded on her. "Not unless Faenwelar wants to lose his soldiers too."

She fell silent, a frown on her face.

"Any other ideas?" Vard wanted to gather a smaller team to continue planning, but not before he had assessed all possibilities.

The king shifted beside him. "If I were Faenwelar, I'd regroup and attack this afternoon. I'd use my dragon where it would inflict the most damage. That will be in the open. I think he will attack again, just as he did this morning. We need archers ready to drive the thing off; kill it if possible. And our soldiers need more shields to protect them from the fire."

Vard and many of the others nodded. Nikolas strode back into the room.

"What have I missed?" he asked.

Formosa spoke. "King Beniel was just saying Faenwelar will attack and use his dragon this afternoon. I think he may wait until tonight."

Nikolas quirked one brow. "What say you, King's Blade?"

"I'd rather hear *your* thoughts, Admiral," Vard said, hands on hips.

Nikolas's eyebrows rose. "Clearly, I don't know Faenwelar, but I think he needs to finish this off quickly. Thus, he won't wait long before his next attack. He'll use all forces at his command, including the dragon."

Vard nodded. "I agree with you. Tactics, gentlemen?"

Formosa looked disgruntled, but to his credit, he was the first to speak up. "If the dragon is to be used this afternoon, we must protect our forces from its fire. Shields are all well and good, but how much protection will they provide? I suggest we could use the trenches to shelter some of our fighters."

"You want to draw the *Sis Lenweri* closer to the city?" Vard asked. "That's a risky strategy if we fail."

"The idea is to not fail, King's Blade," Formosa snapped. "Also, if the elves are closer to the walls, our archers will have a better chance of contributing to the fight on the ground."

Nikolas rubbed his chin, eyes narrowed, but focused on something only he could see. "I don't like relying on trench fighting so close to the city. The trenches were meant as a last line of defense. However, Faenwelar won't expect this. He'll know we like to fight on the open plains. If we make it look as though we have depleted our forces and become desperate, perhaps he'll get sloppy."

Vard could see the pieces coming together in his mind. "It might just work. I've had no word from Kain Arenil or Amitania yet. I worry there are more *Sis Lenweri* who may enter this battle."

"More? Nonsense!" Formosa snapped. "Faenwelar is already stretched beyond his capabilities."

Vard ground his teeth. Formosa's snap judgments really got under his skin. "Regardless, General, I intend to keep my mind open regarding Faenwelar's forces. He has already attacked us on three fronts."

"Yes," King Beniel said. "We hardly want more *Sis Lenweri* coming at us from the west. That would be catastrophic."

Vard nodded and turned to Nikolas. "Admiral, I want your reserve forces stationed to the west of the city and scouts patrolling further out. We must know if the worst happens."

Nikolas nodded. "If we're finished for now, I'll head out and see to that."

Vard nodded, and Nikolas promptly left. At least the admiral seemed to be cooperating. He appeared to realize it was critical to put their differences aside for the duration of the war.

"King's Blade," Formosa said, "I'll see to the trenches and ensure all the shields have fire retardant applied from this point on. I'll also see that the cavalry and elven horsemen carry shields. Do you agree that half our force should be in the trenches and the rest on the open field? We can try to draw the *Sis Lenweri* further from the trees this time"

Vard waited for the man to stop speaking. "I agree fifty percent of our forces should be hidden in the trenches. And make sure the stretcher bearers have protection too. You may go, General."

Formosa saluted and left. The remainder of the attendees also filed out, leaving Isiloe and Ruven with Vard and the king.

"Ruven and Isiloe," Vard said. "Do you have anything to offer besides what we have discussed?"

"This trench warfare is new to me, Vard," Ruven said. "It could work, but. I, too, am concerned about fighting our enemy so close to the city walls. Then again, if it brings the archers more into play, that would be a good thing."

Fierce Isiloe nodded. "Let them come. We will smash them wherever we must fight. Let us not be fearful of losing this war."

Vard smiled. "I wish I had two hundred men and women like you, Ramar."

Isiloe straightened, her eyes filled with pride. "When you have right on your side, it gives you courage, King's Blade." Then her eyes clouded. "I just wish I knew if Gwaethe was safe."

"I'll let you know as soon as I hear anything, Ramar," Vard said. "For now, organize your archers and horsemen, and protect them as well as you can."

Both the elven leaders nodded and saluted before leaving. Vard turned to King Beniel.

"And what think you, My Liege?"

The king smiled, a wicked light in his blue eyes. "I think I would hate to be Faenwelar. He doesn't know what terrors he has in store." The monarch's eyes moistened. "You have done the kingdom proud, my boy. Alecia would approve. I couldn't have a better second." His gaze sharpened. "Now just give me the chance to fight that bastard, and I'll be a happy man."

* * *

Esta sagged against the doorway of the infirmary. The first battle had only lasted a little over four hours, but she was already exhausted. And she didn't have the stomach to witness more pain and death. Her previous patient had drained the last of her resilience. She gulped and fought back tears at the memory of the boy.

Twelve years old at the most, he'd been running messages for the kingdom forces when a *Sis Lenweri* arrow found his chest. The stretcher bearers who brought him in had expected her to save his life. All she could do was watch as he took his last breath. She blocked out the memory of their eyes as she listened to his chest and shook her head. That was bad enough, but what if the next body brought to her was Sam's?

As if her thoughts had summoned him, her husband appeared beside her. She threw herself into his arms and sudden tears poured out.

"There, there, love," he said, his big hand rubbing her back. "What's amiss?"

"A boy," she cried. "I couldn't help him." Uncontrollable sobs stole her words.

"We'll ensure he's remembered as a hero." Sam pulled away from her and lifted her chin, so she met his gaze. "I promise I'll do everything to help his family. Things will be very different after this war, but there'll still be joy."

She sniffed and nodded, words eluding her. She knew if anything happened to Sam, she couldn't go on. "Just hold me." He did as asked, and she took strength from his powerful arms around her.

"I will look after Esta from here, Samael." Merielle's voice and gentle hands enclosed her. "You must return to your duties, as must we." Her voice was soft, but full of steel. For a split second, Esta resented her strength and the intrusion.

She stood straight and as tall as she could. "I'll endure, Sam. I'm sure you have endless tasks to see to before the enemy attacks again."

He nodded. "I must speak with Lady Alique." Esta had noted that none of them wanted to give Alique a surname. She was no longer Lady Zorba as she had married. For a time, she'd become Madame Jazara until Kain assumed his role as elven prince. All knew she wasn't comfortable with the title Lady Arenil. As far as Esta was concerned, Alique was entitled to all the honor she could claim. Unfortunately, none of it would be settled soon.

Esta nodded and escorted Sam to where Alique knelt beside a pallet. She had a soldier's hands clutched in hers, and her eyes closed, lips moving. The soldier was pale and sweating, but his gaze was riveted on Alique, his lips following the prayer. Esta and Sam waited until Alique patted her patient's hands and stood.

"Stay strong, soldier," she said. "I'll see you again when I make my rounds."

Alique turned and greeted them. "Let's speak in the pharmacy."

She led them to the room where the herbs were ground into medicines, and made a pot of tea, handing a cup to each. Sam slurped his like a thirsty man and wolfed down three rock cakes. Esta had no appetite after what she'd seen and done that morning. Alique nibbled on a cake.

"Thank you for this, Lady Alique," Sam said. "I wanted to let you know we think there will be another battle this afternoon." He told her of their plans, and Esta's heart kicked up to a gallop. How would they manage? "Vard has advised that any injured who can be moved should be taken to another facility."

The queen entered. "I'll have carriages take them to the castle. We need to make room here for more wounded."

Alique smiled. "Thank you, Your Majesty. I'd appreciate you taking the stable patients off my hands. We have more surgery to complete before new wounded start arriving."

"Let us hope the men are wrong, and there is no more fighting this day," the queen said. "However, there is no point leaving those who are on the mend here with the seriously ill. They will recover better in the palace. I'll divert some of my maids to look after them. I'm sure the castle housekeeper won't be pleased at the upset to her routine, but there is nothing to be done about it. Perhaps the nobles also have some staff they can spare."

Alique nodded. "I appreciate anything you can do to help, My Queen."

"Right," the queen said, "you tag all those patients you wish to be moved and leave a note with them as to their care. I'll do the rest." She turned and swept from the room.

Esta sagged. "Thank the Goddess for that woman!"

Sam cleared his throat. "I, too, need to be about my duties. Lady Alique." He bowed to her, then took Esta in his arms for a fierce hug. She embraced him just as passionately, taking comfort from his strength.

He kissed her forehead and squeezed her hands before leaving them. Esta watched him depart, wishing she could go with him and watch his back.

"You don't look well, Esta," Alique said. "Are you coming down with something?"

She shook her head. "I had a moment before. I found this morning difficult, and then I lost a patient before I could get help for him; a boy who was part of the communication team."

Alique stepped toward her and took her hands. "That's difficult, Esta. I remember losing my first patient. And when it's a young person, it's even harder. I've walled my heart off, so I can deal with it, but that's easier said than done."

Esta nodded. "I'll learn, I suppose. It's just so draining. There are many decisions to be made, and I feel if I make the wrong one, someone may pay the price."

"I won't tell you that's not possible, because it is. However, if we become paralyzed with our fear, we can be of no help to those who desperately need us."

"I'll try to remember that." She finished her tea and set the cup on the bench.

"I want you to eat something." Alique reached over and picked up an apple. "This will do for now. And keep up your fluids. Watered wine and tea. You're no help if you drop over from exhaustion."

Alique left her and bustled out as though she'd been merely mending a hem all morning. Esta huffed out a breath and closed her eyes. How had she found herself in this situation? All she wanted was to see Mika and put him to her breast; let the dangers of the day fade away to his noisy slurping. Imagining that scene, she felt better. She took a bite from her apple and went to find Merielle.

CHAPTER TWENTY-ONE

AT DAWN on the morning after the battle on the ridge, Kane, with Elora for company, went to see the dragon. Except the dragon wasn't there anymore.

He checked his bearings to make sure he was looking in the same location and walked over the area the beast had lain on. The grass was still flattened, and he found gore that had dropped from the injured eye.

"Where is it?" Elora asked

"I fear it still lives."

Elora's calm eyes met his. "That cannot be a good outcome, Kain Arenil. Did you not make sure it was dead?"

"I discerned no signs of life," he said, "but it seemed the dragon spoke in my mind. I thought it some trickery, or perhaps the effect of my exhausted state, but the wound, the eye, healed over. The dragon said it used *my* magic, yet I felt nothing. In the end, I convinced myself I was hallucinating."

Elora frowned. "Are you in the habit of hallucinating, High Prince?"

Kain ground his teeth and schooled his response to politeness. "You *know* I'm not."

Elora's eyes narrowed. "This is a strange development. Did it know what you were?"

"I don't know. We didn't have a long conversation. I spent most of it doubting my sanity."

"There is nothing we can do about it now," she said. "Next time, make sure the beast has both of its eyes poked out." She turned and stalked off through the forest, heading back to camp.

Kain spun and walked after her. "You weren't just a little sad at the demise of such a beast? After all, there aren't likely many left."

She threw up her hands. "I want nothing to do with beasts who would fight on the side of the *Sis Lenweri*. They are evil and deserve to die."

"The *Lenweri* must have worked with them, once. We could again."

She spun back to him, eyes blazing. "Don't believe Melandrach when he says Orionkael may have been a dragon lord. I was married to him and saw no evidence of it. You are foolish if you think you might have inherited the ability to speak with dragons."

"Then how do you explain the voice in my head?"

"Perhaps you *were* just tired. I advise you concentrate on the matter at hand which is getting us to wherever we are going."

Kain was about to snap back at her, but shut his mouth. Elora had been a friend to him from the first time he set foot in Selinore. She deserved his respect. He dropped the topic for now.

"How's Rasalar?"

"The same. A stretcher is being rigged to be drawn behind a horse. Have you spoken to Gwaethe today?"

"No. I assume she has nothing to add after leaving Amitania to pursue Gorin. But I've sent ravens to Wildecoast and Brightcastle to warn them. If we can get to Brightcastle, perhaps Princess Benae can heal Rasalar."

Despite the injured, they made good time that day and into the next. The wounded traveled in the center of the column with soldiers surrounding them. Kain feared another attack from the elves they had defeated at the ridge. However, none came. And there was no sign of Nugoriem. Hopefully it had flown away to lick its wounds on some deserted, lofty peak in the northern mountains.

The trek was hard on all of them, especially the injured and those who cared for them. In Rasalar, there was no change. Kain made sure they had frequent stops and sent scouts into the forest ahead to hunt for game and berries, amongst their other duties.

At the end of the second day after leaving the ridge, Kain was dozing after the evening meal when Gwaethe's voice popped into his head.

Brother! Kain!

I hear you. How goes your mission?

Angry feelings shot down the line. *The scum Gorin fled faster than we ever imagined. We have come across some bodies of Sis Lenweri who appeared to have died of battle wounds. They didn't stop to bury them.*

It's good to hear your voice.

Did you not hear what I said? Gorin is leaving his people to rot beside the trail!

Gwaethe, sometimes honor must be discarded in the interests of victory.

Only you would say that, Brother. I am ashamed of you.

Hang on! If I were in the same position, I might do the same thing.

Have you lost any of your people on the march?

No. He thought of Rasalar and hoped she wouldn't be the first.

You see! You care more than you think.

I didn't say I didn't care. You implied it.

Let us stop these stupid games. I sent a pigeon to Brightcastle and one to Wildecoast, but I am not confident they will arrive.

I sent ravens to both cities. One way or another, they'll get the news. Vard Anton is no dummy. How are you?

Tired and angry. Jacques is well. Theoden is also hale along with most of our commanders. Gorin had two dragons, one green and the other crimson, which are on their way south with his forces.

Kain decided not to mention Nugoriem again. Gwaethe didn't need something else to worry about. *We will prevail! Never doubt that.*

I try not to, but this war has been going on for so long. I just want peace in our kingdom. It is all I long for.

All? I can see you are a woman who still has her husband with her. Though I imagine you've had little time together.

Alique will survive. She will be in her element in Wildecoast. I bet she oversees the wounded.

I can't wait to hold her again.

Love surged down the bond. *I will talk tomorrow when we are closer to Brightcastle.* Her presence winked out.

Kain smiled. His sister was the queen of abrupt endings to conversations. He sometimes wondered how Jacques dealt with that.

* * *

The war council was convened at mid-morning, and Alecia hurried toward the small audience chamber with Hetty. Her advisor looked handsome this morning in a deep red velvet dress with cream lace features on the collar and cuffs. Alecia still hadn't become used to seeing her like that, but, still, Ramón and Benae appeared none the wiser as to her real identity.

They entered the room after being announced by the footman and took their seats at the front. Ramón raised his brows at her before beginning.

"Good morning, one and all. I've had birds from Amitania and Kain Arenil this morning."

"At last!" The words were out before Alecia could stop them.

Ramón stopped and frowned at her. "Kain Arenil won the battle after he fled Selinore. They found a small ridge from which to mount their defense. A dragon attacked and was downed."

There were cheers from some members. Alecia looked for Ramar Reese to judge his reaction. Typical of the elves, Reese showed little emotion. Did she imagine there was a slight tensing of the shoulders? A dragon was an ancient creature, and she didn't know how she truly felt about killing one. She dragged her attention back to Ramón.

"Yes," Ramón said, "it's truly good news that one beast has been eliminated. However, we can only rejoice so much. News from Amitania reveals they had two dragons to contend with there. The beasts and the rest of the *Sis Lenweri* force that attacked the city are now headed south."

A deep silence fell upon the council members. Alecia's vivid imagination fired up, filling her brain with scenes of devastation if the beasts attacked Brightcastle. She swallowed hard and squared her shoulders. If she was to be queen, there was no point in going to pieces.

"Does Princess Gwaethe suspect the force is headed here?" she asked.

Ramón dragged in a deep breath. "That was what she wrote. The *Sis Lenweri* faced too much opposition in Amitania, so they cut their losses and fled south. We must prepare for Brightcastle to be the ultimate destination, though they could head to Wildecoast."

Alecia nodded and the council members muttered amongst themselves. Ramón clapped his hands.

"I'd like to hear what each of you has to say regarding this recent news," he said.

Estevot was the first to speak. "Prince Arenil is likely to make his way here then?"

Ramón pursed his lips. "He didn't give an indication in his missive. His intention was to meet up with Princess Gwaethe, but perhaps he'll make straight for Brightcastle. As for the princess, she'll follow the *Sis Lenweri* to their ultimate destination. Prince Gorin is leading those heading south."

"It is to be regretted that the *Sis Lenweri* prince escaped," Ramar Reese snapped. "We could well do without *him* leading the force. He is a cruel and pitiless bastard. He had Princess Gwaethe flogged almost to death in the previous battle of Amitania."

Most of the council looked at Reese with surprise. It was unusual for one of the *Lenweri* to show so much emotion. Alecia didn't relish Gorin's plight when they caught up with him.

"There's nothing much we can do about that," Ramón said, "except make him pay for his crimes."

Reese nodded his head, his dark eyes burning with an intensity that Alecia hadn't seen before.

"We must make sure we can accommodate more soldiers," Alecia said, "if Brightcastle is to be the staging ground for the final battle in this war."

"Princess," Estevot said, "there's no point making needless preparations if the enemy elven force sweeps past us. We'd be better advised to make plans to move our force to Wildecoast."

Alecia thought of her dreams of the dragons flying toward Brightcastle Keep and the conflict raging outside. This *was* where they would fight the deciding battle. She *knew* it. But she couldn't explain that to these men.

"I think Brightcastle will see the final battle," she said, "but I agree we must stay flexible. I'll speak to the nobles and assess their capacity for taking in reserve soldiers if we're inundated."

Estevot spoke up. "Personally, I hope the last campaign is staged in Wildecoast. I'm not sure we have the means to defeat the *Sis Lenweri* here, certainly not without help from the capital."

"You hoping won't change the course of this war, Captain," Alecia said. "I suggest you prepare for the movement of our forces to Wildecoast. Meanwhile I'll concentrate on preparing for the ultimate campaign to be staged here. I propose more trenches be dug on all sides of the castle, and the storage of provisions be doubled. Arrow and sword supplies should also be increased. Again, I think the nobles could help with this."

Estevot shook his head. "With all due respect, Princess, I'm not inclined to leave the preparation of Brightcastle to one unskilled in battle. You may continue with your previous organization areas, which were elven training and helping the healers with their facilities and preparations. You may, of course, approach the nobles with any specific requests you have."

Alecia's blood boiled, though she refused to show this man the extent of her anger. But what to do? She couldn't afford to lose face before Estevot and this company. Luckily, Hetty stood and cleared her throat.

"Lord Zorba, Captain Estevot and esteemed members of this council," Hetty said, her voice ringing with command and not a trace of the rasp that was customary for the witch. "As we have met an impasse between the advice of the military and that of the princess, might I suggest we prepare for both contingencies? It would be folly to ignore either possibility."

Ramón nodded as Hetty sat down. "Lady Henrietta, your sage advice is appreciated. I'm inclined to agree. I also believe that both Princess Alecia and Captain Estevot should play their part in the preparations, as must we all."

Reese nodded. "This is truly a time when we must be flexible, think on our feet, and pivot as needed. I believe if we take all possibilities into consideration, we will be able to adjust our plans at short notice."

Estevot shot to his feet. "But won't considering all possibilities lead to a paralysis of decision-making? At some stage we must decide on a definitive course of action."

Alecia snorted. "Nonsense! We have no choice but to prepare to defend this city. If it appears the threat bypasses us and moves on to Wildecoast, then we will follow with all haste. As Lord Zorba says, this defense will require the assistance of all."

Estevot looked to Ramón. "Has there been any request for help from the king?"

Ramón shook his head. "Not at this stage, although we sent a small force of archers and rangers to help with defense and tracking. They should almost be in the city. The king has asked that we prepare to defend Brightcastle and the heir to the throne. With the threat of the southern movement of the *Sis Lenweri* from Amitania, it seems prudent to reinforce our defenses, as well as prepare to follow any enemy force to Wildecoast. Only time will tell what the true danger to Brightcastle is."

Alecia studied her friend. Dark smudges lay beneath Ramón's eyes, and he looked pale. His hair was ruffled as if he'd been running his fingers through it more than usual. She felt the stirrings of guilt. She should have been a greater support for him instead of causing him increased concerns. But, then again, her role in this war was not to be dismissed. Ramón had tried to shut her out at every opportunity. Still, she resolved to patch things up with him this day in order to provide the strongest chance of defeating the *Sis Lenweri*.

Alecia stood. "Your orders, Lord Zorba?"

He squared his shoulders. "Estevot, order extra trenches dug, including trench traps around the entire city. Also, ensure our forces are ready to march at the earliest opportunity if it appears the enemy intends to make for Wildecoast. I'll place more rangers and scouts in the north to help with our predictions. Princess, please liaise with the nobles to gather as many supplies as possible, including wagons and manpower. Also, do as much as you can to augment the healer support staff. Ramar Reese, I'd appreciate your help with trackers and scouts, and your guidance with advance tactics to fight the enemy."

All present appeared content with the orders.

"We'll meet again in twelve hours unless I have anything to update beforehand," Ramón said.

The meeting disbanded, and Alecia approached Ramón with Hetty in tow.

"That was impressive, Ramón. You've really matured in your leadership."

He looked stunned. "Thank you, Alecia. I appreciate that more than you could know."

She hesitated, not sure how to say what she needed to say. "I know I haven't been completely supportive of you of late." She held up her hand when he started to speak. "Hear me out, please. I agree we must unite to defeat the *Sis Lenweri,* and I want to call a truce on our disagreements until this war is over. You have a monumental task to complete and can count on my support."

A smile cracked Ramón's stern visage. He instantly appeared more his normal self.

"I accept, Alecia." He took her hand and kissed her fingers. "A truce in our personal battle until we defeat the enemy. Does that include Benae?"

Alecia drew in a deep breath before she answered. "Yes, that includes your wife. Despite our differences, you both have the kingdom's best interests at heart."

Ramón released a long breath and smiled. It seemed like the first genuine smile she'd seen from him in a long while. "Good! That's so good, Alecia. I didn't know how much this situation had been wearing on me until you spoke just now."

She nodded. "I feel lighter, too. We'll discuss the rest after we vanquish the *Sis Lenweri*." She turned and left the meeting room, eager to be off and seeing to the myriad of chores she'd mentally noted.

"Hold up, child," Hetty puffed from behind her. "Not so fast!"

Alecia stopped just outside the door to the audience chamber. "Sorry, Lady Henrietta. I forgot myself."

"You certainly did. I may look fit, but don't forget I almost died recently."

Alecia grasped her arm. "Don't talk about that here. Come along, and I'll make sure I slow my steps. What do you think we should do first?"

"Let's pay a visit to my contact amongst the nobility, shall we?" Hetty said, and they headed for the entrance of the castle.

Six hours later, Alecia was back in her chambers, sipping afternoon tea and feeling satisfied with her day so far. After she and Hetty canvassed the nobles, they had sprung into action, providing more goods, weapons, and manpower than at their first enquiry. Alecia was beginning to understand that nobody ever gave you everything you asked for. Certainly, in difficult times, even the most generous people held something back.

"Thanks for your help, Hetty," she said. "I've learned so much about negotiation since you became my advisor. And all that without Ramón and Benae suspecting who you are. I even think Ramón is quite taken with you."

She watched as Hetty played with Iona on the rug before the fire. If only this war could be resolved, she might even be happy. And then her thoughts turned to Vard, and her heart stuttered. Happiness wasn't possible while they were at this impasse. It seemed she was doomed to conflict with so many people she valued.

She sighed. There was nothing she could do to change that now. After tea, she would meet with her ladies and organize her personal guard and strategies during battle. One step at a time had served her well in the past and would this time, too. She wondered where Vard was and what he was doing. By now, Wildecoast would be at war. She prayed the Goddess would keep him safe.

"I'm going to meet with my ladies, Hetty," she said, getting to her feet. "You're welcome to stay here and rest or play with Iona. Ring the bell for anything you need." Hetty waved at her as she kissed her daughter and left the chamber.

"Well, well, if it isn't the Princess Alecia, come to spend time with us," Arelle said, as Alecia made her way across the practice ground.

She smiled and bowed mockingly to them. "How goes the training?"

Lin stood with her hands on her hips. "I think we've achieved everything we set out to with our charges. And we've honed our skills too. I've been training with Lyam Anton. He's a wily old fox who learns quickly. I taught him a thing or two." She quirked her brow at Alecia, daring her to read something into her words.

Kenna nodded. "I beat the weapons master today. When we started this, I would've said that was an impossibility. I might even best you, Princess."

"We shall see about that." Alecia sobered. "Unfortunately, our next test may be the real thing. Wildecoast has come under attack this day." The thought of Vard fighting for his life weighed her down, but she shrugged the heavy feeling off. "If you have any minor details to finalize, do so now, and say your goodbyes."

Cretia gasped. "That's very morbid, Alecia."

She fixed Cretia with a serious eye. "You know what we face. This isn't a game now. When we come against our foes, they'll be trying to kill us. Remember what it was like to fight the *Sis Lenweri* when we journeyed to Amitania. Magnify that many times over, for several days, and you have what we'll soon embark upon. Are you ready?"

Lin shook her head. "I don't think we can really be ready for that. However, we're strong and adaptable."

Kenna elbowed her. "What about brave?"

"That goes without saying," Arelle laughed.

Alecia listened to them, sadness in her heart. Despite their experiences, they were still naïve when it came to war and fighting. She included herself in that assessment. Vard had done his best to teach her over the months they'd spent together after fleeing Brightcastle and Finus, and again recently when they had spent time together. He was preparing her to survive whatever the war threw at her.

And she had tried to pass all her knowledge and skill onto her ladies. They had taught the children who were running messages how to defend themselves and done the same for the stretcher bearers. She and Reese had formed an elven archery force capable of shooting a dragon's eye from 200 yards away. But would it be enough?

"Let's saddle our horses and take a tour of the defenses," she said, leading the way to the stables.

They saddled up in quick order with the help of the stable hands. Exiting through the northern gate of the castle grounds, the trench defenses confronted them. Everywhere they looked, soldiers and civilians worked in a frenzy.

The northern trenches were reasonably well developed, as they were the first line of defense for the city and the keep. Those trenches curved around the castle walls and along the east and western sides. All the existing trenches were being extended and widened to allow for more men to shelter in them.

The ladies rode along the base of the keep and city walls, stopping to speak with the workers. Trench walls were being reinforced with timber that the servants of the nobility brought in wagons. Food and water were also being loaded into the trenches along with first aid supplies and medicines. The trenches furthest away from the walls were the trap trenches, laid with deadly wooden spikes and covered with canvas and grass. Alecia would have liked two lines of these, but there wasn't time to dig them and get all the other preparations done.

"Arrangements are proceeding nicely," Lin said, gazing at the southern trenches. "You think Brightcastle will see actual fighting?"

Alecia nodded. "I do. Estevot and I had words this morning. He believes the last battle will be in Wildecoast. However, after my dreams, I think our last stand will be here."

Lin nodded. "For what it's worth, so do I. But, if the *Sis Lenweri* skirt past Brightcastle and on to Wildecoast, we'll follow, of course?"

"Yes," Alecia said. "We can't allow the capital to mount the entire defense. But I don't think it will come to that. We must dig in here and ready ourselves for a tough and bloody fight."

Lin looked at her, frowning. "How does one ready themselves to kill, to die?"

Alecia shrugged. "We've all killed before. Our freedom is at risk. This isn't something we asked for, and we didn't start it. However, I'll gladly sacrifice all to see my land free and at peace again."

Alecia could see her words had lit a fire in the hearts of her ladies, and it gave her an idea. "Let's extend our tour to the mess halls and patrol rooms. I want to speak to the soldiers."

They returned to the keep, so Alecia could fetch the regal cloak she intended to wear in battle. She donned it, and they rode to one after another of the gathering places for soldiers. Whenever they found a group of soldiers, they stopped and spoke to the men and sometimes women.

It wasn't always Alecia who spoke. The other ladies took turns walking amongst the soldiers and weaving their magic. Lin, Kenna, Cretia and Arelle were quick studies and soon had their own willing followers.

Alecia drew a crowd to her wherever she visited. Her red, white and black Zialni battle cloak had been created with Queen Izebel's war cloak in mind, and all Thorians were familiar with the battle queens of old. It sparked their imagination, and they asked Alecia if she intended to fight. It amazed them when she confirmed she did. Excitement squirmed like a pail of live eels in her stomach. The spirit of Izebel gripped her heart, making her feel invincible.

At one of the mess halls, the mood was low. Many of the conscripted soldiers ate there. Anger and hopelessness dragged at them as they sat slumped at their trestle tables. A man Alecia recognized from the day she convinced Soma Nuran to help with enlistment, approached them.

"Welcome Princess. At last, a ray of sunshine on this gloomy day. Do you have news?"

Alecia smiled at him. "I'll leave the news to your commanders, but I'd like to speak with you all." She walked to a chair and climbed upon it, flourishing her cloak.

"Good soldiers, my name is Alecia Zialni, and I am a princess of Thorius. I've come to remind you why we fight." There was grumbling at her words, and several men spat on the dirt floor. She eyeballed them.

"Thorius is a peaceful and prosperous realm, or so it was until the *Sis Lenweri* decided to claim it for themselves. Since then, there has been nothing but strife. So many have lost their lives or had them irrevocably changed. Many of you have been plucked from your previous jobs to fight for the kingdom."

This again led to more grumbling and spitting. Her ladies shifted from foot to foot in her peripheral vision, as if expecting trouble. She held up her hand, and the men slowly quietened.

"Please trust me! We will fight, and we will win. And we can all have the life we once had, only better. Once the *Sis Lenweri* are defeated, we'll work with their peaceful elven cousins to restore Thorius and bring prosperity back." They had fallen silent. Some even had hope in their eyes. "And I'll fight alongside you to achieve this, both in the coming war, and in the rebuilding after it."

"Wait, Princess," the man who had greeted them said. "You'll *physically* fight with us? Like the battle queens of old?"

Alecia's heart soared. They weren't her words, but they couldn't be more perfect.

"*Exactly* like that." She spread her cloak out on either side. "I had this cloak made for battle. Many of you have seen me fight. You know I can do this. Others of you have heard how I defended my people long before the *Sis Lenweri* became a threat. If I'll stand up to my father for you, how much more will I champion you against an evil and greedy invader like Faenwelar?"

The room erupted in cheers as she said the last, and all stood, clapping. Four men approached her and lifted her onto their shoulders, parading her around the room as all present cheered. Once finished, they returned her to her chair platform.

"Thank you, one and all. I promise to be *your* princess, *your* champion, *your* leader. I will always fight for what is best for you." She stepped down amidst more clapping and cheers. The entire room bowed as she left with her companions.

* * *

Gwaethe was tired, but she wouldn't reveal the extent of her weariness. Not to anyone, especially Jacques. He was always too protective. As if she wasn't looking after herself for decades before he ever came along. But she appreciated his care, especially when Isiloe was far away.

She leaned against a rock and stretched out her long legs. The fire spread welcome heat to her toes. A hand grasped her fingers, and she turned to find Jacques beside her.

"The camp is secure," he said, "and the scouts say the *Sis Lenweri* have made camp south of the range. It will be interesting to see which direction they take on the morrow. I think they'll make for Wildecoast to reinforce Faenwelar."

Gwaethe gazed at the flames and mulled over the question. What would *she* do? Probably, as Jacques said, head to Wildecoast. However, this war was unusual in that the *Sis Lenweri* had engaged them on three fronts so far. Why would they not include Brightcastle? She said so.

Jacques tilted his head. "Because they're spread dangerously thin. Mind you, there are more of the blighters than I ever thought. Even so, Wildecoast is the capital. They'll want to decimate it."

"Perhaps," Gwaethe said. "I can't help thinking of the elves of old, and how important Brightcastle was to them. Wildecoast is a human city. If Faenwelar won this war, he wouldn't want to live on the coast. He would inhabit Brightcastle. I think it would appeal to him for his ultimate fight to be there."

The more she contemplated the options, the more she was sure that was where Gorin would head tomorrow. A buzzing in her head announced Kain.

Gwaethe? Can you hear me?

She smiled. *I can always hear you, Brother. It is you who struggles with this communication.*

A grumpy spike of emotion slid down the line. *Not true. Besides, you've had decades to learn this magic. Where are you?*

Still in the mountain passes. The enemy is camped south of the range. You?

We're out of the thickest of the forests and heading for Brightcastle. I decided not to rendezvous with you.

Thank you for telling me. Jacques and I were just discussing where we think Gorin will head.

If he were smart, he'd travel to reinforce his father's troops in Wildecoast, but we are talking about Gorin. He has an inflated idea of his abilities.

He has two dragons, Gwaethe said.

Yes, that could make a difference. The dragon we shot down disappeared.

Gwaethe swallowed hard. *Disappeared?*

Yes. The next morning, it was gone. Perhaps it limped away to heal, but I couldn't get any signs of life from it the night before. None of it makes sense.

Perhaps it was magically moved. Dragons are little understood. Have you asked Melandrach?

Yes. He thinks the beast lives. Whether it is well enough to be a threat in this war is anyone's guess. Stay safe.

And you, Brother.

His presence vanished, and Gwaethe felt its loss keenly. All she wished was for this stupid war to be over so she could go back to building a life with Jacques. She would see this finished and soon. She just prayed she didn't lose too many loved ones along the way.

The morning saw them back on the trail early. Gwaethe rode her golden stallion, Rassar, fighting the effects of lack of sleep. Even nestled in the arms of her love, her dreams had been full of death and pain. Gorin featured in most of them. In none of them had she killed him. Or at least she didn't remember any, and she would have. Gorin's death, even in a dream, was an event which would stick in her mind.

Around mid-morning, scouts returned with a report that Gorin's force had continued due south. Unless he started angling east soon, his destination was Brightcastle. She fought the urge to let Kain know. Only definite destinations were of any use. There would be time to warn him later.

They picked up their pace to reduce the distance that separated the two forces. Gwaethe knew Gorin would be watching their progress. She wondered if he would turn and fight if they got close enough. If he wished to attack Brightcastle, it hardly paid to have an enemy force on his tail. She shook her head. What would he do?

At midday, the next scout report had Gorin still heading due south. She touched her ring.

Brother! Brightcastle is the destination. There is no way he is headed east.

Thank you. I'll march night and day in the hope I can help the city prepare its defenses.

Can your force withstand that? You have been fleeing and fighting for over a week.

We'll do what's required, and I suggest you follow my lead.

His words sent anger through Gwaethe. He had fought his destiny for months, and now he was giving *her* advice.

We have already increased our pace this day and intend to get close enough to Gorin to force him to decide between turning and fighting, or fleeing. Hopefully, if pushed, he will make a mistake.

Careful, lest you pull the cat's tail, and it bites you.

Gwaethe sent a sharp slap of anger at Kain and cut the link between them.

"Errrrr," she growled. "That brother of mine infuriates me."

"How so?" Jacques asked, trotting back to her from up the line.

She shook her head. "Never mind. He is going to march night and day to get to Brightcastle in order to aid the defense. I think we should do the same."

Jacques scowled. "Are you sure that's wise? Our forces are already tired. I don't want to push them to exhaustion."

"They can rest when we have defeated Gorin," she snapped. "If your human soldiers can't keep up, they can join us when the battle is over."

Jacques's normally affable face scowled. "Think about what you're saying. We shouldn't split our force, and we shouldn't push our soldiers past their limits. Tired fighters make mistakes." He paused and took a breath. "I don't want to clash with you over this, but someone has to keep a level head."

She guided her stallion over to bump against his mare. "Do not treat me as some flighty novice soldier, Jacques Vorasava. I could best you in weapons or strategy any day of the week. I will not miss my chance to kill Gorin because you would attach restrictions to me. He is mine to kill."

Jacques laid his hand on her arm, but she shook it off.

"I promise you'll get your chance," he said. "I'll watch your back while you fight him. Just don't run our soldiers into the ground. Brightcastle has legions of men rested and ready to take on the *Sis Lenweri.*" He fixed her with an uncompromising stare. "I won't allow our soldiers to be pushed beyond their limits before they even enter the next fight."

Gwaethe glared at him, trying and failing to mount an argument to his stubborn ultimatum. The trouble was Jacques was correct. For the last week and more, their people had been fighting or on the march.

If she pushed them too hard now, some might die in battle merely because their exhaustion undermined them.

She ground her teeth at having to defer to him. She was an elven princess, and he should heed her word without argument. "You have not heard the last of this, Husband," she snapped, wheeling her horse and trotting back into line.

CHAPTER TWENTY-TWO

MERIELLE rode her gray stallion, Storm, beside the litter bearers who were collecting the wounded. The *Sis Lenweri* had attacked after noon, sending the dragon in first. The massive beast swept over the allied troops who had jogged or ridden into formation when the enemy forces advanced from the forest. She closed her eyes at the sight of the charred corpses she had seen since beginning her latest shift. It was heartbreaking and stomach roiling.

Even her sisters would cringe at the suffering the soldiers had endured. Most had taken cover under their shields or in the trenches, but many had been exposed. The two men they were bringing in had horribly burned arms and shoulders. Others she had fetched had breathed in the fire and lay moaning on their hospital pallets or wheezing their last agonized breaths.

She searched the sky for a sign of the winged terror, but only a few fluffy clouds floated over the field. After the golden dragon wrought its terrible destruction, the *Sis Lenweri* had poured out of the forest, their first lines crashing into the wide trench with the sharpened stakes. Many died, but not enough to make up for the devastation of the dragon fire. Fear threatened to swamp her, but she could not allow herself to succumb. Nikolas was out there somewhere, fighting for the kingdom. She would make him proud.

The surrounding battle suddenly ratcheted up a notch. A pocket of four *Sis Lenweri* on fierce elven ponies finished two kingdom foot soldiers and turned toward her rescue party. Fierce grins cracked their faces, and they advanced on the men and women carrying the laden stretchers. Merielle gulped and charged, screaming a challenge before she kicked her horse into the middle of the enemy.

Out of the corner of her eye, she saw those she was guarding carry their injured away toward the protection of the city. At least they would be safe.

Storm wreaked almost as much carnage as she did, striking out with his hooves, sending the elven horses wild with panic. But their riders were masters of horsemanship and calmed their mounts, even as they attacked Meri. She didn't know what came over her. Already stronger than many men, she drew her sword and lay about her, guiding Storm with her knees. Not that he needed much guiding. Her taller horse gave her the advantage of being above the enemy. One lost his head, while the others had already sustained slashes from her sword in the first seconds of the melee.

Meri lost herself in the fury of battle, killing lest she be killed by the elves before her. She gritted her teeth and vowed none would get past her guard. And then Storm screamed and reared. She was thrown to the ground, dancing hoofs all around her. She rolled from side to side, looking for her mount and trying to avoid the hoofs of the elven ponies.

Then, abruptly, growls and snarling rent the air, and fur-covered bodies hurled themselves past her.

A pair of booted feet stopped at her side, and she looked up into Lady Star's face. "Katrine!" she whispered.

Lady Star placed her finger against her lips. "Shhh. Get to your feet. Here's your horse. I'm sorry my hounds frightened him."

She stood, limped over to Storm, and pulled herself onto his back. "Will you be safe?"

Lady Star smiled. "Yes, don't worry. The hounds will protect me. Get back to the city."

Merielle nodded and pulled her horse away from the fighting hounds. She cantered toward the city, eyes searching for danger. On her way back, she found another group of stretcher bearers threatened by *Sis Lenweri* and joined the two soldiers who were trying to defend them. This time, the enemy was on foot, and she easily dispatched the elves. She sent the workers back to the hospital and looked for more.

Meri spent the next few hours patrolling the battlefield, helping protect anyone trying to get wounded to safety, and joining the fighting when she could.

Word spread across the field of the beautiful warrior with hair like fire. Eventually, her actions led her to the thickest part of the battle.

As her eyes swept those fighting near her, she spotted King Beniel, his sword sweeping left and right as he battled *Sis Lenweri* on ponies. Battle rage must have overcome him, for Meri didn't think he was well enough to fight like a demon, even on his best day. S

he kicked her horse into the fray, working from the back of the pack and making her way toward the king.

Nothing could stop her. It felt like she had been touched by the spirit of some long-ago warrior woman. She didn't tire and felt no fear. All who came fell under her sword. She kept watch for the headbands that denoted their allies and fought alongside them, the kingdom soldiers and cavalry, to vanquish their foes.

Finally, she came upon King Beniel and a *Sis Lenweri* she thought might have been Faenwelar. He had a commanding presence, as though the gods had touched him. His haughty gaze flicked over her.

"Daughter of the sea, you have no place in this fight. However, if you persist in killing my people, I will rain vengeance upon you."

Faenwelar's "daughter of the sea" comment jerked Meri from her own battle rage. He had seen her origins! How was that possible? If he could see right through her, who else could?

"Stand aside before I run you through!" Faenwelar charged at her, and she came to her senses just in time to swing her horse aside and avoid his blade.

"Lady Merielle," King Beniel said, "leave the field before they kill you. The high prince and I have a score to settle."

Meri froze as Faenwelar turned to face the king. Beniel's focused gaze had already dismissed her and snapped to the elven leader. The moment would be forever etched on her mind. Chaos reigned around her, but for this small pocket of calm where the two leaders faced off.

Suddenly, Vard was at her side, mounted on his monstrous black and white stallion.

"Lady Merielle, you shouldn't be here."

"And you should fight Faenwelar instead of the king!"

Vard shook his head. "I've tried to tell him… he won't listen to me. Short of having him arrested and imprisoned, I can't stop this. Believe me, I don't like it any more than you do, but he's determined to finish Faenwelar himself."

"He's too ill!"

Vard looked to the heavens. "Everyone but he knows that. Alique's potion has given him a reprieve from his heart condition, and now he's like a man possessed."

As they watched, the king and Faenwelar faced each other.

"Let this fight between us be decided right here and now, Faenwelar," King Beniel shouted. "If I win, your forces will leave the field, never to trouble us again."

"You are insane, old man," Faenwelar sneered. "What if *I* win? You will never give us Thorius, no matter the outcome of this fight."

"You are correct there. I will have to settle for ridding the world of your evil. You have made the last years miserable for so many."

"Prepare to die, human king!" With those words, Faenwelar charged at Beniel, who kicked his stallion into a dead run. The two clashed hard, sparks flying as their shields smashed together, and their swords scraped to the hilts. Beniel was the first to disengage. He pushed off Faenwelar, and his horse swept its rump in a mad circle, smashing into the elven leader's leg.

Faenwelar screamed in pain and slapped the flat of his sword blade down on the rump of Beniel's horse, startling the creature and almost unseating the king. Beniel recovered and turned his horse to face his foe. He charged again, aiming for Faenwelar's injured right leg, his horse's shoulder contacting the damaged limb. Faenwelar shrieked and struck out with his sword, Beniel easily fending the blow with his shield and striking back with his blade.

No sword blows landed, but Faenwelar sagged in his saddle, his damaged leg affecting his balance. Vard hovered near, observing the battle around him, but wanting to be close to rescue the king if needed. The combatants circled each other, Beniel sitting his horse with confidence. He abruptly spun and trotted his horse away before turning to face his foe. Kicking his mount into a canter, he made for Faenwelar, who set himself as best he could. The two clashed, this time Faenwelar maneuvering to protect his leg, which placed him in an awkward position. Beniel struck with his sword repeatedly, Faenwelar managing to prevent the strokes from connecting.

The elven high prince seemed to be the underdog in the fight now, his defense desperate, barely able to keep Beniel's strikes from inflicting injury. Merielle couldn't take her eyes from the contest, so it was just as well Vard was there to watch over her. It appeared Beniel would win the day, and there would be celebrating in Wildecoast. But Faenwelar slid through Beniel's defense and cut the king on the shoulder of his sword arm.

The king flinched, but struck back nonetheless and found Faenwelar's gut unprotected. His sword flashed through the gap, and Faenwelar's eyes widened before he slumped further in his saddle. However, Beniel's thrust unbalanced him, and his horse swayed away from the elven high prince and out of range of striking.

When Beniel spun his mount to finish Faenwelar off, he found clear air where the foe and his mount had been. Meri sought the enemy leader and spotted him being hustled away toward the forest in the center of a group of mounted *Sis Lenweri*. Beniel saw too. He yelled and gave chase with Vard and Meri hot on his heels. Then, as Meri urged her tired horse to greater efforts, King Beniel sagged in the saddle.

* * *

Vard was almost level with the king's charger, swearing under his breath at the folly of monarchs, when Beniel slumped and began to topple from his horse. Vard steered his mount to the left and came alongside, catching his leader as he fell and hauling him across the front of his own saddle.

He glanced around, but saw few enemy soldiers. The battle appeared to have again been won by the kingdom forces. Still, he needed to get the half-conscious Beniel to shelter in case of dragon attack. Calling to Meri, Vard wheeled his horse and made for the city gates, hoping he wasn't killing the king in his mad dash. On their way, they gathered quite a crowd as commanders and soldiers left the field of battle.

Vard reached the gates and reefed on his horse's reins, hurling himself from the saddle and bringing the king with him. He lay Beniel alongside the wall of the city where the sun's weak afternoon rays could warm him. The king's face was gray, and his breathing shallow. The wound on his shoulder didn't appear deep and wasn't bleeding enough to cause this collapse. His gut clenched in fear. If not the wound, then what?

"Fetch Lady Alique!" he said, "and the queen." Two runners dashed off.

Merielle brought a cloak, folded it up, and tucked it under Beniel's head.

"What is it?" she asked. "What has caused his collapse? He was about to win that fight."

Beniel coughed. "I did win," he said, eyes closed and lips blue.

"Thank the Goddess, My Liege," Vard said. "You're still with us."

"Not for long, King's Blade," Beniel wheezed. "This time, there will be no miraculous recovery. But I will die knowing I vanquished the enemy one last time."

"No!" Vard placed his hand on the king's shoulder. "You have much to achieve. We need you."

Beniel coughed, tried to speak, then coughed again. "Not this time, Vard. I don't have long, so listen." He clutched Vard's shoulder and pulled him closer. "Undo my tunic and fetch the letter in my pocket. It will tell you everything you need to know."

Vard froze at his words, but his heart doubled its rate. *What on earth?* He did as he was told and pulled a parchment from the king's chest pocket.

"What's this?" Deep dread filled him at the prospect of what the letter might reveal. He hardly dared read it.

"I named my heir in that letter." Beniel's voice was fainter by the second, and Vard leaned forward to catch his words. "Remember, we talked about the succession recently. It got me thinking. I don't want to leave the kingdom in the hands of a child, or with those who are inexperienced, or can't be trusted. That meant choosing a new heir." The monarch coughed, then continued, "I chose you."

Vard's heart skipped a beat. "What? I don't think I heard you."

"You heard me right enough, my boy. That letter makes you my heir. Adriana knows and approves. She will help you as you require." He clutched Vard's tunic. "You are the right choice, but I am sorry for the grief this will cause you and Alecia. It had to be done."

Alecia! He couldn't spare the time to worry about her reaction now.

Alique arrived and knelt on the other side of the king, listening to his chest and holding his wrist. She met his gaze and shook her head.

"Your Majesty," she said, "your heart has failed again, and I can do nothing for you this time. Do you wish for a potion for the pain?"

Beniel didn't open his eyes. "There is no pain, My Lady. Where is Adriana?"

"I am here, my dear." The queen knelt beside Vard, and he moved to give her room.

"I'm sorry, Adriana," King Beniel croaked. "You have been a wonderful companion and support to me. Know that I leave you with deep regret." The king sagged, and Adriana gripped his hands.

"Beniel?" she said. "Beniel!" She looked at Alique. "Is he gone?"

Alique placed her ear trumpet on the king's chest and listened, her fingers on his wrist." She sat back and met the queen's gaze. "I'm so sorry, My Queen. King Beniel has left us."

Vard saw Adriana's throat lurch and a tear run down her cheek. He closed his eyes and said a prayer to the Goddess that she'd ensure the king's smooth entry into the afterlife. Eyes closed, Vard thought of how his world had been turned upside down in the space of a few seconds. He couldn't conceive how the king had come to make *him* heir. It wasn't right.

He opened his eyes and looked into the darkening sky. "Let's get His Majesty to the hospital and prepare him to make his final journey."

Vard ushered bearers close and helped them place Beniel's body upon a stretcher. He took one end while the other was taken by a bearer. They walked in silence to the hospital, Alique leading the way, and the queen trailing. It didn't take long for people to gather, citizens from all walks of life following them.

Vard hardly had any awareness of the crowd, but his rangers encircled the king's pallet, not allowing anyone too close. When they arrived at the hospital, Vard handed his end to another and turned to face the crowd.

"Good people," he said. "King Beniel, our great leader, has died. He fought Faenwelar and would have vanquished him had not the scoundrel fled. Our king died as a direct result of the fight." Emotion swept over Vard, almost robbing him of his words. "Do not fear! He has not left the kingdom leaderless. The king made provisions for the smooth transfer of power to his heir." He paused again, still not believing his new status, or wanting it. "We still have a war to win, even as we mourn. Keep the king in your prayers as he journeys to the afterlife."

THE END

GLOSSARY

Places

Kingdom of Thorius (Thor- ee- us) – the kingdom of men which encompasses the King's seat of Wildecoast and the Prince's seat of Brightcastle, along with many smaller towns

Wildecoast (Will – dee – coast) – city perched on the top of a cliff overlooking the sea on the east coast of Thorius; climate is mild but windy

Brightcastle – large inland town surrounded by forests and farms, three to four days ride west of Wildecoast

Amitania (Am – it – ay – nia) or *Elvandang (Elle – van – dang)* in elvish – the deserted city north of the Usetar Mountain Range in northern Thorius; once a thriving city and now home to elves and humans under the leadership of Princess Gwaethe Arenil and Earl Jacques Vorasava

Usetar Range (You – set – ar) – the mountain range running across the northern parts of Thorius

Selinore - the forest home of the peaceful Lenweri, in the mountains north of Brightcastle

People

Lenweri – the elven people who are tall and elegant with black skin and pointed ears; live in mountainous forests north and west of Thorius, in places encroaching onto Kingdom lands; also known as dark elves; they welcome males and females in their fighting force

Sis Lenweri – the faction of dark elves that wishes to take the kingdom of Thorius back from men; only males are welcome in their fighting force.

Defender – a race of shapeshifters who are created to defend those in danger; they sense those in need of their help; a Defender can shift into animal form and the ability is inherited through family lines; when they shift back into human form, they retain their clothes from before the shift; their gifts may include the ability to compel others to do their will.

Guardian – a person or people appointed by the king to oversee a part of Thorius.

Ranger – an elite force trained to fight and track to the highest proficiency; may include females.

Characters

Princess Alecia Zialni (Ah-lee-sha Zee – al – nee) – the King's niece and daughter of Prince Jiseve Zialni who once ruled in Brightcastle and was next in line to the throne. Alecia's story began in **Princess Avenger** and continued in **Princess in Exile**

Vard Anton – the love of Princess Alecia's life and a shapeshifting Defender; once army captain of Brightcastle in **Princess Avenger** and his story continued in **Princess in Exile**

Iona Izebel Zialni (Eye-own-ah Is – zee – belle Zee – al – nee) – Alecia and Vard's daughter, born while Alecia was in exile; she has inherited her father's Defender gifts; she is five months old when **The People's Princess** begins

Benae (Ben-nay) Zorba – Princess of Brightcastle and joint Guardian with her husband Ramón Zorba; she was once married to Prince Jiseve Zialni (now deceased) and has given birth to his child; Benae can heal with her mind and has a close relationship with her stallion, Flaire. Benae's story was told in **The Lady's Choice**

Ramón Zorba – Lord of Wildecoast and once squire to Prince Jiseve Zialni; now joint Guardian of Brightcastle with his wife Benae; brother to Lady Alique Zorba. Ramón's story was told in **The Lady's Choice**

Solomon Daire Zialni – son of Benae Zorba and Prince Jiseve Zialni (now deceased); an infant of three months when **The People's Princess** begins

Hetty (aka Lady Henrietta Guiote) – mysterious ancient woman with magical powers; once Alecia's governess and nanny; declared a witch by Prince Jiseve and sentenced to death but rescued by Alecia

King Beniel Zialni (Ben – ee – elle Zee – al – nee) – King of Thorius; lives in Wildecoast; older brother of Jiseve Zialni and uncle of Alecia Zialni; married to Adriana

Queen Adriana Zialni - wife of the King; lives in Wildecoast; Alecia's aunt

Piotr Zialni (Peter Zialni) – son of Beniel and Jiseve Zialni's younger brother; next in line to the throne of Thorius (his father is dead) after Solomon, unless King Beniel or Alecia have a son

Izebel (Is – zee – belle) – a previous warrior Queen of Thorius from centuries ago, when females could rule; Alecia's idol; her daughter Daphini was the last queen of Thorius

Gwaethe (Gway-eth-a) Arenil – Lenweri princess, daughter of King Orionkael Arenil, who was murdered by High Prince Faenwelar of the Sis Lenweri. She has a golden stallion with silver mane and tail called Rassar which means Sunbeam; her love story was told in **Elf Princess Warrior**

Jacques Vorasava – Captain in the Brightcastle army. Jacques is tall with dark hair, beard and moustache; he has an olive complexion; he is married to Gwaethe Arenil and is now an Earl, and their story was told in **Elf Princess Warrior**

Doctor Damald Monive – chief physician in Brightcastle Keep; presided over the inquiry into Alecia's father's sudden death when he was married to Benae

Millie – Alecia's maid who also helps out with Iona's care

Melandrach (Mel-on-drac) Arenil – brother to King Orionkael and uncle to Gwaethe and Isiloe; a hermit who lives in isolation in the remote mountains above Selinore; he is also a Defender and becomes Vard's mentor

Lyam Anton (Lie-am) – Vard's father who has been missing for over fifteen years; he is now a Defender and can shift into hawk or bear

Katrine Aranati (Kat-reen Ar-an-arti) – sorceress and younger daughter of an impoverished farming estate south of Wildecoast; older sister is Esta Aranati; once a smuggler called Lady Star; heroine of **The Master and the Sorceress**; now mistress of the night hounds

James Tomel (James Tom-elle) – master jeweler and oldest son of a farming family; lives in Costa; hero of **The Master and the Sorceress**; spy master for King Beniel

Esta Aranati – Katrine Aranati's older sister; she is head of the Aranati estate and was once a smuggler known as Lady Moonlight; heroine of **The Lady and the Pirate**; married to Samael Delacost

Samael Delacost – once a pirate, was captured by Nikolas Cosara, admiral of the King's Navy and is now sworn to obey the admiral or spend the rest of his life in prison; hero of **The Lady and the Pirate** and now married to Esta Aranati

Merielle – mermaid who has become human; she has vibrant red hair and is not familiar with the ways of Thorian people; heroine of **The Lord and the Mermaid**; good friend of Esta Aranati

Lord Nikolas Cosara (Nikolas Cos-arra) – Admiral in the King's Navy; he is cousin to Queen Adriana and the hero of **The Lord and the Mermaid**; he is married to Merielle

Alique (Ah-leek) Jazara nee *Zorba* - beautiful blonde healer, married to Kain and brother to Ramón; cousin to General Josef Formosa. Her story was told in **The Elf King's Lady**

Kain Jazara – once general of the Thorian army, he has discovered his father was Orionkael Arenil (past elven king); he has taken up leadership of the peaceful Lenweri; he is married to Alique Jazara and is hero of **The Elf King's Lady**; half-brother to Gwaethe Arenil; son of Orionkael Arenil, the murdered elven king; has a black horse called Snow

Josef Formosa – promoted to general of the Wildecoast army after Kain Jazara was forced to resign; he is cousin to Ramon and Alique Zorba

Alecia Zialni's lady guards –

Linnet Perfore – Alecia's second-in-command; talented scout; tall redhead; gray eyes

Cretia – the planner of the group; blonde with baby blue eyes

Arelle – the peacekeeper; inspired by Alecia to learn weapons; black hair, blue eyes

Kenna – scout and fierce warrior; hyperactive; brown hair and eyes

Jules Estevot (Jewels Ess-tee-vow) – captain of the army in Brightcastle; has blond hair and ice-blue eyes

Reid Vetta (Reed Vet-tah) – Master goldsmith in Wildecoast and Esta's betrothed for a short time

Doctor Achan Mosard – Physician to the king in Wildecoast

Master Dunnet – Vard's man servant

Elora Arenil (Elle-Aura Arenil) – King Orionkael's widow and Gwaethe's mother

Isiloe (Iz-il-oe) – Gwaethe's cousin by Orionkael's sister- unlike most of her race, Isiloe is short with white hair and pale blue eyes. She is a captain (Ramar) in the elven army

Chandrelle (Shan-drel) – Isiloe's sister; tall, dark elven woman with long dark hair; warrior

Exmund - Jacques's aide and corporal in the Brightcastle army; youngest brother of James Tomel, hero of **The Master and the Sorceress**

Elvor Faenwelar - High Prince of the *Sis Lenweri*; enemy of Gwaethe and the humans

Niel Gorin Faenwelar – of the *Sis Lenweri*; Elvor's son

Rasalar (Raz-a-lar) – Isiloe's mother; sister to Orionkael and Melandrach; once a soldier and still trains recruits

Sergeant Dodlan – second in command to Jacques in his trek north and remains with him in Amitania

Master Jenkin – Brightcastle weapons master

Tyra – Benae's maid- stocky, blond; helps with healing

Julli (Ju-lee) Dovara – Alique's maid; gifted helper and healer; not a great horsewoman; gentle and caring

Alia Kelsis – the elven woman who leads the female Sis Lenweri in Selinore

Ruven Magbalar – Sis Lenweri soldier rescued by Gwaethe and became a loyal supporter; he is now elven army commander in Amitania

Théoden Leovaris – Sis Lenweri soldier rescued by Gwaethe and became a loyal supporter and captain of her guard

Vortek Cruzen – Defender who trains with Melandrach

Soma Nuran – a mercenary Alecia convinces to help enlist dissenting army conscripts

Night hound – a beast the size of a wolf, with short grey, black or red hair, heavy snout, and stumpy ears; the eyes are red; there are six toes on each paw and the back feet have retractable cat-like claws, huge and razor sharp; have not been seen in Thorius for at least fifty years

Nugoriem – the black dragon; name means 'eternal fire'

Elven terms

Alen – Lord

Gir – Sergeant

Ade – Corporal

Ramar – Captain

Saleh – attack

Elrie – half-blood

ABOUT THE AUTHOR

Bernadette Rowley is a lover of epic fantasy who is a veterinarian by day and an author by night. She is currently published in the genre of high fantasy romance with nine books and a box collection, all set in her fantasy world of Thorius.

When she was a young teenager, an aunt gave her a copy of The Sword of Shannara by Terry Brooks and Bernadette has lived in various fantasy worlds ever since. The author who has influenced her writing most is Robert Jordan (Wheel of Time series). It's no surprise that her chosen genre when writing romance is fantasy.

"I can see these settings so vibrantly in my mind and hope my readers can too."

But Bernadette has no desire to spoon-feed her readers by laboriously describing her fantasy settings. She would rather the reader use their own imagination.

Along with sword and sorcery, dashing heroes and stunning heroines, this author includes strong healing themes in many of her books- an element which is central to her everyday job.

"When I started writing the Queenmakers Saga, I never imagined my day job would force its way into my stories as it has."

And of course, there are animals, especially Bernadette's beloved horses.

Bernadette lives in Southeast Queensland, Australia, where she enjoys a great coffee, walks in nature and catching up family and friends.

CONNECT WITH THE AUTHOR

Website: www.bernadetterowley.com
Subscribe to the Bernadette Rowley newsletter and
get a free map of the world of Thorius

Facebook: www.facebook.com/bernadetterowleyfantasy
Twitter: www.twitter.com/bt_rowley